BEFORE THE

MANGO RIPENS

BEFORE THE

MANGO

RIPENS

A NOVEL

AFABWAJE KURIAN

DZANC
BOOKS

2580 Craig Rd.
Ann Arbor, MI 48103
www.dzancbooks.org

Library of Congress Cataloging-in-Publication Data Available upon Request

ISBN 9781950539994
First edition: September 2024
Cover art by Michelle D'Urbano
Cover design by Steven Seighman
Interior design by Michelle Dotter

Printed in the United States of America

10 9 8 7 6 5 4 3 2 1

TABLE OF CONTENTS

In memory of my great-grandfather,
Wanwyegni Jatau

PART ONE

1971

CHAPTER ONE

By sunrise, the town knew. How the news drifted from Yawari to Rabata through the moonless hours of night, people did not question; but early on Sunday morning, most of the townspeople donned their church clothes, and those without such attire wore their cleanest. Serpentine paths leading to the primary school, where the Americans held their church services, were crowded with those eager to hear if the story was true—that the Reverend's translator had been set on fire in his village and survived.

The whole town whispered about the fire, and there was nowhere one could go without hearing how the ropes around Zanya's hands miraculously loosened like the chains of Paul and Silas, the apostles the white Reverend had preached about one Sunday. Imagine, people were saying, here in Rabata, they had their own miracle, their own story others would speak about for generations. Childlike excitement thrummed inside and outside the classroom. People squished into desks intended for children. Some perched on top of wooden slats or stood in narrow aisles, waiting, their shoes, sandals, and bare feet striking the cement with impatient taps. Women sat on the veranda, their backs supported by columns, as they shushed and rocked puling infants.

Reverend Jim, who had come to Rabata before the war, paced in front of the congregants. "I'd like to welcome all of you here this morning," he began. His voice was grave, as if his pacing had allowed him to absorb a solemnity required for the occasion. He dabbed the perspiration on his forehead with a handkerchief he unfurled from the pocket of his suit, and the congregants felt pity for him and for his pale skin, which had erupted in small amoebic flares. His mane of gray was edged with wisps of white, and he surveyed the assembly with an expression of disbelief. Three or four times the usual number, the crowd must have totaled close to two hundred, counting those outside straining to see in.

"Some of us," he continued, adjusting the temple of his black-rimmed glasses, "might be tempted to doubt the veracity of the miracle, but let us recall the Book of Daniel. Let us recall how God saved the lives of Shadrach, Meshach, and Abednego, three Hebrew men thrown into a fiery furnace. Did they burn? No, church. They did not burn as the flames raged around them. These men walked out unharmed—"

A slow chorus of groans arose from a raucous group of adolescent boys standing outside. "We want Zanya!"

Laughter followed from those relegated to an outside view. Another youthful voice chimed in, and soon the room filled with echoes:

"Where is Zanya?"

"Fire Boy!"

"It's Zanya we've come to see!"

"And you will, church. You most certainly will," Reverend Jim said, and kept on preaching through the shouts and snickers. If anyone thought his apparent discomfort—due to the heat and the crowd's palpable impatience—would shorten his message, they were mistaken. Disgruntled murmurs receded as he preached from the thirteenth chapter of Zechariah, urging the church to seek refinement through fire, to be purified as gold.

Finally, to the crowd's relief, Reverend Jim said, "Let us praise the Lord. Persecution has once again revived the church. Let's hear from Zanya."

With his long limbs and slenderness, Zanya resembled the limber trunk of a paw paw tree as he walked from behind the Reverend, where he had been translating, toward the podium. He wore a loose collared shirt with cuffs an insufficient length to hide his wrists. His trousers rose one or two inches above his ankles, and on his feet, scuffed brown platforms seemed to fit a size too small. None of it detracted from his handsomeness—the strong jawline and angular nose, the effortless saunter, the natural elegance of his movements. His skin was clean and smooth, as if he had been molded with forest clay. His face unmarked, save for an old scar above his left eyebrow. He looked, to them, like he had never seen fire.

"Why did I not burn, church?" Zanya asked, facing the crowd. He stared straight ahead, and a sly, impish smile played on his lips. "This is what you are asking yourselves? I know—I see the way you are eyeing me. Seeing my face. Looking at my hands and arms." He stretched out his arms and wriggled them, as though disposing water droplets.

"I'm seeing new faces that I've never seen before," he said, smiling at the crowd. "You new people, you have come to see me but now you're saying, 'Why did I waste my time coming? It does not look as if anything happened to him. Why did I wake up early and come instead of working on my farm?' Some of you, you still want to be sleeping."

They laughed, and Zanya laughed along with them. His laughter was appealing in its expansiveness, in how it swallowed any invisible doubts about the veracity of the fire.

"You are here wanting to see me come before you like Lazarus? To see me in bandages to prove that I burned, so you can say, 'Yes o. God has done a miracle.'

"Church, are you not understanding?" he said, spreading his arms apart. "*This*—me standing before you unharmed—is the miracle."

Soon he was weaving together—in Gbagyi and English—the story that had come to them in fragments. There had been dark-

ness without moon on the night of his persecution. He had gone
to visit with his eldest sister Pema, who was ill. After leaving Pema's
village, he decided to travel to Yawari and see his parents, whom he
had not seen in years. When he arrived, his relatives had dragged
him out of his pickup truck.

"Fear gripped me," he said. "They tied my wrists and ankles. I
began to know they intended to kill me. They threw guinea corn
chaff around me. Do you know what they said to me? They shouted, 'Let the white man's god come and save you!'"

His glance swept the room, finding those near the windows,
those sitting at the desks, those near the entrance, those huddled
in corners.

"Then," he said, eyes sadder than a moment before, "these
cousins, these uncles of mine, took kerosene, poured it on the
guinea corn chaff, and lit the bundle on fire."

Kerosene fumes seemed to suffuse the air with his telling, and
the congregation heard the phantom crack of a match, as loud and
dreadful as thunder, and saw the flames undulating to the whims
of the wind that night.

"Your grandfathers," he said, walking toward the first row of
desks, "have told you the tale of Fyilumawye. In her anger, Fyilumawye dipped a finger into the middle of the village river, and the
river dried. In the whole village, no water could be found. Searching for water, one old woman fell under a tree and cried out in
desperation."

He looked to the window again as he spoke, and his eyes had a
distant, faraway glint, as if he were looking beyond them, recalling
his anguish.

"This old woman desperate for water was what I had become
that night in my village." He stopped and looked out at the congregants again, and his mouth parted into a victorious smile. "But
Shekwoyi, our God," he said. "Shekwoyi came and saved me."

"Yes o!"

"Hallelujah!"

Dust motes twinkled starlike in the yellow band of sun falling across the classroom floor. Zanya took a deliberate step into the strip of light. He lifted his hands and proclaimed to the mounting enthusiasm, "Our Heavenly Father saved me."

"Tell us how!"

Zanya's face shone from the film of sweat on his brow. He reached into his pocket and opened his right hand to reveal a thin glaze of ashes coating his palm. "Come and see—these are the ashes from the fire. A miracle of wind blew the fire. The ropes came undone. My shirt had not burned. My trousers had not burned. Church, my body had not burned—"

"Amen!"

"Stand with me," he said, "and let us praise His name!"

The congregants leapt to their feet. Clapping reverberated throughout the classroom. Those outside clapped, too, quick and loud, so that the sound echoed throughout the church like great bundles of sticks clattering to the ground.

CHAPTER TWO

JUMMAI DRAPED A PAIR OF TROUSERS on a clothesline looping the branch of a lemon tree and circling the trunk of a palm in the back-yard of the Parsons' house. She imagined the singing and dancing in the church after Zanya's testimony, and the women's choir strik-ing the kacha-kachas against open palms, the net of cowries hitting the gourd in rhythm to the drums.

She could have been there, sitting with everybody, hearing again about the miracle of fire that happened in Yawari. Instead she had stayed on the mission compound to care for Elijah, the Parsons' eleven-year-old son. Elijah's schoolmates had fought with him on Friday afternoon. If he could not cope with seeing these boys during the week, his mother had said, she did not want him running into them on Sundays, which was why he had been al-lowed to miss service this morning.

Sooner or later, Jummai thought, Elijah would see these boys in town. Sooner or later, he would need to return their knocks and insults.

She dumped the bucket of soapy water on the vegetable gar-den, ignoring the splash on her feet, and walked across the com-pound, back inside the Parsons' kitchen to rinse rice and beans for the afternoon meal. Elijah, who had been restringing his slingshot, followed her and shuffled in bored circles, pulling out drawers and opening the curtains covering shelves of plates and tumblers. He left long, dirty streaks on the kerosene fridge and poked his finger into a tear in the cloth bag holding the beans. Beans—the kind she used for kosai—trickled out and scattered on the counter and floor.

"Abeg, Elijah!" Jummai said, lifting the bag before more spilled.

"I'm sorry," he said, kneeling to gather them.

"Stop touching things before you go and spoil them—"

"I didn't mean to do it." Elijah pushed the beans back into the torn bag. When he finished, he stood and said, "Guess what, Jummai? Mom says astronauts went to the moon. Did you know that?"

"Astro-what?" Jummai said, checking the floor for any stray beans he might have missed.

"Mom says we'd have gone to see the rocket if we were in America. Dad said we'd have seen Apollo 14 go up in space."

"Is that so?" This was what Jummai said to him when she did not know what he was talking about, which was often. Nami, the primary school teacher Zanya planned to marry, a woman Jummai did not care for, usually came to the mission compound to tutor Elijah. If Nami were here, she would have listened to him and nodded, saying, "That is very good, Elijah. What else can you tell me about space?" as if he had said interesting things. Nami liked asking Elijah questions so that his stories grew longer and longer while Jummai looked for ways to get him to stop running his mouth.

"Not like here," he said. "No one's gone to space here in Africa."

God forbid, the child was still talking to her. With his voice like a mosquito's!

"How do you know?" Jummai said.

"Because I do." He shrugged. "Well, Mom said so."

The child liked to tell her things about America. She had listened to him in the beginning until Gary Parson said his son had little memory of his birthplace. Elijah was two when they left

Missouri to their first mission assignment in Malaysia, and eight when they came to Nigeria four years ago in June of '67. Elijah talked of America with the same longing as his mother, so Jummai knew it was Mrs. Katherine feeding him her memories. Jummai felt like she had traveled there, with how Mrs. Katherine talked about Springfield, Missouri. Jummai envisioned a town similar to Rabata, except full of white people like the Parsons, and houses as neat, square, and clean as the ones on the mission compound. She had no wish to visit Missouri. She might feel in America as Katherine Parson felt here in Nigeria—out of place and ready to return.

"Oya, go outside, Elijah."

"I want to stay here with you. Please? I can help."

She felt annoyed with him, standing here expecting things from her, unlike her younger brothers who knew how to entertain themselves. She tried not to dwell on Elijah's faults: his timidity and thinness, his body, a thing easily snapped like kokoro. She thought he would develop into a tall, skinny man in adulthood, and in him would reside a river of insecurities, and his handsomeness—for she could see he would be moderately handsome—would hide these insecurities, and the woman he married would be the one to deal with them when they washed upstream. She knew he must miss his older sister, Allison, who was enrolled at Hillcrest International School in Jos, and this might be the reason for his behavior and the fighting at school, for him wanting to be near her all the time when she was working. But she would not be able to concentrate on cooking if he stayed here in the kitchen.

"Go and play," she said. "Let me finish what I'm doing."

He went quietly, dragged his slingshot from the counter and slipped it into his pocket. He trudged out with his head down.

Within an hour, Jummai had fried the chicken stew. She had rinsed, salted, and seasoned the rice and beans and had them simmering on the stove in separate pots.

The compound gates opened minutes later, and she went to the front door and watched Nelson Landry swerve into a grassy area and park the Peugeot near the black iron gate. The mission owned three vehicles: the blue Peugeot, a van for the mission clinic, and a pickup Zanya used for construction, which he drove around town as if it were his own. The four of them—Gary and Katherine Parson, Reverend Jim, and Dr. Landry—often drove around town on Sundays after church, as if they needed to remember that Rabata was where they now lived.

Gary Parson had stepped out of the car to unbolt the gate for Dr. Landry and was closing it now. No gate or enclosure had existed the first year the missionaries came. One day, Reverend Jim instructed Zanya and his laborers to construct a barrier to separate the mission's property from the surrounding homes. According to her sister Jecinda, Miss Delores, the unmarried missionary, had spoken against the wall when she began working with the mission. Miss Delores said it made the missionaries seem like kings and queens, distancing themselves from the locals.

Miss Delores—who everybody called Mai Mulo because she played the guitar or Malama Delores because she served as the primary school headmistress—lived alone in a small house near the school, and she behaved as if she had been born in Rabata. She had asked the machine boys to teach her how to handle a motorbike, and it was not uncommon to see her practicing on the side roads. "If this nasala woman breaks her head open," one townsperson had said, "let her blood not be on our land."

Chickens fanned their wings around the wheels of the car and scattered when Elijah ran out to greet his parents. Elijah threw his arms around his mother's waist, and the look on his face would have one believe Jummai had mistreated him while they were gone. The compound filled with the patter of the missionaries' footsteps and their foreign American accents.

Jummai retreated to the kitchen. Mrs. Katherine soon entered, placing her purse and Bible on the counter. "I'm so sorry, Jummai," she said. "I didn't expect us back so early. Listen, Nelson and Jim will be joining us for lunch. Is that all right? Can you handle it?"

"There's food, ma," Jummai said.

"Well, I know there's food." Mrs. Katherine lifted the lid on a bowl where Jummai was storing peeled red onions. "Is it enough, is what I'm asking?"

"There is plenty," Jummai said.

With all her brothers and sisters, she had never learned to cook for only two or three people. She had made enough rice and chicken stew for twelve.

"How was church, ma?" Jummai asked.

"What was that?" Mrs. Katherine speared some beans in the pot with a fork and mashed them on a small plate and tasted it. "Oh, Jummai, this is lovely. What'd you do differently this time? You'll need to show me your tricks now, won't you?"

"Yes, ma. I will show you."

"Now, what were you asking me?"

"Church, ma. How was church?"

"It was a packed house, as we like to say back home—"

"Packed house?"

"Oh yes, the whole town was there. I wish you could've seen it."

Jummai stirred the pot of stew and waited for more. She wanted to know how Zanya had sounded in that classroom, where dust rose to sting your eyes and where men smelled of sweat and the tangled roots of the earth and the women and babies smelled of talcum powder. How had Zanya looked standing in front of the congregation with the kind of confidence that always seemed to power him, to make him taller, more limber and sturdier? He lacked the lank of her brother Yakwo, who was growing into adolescence. When Yakwo walked or ran, it was easy sometimes, in his inelegance, to think he had suddenly acquired several arms and legs.

She wanted to ask Katherine Parson if Nami, Zanya's woman, had come.

But Mrs. Katherine was distracted, bringing plates and tumblers off the open wooden shelves. "Could you put these out on the table, Jummai?"

"Yes, ma."

"And make sure the silverware is there, all right? Thank you, dear."

The missionaries had claimed their seats around the dining table when Jummai walked out to serve the meal and bring out the pitcher of water. Back in the kitchen, she began preparing the evening meal. She moved a stool closer to the door and cracked it open so she could see them. She chopped tomatoes noiselessly, preventing the knife from making harsh sounds against the cutting board. If Dr. Landry and Reverend Jim were not there, Gary Parson would have said, "Take a break, Jummai. Come and eat with us."

"Did you see the young boys?" she heard Mr. Gary say. "Did you see how they hung around until the end? Usually they're gone before the sermon gets started—"

"Usually, they're not there at all," Dr. Landry said, in his booming voice. The man talked as if a person were on the other side of the room, not standing inches in front of him. The dining chair and table had imprisoned him, cutting into his stomach. His large size presumed slowness, movements as unhurried as an elephant. It was not so. The locals often shouted to him in Hausa, "Likita! Ina kake gaggawa zuwa?" when he passed them on the road. He was never rushing. It was simply his normal pace.

"Now," Reverend Jim said, "I wouldn't say the young men have never come to church."

"That's right, Jim, they'll come for Boys' Brigade or a youth service now and then," Mrs. Katherine said. "But this time, I'll admit they were more engaged, don't you think?"

Mr. Gary said, "That's because Zanya's got something—"

"He reminded me of a young George Whitefield, truth be told," Reverend Jim said.

George Whitefield. Jummai would remember this name for Zanya. He had liked hearing the stories she reported to him when they used to see each other. "*Hawaii Five-0*," he would say. "Are you one detective?"

Reverend Jim continued, "Some of Whitefield's critics didn't care for his theatrics, the distraction from the core spiritual message. We ought to be careful about that sort of thing. I'd hate to fan the flames, so to speak, of the superstitious."

Jummai did not like how the Reverend sounded, how his mouth moved as if he had tasted bitter leaf in the stew.

"Ah, c'mon, Jim. This was different," Mr. Gary said. "Zanya is coming into his own. I've seen that kind of zeal in the young men these days. I rather like to think it's the feeling of independence in a young nation. Nationalism as it's been in other African countries—"

"Nationalism?" Reverend Jim said.

"—independence in Mauritius, Equatorial Guinea, most recently. You know, I've got a couple of friends working with Africa Inland Mission in Kenya, been there over a decade. They've been facing resistance with nationals since independence."

"Shouldn't surprise us, should it?" Nelson Landry said.

"Well, things are different here in Rabata," Mrs. Katherine said.

"I don't know," Mr. Gary said. "We need to keep these opinions in mind, that's all."

"Once the church is built," Dr. Landry said, "what would be better than a national as your right-hand man, Jim? Listen, this is what I've done with Dr. Awyebwi at the clinic, and that partnership is as good as ever. Isn't that right, Katherine?"

But Mrs. Katherine had taken a sip of her water and did not respond immediately, so Reverend Jim spoke again. "Well, you see, I'm not so sure nationals are ready to lead a church, spiritually or otherwise."

"You sound like the Brits, Jim," Mr. Gary said.

"I believe in gradualism, is all," Reverend Jim said.

"Well, I think Zanya would do anything to work under you."

"Oh, I don't doubt he would."

Mrs. Katherine raised her brows. "How do you mean?"

It took such a long time for Reverend Jim to answer that Jummai pushed the door farther ajar to see if he had fallen asleep. He was wide awake, spooning more rice on his plate. She could see, even from this distance, the curly white hairs springing out of his earlobes.

"Well, you know I grew up on a farm," Reverend Jim said, allowing his spoon to clank on the plate, "about twenty miles south of Rockford, in Ogle County."

"Yeah, that's right," Dr. Landry said. "Not too far from where my folks used to be."

"Right. Well, when I was a child, about eight, maybe nine," Reverend Jim continued, "my father gave me the job of milking the cows and carrying the milk in tin buckets to the springhouse, that's what we used for refrigeration back in those days. One morning, I spilled it, carrying on and fooling around, doing a trapeze act on an old, rotting log."

"I would have loved to see that act," Mr. Gary said.

"I knew I'd be in for a spanking," Reverend Jim said, "so I told my father that a couple of coyotes had been sniffing around the farm. They scared me, I said, and that's why I spilled the milk. Wouldn't you know I had my father and his friends searching the farm all morning with their shotguns before they figured out I'd sent them on a fool's errand."

"Isn't that something," Dr. Landry said, laughing.

"*Then* I received a well-deserved spanking," Reverend Jim said, chuckling along. "What I'm saying is quite simple: sometimes you create stories to get what you want or to get out of what you don't want."

"You don't think Zanya's testimony…" Mrs. Katherine began.

"C'mon, Jim," Mr. Gary said. "You're not saying what I think you're saying about the fire, about what we just heard? Not after the message you gave before Zanya spoke."

"I stand by what I preached," Reverend Jim said. "I'd like to verify it, that's all."

Laughter filled the room, and they spoke at once, voices over-lapping. Jummai had missed something, a whisper or an expression. Zanya would have wanted to know what was said. Quickly, Jummai scooped more chicken stew into another bowl. She looked around for the second water pitcher, grabbed it, and walked into the dining room.

"What's the matter, Jummai?" Mrs. Katherine asked when the door swung open.

"Ma," she said.

With these white people staring at her with eyes like cats, she sometimes found that her words stubbornly refused to come. Away from the mission compound, she could talk freely.

"I brought more stew," she said finally.

"Oh, I think we're fine." Mrs. Katherine gestured at the food on the table and the empty plates that glistened with streaks of oil. "You're a first-rate cook, dear."

"Actually, Jummai," Gary Parson said. "Just a second, now that we have you."

"Yes, sir?"

"I take it you've heard about the fire?"

Who had not heard? But these were the things she could not say bluntly to these people.

"Yes, Mai Hankali. I have heard."

She waited, holding the pitcher of water in one hand. The bowl of stew in the other warmed her fingertips.

"So what'd you think?" Mr. Gary said. "Do you believe it happened?"

"Oh gosh, don't ask her that, dear—" Mrs. Katherine said.

"Why not? Doesn't matter what we think, really."

He beamed at Jummai, waiting with one arm slung around his wife's shoulders. Elijah told her that on some mornings, he found his father asleep on the orange and brown cushion in the parlor and not in the bedroom with his mother. The other day, she overheard Mr. Gary and Mrs. Katherine arguing in their bedroom. Mrs. Katherine said it was time for them to leave Nigeria. She had kept saying "this country."

Mr. Gary said the only reason Mrs. Katherine wanted to leave was because she had not made friends in Rabata. "Oh for crying out loud, Gary," Mrs. Katherine had said. "That is *not* the reason."

"Tell me then, honey," Mr. Gary had said. "Why don't you talk to me, tell me what's going on?" Jummai had hurried out of the corridor when the doorknob turned.

Here, in front of everyone, they were fine.

"What I think?" Jummai said.

"Yes," Mr. Gary said, encouraging. "You believe it happened? It's real?"

The true things Jummai wanted to tell Gary Parson about that night, she could not say. These white people had come with their Holy Spirit, but they did not know that other spirits existed. They did not believe that things like this could happen. A person could be set on fire and survive without a single blemish.

"For our people," she said, "anything can happen. Even things like this."

"Well, there you have it, Jim," Mr. Gary said, drumming the table.

"I guess that's all the proof we need." Nelson Landry wiped his forehead with the crook of his elbow.

Jummai had liked answering Mr. Gary's question; she remained standing close to the kitchen entrance in case they asked more questions.

"Jummai," Mrs. Katherine said, "be a dear and bring out the lemonade, would you?"

"Yes, ma," she said.

She had done well for Zanya. She would tell him this when she saw him again.

Months ago, when he began befriending Nami, he had told Jummai to stop coming to see him at night. She had listened, and they had not seen each other again. Until the night of the fire.

But she needed to tell Zanya what she had gathered for him this afternoon. About how these missionaries said Zanya was like one man, one George something. She had already forgotten and was mispronouncing it in her mind. She would tell Zanya how they had talked about him being the one to lead the mission church along with Reverend Jim. If she told him these things, he would remember how she helped him. And he would change his mind about having sent her away, and would say she could come see him again.

CHAPTER THREE

As HER FAMILY'S DRIVER, Benedict, approached the mission clinic, it looked to Tebeya an oasis, a powder-blue building in the middle of a grassy field, a copse of maize growing behind it. The sun was not yet potent enough to obliterate the mist haloing the clinic. The sight reminded her of childhood, when farms outnumbered roads and there had been little to see in the five miles it took to drive through Rabata and into the viridity of forests and hills toward Keffi.

These days, there were more flats and houses and businesses being built in Rabata. More commercial vehicles like buses and taxis ferrying people to Jos, Lagos, and Kaduna, and motorbikes roaring down the roads and winding through the new roundabout. A burgeoning row of shops had risen behind her parents' provisions store, which sold non-perishables such as powdered milk, sugar, biscuits, lotions, soap, and other personal use items. The store was painted an optimistic blue and yellow, distinguishing itself among the shops constructed from tin or planks of raw, unpainted wood. Not many stores had strong doors and tiled floors like her family's. On the storefront, in white paint, the laborers had stenciled GLORIES AND BLESSINGS LADIES' PROVISIONS STORE. As an afterthought were the words AND GENTLEMEN ALSO WELCOME. The last four letters of "welcome" were not visible unless one went around the right side of the building.

What a lengthy and torturous name for a store. If Tebeya had been consulted, she would have called it Mama Bintu's Provisions Store and left it at that. It was maddening to her that you could not see the full name if you drove down the main road.

She knew her family had been too worried about the viability of the provisions store and her father's Glories and Blessings Transportation Company, when the war with Biafra began in '67, to bother about a new name. The war had officially ended a little over a year ago, and the country was paradoxically at peace under a military regime, with General Gowon serving as head of state. Rabata, situated in the Middle Belt, not fully north nor south, had been shielded from the war. Now, the town buzzed with more inhabitants, and this was good news all around since many of them frequented the mission clinic. Nelson Landry—whom Tebeya was trying not to think too much about this morning—said the clinic would likely expand and become a primary health center in a few years' time.

Benedict maneuvered to the entrance to drop her off in the usual place, close to where the patients lingered in restless groups, sitting on concrete benches or recumbent on the grass, resting upright on the trunk of trees. Tebeya could see that the crowd already totaled about thirty patients at half past seven. She and the staff often examined sixty to eighty patients a day, and there were dozens they turned away. She had in mind a shaded outdoor waiting area as a future project to prevent the patients, mainly women, from suffering in the sun. Men came to the clinic too, but most often it was women, entering with dusty feet and stoic faces.

Tebeya looked beyond the crowd and did not see Nelson, or Goliath as her mother had christened him due to his height. Tebeya had scheduled a preparatory meeting with him—an intentional early morning meeting to get him to the clinic on time for the tour and inspection today with Edward Hayes, the mission's regional coordinator.

Benedict slowed to a stop. "What time should I come back, madam?"

"The same as yesterday," she said, and shut the door.

"Ina kwana, Dr. Tebeya," patients called in Hausa.

She returned good mornings and stopped to greet new faces and speak briefly to those in the queue. One intake coordinator stooped near the door to the clinic, scribbling a patient's medical history on a clipboard. Tebeya searched the grounds for the second. Two intake coordinators helped move things along smoothly in the mornings.

She still had not sighted Nelson. The white mission van they sometimes used for medic transport was parked on the east side of the building, but it offered no information about Nelson's whereabouts, given his preference to walk the mile to the clinic from his house.

Tebeya made her way to the office she shared with him and Katherine Parson, senior nurse. It was located past the medication supply closet, patient ward, and the two private examination rooms reserved for patients willing to pay more. The office was the final door in the corridor before one turned left toward the operating theater.

She knocked first, hoping she'd hear a cheery "Come on in!" from Nelson. There was no response. It was possible that he was behind the desk, reviewing their operational expenses or addressing issues with staff salaries. *Please let him be here. Let him be on time.* She searched the bottom of her bag for the office key, jammed it in, and unlocked the door.

The office was empty. The desk unmanned. A nervous spasm traveled along Tebeya's lower back like a jolt of electricity. She sighed, tossed the keys on the desk, and inspected the room. Anyone else would have pronounced it clean and disregarded the smattering of dirt atop the file cabinet from the potted plant Katherine insisted on coaxing to life despite its wilting, perforated leaves.

They would not have noticed the overfull dustbin or the strip of grime behind the desk, where the wall met the floor. A quick, firm swipe of a wet mop or rag would have taken care of this and also removed the amorphous stain on the door's hinge. Someone else may not have noticed the three-day-old mugs of tea and coffee, partially consumed and cold. The pastel pink lipstick on a white mug belonged to Katherine Parson. Across from the desk, a procession of ants scurried near the hem of the blue curtains and crept up the windowpanes. Monday was the name of the clinic's custodian, and Tebeya found his laziness and inattention to detail inexcusable in a medical environment. She had talked to Nelson about replacing him. "Monday's a great fella," Nelson said, as if that should pardon Monday's abysmal cleaning skills. "He's my tennis buddy, you know. You'd never believe how good he is on the court. Not sure where he learned to play—"

"Dr. Landry, he's not doing his job well."

"Right, so, let me talk to him, all right?"

That had been two months ago, and nothing had changed. Nelson struggled to fire locals even if they underperformed, like the anesthesiologist who, during operations, fumbled airway techniques he should have mastered in basic training. Nelson protested that he had taken an oath to care for the sick and vulnerable, and it included any member of his staff, not his patients alone. Did Tebeya know that Francis, the anesthesiologist, was in the midst of building a new house for his family? "Would you fire him if you were in America?" Tebeya had asked, and Nelson paused, then said, "Yes. Yes, I would."

It would have taken ten minutes to bring the office to her sanitary standards. She had warned herself before accepting the clinic position: *do not become the person that does everything*. Yet, here she was, doing everything. She set her medical bag on the desk and considered what tasks to complete before Edward Hayes arrived.

Her sister Bintu, who had come to Rabata unannounced from

Jos the other day, would say Tebeya enjoyed the control and affected misery when she derived pleasure in bustling behind others
and overseeing their work and redoing it properly with irritating
precision. Bintu said Tebeya had liked being the sibling her parents gave responsibilities because Bintu had abdicated the duties
of a senior sister and been absorbed in her own interests instead
of caring for Tebeya and their youngest brother Patrick. Once,
when Patrick was three and under Bintu's care, he had wandered
away from the smaller house they once lived in and gotten lost.
Tebeya had searched and found him tangled in bramble, crying to
be freed, and Bintu had said, "It's nothing. Small-small scratch. Is
he not alive?"

In adulthood, Bintu had reclaimed the firstborn role. She
married and had children as their parents expected. She lived in a
house similar in size to their parents'. At moments, Tebeya thought
she desired the life Bintu had created for herself. Envy made one
want the trappings of another because it seemed the person in possession of them lived a fulfilling life. What you wanted was the
fulfillment, but jealousy made you think you needed the trappings.
Tebeya had her position in the mission clinic. She had the respect
of her staff. She had her father's pride in her work. She reminded
herself of this as she wiped the dirt from the file cabinet and carried
out the dustbin to be emptied.

An hour later, the clinic employees assembled in the staff room
to welcome the regional coordinator. Nelson was still nowhere to
be seen.

The staff stood in an anxious circle, shooting confused glances
in Tebeya's direction. Morning delays made for a longer day. Since
he was responsible for the Rabata mission station, Reverend Jim
was also in attendance. He had come for the clinic staff's standing morning prayer session and to speak with Edward Hayes. He
would participate in the tour before leaving for his pastoral duties.
He wore a gray suit, and the black clerical collar he was rarely with-

out hugged his neck. The sleeves of the suit were wrinkled. Had the Reverend's house servant Manasseh not seen fit to iron it out? Tebeya shook the thought from her mind. What did it matter? He was here, waiting with more patience than Edward Hayes.

Tebeya avoided Edward's swelling brows and instead watched the moving hands of the clock tick down to 8:30 a.m. Was it possible to find Nelson and kill him for this embarrassment? Of all the days to be late, when Edward Hayes only came twice a year for review: this month, and six months later in September.

Nelson had arrived late for staff meetings over the past two weeks. He had also been absentminded yesterday, and she caught him making minor clinical errors. And yet she had convinced herself he would be punctual and prepared for the tour and inspection.

On the way here, she had held back from commanding Benedict to drive in the opposite direction so she could pound on Nelson's door and see to it that he was dressed, shaved, and gulping a caffeinated drink.

She sighed in annoyance at her own self-restraint.

"Dr. Awyebwi," Edward Hayes said. "Shall we get started?"

His face was endearing, like an inquisitive animal—a handsome, slight face with kind eyes. He had narrow shoulders and a healthy fluff of dark hair, and the tautness of his skin made it nearly impossible to guess his true age. He could have been thirty or forty-five.

"Dr. Landry will be here soon," she said. "He knows you're coming."

"I'm giving my morning to your clinic, Dr. Awyebwi," he said, "and I've got a two-hour drive to the next appointment—"

"I have some appointments myself," Reverend Jim said.

Katherine Parson poured a steaming cup of tea and clinked the spoon against the side. "Now, listen, Edward," she said, "we do tend to run into patients on some mornings while trying to get here. I'm sure Nelson got a little sidetracked."

"It's true," Tebeya said in rare agreement. "We can never predict our mornings."

"Jim, Edward, I'd be happy to start the tour until Nelson arrives." Katherine handed Edward the cup of tea along with a napkin, prepared to take him by the elbow and lead him off.

Tebeya wished she had a more favorable opinion of her senior nurse. In Tebeya's first month at the clinic, Katherine trailed after her, offering unrequested advice. If Tebeya ordered a treatment for a patient, Katherine Parson would say, "Well, actually, back in America, we'd…" Everything was *back in America*, as if America dictated how things should be done in every other country around the world.

"There's no need, Nurse Katherine," Tebeya said, not moving from her position. "I'll conduct the tour with Edward."

Katherine adjusted her white nurse's hat, a miniscule overturned boat on her head. "Well, I suppose I'll wait with the others, then."

"Yes, that will be good." Tebeya turned to Edward and Reverend Jim. "Please come with me. Let us begin the tour."

She directed both of them to the twelve-bed ward and handed Edward the report she had compiled, which included statistics of patients seen, maternity deliveries, and number of surgical procedures performed. She discussed the most prevalent cases: malaria, tuberculosis, typhoid, and guinea worm. She showed them the dispensary, informing them about the quality and expense of the medications they imported from England, the Netherlands, and America. Her shoes made powerful, satisfying noises as she led Edward Hayes and Reverend Jim through the corridors, which felt confining with so many patients lining the walls. She greeted them and calmed those fretting over their illnesses. They were pleased to shake hands with Reverend Jim, and some asked him to pray over their sick children. Their requests held him up, and he soon waved Tebeya and Edward on to continue without him.

She led Edward to another room where they housed a large,

expensive stationary X-ray machine, a brand new and essential purchase. She discussed their recent in-country equipment purchases—beds, operating tables, autoclaves, and lamps.

"This is swell," Edward said, leaning a hand against the smooth bed of the X-ray machine. "You've all been running this clinic seamlessly for three years, seeing more patients than some of our other clinics."

"Yes, Dr. Landry and the architect the mission sent—"

"Tom Wright, came here from Michigan—"

"Yes, Mr. Wright. They planned the clinic building and operations very well."

"Don't be modest, Dr. Awyebwi. You're integral to the success of this clinic."

"Let us continue," she said. The generator droned outside as she showed him to the operating theater with its clean windows and sterilized instruments.

Nelson rushed in then. His hair was wet and mussed, his face glowing from exertion, and his shirt belted into trousers instead of the shorts and tennis shoes he generally wore around the clinic. He donned trousers a handful of times during the year, on occasions such as this, or when the Benue-Plateau state medical officer visited.

He pumped Edward's hands and said in a long, voluptuous exhale, "You wouldn't believe the morning I had. I tell you what: someone's gunning for me. How are you, Ed?"

"It's good to have you join us," Edward said. Despite his height, Edward leaned his head back to have a proper look at Nelson's flushed face. "Dr. Awyebwi's handled things perfectly well so far. What was the delay?"

"I'm afraid I'd bore you with the details," Nelson said, adjusting his stethoscope. "Just one of those mornings. I'd tell you more, but there's a lot we've got to get through—"

"I was just showing Mr. Hayes the operating theater," Tebeya said.

"Wonderful," Nelson said. "Let's get a move on then, shall

we?" He assumed the charge, speaking fluidly about the operations they performed, and smartly guided the conversation to the need for more equipment and staff to better serve their patient population.

Tebeya's time with Edward Hayes was over, and its brevity left her stunned. She followed the two men and tried not to remember that she had been recruited to stay in Dublin, and when she returned to Nigeria also recruited to keep practicing at a hospital in Mkar—a three-hundred-bed building boasting local and expatriate doctors—but instead had chosen to serve this clinic in the town of her birth under an increasingly unreliable director.

She had interviewed with the mission while working at Mkar, and Nelson offered her the position as soon as her interview ended. "I can't think of anyone more fitting to work side by side with," he had said, enfolding her hand in his massive ones and shaking it with vigorous enthusiasm. He offered her his medical tomes from America and encouraged her desire to change clinic culture. Clinics and health centers typically trained male primary school leavers as junior nursing assistants or aides. She had advocated for training young women at theirs, saying to Nelson, "Why should the men in this town be the only ones with opportunities?" Nelson had said, "Listen, of course, I'm on board. Ask Jim. He'll tell you I was one of the first physicians in Rockford to have Black nurses on staff." Tebeya had said, "Good, then me and you, we'll be fine, won't we?" She reached for these memories on days like today.

"What happened this morning, Dr. Landry?" Tebeya asked when they were alone on the front steps of the clinic, after seeing Edward Hayes off. "We were all waiting for you."

"Rough start to the day." He turned toward the passel of patients sitting on the grass and benches. "I'm sorry, really, that I put you in such a bind. It wasn't my intention."

She ventured to ask, "How is your wife?"

He blinked. "Oh, Virginia? Why do you ask?"

"The letters, no? They came here for you some days ago—"

"You know, I'm not sure why Jack keeps delivering them here when I've asked him to send it to the mission compound with everyone else's."

"Is Virginia doing well?"

"She's great, just fine."

"Okay—that is good. Give my regards to her when you next speak." She studied him for any angst, wondering how she managed to find herself in an investigative role. "Those-your judgmental eyes. I can do without them," her sister Bintu had said the other day, when Tebeya asked why her sister's husband Thomas and her niece and nephew had not come to Rabata with Bintu. Is this what Nelson thought as he stuttered over her simple inquiry?

She pressed, "Is Virginia planning a visit to come and see us in Nigeria? She must want to see the clinic you built."

"Come here? To Africa?" he said, his mouth in an uncertain twist.

"She should travel to Rabata so we can meet her."

An intake coordinator pushed the entrance open, and Nelson stepped to the side to avoid the swinging door. The coordinator announced five new admissions were waiting in the ward and a returning patient in the first private examination room.

"I'm right behind you," Nelson said, and followed the girl inside with an alacrity Tebeya interpreted as relief that he had escaped further probing.

It was Virginia, Tebeya decided, as she walked in after him. Virginia was causing trouble across the ocean in America. This faceless woman who had allowed her husband freedom to travel the world and come to Nigeria to launch this mission clinic, without intentions of ever joining him. Tebeya should have sympathy for Nelson, but she carried little. She mustered sympathy for herself, for the fear that the issues cropping up in Nelson might be deeper than she knew. For the certainty that she would be the one tasked to deal with them.

CHAPTER FOUR

ZANYA TOOK QUICK, CONFIDENT STRIDES across the road toward the church construction site, the uneven hem of his trousers striking his ankles. In a few minutes, he'd have them rolled to his knees, stomping barefoot in a shallow pit mixing clay-rich soil, water, and grass for a sludge that would be poured into wood molds for bricks. He did not mind the walk but would have preferred to drive the mission's Bedford pickup this early morning, fiddling with the radio, desperate to hear a song that mirrored his cheerful mood. Gary Parson oversaw maintenance of the mission facilities, and he had borrowed the pickup for an errand to Keffi. He volunteered to bring back materials the laborers needed from their supplier and would return the pickup to the site later today, the bed of it filled with heaps of sand and gravel.

All this week, Zanya had seen admiration in the eyes of the young boys on the street, the men who greeted him at Shigudu's or Flo's restaurant. Mothers in the marketplace had called out to him, hoping for an anecdote he had forgotten to mention on Sunday, one that they would be in possession of to share with their children. He talked to them though he did not retell the story. He did not want to relive the memory of that night. If he thought too deeply about what could have happened to him in Yawari, a pit of fear took shape inside his mouth, one as hard and grainy as a cashew seed, and it would seem intent on going deep into his body, seeking to lodge.

And Nami. This sweet, beautiful woman. What would have happened to her if his relatives' scheme to burn him alive had succeeded? She had been patiently waiting for him to ask the Reverend about the associate pastor position, which would put him in better standing when he approached her family for her hand in marriage. After his testimony, she had said Reverend Jim would begin to see him differently, to consider him for leadership in the mission church, and of course, he had thought the same. He had ideas about evangelism and the structure of the church and what traditions from their people the church could begin to incorporate into their worship. There were rules against drinking and polygamy that he would have done away with, like the Anglicans. Rules he did not think the Americans had considered when they came to Rabata to minister to their people. He carried a notebook of these ideas, and sometimes he fished it out of his trouser pocket to jot notes. "This is why the church needs Nigerian leaders," Nami had said when he shared his ideas, "someone like you, Zanya." He smiled when he heard these sentiments from her, when she made him feel like more than his parents or family had, like he was not only a laborer, but also a man of brilliance and purpose.

His uncle, who had paid for him to go to secondary school, were he still alive, would also have wanted Zanya to advance with the mission. Zanya remembered the drive to Kunama over a decade ago when he was a fourteen-year-old boy, leaving his village for the first time. He and his uncle had driven on the Saturday before the first term commenced. His uncle lectured him about the opportunities he would find as a scholar, advising him to study in England or America for university and return to serve a new Nigeria as a civil servant or parliamentarian. The responsibility of the nation was going to come to the youth, he said. It was September of 1960—Nigeria had formally petitioned Britain for independence. Abubakar Tafawa Balewa was to be the prime minister in the North, and Nnamdi Azikiwe the appointed president of the new republic. The country was poised for independence, for the coming together of disparate regions.

To this day, he recalled the beauty of the campus. KUNAMA SECONDARY SCHOOL was written in large block letters above the archway, two paths intersecting at the entrance and leading up a hill toward the school dormitories and buildings. Boys strode by in groups, jabbing each other and laughing with such familiarity Zanya deemed it their intention to make him feel a foreigner to their campus. He had looked on at the tableau of boys Kunama had fashioned, and they had all looked cleaner and sharper than him. Their hair shaved low and edged, their socks taut and unblemished, their white shirts ironed and neat; they all belonged together in an advert for Omo detergent. The boys had flashed telegenic smiles at the new and nervous students.

"Soon, Zanya," his uncle said, before he left, "you'll be like one of those boys."

When Zanya's uncle died at the end of his fourth year at Kunama, his father withheld the money his uncle had intended for his final year of schooling. Zanya had come back to work in Yawari, building houses with his father again in different towns and villages, knowing his path would not look the same as his former schoolmates. He would need to fight to progress in life, as he had fought for other things. Although he had worked with his father before going off to secondary school, the task of brickmaking and construction became laborious and monotonous when he returned, after he had experienced Kunama and seen boys who would go on to be barristers, clerks, engineers, doctors, and civil servants.

He could have taken exams and gone to university in the Soviet Union with a full scholarship, like his former dormitory mate Bashiru, or gone to the UK and America like some of his other classmates. Whenever he remembered the day his father told him he could not return to Kunama, whatever he was looking at or doing in the present became colorless or wearisome, a sudden homage to his failure. Bashiru had become a big man now. He had finished his university degree in Moscow and lived in Kaduna, working as a manager of operations at Nigerian Food Storage Ltd.

It was unfair how life happened, how diligence and desire could fail to yield opportunity. He and Bashiru used to compete about being first in class, and Zanya had often surpassed Bashiru with his high marks. He had studied more than Bashiru. He would sit in the top bunk with his textbook, reading pages after pages, while Bashiru lazed on the bottom bunk, disrupting Zanya and hungering for a game of cricket or Fives.

There was a verse in the scriptures he had pondered for days when he first read it. *For to him who has will more be given, and he will have abundance; but from him who has not, even what he has will be taken away.* Gary Parson said the scripture was in reference to spiritual truths. Those who yearned for God would be given more revelation of God, and those that did not hunger for God, even the knowledge they had of God would be taken from them. Zanya had liked his own interpretation, that the verse reflected the injustices of life. People like him who did not have much could have even that little taken away from them.

As he walked closer to the site, sweat from his armpits leached into his shirt, as if in anticipation of the labor awaiting him in today's heat. He was close enough to hear the clanging of pots and the chatter from the women who came in the mornings to sell fried yam and kosai to the laborers. Soon, they would begin frying, and the aroma of spiced beans and pepper and the crackling of fire would heighten the hunger of the men.

Piles of bricks, sand, and gravel had overtaken the land. Two weeks ago, the perimeter of the building had been marked with timber pegs and string lines before the laborers dug trenches for the foundation. Now, brick by brick, the walls were slowly rising into the sky. When Zanya first started with the mission, he had savored each construction project—the houses, the renovation of the school, the clinic. But when he worked on the church these days, he sensed his impatience to quickly finish, for it seemed to be keeping him in the same role.

Kago and Betabwi, two of his laborers, stood near the mixing pit for bricks when he arrived. The ditch held about four gallons of water, six gallons of chopped straw, and more than twice the amount of soil as water and straw. Kago's red-capped head was close to Betabwi's bare one, and the two of them whispered, glancing around as if the women sellers might overhear their words.

"Wetin happen?" Zanya said when he reached them.

"Fire Boy!" Betabwi clapped Zanya's back.

"Ah, stop, Betabwi," he said. "Wetin be the matter? The way una dey stand so."

"Wahala dey o," Betabwi said. He had no sleeves on his shirt, and the large gaping holes showed off his hairy chest and muscular arms.

"Dem never bring today goods?" Zanya surveyed the site. A lorry was scheduled to deliver water tanks this morning.

"We hear say dem other laborers dey make more money than us," Kago said. He lifted his cap slightly off his brow. The words RIGHT ON! were emblazoned on the front panel. "My cousin wey dey work for mission for Jos, na him wey tell me this."

Zanya looked from Betabwi to Kago. "Our same mission?"

"Almost double for the same type of work wey we dey do for here," Kago said.

Zanya whistled. "That cannot be. Double?"

He could have done much more with that kind of money.

"I didn't know this. Kago, you sure say wetin your cousin tell you na true?"

"No be lie," Kago said. "Them dey do the same thing we dey do."

"We want better money," Betabwi said. "We come meet you so you go tell Reverend."

"You know our situations," Kago said.

"I'm hearing you," Zanya said. "I'm hearing you."

It was serious if Kago was here asking with Betabwi. Kago was not the kind of person to complain against the mission. He was one of Zanya's most dependable laborers. He taught language learning to the missionaries and had worked as their driver. Years ago, he had risked his life to help Gary Parson transport war refugees to the Cameroonian border. He had proven to be serious-minded about the church, and he and his family had taken to the Christian faith.

But this morning, Zanya had hoped to speak to Reverend Jim about the pastoral position after the Bible study. So whether it was Kago or not, this talk about wages would have to wait. The Reverend was due to arrive in the next half hour and lead the Bible session with the men, as was his custom on Wednesdays.

Betabwi said, "When Reverend come, you go tell am abi?"

"Ah, Betabwi," Zanya said. "We must see if this is true."

"It's true. If you no go ask Reverend, we go ask—"

"No, no, I will ask, but not today," Zanya said. "Let me find the proper time."

⁂

Zanya led Reverend Jim around the perimeter of the church foundation. They came upon the side of the foundation where the administrative offices would be, behind the sanctuary. He visualized wooden pews and a corridor that would lead to the pastoral offices, one for Reverend Jim and the other for the associate pastor. The windows would look out on the land closest to the river, where a jumble of shoots, thorny brush, orange, paw paw, tamarind, and palm trees grew. Land on the other side was a bald, sunbaked surface. Zanya had gone up to the Awyebwis' grand mansion with Reverend Jim and Gary Parson when the mission purchased the seven acres from Baba Bintu.

"How much longer before the building is complete?" Reverend Jim asked.

"Two months' time," Zanya said.

"Two months?" Reverend Jim beheld the clear blue March sky. Calm today, but with the approaching rainy season, a haven for storm clouds.

"Before the rains come," Zanya said, noticing.

Dry season was the ideal time to build. They should have begun in October or November of last year, but funding had not come from headquarters until last month, February, and Reverend Jim had not wanted to wait any longer to begin construction.

Zanya indicated an area farther behind the marked foundation. "We can build an outdoor structure here, a place for mothers, if we have additional material after the church is complete. When the children cry, they can have a place to go and sit comfortably."

"That's a wonderful thought," Reverend Jim said.

"I was also thinking," Zanya said, leading them along, "that local farmers in the church can help us to cultivate the land around the building—"

"I hadn't thought of this."

"See, we can plant money-producing trees—mangos, locust bean, and shea butter. We can use these funds to support the mission church."

"Very good. I like how you're thinking. Keep this up, Zanya, and we'll have you overseeing the building of our guesthouse next year."

"Guesthouse? Here in Rabata?"

"That's right. The mission has plans to build a hotel for mission travelers, and it'd be open to other guests too, non-missionaries. They're in the process of solidifying the plans, securing the funding. It'd be the perfect project for you to take on next, I'd think."

It was not what he wanted to be doing in a year's time. In a year's time, he wanted to be standing behind the pulpit, preaching, not holding a brick in his hands.

He nodded. "Oh. Okay, sir. Thank you."

"Let's gather the men for prayer," Reverend Jim said, settling comfortably into a chair Zanya had set up for him under the shade of a pear tree.

Zanya called to the men, and the laborers cast their shovels aside and left their wheelbarrows and came toward the circle of trees. They mumbled incoherent greetings, and they either flopped down in the grass with muddied legs outstretched or arranged their bodies against tree trunks with hands behind their heads.

"Before we build the Lord's house," Reverend Jim said, his red leather Bible on his leg, "we must ask Him to bless the work of our hands. Second Timothy says we ought to purge ourselves from dishonorable practices. Let us be sanctified so we may be fit for the master's use and prepared to do every good work. As always, let us begin by confessing our sins—"

"Palm wine," Betabwi said, cutting the Reverend off.

"Yes o. Pammi," another agreed.

Zanya frowned. Normally, the men bowed their heads and said their confessions quietly. "To ourselves," Jim said, "as we usually do."

Another laborer ignored his ask. "When I drink pammi, I wan kneel down begin dey praise God. Because na him make something wey sweet like pammi, ba?"

"When my wife vex me," Betabwi said. "How you wan make I calm down—"

"If you no take pammi small?" someone interjected.

The other men chortled. Betabwi once had three wives. Reverend Jim, in upholding mission tenets for baptism of new believers, had required Betabwi to divorce two of his wives. Their laughter held long enough for Zanya to hear the frostiness undergirding it. It was not a pure and affectionate sound. He detected a mockery in their eyes, and his stomach sank. They were going to bring up the wages.

Reverend Jim looked uncomfortable as he twiddled the clerical collar around his neck. Zanya decided to speak up. He could change the direction before it devolved. "Men, we have work to finish. Please, if we can pay attention—"

"It's fine, Zanya." It seemed Reverend Jim would entertain their unusual decision to publicly air their sins. "Palm wine, women. Yes, what else shall we confess? Dishonesty?"

A new laborer grinned, a glint in his eye. "Which one be dishonesty again, Reverend?"

"It's deceitfulness," Reverend Jim said cautiously. "Falsehood when truth is required."

The man twisted his mouth, contemplating the Reverend's definition. "Ehn, so I go tell my wife one thing and then commot go do anoda thing?"

"Yes, that would be one such example," Reverend Jim said. "What else, fellas?"

"Na only us get sin?" Betabwi said. "Reverend, every day, you dey make us talk our sin. You nko? Wetin be your own sin? Na God you be wey we no fit ask you?" He heaved himself up, snapped a twig and chewed it. "So wetin be your sins, Reverend?"

"My sins are many," Reverend Jim said, "and if we were to go through each of them, ponder my own failings, well, I'm afraid we'd be here all day."

"This is not the type of question you ask a man of God." Kago wrung the bill of his cap and fixed it back on his head. "You no suppose ask am to open him mouth talk all his sins."

"No, it's all right, Kago." Reverend Jim set his unopened Bible on his lap. "James 5:16 does say, *Therefore confess your sins to one another and pray for one another so that you may be healed.*' I confess to you, fellas, to harboring uncharitable thoughts about some of the people I come into contact with in my day to day—not any of you, of course."

Some of the men grunted, others laughed a little.

"I confess that from time to time, there comes over me a great reluctance to do the hard work of preaching. I confess to anger, anger at His plans, which appear misaligned with my own. I have wrestled with anger that God saw fit to take my dear wife too early."

There was a silence, and the men nodded, surprised that he had answered with candor, embarrassed by the catch in his voice.

"Now, I'd like us to get through the scripture," Reverend Jim said, leafing hurriedly through the pages of his Bible. "David said, *'Behold, I dwell in a house of cedar, but the ark of the covenant of the Lord is under a tent.'* We, like King David, are residing in houses of cedar, in palaces, and the Lord's house has not been built—"

"Reverend, na us you dey talk to?" asked a long-faced man with a pleasant smile. "No be you wey dey live for dat big house?"

"Am I not seeing it there?" Betabwi pointed with his lips toward the mission compound. "House wey we build you."

Another laborer thrust his body forward. "Reverend, make you come see where me, my wife and my pikin dey live. After you see am eh? You no go count us as people wey live for palaces. You even get well inside compound."

Zanya crossed his arms and looked at the laborers. Betabwi must have put the others up to this. To prove a point about his capabilities and show Zanya he had some authority. He must have spoken to the laborers and stirred their frustrations. They would never have done something like this when Zanya first hired them. A twinge of worry surfaced because, like children, they were outgrowing their dependence on him, and like children, this new understanding of their power might lead them to distrust his guidance.

"Gentlemen," Reverend Jim said. "Today, we're speaking of David's call to build God's palace, and how God has chosen you to do His work. We are not here to discuss the mission compound, the houses we have."

"Increase our money," Betabwi said, with a quick glance toward Zanya. "Then we go come build God house like we build your palace for you."

"More wages?" Reverend Jim frowned. "What are you speaking of?"

Zanya walked closer to the Reverend's chair. "This is not the time to discuss such matters." Had he not asked Betabwi to wait? Had he not said he would be the one to ask at the appropriate time?

One laborer pulled himself up. "Reverend, we know say you fit add more money for us."

Betabwi said, "After all the work we don do for you—"

"Kago agrees," another laborer said. "Even if he no wan talk."

Kago, who had kept his word and not said anything, glowered at the man who had spoken but did not refute his claim.

"Men, please," Zanya said in Gbagyi, commanding their attention. Reverend Jim was moderately fluent in Hausa, and Zanya did not want the Reverend to understand fully. He spoke softly, like a teacher taming a classroom of boisterous children and tried to ignore the dread, the whisper in his mind that what he was saying was not enough to allay their frustrations. "I'm hearing your complaints. Please, don't spoil things now by asking for more pay when it is not the right time. Let me talk to the Reverend. What if he is angered? What if he insists that other laborers take your place? Let us wait."

After a silence and what seemed like reluctant nods of agreement, the men grudgingly turned to face Reverend Jim. The rest of the session proceeded without interruption. After the session ended, the men loped back across the grass to the construction site in twos and threes.

"I'm sorry." Zanya crouched beside the Reverend's chair.

"You knew?" Reverend Jim's tone was accusatory. "What is this about?"

"The men learned the mission is paying its workers more in Jos."

Reverend Jim fluffed a white handkerchief loose from his pocket. The helices of his ears shone pink. "What do you mean they learned of it?"

"They have relatives who work for the mission in Jos—"

"Is that right?" Reverend Jim was quiet a moment.

Zanya studied the Reverend. "Is it true? Is the mission paying them more money for the same work? This would be good money for our laborers."

"Listen, laborers in Rabata should not expect to receive pay equivalent to laborers in Jos. I'm also not at liberty to discuss what the mission pays laborers at other stations."

Zanya stood and dusted his palms before putting his hands in his pockets. The laborers would not be happy with such a response. He imagined Reverend Jim in his office radioing headquarters or the other mission stations to warn them against disclosing wages.

"Just know," Reverend Jim said, "that what the mission pays its laborers in Rabata is fair. I trust you to relay this to our men and take care of this situation."

"Laborers will always complain about their pay, Reverend. If you took every complaint seriously, you would never have time to work."

"Well, if today was any indication of how serious they are—"

"But you see that they're still working," Zanya said, as if reassuring a child. "None of them have left. I'll speak with them."

Reverend Jim tapped his foot against the leg of the chair in rapid movements and brushed invisible crumbs from his trousers. Zanya would leave him alone with his thoughts. Clearly it was no longer the right time to ask about the pastoral position. He walked off to work among the laborers, who were testing the bricks for dryness and turning over those in need of the sun's heat.

CHAPTER FIVE

MANGOES, THICK-SKINNED AND RIPENED, offered a sweet aroma to the night. Zanya plucked a large one from its branches and offered it to Nami as they sat next to each other on the ground. They bit into the pulpy flesh, the mango slippery in their hands as they savored the syrup dripping between their fingers.

Their routine was to meet outside the primary school after she finished teaching, but today Nami wanted to meet near the old well, under this tree. Zanya stretched his legs on the grass and pressed his back against the scaly trunk. Just sitting next to her, seeing the familiar slant of her neck in the darkness, caused him to feel as he had not throughout the day, like he had once again found refuge simply by being in her nearness.

"You're angry with me," he said.

She sighed. "I'm here waiting and waiting."

"You have to trust me, Nami."

"Everybody is asking me when we will marry."

"I'm working very hard. You just have to—"

"I just have to what? Wait and wait? You should have asked about the position regardless of the men. Can a person not ask for two things at once?"

"It wasn't the right time."

Zanya threw the mango pit aside, and it landed without noise in the grass. He pictured a colony of ants sniffing the sweetness of it in the dark, their tiny bodies tunneling toward the oblong seed.

"My father is wondering if you're serious. He's wondering what kind of man you are."

"Haven't I proven myself already?" Nami's father, a bank clerk at Standard Bank in Keffi, had yet to take a liking to him. During the formal introduction, he sat with arms folded and eyed Zanya with skepticism. "What else must I do?"

"He says he doesn't know why things are taking so long—"

"But he knows the things with my family."

"I've told him."

His family was supposed to bear the responsibility of the wedding, but he knew his parents would not contribute anything. Since Zanya's uncle had long died, his brother-in-law, Shagye, had represented him and visited Nami's uncles to tell them of Zanya's interest in marrying her. The introduction had followed with them bringing a set of dishes, drinks, and kola nuts to Nami's relatives. He had been saving since then so they could plan the wedding, and he could pay the bride price and buy the list of gifts Nami's family had requested.

"Nami, I will need more time," he said.

"Well, you better hurry before another man comes and asks for my hand."

He turned to her, reassured to see the outline of a smile, the moonlight glistening on her lips. He had never counted money this intently before, each shilling, each pound. Being with a woman in such a serious manner had produced new worries. An amount that had seemed sufficient became a pittance for two. A mate of his in Kunama used to say, "The handsomeness of a man is in his pockets." Alone in the small room he rented at the edge of town, he went without meals every now and then and could stretch his money. He could, in the morning, consume a portion of fried yams purchased from one of the women on the construction site and not eat again until night or the following day.

When he thought about the amount he needed to wed Nami, his head filled with a pressure he had never felt, like standing in a room full of smoke, wanting to breathe and not finding a way to breathe.

He and Nami had met one morning when he had forgotten to clean the classroom after service on a Sunday afternoon and so arrived early to do it the following Monday. It was the classroom where she taught mathematics to her class five students. She had rearranged the desks by then and bagged the forgotten items—a child's shoe, a pack of cigarettes, a forgotten Bible.

"Our people know God, but they don't know how to clean?" Nami had said.

"Ah, so," he had joked, "you're not one of my admirers, then."

She laughed. "Kai, these admirers, they'll get themselves into trouble for you."

Something had reared within him in hearing her laughter—an aching desire to be near her laughter always. Nami had completed her studies at the Government Teacher's College in Keffi and come to work for the mission primary school. In the past two or three years, when he was not paying attention, she had become a full-figured young woman with shapely hips and a decisive sway. That Monday morning, she wore her hair in a sleek braided bun, trussed with a white and blue head tie. His gaze traveled from the sunburst of blue petals on the collar of her blouse to the birthmark on her neck up to her remarkably high cheekbones. He asked to see her again, outside of the primary school.

"Come now, Nami," he said, breaking the silence in the darkness and reaching for her hand. "You're not going to leave me for another man. I won't allow it."

"I'll remind my father of how serious you are," Nami said, in a voice soothing to his ears. "That you know what you're doing."

"So, you will wait?"

She teased, "Where else can I go?"

He thought this was how her students must feel in her presence, a little renewed or rejuvenated by her optimism and care. He was a lucky man to have her, and he should not play with the luck he had been given.

"Things will be well, Zanya," she said.

He rose from the ground and extended his hand to help her rise. He was about a foot taller than her, and she came up to his chest when she stood.

"You are right," he said. "Things will be fine."

"Am I not always right?" she said.

How was it possible to feel both hollow and comforted? He would do what he needed to marry Nami, to have her at his side. He reached for her hand and enclosed it gently in his.

CHAPTER SIX

JUMMAI WALKED THROUGH A PASSAGEWAY between the shops and salons on the main road, stepping over pools of fetid water to reach the path home. The night smelled of dust and exhaust, and something calming and sweet ran through it—the scent of blossoms, like the flowers that grew along the wall of the mission compound. She lived with her family in the center of town, not too far from the Glories and Blessings provisions store, in a two-room house with a cooking area and latrine outside. She shared a room with her five siblings, and her mother and her mother's husband, Tin City, slept in the other.

Whenever she returned from the Parsons', she compared her home to the mission compound. The homes on the compound had freshly cemented verandas, generators, and big, sweeping yards. In the mission garden grew rhubarb, cucumbers, zucchinis, carrots, cabbage, and radishes. Lemon, mango, grapefruit, guava trees, and banana plants populated the compound, and the storage room had mountains of onions, cassava, yams, sweet potatoes, and rice. The kitchen held shelves of Mrs. Katherine's strawberry jams, sugar cubes, tomato sauces, and the canned bacon and spices they brought back from Missouri when they went on furlough. Almost every week, as they had this evening, the Parsons sent her home with food—onions, oil, biscuits, spaghetti, or vegetables from the garden. It made her grateful for the Parsons, and at the same time, the sack of food reminded her of how much more these people had. Imagine, the three of them, four when Allison was here, having more food to eat than her bigger family.

She reached the entrance to her family's house and heard but did not see her brother, Yakwo, shouting behind the compound to their brother Innocent and another boy who sounded like Elijah. Yakwo was saying if he were Zanya, he would have taken a cutlass and whacked the villagers. No one would have captured him or tried to kill him.

"Yakwo, you would have burned," Elijah said.

"I would not have," Yakwo said. "Just like Zanya, I would have lived!"

"We will burn you now and see!" Innocent said.

More shouts and chuckles followed before the three of them raced out from behind the house. Elijah was unable to match Yakwo's speed, and he tripped and fell in his attempt, calling out, "Yakwo, wait!" Yakwo did not wait. He snickered and ran ahead, nearly colliding with Jummai when he leapt to avoid an old tire.

"Where are you going?" she demanded, grabbing his collar. He smelled of smoke. "Are you misbehaving, Yakwo? Don't go and misbehave o."

"Ah, Jummai, leave me—" Yakwo said, wrenching free.

"If I hear that you went and caused trouble—"

"We didn't do anything."

Elijah and Innocent supported Yakwo. "We're not doing anything, Jummai!" Which meant they were doing something.

"What did you bring us?" Yakwo said, pulling the bag open on her shoulder.

"Leave it," she said. "Elijah, why are you here when your mother is looking for you? Go before she worries."

The three of them ran off from her, down the path to the river and not toward the mission compound. Yakwo and Innocent were always doing something, and it was never something useful or good. At a naming ceremony, Yakwo had once boasted to guests that Innocent and Sayi possessed miraculous power because they were twins. They can harm anybody who is mean to them, he had threatened. "Who told you?" Jummai asked when she discovered the three of them crouched near a bush, their teeth and tongues orange-stained and mouths shining with oil from the spoils they had gotten after frightening other children. Their mother still believed the old saying that twins could curse a person who wronged them. This was where Yakwo, Innocent, and Sayi had learned it, and that night, they had gotten a good amount of Fanta and meat with their nonsense threats.

Jummai surveyed the cooking area outside the house. No firewood burned. No peeled yam waited to be boiled or fried. No onions or peppers. Nobody had cooked. Her grandmother often said, "It is only a lazy person that sees the first sign of rain." This was her mother every day, looking for rain. Her brothers and Tin City, too. They waited for her to come home after cooking and cleaning for the Parsons to cook and clean again. Her grandmother, who had lived with Jummai and her mother after Jummai's father left, would never have permitted such idleness. She would have taught Innocent and Yakwo to wash, cook, sweep, weave chairs, and fry kuli-kuli, no matter that they were boys. She would have disciplined them, swatting their bottoms or mouths.

Jecinda helped Jummai when she could, but often she walked away with her books and hid behind the house to finish her assignments, or she left to work at the mission clinic in the afternoons. Nobody in the family disturbed Jecinda, but everybody could disturb Jummai. If somebody learned Jecinda worked at the mission clinic, they would say, "Kai, you're secondary school girl, and you're working like an ordinary person?" If not for her mother and all her siblings, Jummai could have attended secondary school like her sister, who was doing so because Miss Delores had written letters to her Pennsylvania church and asked them to support Jecinda with donations.

Jummai peered inside the house and saw Tin City lying on the wooden bench. He had his feet propped on her mother's lap as she trimmed his toenails, collecting the jagged clippings and throwing them on the floor, nudging them in a pile with her foot. Tin City had come home from the tin mines for a few days and would return soon. He was a thin man who sniffed smokeless tobacco, littering tins of J&H Wilson around the house. She resented her father each time she returned and found Tin City in his place. She had been very young when her father left. He had departed for his farm one morning and never returned. They had stopped fearing him dead when they discovered he had gone to live with another woman and work on a cocoa plantation in the Western region, in Yorubaland.

Soon after, her mother had married the man who became Jecinda and Yakwo's father. Jummai had liked this new father, for he had sent her to primary school in the neighboring town and sent her for one year of secondary school before her mother divorced him, too.

The twins, Sayi and Innocent, were birthed in her mother's third marriage. Tin City was her mother's fourth marriage. He was a man who was as terrible as Sayi and Innocent's father and more absent than the others, working months at a time in the tin mines in Jos. He had brought their youngest brother, Walu, from his previous marriage. Her mother was now pregnant with her sixth child, Tin City's second. Jummai carried sadness for her mother and had visions of her as a young woman with a strong back, and arms and legs as fat and healthy as tubers, skin as smooth as a melon, before Jummai's father and all these other men entered her life. With each passing year, she realized her mother's walk—stiff on such a short, lithe body—and the wrinkles on her neck were physical manifestations of the pain she'd suffered.

"Who's there?" Tin City shouted, peering in the direction she stood. "Jummai, is that you? Standing at the door like one common thief?"

"I'm the one," Jummai said.

"Oya, come and give us the money."

"Ah, don't move," her mother said, pinching the biggest toe on Tin City's left foot and steadying the nail clipper in her hand, resting it on her pregnant stomach. A sleepy Walu sat by their mother's side, leaning on her arm, his head lolling forward in tiredness.

Tin City said, "How much have we made today?"

Imagine him saying *we*. Jummai cleaned, cooked, swept, washed, and yet at the end of the day, her mother and Tin City collected her money as their own.

Tin City threw his feet to the ground and bounded up at the sound of the coins jangling as she removed the sack from her pocket. He wore a ragged white shirt, stretched and loose at the neck, and he scratched his stomach under the thin, cheap material.

"Bring, let me see," Tin City said.

"Wait until you see the small money they paid me," she said.

It was not true; the Parsons paid her well, but she had to pretend. So she went through the pretense, bringing the coins out of the bag and counting them, pressing each one into Tin City's open, callused palms. The money would be used for things they did not need, like more tobacco and Tin City's gambling. They would not use it for food or clothes or to fix the house. So after Mrs. Katherine counted the money she owed Jummai for the week, Jummai would go into the kitchen and put some coins into a sack for her mother and Tin City, then hide the rest in her shoe.

"Is this all the money?" her mother asked.

"Yes, Mama. This is all," Jummai said.

Her mother sucked her teeth. "My daughter, this small money?"

"You have more money than this, Jummai," Tin City said.

"I don't have—"

"Shut up! You have. You can deceive your mother, but you won't deceive me."

"I have given you the money," Jummai said. "Where is your own?"

"Am I your age mate that you're talking to me like this?"

She did not move when he came closer to her, as if to grab her shoulders and shake them until more money fell out of her wrapper. She was unafraid of him, and she did not lower her gaze to show respect as she should have done. She looked at him without blinking so he knew that he was not her father. He was like all the other men her mother had married. He would soon be gone, and it would be her mother and her brothers and sisters again.

"Are you trying to cheat me?" he said, eyes flashing with anger.

Jummai said, "How can I cheat you with my own money?"

"This-your mouth!" He narrowed his eyes and lifted his hand as if to slap her. "Listen to this daughter of yours—she should not be living in this house anymore. Haven't I told you?"

"My daughter, please," her mother said, frightened by Tin City's anger. "Answer him."

"I'm not cheating anybody, Mama."

Her mother said, "Jummai, you know there is a hole in the floor in me and my husband's room, where the cement has broken—"

"I know," she said.

"If there is more money—"

"Mama, this is all they gave me today," she said.

The house needed many repairs. She had heard that Zanya fixed the roof for Nami's family last week, and not once had he ever stepped foot in Jummai's family's compound. Nami's family could have afforded to fix their own roof. Had Nami asked Zanya, or had he done it without her asking? Or did he believe Jummai would have saved the money and done it herself? These are the questions she wanted to ask him the next time she saw him. She had wanted to go to him many days ago and had not yet gone.

Tin City went back to the bench with the money. "If you are lying to me, Jummai, you will suffer. The day I catch you, you will suffer."

"Oya," her mother said, "go and peel yam. Take Walu. Walu, go with Jummai."

"What of Jecinda?" Jummai said, lifting Walu. He was two and a little heavier now. Her fingers radiated with pain as she held him, and her back was sore. She had aches down her thighs and calves from the work she had done at the Parsons' house and from helping Manasseh—who was many years her senior—wash the Reverend and doctor's clothes.

"Don't disturb your sister," her mother said. "See how hard the girl works."

Jummai said nothing. She nestled Walu's warm body against hers.

The remaining coins, what Tin City had not taken, pressed against the soles of her feet. She liked how they felt, hard and cool, as she walked to the room she shared with her siblings. It would not be long before she saved enough to leave this house. Inside the room, she crouched, Walu's arms tight around her neck, and removed the money from her shoes, hiding it in a bag and locking it in a trunk the Parsons had given her.

CHAPTER SEVEN

"Now, WHICH HOUSE are we going to first?" Reverend Jim asked, seated on the passenger side of the pickup. It seemed as if he wanted a map in his hands to trace the roads.

"The family with the sick father," Zanya said. "He's been in and out of the clinic."

They had two visitations in a village past Keffi. As he drove, Reverend Jim relaxed next to him, his suit jacket off and thrown across his lap. The Reverend placed his elbow out of the open window. The hot metal must have stung his arm because he dropped it immediately and unhooked the cuff buttons of his shirt to rub the skin.

Before he could second-guess himself, Zanya said, "Reverend, you mentioned you are making a new position in the church."

Reverend Jim turned to look at him. "What's that, son?"

"The associate pastor position."

"That's right. I did say so, didn't I?"

"Many people came to hear me last Sunday," Zanya said, hearing a hunger in his voice. "I feel God calling me to do this work—"

"Preaching, you mean?"

"Yes, preaching." Last year, Zanya had approached Baba Bintu with confidence about purchasing land for the mission church and secured it without problem. Why did he feel anxious and uncertain making a request to the Reverend?

"Son, a calling is not as ephemeral as a feeling," Reverend Jim said, resting a hand on Zanya's shoulder. "To be called is to be haunted by a deep, urgent, and unshakeable power."

Zanya said, "I think I have it, Reverend, this urgency—"

"Well, that's just it, isn't it?" Reverend Jim said, extending his hands to capture the magnitude of his point. "Thinking won't keep you."

"Sorry, sir?"

"You can't *think* you have the calling, son. You must *know*."

It had been different that Sunday, standing at the pulpit. Instead of translating the Reverend's sermon in Gbagyi, he had spoken his own words. He could have stayed in the classroom the whole day. What food would he have needed? For when he became as he had that day, the Word of God became his bread, and he could have found new verses and remembered more stories his uncle used to tell him. When he had preached, it seemed as if the walls crumbled, and he stood in an open field, speaking to the congregants beyond the desks and chairs. When he thought about the ministerial work of speaking to others in their sufferings, doing it as his life's work, it filled him with meaning. It would entail long days, sinuous drives to remote, small villages, the work of convincing people of a truth that had once sounded to him like mythology—a son of God not of their own people who lived centuries ago, in a nation not their own, and claimed to be a deity. Yet, this Christian faith had upturned his life, and he had been drawn to it more than the faith of his father or family. It had humbled him into a weeping posture on the Reverend's floor—this promise of renewal and a new beginning, this promise of being born again. He had wanted to be born again since he had been born.

"Are you unhappy with us, Zanya? Is that it?"

"No, sir. I just think I'm capable of helping the mission in other ways. This is why I'm asking to become a preacher, like you."

Reverend Jim laughed, a friendly, noncommittal laugh. "You

didn't think I'd just give you the position, did you, Zanya?"

It was exactly what he had thought. After working four years for the mission, he had thought he would ask, and Reverend Jim would say, "You have become like a son to me. You may have what you have asked." He had failed to anticipate laughter and questions.

"What of training?" Zanya asked. "If I can receive pastoral training—"

"I'd have to look into the feasibility of it," Reverend Jim said, as if it would be an impossibly arduous task. "I hadn't thought about this for you—"

"Is now not the time for our people to start leading? Doesn't the mission have vision to become like SIM ECWA, where nationals are the ones directing and leading?"

"Well, let me be honest, Zanya. I think you're hungry for solid food while you're still in need of milk. Don't rush into leadership when you're an infant in the faith."

Zanya wanted to roll the pickup to a stop in the grass. He wanted to twist his head and say, "Me, Reverend? An *infant*?" But the Reverend would have raised his unruly white brows and put his finger in the groove under his nose and looked at Zanya as if he had confirmed his point about maturity.

Zanya did not do any of what he wanted to do. He repeated the words as a whisper, and his tongue smacked the back of his front teeth. Is this how Reverend Jim saw him? After all he had done for the mission and church? He could do nothing else but keep his eyes focused on the road ahead while holding the steering wheel so forcefully that he was certain when he released it at their destination, there would be imprints of his fingers denting the metal and plastic.

He turned on an unpaved road leading to a cluster of houses. A herd of cattle crossed the road with a herdsman who walked ahead, a traditional stick jutting over his right shoulder. The cattle's black snouts bobbed, and the sum of their white humps looked like mountain peaks. Zanya drove around the lagging cattle and parked in front of a house with a single palm tree in the front yard.

He found his voice again. "There is much I have learned from you in these four years. This is why I'm asking, Reverend."

"Tell you what. Let's do this slowly," Reverend Jim said. "There's a regional conference in Jos at mission headquarters the last weekend in April, Friday to Sunday. Why don't you come along? You'll get a sense of a pastor's mission. Let's start there."

"Please, Reverend, isn't this what I do with you every day? Isn't that what we're doing now?" He indicated the ailing man they had come to visit, lying on a pallet his family must have dragged outside. "I already know what the work is like."

"You'd sit in the sessions. Get a sense for what ministry demands of you. After you attend, we can reconsider your request. How's that?"

"Yes, sir," he said. "I will come to the conference."

"That's the spirit," Reverend Jim said.

Zanya cut the ignition and said what he did not feel: "Thank you, sir."

He had learned over years of working with the mission that these missionaries expected him to show a deep, expressive gratitude for the small things they gave him or did for him. When he lived on the mission compound, Reverend Jim had given him a gadget he could not use, and Zanya had had to thank him as if it were the most thoughtful gift he had ever received, and not a nonoperational dictaphone.

The sick man had propped himself up on his elbows and was waiting for them. He called out, "Fire Boy! Did you see me at the church?" as they drew closer.

"Sorry," Zanya said. "I didn't see you."

"I was there o."

Zanya squatted next to the pallet while the man's heavily pregnant wife walked outside with a chair for Reverend Jim.

"You came that Sunday?" Zanya said to the man. "Were you not sick, sir?"

"I made my eldest son come and carry me. I said I had to see for myself."

"Good, good." Zanya grinned. "Come again and see us."

The man waved flabby, thick-haired arms and let out a hearty laugh. "Let them set you on fire again, then I will come!"

The three of them spoke about the man's illness and the needs of his family, what the mission might provide to them. Zanya's mind wandered from the conversation and returned to the one he'd had with Reverend Jim in the pickup, which had left him dissatisfied.

He thought Reverend Jim would remember that when he had first come to Nigeria, in February of '67, Zanya was the one who rescued him after a robbery. It was the day he had decided to leave his family and village. Not knowing where he was going, he had walked for a couple of days, receiving lifts on lorries, sleeping behind shops, and wandering east without a destination in mind. He did not know what led him to that tree where he found a disheveled and bloodied Jim Clemens and a badly wounded mission driver, a vicious cut on his arm, and their Opel stalled and emptied of their luggage.

"Our car—these men came and took everything," the mission driver coughed out. "We thought they were helping us—" He struggled to push himself up and winced from the gashes on his palms. "Abeg, take Reverend," the driver said. "You fit carry am?"

Zanya had strained to lift Reverend Jim onto his back. His arms locked under the Reverend's thighs, and the Reverend's head rested in the crook of his neck, his chin on Zanya's shoulders. He had walked and walked until the flat-roofed houses of Rabata came into view. No clinic existed then, so the locals had directed him to the diviner. She had given Reverend Jim local medicine and fed him zhepo until he regained his health.

Reverend Jim would not have survived if Zanya had not come upon him that day. If he had left him at the base of the tree, the Reverend would have died. He had thought Reverend Jim would remember these things. He had not thought that these were things he needed to say.

CHAPTER EIGHT

TEBEYA HAD GONE TO LOOK at a block of newly developed flats the other day, and she wished now, sitting at the dining table with her mother and sister, that she had leased a place immediately instead of spending another evening in her parents' home.

Bintu's three-day visit had somehow extended into two interminable weeks. Tebeya had asked Bintu when she would return to her family, and Bintu behaved as if she could not conceive of journeying the three hours north to Jos. Thomas is in London for work, and the children are with their other grandparents, Bintu had said, as if that explained her presence.

Tebeya now understood that her mother had summoned Bintu to Rabata and asked her to speak to Tebeya about the dearth of suitors in her life and her incomprehensible preoccupation with the white people's clinic. Until last week, Bintu had been unhelpful and not broached the topic of marriage, for which Tebeya had been grateful. But a few days ago, a couple of men that Bintu introduced as acquaintances of Thomas had come to the house. Sensing what was happening, Tebeya had volunteered for night shifts at the clinic. Except for this evening, which she was soon coming to regret as she listened to her sister.

"People have been asking about your situation," Bintu said.

"Yes o," her mother chimed.

"Which situation is this?" Tebeya asked. "Which people?"

"*Which* situation?" her mother said, incredulous.

Her mother said their relatives wanted to know if something were the matter with Tebeya. Why had no man asked for her hand in marriage? Why did she not want to marry and bear children like other women? Women in Rabata had birthed four or five children by Tebeya's age, and Tebeya seemed content to live in her parents' mansion, unwed and barren.

Her mother had diagnosed the issue. How could Tebeya think of marriage when she concerned herself with those indigents at the mission clinic? Though the cleverest of her three, Tebeya was also the most stubborn. Perhaps, her mother mused aloud, brilliance and obstinacy were inseparable traits.

"Mama, I don't care what anybody has to say," Tebeya said, retaining a calmness she did not feel. "What do they know?"

In this town, she was not as important as a married woman despite her accomplishments abroad and her role in the mission clinic, and she had come to accept this status. Delores, here without husband and children, shared the same ranking as Tebeya. The town did not know what to do with Delores, and so they offered their sons or told her to return to America to find a husband and to come back when she had married.

"My daughter, how can you say such things to your own mother?"

"What did I say?" Tebeya said.

Bintu clucked. "Mama, see—what have I said to you. This is how she thinks, like these foreigners. This is how she goes about talking to people these days."

Tebeya exhaled. Let her not blast Bintu right now. Let her forgive her sister's insufferable presence. Where was Duza with this food? Eating would have curtailed this conversation. She wished her father had not traveled to London for work. He seldom said anything to her about marriage. He left her to do as she wished, and if he were here, he would have sided with her and counseled her mother and sister to leave her alone.

She used the back of a teaspoon to slide a teabag up the side of her teacup. She handled the bag roughly while squeezing out the excess water, and the casing tore. Crushed leaves floated like ants on the scalding water.

"Have your father and I not supported this mission clinic?" her mother said. "When you came and requested funds, did we not give them to you?"

"Yes, Mama, thank you."

Her parents' donations constituted about a fifth of the clinic's funding. Their wealth came from her father's company and properties they owned in Rabata, Keffi, Nasarawa, and other towns. They had shares in Alumaco and Wiggins Teape.

"So, why have you shamed your father and I?"

"Mama," Tebeya said, "I didn't know you were giving us this money in exchange for me to marry. Is that why you supported the clinic?"

"Eh! You think that's what we were doing? Shame on you to suggest that this is what your father and I would do."

"Then why are you reminding me of how much money you're giving?"

"This-your sister." Her mother turned to Bintu, as if Tebeya were no longer present. It was what she did when someone had offended her. She ignored you and spoke to the air or whichever other person happened to be in close vicinity. "Why did we send your sister to Dublin if she's going to work at this small-small clinic for the rest of her life?"

"Mama, leave her." Bintu smiled, showing off perfectly aligned teeth. She lifted her elbows to the table, and thin gold bangles shimmered down her wrist. "She'll marry one of those indigents in her clinic. Are those not the only people she sees these days?"

"Talk to your sister again, Bintu. I cannot speak to her."

"Well, you know Thomas's friend asked after her." Bintu's face was like their mother's, intrusive and gossipy in the light. She enjoyed the pretense that Tebeya was not there.

"What does this friend of Thomas do?" her mother asked.

"He's a barrister," Bintu said loftily.

Her mother pursed her lips, impressed. "Barrister?"

Bintu said, "Let me talk to Thomas and ask him to talk to his friend—"

"Can both of you just free me? I don't want to meet anybody," Tebeya said.

Imagine marrying someone like Bintu's husband. Thomas never held conversation with people—the man lectured, adopting a practiced professorial tone. Her brother-in-law liked to hear his own reasoning and analysis; he also did not care for the opinion of another if he considered himself more intelligent than the person with whom he was speaking. He should have been an academic, not working as a director for Shell-BP.

"I'm not interested," Tebeya said.

"Not interested," Bintu said. "Can you imagine? I've asked myself what happened to my sister in that Dublin? That Irish man—what was his name? Was it Geoffrey?"

Tebeya said coldly, "Who do you mean, Bintu? Which Irish man?"

"Eh? Irish man?" Her mother searched both of their faces.

"Yes, Bintu," Tebeya said. "What are you talking about?"

She would not forgive her sister if she mentioned Gerard's name. It was as if they were adolescents again, protecting a secret relationship from their mother's ire, and not women in their thirties with professions or families. Bintu grinned and let the tension escalate a little more, and the red lacquer on her nails flashed in the light.

"Nothing, Mama," Bintu said finally. "Okay then, what of Zanya?"

"Zanya?" Tebeya said. What was the town's obsession with this

boy that even Bintu had heard of him? She'd been illogically annoyed with him since children had taken a dangerous interest in
lighting matches after his persecution, adding to the clinic staff's
caseload. She had not attended the service where he spoke. She had
nothing against him. She generally did not attend on Sundays. She
believed the God she served was a merciful God who rewarded
the work of those tending to the sick. Instead of wasting time in
a church, hearing what she should be doing, she wanted to be the
one who got on with the grueling work of tending.

"No, not that one, Bintu," her mother said. "We don't know
anything about his family. We don't know where he comes from."

"I heard he'll soon be pastoring the mission church," Bintu
said. "That's what people were saying—"

"How did you hear?" Tebeya said. "When have you left this
house or stepped outside of the car to even hear?"

Bintu's mouth became like a clothesline tugged at both ends.
Bintu had dressed for the evening meal as if attending one of her
husband's functions—a powdered face and bright red lips, her
hair a voluminous net of black strands brushed into a cumbersome style that did nothing to emphasize her beauty. Her garment,
embroidered with pink thread at the sleeves and neckline, was the
subtle green of sweet melon. Her face had softened with age, losing the fine, sharp features that had made her a contender for the
affection of many men in university.

"Me, I talk to people," Bintu said. "That is how I know of
Zanya."

"Haba, Bintu. I'm not interested—not at this age."

Her mother said, "Tebeya, you are nearly thirty-six. An old
woman! You are an unmarried woman. Childless. Just there running the clinic with that Goliath—"

"He's marrying Nami," Tebeya said.

Her mother said, "*Goliath*?" at the same time Bintu said, "*Dr.
Landry*?"

"No."

"Then *who?*" Bintu said, annoyed.

Tebeya rubbed her left temple and negotiated a comfortable position, which felt impossible in this chair, with its wooden slats. She should go into the clinic. She was not supposed to work tonight, but the clinic could use another physician, and she could use the escape from this interrogation.

"Zanya," she said. "He's marrying Nami."

"Isn't that all you had to say?" Bintu snapped.

Their house girl, Duza, entered carrying a plate of fried potatoes. Her pupils shone like black marbles, and her upper lip revealed a prominent yet attractive gap between her two front teeth. A distant cousin, her family had sent her to Rabata because they could not finance her education. Without Tebeya's mother's sharp, discerning eyes, their father would have accepted anybody asking them to take in a son or daughter (and there were many requests).

Her father lived as if a single act of refusal to the destitute might result in the loss of his wealth. He often traveled to Kulo, deep in the hills, past Yawari, to deliver bags of rice and canisters of oil to his relatives. Her mother did not harbor such fears or beliefs. She refused relatives left and right but had consented to Duza—this eager, hypervigilant child who was not a child really but a maturing, slightly underdeveloped adolescent.

Tebeya could have adopted someone like Duza, had she stepped foot inside the orphanage Benedict had taken her to last month at her behest. "Shall I stop here, ma?" Benedict had asked, pulling up to the circular drive and parking in front of a signpost: DORCAS MINISTRY, AKWANGA. GOD KNOWS THE BEST.

Overwhelmed with nerves, she had said, "Can your eyes not see? This is not the place."

"No, madam. It is the place. See."

A gaggle of boys and girls trailed out of the tin-roofed building and ogled the sleek, monstrous sedan. They had stared directly at her, sitting against the leather seats, and foresaw with their know-ing eyes her indecision and cowardice.

"Turn the car around," she had ordered.

"Madam?"

"Please, let us go."

How could she go and see about caring for an orphan at this time in her life, with her clinic responsibilities? She desired a feel-ing of accomplishment in improving a person's life, delivering them from an unfortunate circumstance and exposing them to the same opportunities she had been given. She had considered if her motivation stemmed from a true desire to offer support or to satisfy a selfish want of accomplishment. And if it were partially a reflection of her self-interest, where was the fairness in bringing another person into her life?

Duza curtsied and served the plate of fried potatoes and plan-tains on the dining room table, wiping drops of oil from the rim with a cloth.

"Eh heh, you see, that's better." Tebeya's mother wiggled a po-tato wedge. "I want to see this from now on. Every piece should be the proper size."

"Mama, let Duza rest," Tebeya said. "She'll go back in there now and be sorting through your potatoes, trying to see which ones to give you."

"You can't be there cutting potatoes anyhow," her mother said, hooking her cane on the chair. "See how I taught you to cut pota-toes properly, and now, you'll be doing surgeries."

Tebeya sipped the dregs of her tea and handed the teacup to Duza. "Wash it well. You're doing good in this house."

Duza gave a startled, serious smile at the praise before leaving.

"That's how you spoil them," Bintu said. "Praising them. She'll go and get a head so big she won't fit into the kitchen anymore."

Tebeya ignored Bintu and glanced at the clock. "I have to be going."

"You're going at this time?" Her mother did not hide her disappointment. "My daughter, you won't eat? How many hours are you in that clinic? It's too much."

Bintu clucked in agreement. "Tebeya, body no be firewood."

"Firewood or not, I have to work."

It was a relief to stand instead of sitting captive to her mother and sister. She wanted to go upstairs, put on a wig and a little lipstick, but she feared that any lingering would pull her into another conversation.

Before she walked out of the front door, she overheard her mother speaking to Bintu. "A barren woman goes to the stream and comes back faster than a woman with children. Let me be the one to deal with your sister."

CHAPTER NINE

THE NIGHT WAS WARM and the mosquitoes unobtrusive, their presence announced only when they pricked the bare legs and arms of a patron at Shigudu's. Around Zanya, customers buried their heads in steaming bowls of pepper soup, and he caught a glimpse of their faces when they needed to wash down the ganda or cool their tongues with a swig of beer. Zanya and his laborers did not eat, though they occupied two of the seven tables and congregated under the light bulbs hung across the bar's tin roof.

Victor Uwaifo's voice came from a radio somewhere above their heads, singing in tune with the twang of his guitar. Two women arched their backs as they pounded yam, their chests heaving with each rise of their arms, pounding in tune with the song, while Shigudu's son grilled moist flanks of grasscutter, fanning smoke that blew in his direction.

Shigudu stopped at their tables to see what the laborers wanted to eat and drink.

"With which money?" Betabwi said.

Shigudu said, "No money? And all of you are here?"

The rumblings of his men's stomachs reached Zanya. He placated Shigudu by ordering beers for the men and a mineral for himself.

They had come to Shigudu's since their first building project, and though the laborers felt the tightness of their pockets now, they came for the atmosphere and the ritualistic aspect. Zanya drank his Coke and listened as his laborers argued about the Igbo returnees coming back to reclaim their homes and businesses in Rabata and attempting to reenter their roles in universities and the military. It was too early to know how they would reintegrate into Rabata and other cities and towns in Nigeria. The war had bred animosity and distrust.

"Biafrans made a good attempt at this war o. They should be treated with respect when they return," Kago said. "War is war, but their efforts should be rewarded—"

"Who said we would not respect them?" Betabwi said, as if he were the head of a university determining which person to employ.

"He's not saying we won't," Zanya said in Kago's defense. "Three years was long for those soldiers to fight, for them to have resisted federal troops. Chubz will tell you."

His friend Chubz worked for Glories and Blessings Ladies' Provisions Store and had yet to be convinced about the Christian practices of the mission. He was the only person most people in Rabata knew who had fought in the war, so they called him General. He had come home with a pinned shirtsleeve flapping against his side like a folded pillowcase where his left arm used to be. "Shrapnel in Okikra," he said when people asked. Chubz had the somber and dignified expression of a soldier, and one could picture him with the hard helmet and military uniform, shouldering an AK-47. Chubz was fond of saying he had gone in whole and returned seven-eighths. He would say he counted himself lucky to have only severed his left limb, and the townspeople would know he was thinking of the misfortune that befell his comrade in the explosion of a bridge connecting Obot Akara and Umuahia. *I saw the whole thing with my koro-koro eyes*, Chubz would say. Chubz had told Zanya that the military training he received in Accra had been preparation for peaceful times, not war. As a result, they had not had enough trained men in the Federal army to quell the regional rebellion.

One of the laborers said, "Ojukwu was lying to this country. Tricking all of us. He was collecting his weapons for war while people were laughing at him."

"Like the Reverend," Betabwi said, taking a swig of beer.

The men laughed and one agreed, "Yes. Like Reverend."

A laborer said, "You go compare Reverend Jim with Ojukwu?"

"Liars, the both of them." Betabwi looked around at the other men and licked his lip, gearing up for a rant. "Reverend get money and him no wan pay us."

"Monkey dey work, baboon dey chop," one of the men called. The others laughed, and a couple of them said it was true.

Zanya thought his laborers' silence over the past week meant they had accepted the situation. They had made progress on the church, raising wooden scaffolds to continue building the walls. A church member felled a tree on his farmland, and they had sawed the wood and transported it to the construction site. He and Betabwi had hauled the timber from the pickup one afternoon, while the sun, a brutal force, piloted its rays on their perspiring foreheads and backs, and sawdust specks blew into their eyes.

Perhaps the laborers desired more, like him. Maybe the learning of new trades or skills when construction projects were unavailable. The mission could help the laborers in this way. He reached for the pen and notebook in his trousers.

"You and this-your notebook," Betabwi said, scoffing. "What does it say? You dey write: Make Reverend give wages to dem laborers?"

Zanya laughed with the men and put the notebook away. "Betabwi, we suppose work. Even if money dey small."

Kago said, "I no for complain if dem dey pay us better money na, but dis money, e no do."

"Kago," one of the laborers said, "since the first day, you've been siding with Reverend Jim. Anything Reverend wan do, I go see Kago there first. No be so?"

"I've changed," Kago said. "I've changed. I'm seeing things now."

Another man, one week on the job, spoke up. "Ehn, Zanya, make you go talk to dem for us, na," he said. "That's why you be oga. See as you tell me make I come join in this work and I agree. Na you wey we dey look o."

"You that have just come," Zanya said, "see you asking for more money."

The laborers chuckled, and the man was briefly embarrassed. He conceded, "No problem. I no stay for here long, but I dey see how things dey work for here."

One of the women who was pounding yam earlier came and collected their empty bottles from the table. As she strutted off, Betabwi swiveled in his chair, and his lips curled in lascivious pleasure, appreciating the bounce of her bottom.

A laborer next to him said, "Betabwi, you wan fourth wife? Wetin you dey look, na?"

"Man get eye," Betabwi said. "I just dey admire dey work of God."

"Reverend talk say make we remove our eye o," someone said. "If eye go cause sin."

Betabwi laughed. "Ehn, make God come knack me for eye!" He turned back to Zanya. "You go talk to Reverend about this money matter? See how I dey work with this my body. If you don't do something, Zanya, this church will never be built."

"Wetin you dey talk?" Zanya looked around at the other laborers. Some stared at their half-drunk bottles and rolled the bottle caps in their palms. A couple gave him defiant looks and leaned against their chairs, arms folded. "You'll stop building the church?" Zanya said, catching the drop of Coke that almost trickled down his chin. "Is that what you're saying?"

"Make you tell Reverend," Betabwi said, staring at him, "and he go do am."

"I dey hear you," Zanya said.

"Fire Boy," Betabwi said, raising his bottle. "Na God wey save you from de fire wey dey your village. Na you fit handle dey Reverend."

"Fire Boy!" another man called.

"Fire Boy!" the men shouted in unison and clinked their bottles to Zanya. Women carried more pounded yam, egusi soup, and pepper soup to the surrounding tables. Music flowed down from the speakers as the laborers' chant rose into the night.

Fire Boy. The words echoed like a taunt in Zanya's ears as he sipped the dark, sweet liquid and eased himself into the shadows of men.

PART TWO

CHAPTER TEN

THE PEUGEOT BETRAYED JIM with a whine as he reversed out of the mission compound, praying neither goat nor rooster strayed behind the car. Or a sheep. He considered the irony of slaying a lamb two weeks before Easter. His domestic worker, Manasseh, was sweeping the compound and must have heard the noise; it was a distinctive screeching sound. But Manasseh did not look up, which was fine with Jim. More scrutiny might have led him to abandon his plan to drive alone into the villages in the hills.

Manasseh had given him an earful about traveling unaccompanied. "I'll be fine," Jim had said. He had seen, in his house servant's eyes, a judgment of his naïve stupidity.

"If you say you do not fear," Manasseh had said, shaking his head, "it is because you have not seen a fearful thing."

Jim flexed his fingers as he shifted gears, nervous over the unfamiliarity of the vehicle. This wasn't his old Ford Deluxe Tudor. He had known every inch of that car. He and Edna had purchased it in the early years of their marriage, and their sons, Walter and Pete, had ridden in it until they were teenagers.

He had only driven a handful of times since arriving in Rabata. Zanya, Nelson, or Gary drove him where he needed to go. He had not trusted any of them for this outing.

Gary would have asked too many questions if Jim had told him he was traveling to Zanya's sister's village. He found Gary Parson

keen to believe the good intentions of the locals and too enamored
with them (and Gary's wife, Katherine—a bit of a sourpuss—not
enamored enough if he were being honest). Nelson Landry, however, had said absolutely nothing about Jim's trip. Jim had gone to
Nelson's after supper last night to learn more about Zanya's sister
Pema and her current health condition. Nelson had opened the
door groggy and hair askew, outfitted in a blue waffle bathrobe,
the sleeves short on him, and a little too disoriented to see Jim on
his doorstep at an early evening hour. He'd been keeping to himself
since his divorce from Virginia, and Jim had in mind to check in
on him a little more, counsel him through it.

Nelson told Jim that Pema's disease had to do with kidney
malfunction. He planned to drive to her village for a medical visit
next week, and if Jim wanted to wait, they could go together.

"Thanks, Nelson, but actually, I'd like to go on my own," Jim
said.

Nelson had yawned and looped the ties of his robe into a knot.
"Suit yourself."

"I'm concerned about you, Doc. Are you doing all right?"

"Right as rain, Jim."

But "right as rain" did not reach his eyes or hide the slope in
his stance. Jim too had braved the well-meaning questions after
losing Edna. "I'm doing fine, thank you" had been his version of
"right as rain." Depending on the day, it meant no more than he
had somehow found the strength to shave that morning and don
a clean shirt.

Almost six years had passed since Edna's death. Remembering
those early days after her loss, his body still delivered a spasm of
grief as acute as what he felt then.

Coming to Nigeria with the mission had saved him. Both of
his boys thought it an impetuous, ill-formed decision. Here in Nigeria, among the Africans, he had become important again. He
had feared languishing without Edna, like Bob Cassell, a congre-

gant at his former parish, First Presbyterian, who had succumbed to a heart attack six weeks after his wife's death.

Yet here Jim was—living, preaching, and thriving in Africa. Rebirth, when most of his acquaintances had contented themselves with retirement.

Jim's bifocals skidded to the tip of his nose, and he pushed them up with a quick gesture and adjusted his hands on the steering wheel. Rocks crunched underneath the tires as he turned.

He wasn't done living; that's what he had felt after Edna passed, that's what God had whispered to his heart after Dave Turner's installment at First Presbyterian. Less old-fashioned, the board said about Dave, his preaching keeping with the political times. They weren't getting rid of Jim because of what Pete had done. Dave was supporting desegregation efforts, pushing for racial equality in the greater Presbyterian body.

All hogwash. Jim was not against civil rights matters, of course. He had only questioned the wisdom of such rhetoric being preached to a congregation he had pastored for two decades, one he did not believe was ready for such a message.

The winding road wrapped behind houses painted the green and blue of Easter eggs, a few with gabled thatch roofs or others with roofs of corrugated steel. Some of the neighbors he passed waved at him, but he could not concentrate on them nor did he dare lift a hand to wave back. Edna would have loved driving through town with him. She would have known every face—animals included—within a few months. She had the natural ability to make people comfortable in her presence. He'd love to have her along today. She would have had the right words to put Pema at ease. She was better than Jim at this sort of thing, though she would not condone the reason behind his visit.

No word other than embarrassment could describe the slow frothing of blood in his limbs as he had sat, as an audience member in that dusty, clamorous classroom witnessing the congregants' infatuation with Zanya. Embarrassment—an emotion so infrequent these days he had misidentified it as a physical malady, a heat stroke, perhaps. There were stories here and there of townspeople new to the faith who had to sever ties with hostile families or whose relatives took advantage of their Sunday morning outings to church services to sabotage their crops. He believed all of this. Zanya's testimony, however, he simply could not. If he learned the truth and the truth was the truth as Zanya had said, so be it. If it were false, then he'd know not to place Zanya in a position of leadership.

Edna would have said, "Zanya's just a kid, dear."

But Zanya was not just a child. He was a bright and capable young man, gunning for progress and seeking to undermine Jim's position.

"Out with the old," Jim muttered to the road.

He must look nutty to the locals, driving along, talking to himself like this. The gears creaked their rebellion as he shifted. He turned the wheels to get on the main road heading west and narrowly avoided two women carrying bundles of calabash dishes on their shoulders while guiding their children along the path to the marketplace. Had he never noticed the number of denizens in this town? As a passenger, he merely concerned himself with the conversation at hand or questioned if the windows offered enough of a breeze.

The other night he had settled on the problem. Zanya reminded him of his youngest, Pete. Had he interrogated Pete years ago, he'd still be pastoring at First Presbyterian, not here in West Africa. It shamed him that he held fond memories of his former parish, and they sprung upon him when he least expected. When he wished to be incensed at the unfairness, his spirit turned mournful. He remembered with pleasure how he had woken up on Sunday mornings and enshrined himself in a white pulpit robe with a deep violet sash around his neck to prepare for service. In the structure to the service, precision proffered peace: the lighting of candles, the ringing of the bells, the call to worship, and the doxology. He recalled the rich red oak finish of the pews and the limestone interior of the church. Long, dark beams gracing the ceilings. Stained-glass windows engraved with cubist angels.

And he'd lost it all.

Kierkegaard had written with a dry, honest sort of certainty about the anxiety of the past—that if one was anxious about a past misfortune, one's apprehension was because the past might repeat itself and become the future. That was why he was driving to see Pema in her village—to know what he needed to before *not* knowing led to much worse.

The sky did not look real to Katherine. It looked like an eggshell painted blue—a brittle stretch of sky that might crack. She had thought sky was sky everywhere. But American sky was lovely, how the sun ringed the clouds with gold. Sky in West Africa was harsh and unforgiving, wide and untamable. There seemed an endless amount of it.

Behind the clinic, sheets and uniforms Jecinda had soaked and washed in the wringer machine and hung to dry on the clotheslines flapped languorously in the breeze, releasing an acrid smell of chlorine. Her husband, Gary, was here this morning to dig and fence a deeper disposal area for biomedical waste—surgical refuse and tainted needles and bandages. Clinic staff burned medical waste in the pit when they could, but in rainy season, the unfenced, shallow hole collected water, and needles and other detritus floated on the surface.

Around the corner, a horde of patients waited. Here, in the back, one could steal a restful minute. Katherine navigated past the empty tubs and buckets and rinsed her white leather shoes under the outdoor faucet. She had just started her examination on a febrile fifteen-year-old male when he turned over and retched. Wet, clumpy vomit had congealed on her shoes, and bile seeped into her stockings.

She was sick of this—the blood, the fluids, the coughing, the insects, the long, exhausting hours. She'd resisted leaving Malaysia for Nigeria, but she had loved returning to the nursing duties she had not been able to perform in Penang. Somewhere in these past two years, the novelty had worn off. It seemed people died from curable illnesses instead of getting better like they had before, and there were more patients than hands and hours in a day.

She poured water on the bar of soap and lathered her bare legs, wondering if she was really just upset at how Tebeya had cornered her moments ago to voice ridiculous concerns.

"Dr. Landry is displaying poor judgment," Tebeya had said. "When he arrives to work, the way he looks and smells, the way he's sweating. He seems…" Tebeya did not utter the words, and because she did not, the word had drifted like skywriting: *drunk.*

"Nelson, dear? Drinking?" Katherine had chuckled. "Oh, for goodness' sake, of course he's sweating. He's like the Green Giant." Nelson was a large, ruddy man, squeezed into his white shorts and shirts like the fabric was insufficient to hold his girth.

"Green giant?" Tebeya said.

"It's a commercial for peas back in America and—well, never mind."

Tebeya had looked at Katherine with a dark, blistering glare. "I'm serious."

Tebeya was unlike other nationals. She was not as deferential as the Nigerian nurses under Katherine's supervision, and neither was she as anxious as the colored nurses at St. John's had been whenever she supervised the colored wing of the hospital. When Nelson hired Tebeya, Katherine had realized with a start that Tebeya was *her* superior in the clinic.

"I doubt," Katherine had said to Tebeya, testy, "it's anything to fret over, that's all I'm saying."

"He's made many mistakes," Tebeya said with equal tetchiness. "Talk to him so these mistakes do not happen again."

"If it's never happened before, you've got to assume he was tired or sick—"

"You don't think I would know if he were sick?" Tebeya said in a voice that dripped with something Katherine could not put her finger on—something tedious and resentful. "What are *you* going to do, Nurse Katherine?"

Nothing. Katherine wasn't going to do a single thing about it.

She pushed her feet into her now-soaked shoes and ignored the squishing sounds. She called to Gary and waved him over. Gary put a hand up to say "Just a minute," pointed to the pit and said, "Be n zukwo n ya. Nyin bokun n sopa ye," to Kago, who was working with him today instead of laboring at the construction site. Bring a shovel, dig the pit here, Katherine inferred. She could never be sure. These languages left her befuddled and still in need of an interpreter.

"Are you happy, Gary?" Katherine asked, when he plodded over to her, shovel in hand. Back home, he sported a suit and tie to work at his father's car dealership. In Malaysia, he had gone on visitations with ministers and led youth programs. Here, he served as facilities services manager, overseeing landscaping and building maintenance efforts.

"Is this what you wanted to talk to me about, honey?" Gary said, pushing up his goggles. "You want to know if I'm happy?"

"Well, no," she confessed. "I guess I was thinking about you and the dealership. I thought maybe you missed it, you know."

"Not at all." He rested his foot on the shovel's blade. "You all right?"

She recounted the brief incident with Tebeya. "It's terribly dramatic," she said. "We're all exhausted—I'm at my wit's end some days. That's all it is."

"You should have reassured her." Gary nudged his ear with his shoulder to get at an itch. "We both know why Nelson's, you know, not himself. You should've said you'd look into it."

Nelson and his wife Virginia had divorced when he went home on furlough last November. They had all vowed to keep it under wraps from the locals. Gary did not understand why. The locals permitted divorce in their culture, and had the church not asked some of the men to divorce their second and third wives?

"You know what I thought? It wouldn't be like this with Carole." She paused, recalling the ease with which that friendship had flourished in a Malaysian village where armed police patrolled the perimeter. Carole Brigham had arrived with her brood of six a year before, and they'd become instant friends. They had sent their children to buy bowls of fried mee hoon and laughed at their delight, the toothy grins and crinkled eyes, as the thin noodles greased their mouths. To celebrate American Thanksgiving, they had bought rambutans and made a version of cranberry sauce to go with roasted fowl.

"Carole was British, for one," Gary said. "Dr. Awyebwi's not."

"Still, it shouldn't be this hard." She ran her fingers through her hair. It had grown out of the chin-length style, down to her shoulders now, and was in desperate need of a good trim. She could not describe its color as anything other than sandy, and it was drier and thinner with the sun crisping it daily.

"Delores said it might help if you got to know the other nurses and staff, you know, outside of the clinic."

Katherine raised her eyebrows. "Delores?"

"Yeah, well, that's what she's done with her teachers. You could have your staff over to the house or visit their homes. You haven't done any of this, Katherine, and I'd like to think it could help you, you know, feel a little less lonely."

"Oh, well, okay."

"She's got good friendships here, that's all, with the Nigerian women," Gary said. Katherine heard an unusual note of admiration in her husband's voice. "She's swell, Katherine—"

"Well, that's nice, Gary," she said. "That's really nice."

Delores Boyd had joined the mission in '69 and requested—or more appropriately, demanded—to be housed separately in a home closer to the primary school. Her slender figure had not gained an ounce with nearly two years of the locals forcing fufu and egusi on her. Meanwhile, the elastic bands of Katherine's skirts often slipped cozily underneath a pillow of flesh, and when she sat, her stomach rubbed against the starchy white fabric of her nurse's uniform. Gary had said nothing about the recent weight gain or the new pliability of her stomach. He would not have noticed because he had not touched her in months.

"If you won't take it from me," he said, "invite Delores to supper. Hear her out. All right?"

"I'll think about it."

"Attagirl. Give it time with Tebeya, love. It'll blow over before you know it." Gary popped the blunt tip of the shovel out of the ground and kissed her forehead.

"Sure, thanks Gary," Katherine said, as her husband walked back to the ditch She rearranged her stockings on the clothesline and turned to go back inside. She had come to dislike this phrase of his, about giving it time. Ever since they'd met in her third year at the University of Missouri, she'd observed Gary as a man who refused to give up on things that had run their course.

Malaysia had been the rare time Katherine saw the wisdom in giving it time. During the Malayan Emergency, the British had relocated close to half a million Chinese refugees into new villages in Malaysia. Their mission agency, like some of the others, had sent missionaries to the island. Katherine had feared the police, and the barbed wire fence running the perimeter made her feel as much a prisoner as those they had come to serve. Eventually, she acclimated to the strangeness of their assigned village and to the island of Penang, to the white shore and the soughing wind in the coconut trees. She walked along the beach each morning, observing schools of bluespot mullet swimming to the shores under the wooden walkways interconnecting the houses. Allison and Elijah dug for sea worms and ran to catch black crabs that scurried across the beach like tiny bowlegged old men. At dawn, Gary drifted along in a sampan with an elderly villager for a fishing excursion.

They had arrived in Nigeria after the coup leading to Yakubu Gowon becoming head of state and after the pogroms in the North. Months later, Biafra seceded and the Civil War began. Edward Hayes sent word over radio, informing them and other missionaries that they could leave Nigeria for reassignment in another country or return to the US.

"Katherine," Gary said then, "we can go back home if that's what you want."

He had meant it. They could have packed their suitcases and left Africa, if she'd been prescient and could have known the hold this town would have on him. That night, she had imagined the whispers at their sending church in Springfield if they returned so shortly after reassignment. The women in her Sunday school class would have judged her: Katherine Parson, modern-day Jonah, recalcitrant wife.

"We can stay in Rabata," she said, "for a year. But that's it, Gary."

"Are you sure? If you're not—I'm not forcing you."

"I know, and it's fine."

"You're brave, sweetheart. I love you for this."

She liked him thinking her brave when she wanted nothing other than to curl up in his arms. Gary had hooked his arm around her waist, hugged her so close she inhaled the traces of rosemary from the roast chicken she had made for supper on his breath. He had taken her hand and led her into the bedroom, where they'd made love.

Now, they hadn't made love in months. *Seven months.* Over half a year. Were they to accept this after fifteen years of marriage, or was it a consequence of serving the mission?

A new patient waited for her in the ward when she returned. He was presenting with a broken index finger.

"God spared my life!"

"It's only your finger, right?" she said, nodding sympathetically as she studied the index finger, which was at a peculiar angle. "Let's see if we can take care of that for you."

"It was where I was sitting that saved me. My head would have been chopped—"

"Ah," she said, finding the medical tape to splint the fingers. She tried not to look at the clock above him to see how much longer she had on her shift. "Just hold on for me, would you?"

Pre-field training had not prepared her for any of her emotional hardships. She could not sit with anyone and say, "My marriage is on the fritz." She had cultivated no true friendships in Nigeria. Frankly, she was wary of friendships with the African women or missionaries at other stations. She was Goldilocks when she met them: too loud, too quiet, too shifty, too trusting, too gossipy. Tebeya could have been a friend, but goodness, the woman had that prickly egoistic personality, and a question stamped on her forehead that seemed to say: *What are you doing here?* Delores could have been a friend, but she, like Gary, fostered a nauseating enthusiasm about Nigeria.

She had not expected Gary to love Nigeria more than Malaysia, to be so at ease with the people. The locals had nicknamed him Mai Hankali to signify a gentle and considerate person, and Mai Mulo for Delores. Katherine had ceased wondering why the locals bestowed no nickname upon her. Once, she walked into the kitchen to find her husband looking absurd with his long, white arms lifting the pestle up to pound boiled yam in the mortar. Jummai had been chuckling at his attempts, saying, "Mr. Gary, I will show you how to pound yam properly like our people do." Or Gary would teach Jummai how to pronounce a word like "chutney." It would sound wrong to Katherine, coming from Jummai's mouth, the heavy Nigerian accent making the word cumbersome: *choh-tee-nee*. It had cracked Jummai and Gary up. Jummai rarely laughed like this with her. It made her feel buttoned up and prudish.

Gary was certain Nigeria was where they belonged. Never had he been so committed, so certain of God's calling. The notion of hearing from God—this nebulous experience other believers seemed so adamant on seeking—confounded her. She doubted she could bear the loneliness much longer, but did not know how to force her husband's hand.

CHAPTER ELEVEN

PEMA'S HUSBAND SHAGYE welcomed Jim inside the home and offered him a meal of rice and stew, which Jim declined. He led
Jim down a short hallway and into a stuffy, unlit bedroom, where
natural light streamed in through the uncurtained window. On a
cot pushed into a corner of the bedroom, Pema sat upright with
her back against the wall.

Jim noted little resemblance between Pema and Zanya besides
the shape of their heads and their flat noses. Pema would have been
a lovely woman—the searching eyes, the strong, stately chin—but
her illness had scarred her features. Jaundiced skin had replaced
all vibrancy or smoothness. In good health, she seemed the kind
of woman who would have shunned indolence. He pictured her
running to the market for the Knorr cubes the women here were
so fond of and a jug of vegetable oil.

They all spoke softly because the illness, it seemed, demanded
a reverential quietude. Jim asked after Pema's sickness, giving the
impression that this was the main purpose of his visitation. He assured her that Dr. Landry or Dr. Awyebwi would come to examine
her next week. "They'll bring the medication you need, I'm sure,"
he said.

"My wife is very wise, Reverend," Shagye said. "She does
not want the medicine. She knows the white man's medicine is
faster, but the illness comes back quicker. Our people know that

sometimes you cannot cure Black man's illness with white man's medicine."

"Well," Jim said, "I'll let the doctors know," before bringing up the miracle of Zanya's persecution, the real reason for his visit.

"My wife's cousins and uncles were the ones," Shagye said. Light from the bedroom window filtered through Shagye's straw hat and marked his face in sun stripes. One long dark tribal line scored his left cheek, and it undulated as he spoke. "They were the ones who wanted to set Zanya on fire."

Pema said with slight suspicion, "Did Zanya not tell you these things already?"

"You see, it was such a powerful recounting," Jim said. "I'd like to learn more for the purposes of ministering to the people in that village." This was not untrue. Whatever he learned here could be massaged into a future sermon.

Pema spoke again, and it was hard for Jim to hear it. "There is nothing we can say," he thought she said. "Were we there to see?"

He cupped his right ear. "Pardon?"

"It happened as Zanya said it happened." Shagye sat on the edge of the cot. "You will know the ant that stings you through its speed. If Zanya is not telling the truth, you will see it. Zanya is going to marry soon, and we have gone to the girl's relatives. Are you coming to bring trouble?"

"No, not at all," Jim said, raising his hands as a sign of peace. "Please understand that my desire is for the full truth of the story. I'm wondering why your relatives chose your brother."

"What do you mean 'why'?" Pema said.

"I'm not sure if he's the only person in your family who has chosen Christianity. Most families have fraught relationships, bad blood, if you will, between relatives. The cruelty, the intended immolation of a family member—it's just, well, it raised a lot of concern."

"Have you gone and asked him yourself?"

Jim had not asked Zanya directly. What would be the point

when Zanya was likely to cling to his original story? "From what I've gathered, you're the closest person to him, Pema," he said. "I thought you'd offer more context—"

"My brother saved your life when you first came to our country. Did he not?" Pema said.

"Sure, but I think we're getting a little off topic here."

He hooked a finger in his collar and pulled against the material for air, suddenly irritable and famished, despite the heavy breakfast Manasseh had prepared before this outing. He disliked the reminder of how Zanya had saved his life, as if this singular act absolved him of any wrongdoings.

Jim's clearest memory was not of the actual robbery. It was the lone symphony of his driver's urine striking a tree as they waited, stalled, on the side of the road. Three hours later, the car of the two assailants had inched up the road. The men offered to drive Jim and the mission driver the final miles to Rabata. They removed Jim's luggage and boxes out of the Opel and into the backseat and trunk of their vehicle. And when Jim asked, "What about us, gentlemen? Where are we to sit?" the men attacked, clobbering his driver and then him. Jim recalled the mortification of being carried like a newborn on Zanya's back. They had saved each other was how Jim liked to think of it these days. Zanya had saved his life so he could save Zanya's soul. Still a private thought festered: he should have saved Zanya first.

That fateful afternoon, he had protested to Zanya that he could walk, but the words never traveled from the nerves in his brain to his larynx to form the plea. He had fought not to drink the bitter, warm liquid in the diviner's home, not to have it trickling down his throat, the specks of leaves welding to the inner linings of his cheek and the roof of his mouth. "You were dead, Reverend," the locals were fond of saying, "we were certain you had passed to the other side. If it had not been for Zanya and the diviner, you would have died."

Pema said, "Was it true? That Zanya saved your life?"

"Yes, he did—"

"Then this, too, is true," she said. Their faces became shields.

Shagye rose. "My wife is tired now."

"Oh, yes, yes. Well, I'll get going then."

Shagye closed the door once Jim was outside. Cornstalks high-er than Jim's head grew in the bramble near their house. Under a wooden bench, two white-footed puppies had fallen asleep with paws outstretched. The heat and humidity had siphoned energy from the day. The other animals, in their lassitude, had stopped grazing and collapsed on their hooves.

A couple of men relaxed in chairs underneath the same tree, eating from a bowl of boiled peanuts. They stared at Jim as he walked to the car. He stopped before he unlocked the door. It was worth asking these men since he was here, so he doubled back to speak to them. He asked in his best Gbagyi: "Do you know Zanya? Did you hear about the fire?"

"We heard," they said, and their faces turned cold, like Pema and Shagye's.

"Well, good day, gentlemen," he said, knowing he'd get no more from them.

The engine failed to cut on when Jim turned the car keys. It coughed and sputtered, and all the while the men watched from under the tree. Jim pressed the gas in panic and turned the key in the ignition again, halfway, then fully. "Come on, come on," he whispered, pushing in the key again.

The engine roared to life after a couple of false starts, and he clapped a hand to his forehead with relief. He drove off from Pema and Shagye's house with a halfhearted, modest wave to the men sitting under the shade.

As he approached the end of the road leading out of Pema's village, a shadow came from nowhere in his periphery vision, bolt-ing toward the door so that Jim slammed on the brakes, thinking whatever it was would cut across the front of the car. It was a villager, and the man banged on the hood of the car for Jim to slow down. He dithered before rolling down his window, sticking his face out a bit.

"Yes? May I help you—"

"Go to Yawari," was all the man said.

❧

"Yakubu is still there," Chubz said. "Rehabilitation, reconstruction and reintegration—" He turned down the radio blasting news about Major General Yakubu Gowon, and his recent tours across the continent.

"They will begin reconstruction on the Third Mainland Bridge," Zanya said, sinking into the sole cushion in Chubz's flat. He was disconcerted that it was just him and Chubz in the small parlor, which felt capacious without men and women crammed inside, smoking and drinking as they did during Chubz's parties. Jummai had often danced in the middle of the room, as if music flowed to her ears alone, unaware or unconcerned that the men's eyes followed the jiggle of her hips and that she solicited jealous glances from the women.

Chubz pinched the wiwi, which he had rolled and filled minutes ago, with his right hand. "Have we seen anything yet?"

"Before he returns the country to civilian rule."

"Civilian rule? Old boy, you think Gowon will give back power? Once you taste power—atoh, you will keep power."

"Na people like this dey make life hard for us wey no hold power."

"What is troubling you?" Chubz reclined on the cushion with his good arm slung behind his head as if protecting it from being taken, the wiwi perpendicular to the ground. Zanya pictured Chubz in his youth, sleeping with both arms angled like wings un-

der his head, relaxed and confident, unaware that he would enter
a war that would disfigure him. Chubz's left arm, the one blasted
off at the elbow, bore a face in the dark, hazy room. The skin was
shiny and pinched where it had sealed, and a pinkish ring enclosed
the wound.

"Reverend is troubling me," Zanya said, and told Chubz about
the laborers' insolence. They were coming late to the site and had
slowed the brickmaking process. Last week, it had been an insufficient amount of water in the mortar. He had pulled Kago aside
and learned Betabwi was the one who had mixed it. Zanya worried
that Betabwi, in his quest for higher wages, might sabotage construction efforts. Kago had laughed. "Na small mistake."

"Reverend blows fan and at the same time produces smoke,"
Chubz said, pushing out smoke from his mouth to make his point
about Reverend Jim's duplicity. The smoke diffused in the dimness.
He continued, "You get plenty wahala." Chubz told Zanya he had
eaten at Flo's the other night and overheard the laborers discussing
a strike. "They didn't see me. But me, I saw them, and I listened."

"Strike? No, General, they would tell me," Zanya said, ignoring his quickening pulse.

"Tell you what, old boy?" Chubz laughed, and the laughter
turned into hiccups. He recovered. "You? Who oversees them?"

"I'm with them, on their side. They know, na."

Chubz took a drag of the wiwi and closed his eyes. It was of no
consequence to him. The flaccid cushion sagged under Zanya, and
he shifted to a sturdier side.

Zanya said, "Who was talking—at Flo's?"

"One big-big guy."

"Betabwi?"

"If the man ate people, he would eat you and me, no problem."

"That's him. He's the one you heard."

Chubz opened his eyes. "The man sounded serious."

꧁

The next morning, Zanya splashed his face with water, allowing the water to dribble down his nose and chin before lifting the bottom of his shirt to wipe it off. He lifted the tin cup over his mouth and swished before spitting the water out. He threw the cup back in his pickup then snapped a twig from the neem tree and used it to clean his teeth as he waited for his men to come. This morning, the church looked more unfinished to his eye than it had yesterday. He could not leave it unfinished. This could not be the pattern of his life. Kunama, unfinished. The church, unfinished. He'd finish it himself, brick by brick, layer by layer, wall by wall.

Restless, he chewed on a short stalk of sugarcane and waited. His father could suck on a bundle of sugarcane for days, leaving mounds of fibrous pulp at his feet. One afternoon, when Zanya must have been no older than the age of Pema's youngest now, his father skinned one of his sugarcanes for Zanya. He had used his teeth to remove the green bark for Zanya. "Take it," his father said when Zanya, confused by the rare generosity, had not immediately reached for it. The two of them sat together on the ground, their backs against the wall of the house, chewing and swallowing the sugary sap. The sugarcane had been especially sweet that day, and Zanya had chewed slowly to savor it, to absorb the stillness of the afternoon with his father. He remembered that stillness—a stillness weighted with pain and uncertainty. He remembered how pain lined his father's face, how pain lined the movement of his father's hands as he stripped the sugarcane barks. How uncertainty marked his own movements as he sucked and watched the dexterity of his father's hands.

This morning carried the same stillness as that day with his father. Sun came slowly, pushing its way through the clouds like a person emerging reluctantly from his covers. Blackbirds flew listlessly, alighting on the stems of paw paw trees growing near the site.

Kago arrived first, his cap visible before Zanya even saw his face. He was followed by a group of four men that had walked together. Zanya spat the sugarcane fibers out and stood from the bed of the pickup.

"Kago!" he called in greeting, his voice overjoyed, waving too eagerly.

Within the hour, all the men had come, including Betabwi, and the sun had fully woken up and was doing its duty to bring heat to the day. Chubz must have heard the same complaints that the men made every night after a long day's work. This morning, they were themselves again—he thought and hoped—pushing the wheelbarrows, clay pliable in their hands.

He had to talk to the Reverend even if Chubz's claims might be wrong. He owed it to them, to let them know that he had tried, before their discontentment morphed into something uncontrollable.

CHAPTER TWELVE

IT HAPPENED TWO MORNINGS LATER. A knock at the driver's side window of Zanya's pickup stirred him awake. He opened his eyes in drowsy slits and spied Kago's bright red cap before he noticed Kago's cloudy-looking eyes staring back at him. A rush of sunlight blinded him when Kago moved aside. Zanya fumbled for the door handle.

"Why are you disturbing me?" He stood bare-chested, the rays warming his skin. He tugged his shirt off the seat and pulled it over his head.

"See all that you've done for my family," Kago said. "When my daughter Miriam was sick last year, you came and took us to Keffi. You remember?"

Zanya stretched his arms above his head. What was Kago running his mouth about? Sleep beckoned to him, and there was much they had to do today.

He listened as Kago recounted the day Zanya had transported three-year-old Miriam to the hospital in Keffi. Discolored skin folds bulged under the girl's eyes, and her breathing had been shallow. Typhoid fever.

"Wetin you dey talk, Kago?" Zanya said.

"As the ear hears," Kago said, "the head is safe—"

"Kago!" Zanya snapped. "What is it?"

His sharp tone rattled Kago. "The men are not coming. We

dey go strike. I came to tell you because we are friends. We're not coming until Reverend increases our money—"

Zanya did not wait for the rest of Kago's sentence. He jumped into his pickup and swiped the keys off the dashboard for the ride to the mission compound.

⁂

Zanya shook the rods of the locked gate. Through the bars, he saw Manasseh walk out of the Reverend's house, heading to the cowshed.

"Manasseh!" he called, rattling the gate. "Please, come and allow me enter."

"Who is it?" Manasseh said.

Was the man blind? How could he not see from that short distance?

"It's me. Zanya."

"What is the matter with you that you're coming this early morning?" Manasseh said when he reached the gate. Manasseh's portly face, incongruous with the slenderness of his body, had never known a wrinkle, though he must have been sixty. He folded his arms and stared at Zanya.

"I have to talk to Reverend," Zanya said.

"You cannot disturb Reverend when he is sleeping—"

"Manasseh, I must speak to him."

He wished he had the keys to unlock the gate or break them open with force. Manasseh had never cared for him. From the moment Manasseh came to work for Reverend Jim, he viewed Zanya as his competitor and was protective of the Reverend. Zanya had said this to Jummai, and she reassured him it had nothing to do with Zanya. This was how Manasseh behaved with her, too, and anybody who was not the Reverend.

"It is very important," Zanya said, gritting his teeth.

"What is it?"

"How can I tell you before I tell Reverend?"

Manasseh tarried, twisting the key in the lock and unlinking the chains as if he no longer knew which direction to uncoil them. He ushered Zanya through the mission compound gates and asked him to wait on the Reverend's veranda.

As soon as Manasseh left and Reverend Jim arrived outside to meet him, Zanya blurted, "The men, they're striking," and his voice came out strained and soft.

"What?" Reverend Jim said.

"They're striking. Refusing to work today—"

"Have a seat and tell me what happened."

Zanya thought his bones might not bend and his muscles would stiffen. He settled into a yellow chair, finding that his body ignored his emotions and bent as usual.

"We have to do something," Zanya said. "This morning, Kago came to me to tell me that none of them want to build the church."

Reverend Jim took the chair near the window. "It can't be true. They'll show up."

Manasseh had set the small table on the veranda with a can of Milo, sugar cubes, powdered milk, and a flask of hot water. He served a tray of sliced oranges and a loaf of bread and arranged them on the table. Reverend Jim reached for the flask and motioned to Zanya. "Eat something."

"I'm not hungry, sir."

He was suffering shock with this mutiny, and he could not simply eat as if the day were unfolding as usual. The laborers had not given him another chance to negotiate with the Reverend. He would have worked alone all morning wondering where they were, trying to understand what had happened if Kago had not come. He sat unmoved with his feet wide apart and his hands clasped in his lap.

"It'll do you good." Reverend Jim pushed the plate toward him.

Reluctantly, Zanya picked up an orange slice. The taste was sour, that of a lemon's, and he glanced down to remember that what he held was supposed to taste sweet. He set it aside on a small plate Manasseh had provided for the rinds.

"The men cannot quit. If the rains come—all our work, our efforts will be damaged. If we cannot give them what they're asking for—"

"We're not giving in to these demands, Zanya." Reverend Jim spoke in a firm, impolite tone. "You should be careful, son. Sometimes, greed masquerades as need. I need you to trust me on this."

A bird, gray-cheeked and homely, flew toward them, alighting on the ground near one of the columns. It surveyed the veranda in coy steps, digging its sharp beak into its body to preen its feathers. Zanya studied the bird; how oblivious and calm it was in its environment.

"So I'll have to hire other people," Zanya said. "In order to finish this work."

"No, no. We're not going to do that either."

"But we need to finish the church before the rains—"

"We're going to wait this out, son," Reverend Jim said. "Don't give into their demands without pushback. Money is never the heart of the issue, you understand?"

"What they're asking for is fair," Zanya said. "If we want to maintain their trust, we must take care of them."

"What the mission gives the men is fair," Reverend Jim said. "If you can't handle this small opposition, Zanya, how can you handle the pulpit? The immensity of people's spiritual problems, the bickering, the falsehoods—"

"I understand, but is this not a different matter?"

Reverend Jim did not stifle a small laugh. "Yes, this is far easier than the pulpit."

Zanya looked at where the gray-cheeked bird had landed earlier. He caught a glimpse of Jummai across the way in the Parsons' house setting a thermos on their dining table. A shiver of jealousy shot down his spine. Jummai had intimate knowledge of the compound as he once had when living in Reverend Jim's home. He recalled an afternoon when Allison Parson played "Twist and Shout" from her American records on the days he and his men constructed the wall surrounding the compound. He had enjoyed those days until he and the laborers completed the mission houses and Reverend Jim asked him to find his own place.

"This is a test for you, Zanya." Reverend Jim removed his glasses and cleaned the lens in slow, measured circles with the corner of his handkerchief. "Can you lead this group of laborers? Redirect them from self-will to God's will?"

"I don't know, Reverend. This is very serious—"

"Well now," Reverend Jim said. "That's not the Zanya I know."

Zanya swallowed and cleared his throat. "Yes, I can lead them."

"You said yourself the church would be built before the conference. Make it happen."

It aligned with the original timeline he had confidently given the Reverend weeks ago. The construction site flashed in his mind, along with all the work that needed to be done: laying of more bricks to complete the walls, installing windows and doors, the pipework for the drainage system. What had seemed feasible when he surveyed the site yesterday had become suddenly overambitious and impossible.

"Will you meet with them, sir? Talk to them?"

"Until they return to work, there'll be no negotiations," Reverend Jim said. "Tell your laborers to be content with their earnings. Finish this building, and I'll put your name forward with the mission to serve as my right-hand man."

"You're serious, Reverend?" The internal turmoil of worry and frustration was still there. "You will give me the position if the men return to work?"

"Convince them to return, Zanya. Finish the church."

CHAPTER THIRTEEN

JIM WALKED BACK into the house after Manasseh closed the gates behind Zanya. So, this is what the men wanted to do. A revolt? When they were so close to completing the new church?

He passed the living room and went down the short hallway toward his office in the second bedroom. The office was small and sparse, a monastic bent to its decor. A desk and chair. Two wicker chairs for guests. A five-shelf bookcase abutting the window. Behind his desk was Doré's *Landscape in Scotland*, a painting he had brought back with him the last time he was on furlough. In the weeks following Edna's funeral, he had wandered through the manse seeing his wife's touch everywhere—paisley wallpaper plastered in the foyer, tchotchkes from outdoor country fairs, the puffy, tufted recliner she fell asleep in while crocheting. After her death, the manse had become a cold, unwelcoming place with dark, heavy wood paneling, and he'd never realized how little sunlight filtered into it.

He thought he would welcome the change of environment in Nigeria, where nothing in the spartan house reminded him of theirs in Rockford. He found that he wanted to be reminded of Edna more than he wanted to escape grief, and so he had returned with the painting.

He reached for the ledgers in the top drawer of the desk. He knew what he would find, but he wanted to see it anyway, the figures the men had originally agreed to. He wasn't too worried about their refusal to come to work this morning. This strike, if he could call it that, would be an opportunity for him to see how serious Zanya was about leadership, a test of sorts to see how true the calling might be. Zanya could not know that a day's soliloquy was insufficient to bolster one through the inevitable trials in ministry, and there'd be temptations to disobey the original call. Stand long enough in the pulpit, and how quickly the choir of praise becomes the gallery of critics, how gratitude curdles into spite. With the men revolting now, Zanya might see what Jim aimed to teach him about leadership and ability. A Hausa saying captured well the trials of ministry: *I'd rather a thousand cows than ten people to shepherd.*

Jim had been studying at Presbyterian Theological Seminary at Zanya's age. He had not yet known the spiritual turmoil of carrying others' afflictions or the sleepless nights spent in perpetual prayer, bearing burdens that thinned and stretched the walls of your heart. You neglected spouse and children, and in the end, saved others' souls but not the souls of those closest to you. Look at his two sons. Walter was a history professor at Amherst College. He and Walter had fallen out of an amicable father-son relationship in Walter's teenage years, when he'd quit showing up to Sunday school because he no longer believed any of it. To him, Biblical stories were legends written by man and full of contradictions. *There's nothing much there, Dad.* Jim remembered how he'd said those words about the Bible, in that hubristic manner of a teenager who believed himself superior in intelligence to his parents. When Jim countered Walter's doubts, Walter would look up from whatever book he was reading with a look of annoyance and a smidge of hatred—Jim had sworn to Edna it was hatred—and say in a patronizing tone, *All right, Dad,* as if Jim might be the greatest idiot he'd ever encountered. It had put a deep fear in Jim to hear those atheistic views, and he had not handled his son's questions with aplomb. These doubts had shaken him to the core—the gradual disillusionment and disintegration of his son's faith.

Jim's youngest, Pete, now bounced from low-wage job to low-wage job in San Francisco, wearing ripped jeans and growing his hair in an embarrassing mop like the hippie youth out there. It was a look befitting a vagrant, and one Jim found hard to tolerate on an adult male in his thirties. The scandal with Pete had led him to be more discerning about financial matters.

Jim opened the ledger for the church construction and scanned the numbers, going down each line. He had reduced the wages the mission allotted for the laborers to free up monies for other ministerial efforts. He had quoted a price, and the laborers had agreed to it without complaint until the tip from Kago's cousin. Finding labor at a lower cost had put Jim in good standing with Bill Kent, the country director, who was impressed with his stewardship of mission resources and his ability to save on expenses compared to other station leaders.

Renegotiating with the workers might lead Bill to distrust Jim's governance of the Rabata station. "Build a church," Bill had said. It was the main project Bill assigned Jim when he came on board, and he had no intention to invite any doubt that he'd been wrong in his management of the construction or the financial affairs thus far. Give it a week, and he was confident the strike would wither on its own.

He closed the ledger to put it back in the first drawer on top of the other records and decided—for safekeeping—to lock it in the bottom drawer instead.

※

The muggy, dense air in the operating theater gave Tebeya the sensation of being sheathed in an enormous steamed towel. The surgery was closed to nurses undergoing training, which meant the theater contained only the necessary clinicians—the nurse anesthetist monitoring the woman's breathing, the scrub nurse waiting with an anxious sort of stare to hand over a sterilized instrument at Tebeya's or Nelson's request, the nursing assistant poised to leave the operating theater for additional medical supplies. Tebeya's eyes tracked Nelson, who stood across from her, hand poised to begin operating on the patient's lower extremity.

"How are you doing, Dr. Landry?" she asked for the second time.

"I've said I'm doing fine."

"Are you sure?"

"Dr. Awyebwi, please. What's with the interrogation?"

"Okay, if you're fine…"

Her mask made it sound like she was speaking into a balloon, which she thought an adequate description for her current state. She felt trapped inside an inflated balloon, inside a room with elastic walls that might collapse once the air was expelled. Nelson Landry had bleary, tired eyes, and it seemed as if he would have liked nothing more than to be in a parlor with low lights and a fan running at full blast with a bottle of Heineken in his hands, not operating on a patient who had come to them in severe pain. The patient, an ailing grandmother, had arrived in the back of a lorry, riding atop a load of benniseed with her granddaughter and a friend. Tebeya had examined the grandmother's leg, a purple mass no longer embodying anything human, the infection having spread from the woman's foot to her thigh. The grandmother had spoken in soft, indecipherable words with each difficult breath she inhaled. Her friend explained that they were unable to save and borrow enough money for the clinic fee until now.

Before the operation, Tebeya put on her surgical apron and said to Nelson, "We need to delay the procedure. See how weak her body is? We can do the surgery in a couple days' time."

The patient needed to stay a couple of nights so that an incision could be made for pus to drain from her leg for a day or two.

She required proper hydration, and they had not given her vital preoperative antibiotics.

"No can do, Dr. Awyebwi," Nelson had said. "We've got to move forward today."

Now, as Nelson raised his hands, her eyes were fixed on him. Sweat pooled in the creases near his eyes, soaking the rim of the mask covering his nose and mouth. She itched to seize the ten-blade out of his hands. Yesterday, Nelson Landry had smelled faintly of alcohol, so faintly it could have been the result of a strong aftershave. When she inquired, he blamed the scent on a new liniment he had used for a patient. "Must've gotten all over me," he said. In Dublin, Gerard Nolan and the few medical school classmates willing to partner with an African student had nicknamed her "Scalpel Eyes" for her astute observations.

Under the glare of light, the grandmother's leg was swollen beyond recognition, and the wound had not been properly cleaned. Tebeya could only assist Nelson. Eventually, she would begin performing minor surgeries, a responsibility not many female physicians were given. To stand observing him without the ability to intervene was agonizing.

"Dr. Landry!" she cried.

He had gone too far, beyond the line to incise, centimeters above the circle she had drawn around the woman's pus-infected thigh.

"Gauze, now," Nelson said. "Hurry up, please!"

The scrub nurse produced it within seconds.

"Quick, put pressure on the area," he ordered, though Tebeya was already sponging the incision with a pair of forceps. She pushed the gauze against the wound, and the white netted cotton turned a bright red. She held it until the bleeding was under control.

"All right," Nelson said, looking up at the team. "Let's take a deep breath. Listen, nothing happened. It was just a nick, you know. The patient's fine."

"But Dr. Landry," she said, "you're not looking well—"

"It is very hot, Likita," said the scrub nurse to Tebeya, as if to excuse Nelson. "That must be why Dr. Landry is looking as he is."

"That's right. It's got to be these temperatures," Nelson said, as the scalpel reflected the overhead lights. "Must be in the hundreds, am I right?"

"You're the wrong color for this kind of heat, Dr. Landry," the nurse anesthetist, who had come from Ahmadu Bello University Hospital, said. All the others tittered.

Tebeya wanted to tape their mouths shut and push them all out of the theater for their flippancy and traitorous snickers. There was nothing humorous about the situation, and if they had known the truth, none of them would be laughing about the heat or Nelson's paleness. He had them deceived. The man had such a kooky personality that the staff would have readily attributed any strangeness to this and to his whiteness.

"Well," she said, because Nelson would not quiet her so easily, "if you're not fine, Dr. Landry, if the heat is causing you problems, we can stop."

"For the last time, Dr. Awyebwi, you are here to assist! You are not to perform this surgery. Do you understand?" He looked from her to the nurse anesthetist and to the scrub nurse. "Does anyone else object to my continuation of this surgical procedure?"

A long, uncomfortable hush ensued. No one offered a rejoinder.

"Good," he said. "Let's continue. In silence."

She ignored the stares in her direction—the obvious curiosity about what had happened between Dr. Tebeya and oga, senior doctor, the one in charge from America. She drew her shoulders back and refocused as Nelson pulled the scalpel in a single circular motion on the flesh and pulled back the thin flap of skin. Each subsequent incision produced more and more pus as Nelson searched for the primary source of infection. The grandmother's breathing had changed, and this was another warning to Tebeya, a sign for them to stop. Nelson steadied his hands and moved gingerly into the tissues, and she heard his shallow, uncertain breaths as he lowered the scalpel again.

CHAPTER FOURTEEN

JUMMAI STOOD UNDER the Parsons' veranda, wringing her hands on the apple-dotted apron Ms. Katherine had recently insisted she wear when cooking. Her eyes raked the compound for Elijah. He liked to doze in the hammock behind the Reverend's house or she'd find him crouched against the cowshed, playing a game in the dirt.

She spotted him in the grapefruit tree, his whitish-looking hair peeking out of a cluster of leaves like a rooster's comb. She waved at him to come down. "Elijah! You know Nami is coming."

"I know, I know," he said.

"You have to be ready with your books."

"I already am," he said, hopping out of the branches. A green-skinned fruit plopped off a limb, thumping the ground and rolling down to rest near his shoes.

He sprang up, brushing the little stones and dirt from his knees. "Jummai, I found something. Can I show it to you?"

"No, you have to soon eat," she said.

"Please?"

"Elijah, if you make me burn my yam porridge—"

"It'll be quick! I promise."

She followed him on the path that curved behind the house. Last time, the child led her to a harmless spotted snake he had killed with his slingshot. This time, he ran ahead of her to Dr. Landry's house, which was a short slanted walk from the Parsons', past a pineapple patch and plants with flowers as red and bright as tomatoes. The three houses on the compound formed a triangle. Dr. Landry's house faced the front gate. The Parsons and Reverend Jim's houses, with the same roof and blue-painted walls, flanked the doctor's and faced each other. If you stood on the Parsons' veranda at night, you could see into the Reverend's parlor and find Reverend Jim writing sermons with a Bible at his side or reading at one of his two desks. A cowshed and chicken coop also abutted his house.

On the days Manasseh was not working, Jummai cleaned Dr. Landry and Reverend Jim's houses, so she knew the inside had the same structure as the Parsons: a parlor with enough space for a dining table and chairs made by local carpenters, bedrooms in the back of the house, and the toilets near the bedrooms. The kitchens were connected to the dining room through one door and had second entrances that led outside. Each kitchen had shelves, wood stoves, bottled gas ovens, and kerosene refrigerators.

"Over here," Elijah said, grabbing Jummai's hand.

She fixed her wrapper to her hip and yielded to his pull. They walked deeper into the doctor's yard, between robust stalks of banana plants, whose leaves were tattered from the wind.

"See," Elijah said, giving a stalk an unnecessary kick. "I told you. All the bottles I found. Look—it's a lot of them."

Jummai pushed aside the large leaves. Elijah had unearthed empty bottles of varying brands: Guinness, Heineken, and Stout. The unlabeled ones must have held palm wine. The green and brown glass glittered like beetle shells in the sunlight. Elijah had heaped the scooped-out dirt around the hole, and the pit contained enough bottles to entertain a number of tables at Shigudu's beer parlor. Had someone sneaked into the mission compound and put rubbish in the doctor's backyard? Her second thought— Dr. Landry was drinking—was probably closer to the truth. The doctor did not remind her of her father who used to stumble home late at night after drinking, stubbing his feet against her and her mother's sleeping bodies and cursing in the darkness. Was she not used to seeing things and shutting her mouth? When Tin City beat her mother, had Jummai said anything to anybody? No, she had simply gone and minded her business. They should leave Dr. Landry's yard and go back to the house.

"It's rubbish," she said to confuse Elijah.

His grin lapsed. "No, it's not. It's like *Treasure Island*."

"You're here wasting my time. You're too old for such things."

"Dr. Landry's making something! Like a ship in a bottle."

Jummai did not know what the boy was talking about with ships inside of bottles.

"I'm gonna ask him when he gets back."

"You won't say anything to him, Elijah. I don't want to ever see you here again playing with these bottles. Cover the thing. Now."

Elijah sank to the ground and dug his hands into the dirt he had shoveled out.

He was not as sharp as Allison. He would soon forget the bottles. He would only think Jummai had spoiled his game. To be certain, she added, "Don't go running your mouth, or you'll be in trouble with me. Are you hearing me?"

"But Jummai, what if—"

"Did you hear me?"

He groaned, "I won't," and buried the bottles quickly.

❧

Jummai noticed what Nami wore when she walked through the gates of the mission compound to tutor Elijah. Last week, Nami had worn a blouse and wrapper; the material had been orange with blue squares. Today she wore a white blouse tucked into a green and yellow striped skirt that grazed her knees. Around her neck was a thin cord of fabric like a man's tie, silky and striped green and yellow like her skirt. Nami dressed in simple fashions, and apart from the same pair of small gold earrings, Jummai never saw her wearing any other jewelry.

The more Nami came to the Parsons' house to help Elijah with his school assignments, the more Jummai understood why Zanya had decided to marry this woman. She talked to Jummai as if they were friends. She asked after her sisters and brothers, remembering all of their names, telling her about Yakwo, who she said was a smart boy, if only he would apply himself instead of misbehaving. Nami also did not like Jummai to do things for her. If Jummai said, "Let me go and bring water for you to drink," Nami would say, "No, I am fine. Let me get it myself."

Jummai served them the yam porridge on the back porch with a glass bottle of "catchup," as Elijah called the red American sauce he liked to pour on his meals. They finished the full amount in their bowls, and Elijah, who said porridge was "yucky" and wrinkled his nose at the smell of crayfish, ate all of it and begged for more.

Jummai knew her food was good. Miss Delores had once come to her family's compound to speak with Jecinda, and because Jecinda had not yet returned from the clinic, Miss Delores had talked to Jummai, asking her what she would do if she did not have to work at the Parsons'.

"I wan open restaurant," Jummai had said. "I don't know if it will happen."

"Nonsense, Jummai," Miss Delores said. "I believe you could. I see it now. You'll have a thriving business, and you'll hire others to work for you. You can absolutely do it."

"Ah, Mai Mulo, I don't know."

She could sell food like the women who sold meals in their houses with benches for people to sit and eat. Maybe this is what she would do if her mother and Tin City allowed her to use their house. She had said this to Miss Delores.

"No, Jummai," Miss Delores had said, "I won't hear of it.

You'll have your own restaurant. Raise half of the money, and I'll see if I can find the other half. How about it?"

The money she saved from the Parsons was not simply for her to find a place to live without her family, but so that she might have enough to open a restaurant.

From the kitchen window that looked out into the backyard, Jummai studied how Nami tilted her head and said in a firm voice, "Try again, Elijah."

This was what Zanya wanted: a woman who said things like "try again." She wondered what Nami might have done about the bottles Elijah found. Would she have confronted Dr. Landry or gone and announced it to Malama Delores or shut her mouth like Jummai? She knew the answer already. Nami would not have kept quiet about such a thing. She spoke to these missionaries as if they were her mates.

"You have to know your long division," Nami said, "and how to do percentages."

"I guess," Elijah said.

He put his head down on the table and spun a pencil between his fingers, twisting it back and forth. Jummai could see he wanted to be banging bottle caps with a rock to flatten them or playing with his slingshot, hunting snakes or shooting at birds and lizards.

"It is not 'you guess,'" Nami said, plucking the pencil from him. "You have to learn. Don't you want to be a smart boy who is first in the class?"

Elijah shrugged. "Not really."

Nami laughed at this, and Jummai did not know why Nami laughed when the boy was saying he wanted to be an idiot. Was this how she laughed with Zanya? Did she make Zanya laugh in his flat so that his mouth, full and wide, showed his strong teeth, and lines extending from the curve of his nose to the corners of his mouth deepened? It seemed a long time ago when Jummai used to go to Chubz's flat where Zanya was certain to be found, drinking stout and rolling wiwi with Chubz. She and Zanya had danced and laughed in the darkened room with smoke reaching the ceiling.

One night, he had taken her to Keffi, and they danced in the open-air nightclub among the throng, and they swayed to Highlife music, and to the drum solo of the Ominah Band.

"Fine girl," he had said, his hands on her waist, pulling her in.

"You and your mouth," she said, laughing. He had seemed the only person who could bring laughter out of her.

"No." His voice had been serious, his mouth very close to her ears. "It's true."

This was when Zanya had first come to Rabata in '67, before the Reverend started preaching to him in the evenings and telling him about his Christian god. Zanya had been like the other men in this town. After his conversion, he began to wear more of the European fashions. He was not as stylish as some of the young men in town, with their wide Keep Lagos Clean trousers and solid platform shoes, their open shirts exposing hairless chests and glinting gold chains sinking into the valley of their shirts. But he had purchased new shirts and trousers when he began to translate in front of the church on Sunday mornings.

Zanya was not like some of the locals who pretended to accept the missionaries' religion so that the missionaries might give them money for their businesses or help their children with school fees. He had accepted the things they said and had begun to live like them. Remnants of the former Zanya, the man with the stained shirt and trousers hitched up to his calves, smelling of sweat and tobacco and local brew, had disappeared. She was not surprised he had chosen a woman like Nami; she suited this new person he had become.

Nami said in a firmer voice, "Sit up, Elijah. You must finish these problems."

Elijah pulled himself up straight, and Nami returned his pencil.

"You know that you can learn, too," Nami said.

Jummai nearly dropped the plate in her hand. Nami had looked up and found her staring at them from the open kitchen window.

"Me?" Jummai said.

Nami retightened the knot of her green and yellow necktie. "With how fine you are, if you start learning more eh? All the men will keep following you, they won't be able to leave you alone."

Jummai smiled. Zanya had not left her alone even without her finishing school. She did not like how people thought she was stupid because she had attended only one year.

"If you want," Nami said, "I will tell Malama Delores you want to learn. She will give you books. She has many of them."

"Me, I'm fine," Jummai said.

"I can help you if you do not want Malama Delores to teach you."

"I'm fine, sha." How many times did she have to be here repeating herself?

She did not like how Nami turned her shoulders, as if she pitied Jummai for not wanting to learn. She was sitting there, comparing Jummai to small Elijah and how he went about saying things like "not really." She imagined Nami and Zanya laughing together in his pickup later this afternoon. "Foolish Jummai," Nami would say, "I offered to teach her, and she said she wanted to remain an idiot like Elijah." They would laugh close with each other, and Nami would be fresh and beautiful, her hair styled, wearing her bright teacher clothes.

"You are marrying Zanya," Jummai said.

Nami turned from the paper she was marking. "What?"

"Zanya. You are marrying him?"

"Yes, after the church is built, it is there we want to marry."

Jummai heard the fear in Nami's voice at what she had asked. The pitiful look she had given Jummai was replaced with curiosity and concern.

"How do you know Zanya?" Nami asked in a voice that made Elijah glance up from his composition book at her. "I did not know you knew him."

"Who in this town doesn't know him?" Jummai said. "Everybody knows him." Nami opened her mouth a little as if she wanted to ask questions, but Jummai continued talking. "Zanya comes here to see Reverend Jim. Sometimes, he will come to see Mai Hankali. On Sundays, he will come and eat the evening meal with the both of them. You know the man used to live on this mission compound, in Reverend Jim's house."

"That must be how you know each other," Nami said.

"Before nko? How else would I know him?" Jummai said.

Nami tilted her head like she had earlier with Elijah. Jummai said nothing for a while, and then she said, "You want water, Nami? You are looking thirsty."

"Yes," Nami said this time. "Yes, thank you."

CHAPTER FIFTEEN

ZANYA STRETCHED OUT across the seat of the pickup, parked on the church construction site to guard the materials. He could not believe the laborers had stayed away for the past three days. He had expected them to return the next day. When this did not happen, he had expected commotion. A protest at the construction site. But they did not seem to have organized themselves well. They simply refused to work.

It was hard to believe his own men had come against him. Without telling him. Except for Kago. If he stopped to think, he could say that it wasn't against him; they had come against the mission. But it felt as if they had targeted him since they had not involved him in their plans. A knot of indigestion from the kilishi he had hurriedly eaten earlier traveled up into his chest. The laborers were doing it to prove a point; soon enough the absence of wages and the responsibility of caring for their families would bring them back.

Under his notebook on the dashboard was a hat his eldest sister Pema had knitted for him when he was an infant. He had outgrown the tiny, floppy head covering, yet he stowed it in the pickup as if it gave him luck on his drives. He had carried it from Yawari to Kunama Secondary School and back to Yawari. And when he left his village a final time without knowing where he was going, he had tucked the hat into a bag holding his meager belongings. He held the knitted hat in his hands now, thinking it might bring him some peace tonight.

Nights like this in Rabata reminded him of Yawari. If he listened hard enough, he thought he heard the river, the insects, and the su-surrus of night like in Yawari. Back in his village, giant trees, fruited with coconut, tamarind, and mango, stood guard over the houses and compounds with branches splayed. At night, somber musical notes emerged in the branches striking each other. He missed the beauty of his village—the flowering palm trees surrounding each of the compounds and the winding sandy paths connecting the homes.

He might never have left Yawari if not for his family. When he was a boy, his mother had said things that made him know he had to leave. "Child of evil," she cried in a cold, hard voice, as if jolted by something within. She had been like this since he had memory, and since he had memory was when he began to know she did not love him like mothers were supposed to love their children. She both loved and despised him. It would have been better if she had either loved him or despised him, but because she existed in this duality, he suffered.

His sister had shared stories that made him know his mother had lived another life before his birth, but she had taken her for-mer life, folded it, and stowed it away.

"What happened?" Zanya asked.

"You were born," Pema said. "That is when Mama stopped being Mama."

"What about Baba?"

"Baba, too, stopped being Baba."

He knew the truth now. Because of Pema, he had come to understand his repugnance to his mother and father. He was the bastard child of a man whose face his mother had never seen, a man who raped her in the bush when she was washing clothes in the stream. His mother had returned with the basin of clothes filthier than they were before she left.

The day Pema told him the things he was not supposed to know, he had looked at the family's personal god at the base of their door, and emptiness consumed him where there had always been fear and awe. The god of his family was not a god he wanted.

Thinking he'd heard a noise outside, Zanya bolted up. He returned the knitted hat to its corner and turned on the engine to spotlight the construction site. He drove slowly around the grounds and parked closer to the building when he saw that all was safe. What would his mother and father say if they could see him in Rabata? Look at him here, entrusted to guard a church, entrusted to build a church in fact. After his conversion, he had thought himself freed of the memories of his family, but they returned from time to time and affected who he was now, the things he did and said.

Why had he even gone to Yawari in the first place that night? He knew. He had felt compelled to reunite with his parents, to see if things had changed. Wasn't it because of them that he had allowed the testimony about the fire to turn into something other than the truth? Because he had wanted people to see him as something greater since his own family refused to do so?

But it had been unwise to let the story become what it had become. His family would know that he had lied to the mission and to the people of Rabata.

The truth about the night of the fire was there—buried in the vastness, in the miraculous direction it had taken. It was true that his cousins and uncles had grabbed him, surrounded him and demanded he reject his Christian faith. It was true that they threatened to set him on fire. It was *not* true that they had bound him and thrown guinea corn chaff around him. It was *not* true that they had set the sheaves on fire. It was *not* true that he had nearly burned alive and that God had saved him with a gale. His relatives had untied and released him, and Zanya had jumped into his pickup and sped down the road and into the darkness.

He could have stopped the rumors; he knew this now and had known it then. He could have stood in the church and said, "It is not true as they have told it." He had not thought about the things he had already done for the town and mission. He had thought that soon, people would learn of his past and where he had come from, and when they learned of it, people would say all he had done was not enough, and the true story of his persecution would not have been enough.

He did not know he had fallen asleep until a tap-tap against the window roused him.

He blinked into the darkness. "Jummai?"

She knocked again.

He rubbed his eyes to wake himself and wound down the window.

"You won't let me come or enter inside?" she said.

"You should not have come. Didn't I tell you to stop coming?"

"There are things I must tell you."

"Jummai," he sighed.

"You will want to know."

He hesitated before finally unlocking the passenger-side door, and she went around and climbed in. He had not seen her since the night of the fire, and before then, he had not seen her since he and Nami met several months ago. And of course, to have seen her on the night of the fire had been a mistake; it had given her ideas again.

"Take," she said, handing him the keys from the dashboard.

He was fully awakened now. He took the keys from her, but he did not start the pickup as he had done in the past to drive to a more secluded area near the river. There would be no need for hiding tonight. He planned to send her away after she shared what she had come to tell him.

"Come," he said, flinging open his door.

He returned the keys to the dashboard and kept the headlights turned off. A deeper darkness had overtaken the sky. The leaves of tamarind and palm trees on the site were black outlines against the sky, and far behind the foliage, the river flowed gentle and invisible. They stepped outside, and he went up to the bed of the pickup first, shoving two bags of cement to the side to give them room. He helped Jummai up, and they stood facing each other, his hands resting on the firm slope of her bottom. Guilt came, creeping into his fingers and chest. He released her, dropped down and switched on the torch, propping it between the two bags, and it gave them a halo of light with which to see each other.

"Jummai, you know what we did before, it was not good."

She had begun unbuttoning her blouse. She stopped, confused.

He did not look at her. "See the things I'm trying to do with Reverend Jim and the mission. It means this thing—me and you—cannot continue. If I want to do more with the mission, if I want to marry Nami—I must—I cannot do this. You understand?"

Jummai nodded, yet he doubted she comprehended. He knew she thought it a confession of his weakness. He might be saying it but not truly mean that he wanted them to stop. He could not blame her when he did not sound entirely convincing to himself.

"Button your blouse," he said.

"You are sure?"

"Yes. I'm sure."

He looked down to temper the temptation to undress her. His flesh did not operate on certainties. Certainty demanded he concentrate on her imperfections. She was a fine woman—the curvaceous body, the full lips, the round breasts, their size exaggerated by her suggestive walk—but she lacked the sophistication of a university girl or of a woman like Nami.

"There are things I have been wanting to tell you, Zanya."

"Is that so?" This was good. Just talking like this. "What is it?"

"The doctor is drinking."

"Which doctor? Nelson Landry?"

She nodded, and she smiled in the way he liked. And it reminded him of Nami, looking up and smiling at him so many nights ago when they met under the mango tree, and a horrible wave of guilt struck him again. He turned his face from her.

"How do you know?" he said.

She told him a story about Elijah and a burial ground of beer bottles in Dr. Landry's yard. The bottles could have meant anything.

"Have you seen him drinking?"

"No."

"Have you seen any beer in his house? Have you seen him drunk?"

"It's not me that cleans his house. It is Manasseh."

If it was true, he wondered if Dr. Tebeya knew, working in the clinic with this man.

"They said," Jummai continued, "you were like one man called Georges Wallfeed."

"*Georges Wallfeed?*" he said, laughing.

She laughed, too, throwing her head back so that the torchlight caught the roundness of her cheeks and made her teeth gleam like pearls of coconut flesh. It felt good to laugh with her sometimes. Laughter free of expectations. Free of demands.

"Who can know with these American names?" she said.

"Whitefield," he said. "You mean George Whitefield." He had heard this evangelist's name before from the Reverend, and it had been said in a dismissive tone. Sometimes, he could not be sure of the news she brought back to him.

"Yes o. That was the one. It was good, that day. The way they were talking about you that Sunday, especially Mr. Gary, about the fire and the church."

"My *Hawaii Five-0*," he said, looking up.

She had not buttoned her shirt yet. Moonlight shone and the stream of light from the torch shadowed the slope between her breasts. Nami was not so free like this. The last few months had been pleasure with Nami, a different pleasure than Jummai gave, and this physical pleasure Jummai gave, which he wanted with Nami, she withheld from him. He had refrained from forcing it, cherishing the opportunity to hold purity with her.

But Jummai, this buxom woman with those voluptuous hips, those strong, lean legs in a wicked saunter to his pickup. She was like drink, tap-tapping on his window. He lost his resolve when she appeared, forgetting his longing for purity and desire for righteousness. Her hair was as dark as the velvet-skinned tamarind that clustered on trees, plaited tight and woven into one supple braid dipping down her long neck. Her languid smile suggested a preoccupation with something other than the present. These encounters became an unspoken ritual, where she made no demands and asked no questions. Their nights together had not mattered to him before his conversion. She had been like the other women, the ones he met in bars or nightclubs. The forgettable ones who sidled up to him and filled his ears with humorless laughter. But then he had come to this new faith that demanded a purity he tried to maintain.

"Jummai," he repented in a strangled whisper for what he was about to do, reaping already the remorse to follow.

"What is it?" she said.

He drew her toward him. One final time. And as it always seemed when they came together, she knew what he desired without him speaking. He knew it was because of his tiredness, the lure of Jummai's voice, the ease of sitting with her, the momentary reprieve from the demands of the day, the expectations from his workers, the enjoyment of being, however momentary, unburdened.

Touching Jummai was like touching sun. How inflamed he was in his desire for her—such an amorphous and baffling force that it could not be contained. Her breasts, plump and soft as peeled oranges in his hands. Her single braid, dark and bountiful, swishing against the base of her neck. She was both comfort and temptation in his arms, taking him to a place where the purity he sought was unattainable.

How could any god ever make him, born of a ruined woman, clean? Each time he was with Jummai, it reawakened this doubt. The voice insisting he was still a bastard. He was soiled. Soiled as the day he was seeded in his mother's womb.

Afterward, Jummai clothed herself and looked at him expressionless, as if she were accepting of him, of all his weaknesses and hypocrisies. She climbed out of the pickup and walked in the direction leading back to her home. He exhaled his pleasure and confliction, laid his head against the back window, and stared up into the starless night.

CHAPTER SIXTEEN

LESS THAN A MILE from the mission compound, flames lashed against the afternoon sky as Mama Daga's lubu burned. Neighbors rushed toward the property carrying containers of water—cups, pots, pans, and bottles seized from their homes. Water sloshed over the sides, splashing and cooling their feet. Young men, more courageous and convinced of their invincibility, dared close to the lubu to douse the flames. Mama Daga came running shoeless and with her wrapper flying wide open like a cape—the onlookers expected her to ascend into the whirlwind of smoke. Nothing could be done, so the townspeople watched the flames raging through the roof and the smoke billowing into the sky. All the guinea corn and yams that had been stored would be lost. Later, the townspeople said the culprits were two boys, maybe three. They had seen the boys running from the lubu as quickly as the big white doctor walked through town. It could have been no one else but them.

CHAPTER SEVENTEEN

NAMI'S DRESS ROSE AND FELL like a breath above her knees. A faint-ish, sweet fragrance suffused his pickup with her arrival. Her hair, pulled back, revealed the openness of her face. Her lips were im-bued with a soft red like sorrel, and her cheekbones flushed with excitement. She had a quieter beauty than Jummai, less obvious until she sat like this in front of him, resplendent and fresh.

"You didn't have trouble coming?" she asked.

"No," he said, reaching for her hand.

A short, uncomfortable silence prevailed, which occurred sometimes when they reunited, whether after hours or days, both wondering if this new time would bring the same enjoyment as the time before, and appraising the other to see what was new or al-tered. This time, remorse resided in his silence. Remorse about the previous night—the pleasure of his hands on Jummai. He could relieve the physical discomfort of shame. Tell Nami. Tell her about the fire. Tell her about Jummai. His mates in Kunama would have laughed. Chubz would have laughed. Tell a woman what he had done? So she could end his life?

Nami was not like this, he thought. But the truth was that he did not know what she was like if faced with his confession. He knew her in this joyous, endearing state, where she thought what she was hearing and seeing from him was him as he truly was.

He had parked near the entrance of the primary school, close

to the headmistress's office which, like the other doors, was deco-
rated with palm branches to celebrate Palm Sunday, the fronds
like green shutters on the windows. A woman from the choir had
created an arc of branches above the classroom door where the
service was held. Behind a curtain of fronds, Zanya glimpsed Gary
Parson sitting comfortably in the headmistress's office, talking to
Miss Delores. One or two days a week, Nami told him, Gary came
to the primary school to complete maintenance duties, and often,
he spent time in Miss Delores's office.

"He has been there for the last hour," Nami said, "since we dismissed classes." She looked around as if to ensure none of her primary school students were wandering close to the pickup. She whispered, "They're talking because of government takeover in schools.
It started happening in other regions, and now it's coming to us—"

"I've been hearing."

Zanya looked at how Gary Parson was sitting and talking, as if
he could have stayed even if there were other things for him to do,
other people waiting for him. He doubted they were talking about
government takeovers. He had never witnessed any improper behavior between them, but he could see the small things in their
stance or how they looked at each other. He had mentioned it
to Nami once, and she refused to believe anything indecent was
happening. "That's not how Malama Delores is," she said. He had
thought the same about Gary Parson, but then he would think
of himself, and the indecent things he had done, and he thought
that this is how others might be too—their sins camouflaged in
darkness.

"Malama Delores said she's going to talk to the Reverend
about the men."

"Good. Maybe he'll listen to her." Neither side had budged so
far. He felt as if he was going from person to person, and no one
was interested in compromise.

"What of Gary Parson? Did you ask him?"

"He's gone and tried to talk to Kago."

Nami tugged her dress over her knees. "Why can the Reverend not just pay them more? It does not make sense to me. Why does he keep saying 'no' when our people ask for more?"

"He might not have the funds."

"He has. The mission has."

In the distance, across the field, a plume of black smoke rose to the sky. It was not the wispy, dissipating smoke from a cooking fire. It would not reach that high. He leaned toward the windshield to see, though he could not make it his problem to solve. There were other things he had to worry about now. He turned back to Nami. She sat with her mouth locked and her long neck angled to the side.

"So, you know Jummai," she said. "How do you know her?"

"What?" He had not expected Jummai's name out of her mouth.

"Give your answer, Zanya."

"Answer you? What are you asking, Nami?"

Nami stared straight at him. For a moment, it seemed she could see into his mind, to last night with Jummai. Chubz had said women were clairvoyant like this—like witches. It was one kind of power men lacked. Women could have eyes in other people's eyes, he said. They could jump from one pair of eyes to another and catch you in whatever you were doing. He had laughed with Chubz at the foolishness.

"I won't have it, Zanya—"

"What is there to have?" His nerves came out in the thumping of his fingers against the pickup's steering wheel. His heart raced. Had someone followed Jummai to his pickup and told Nami? Had a laborer been on the site last night and seen him? "You're the only one I want. Why are we even speaking of this?"

"I'm lying, abi? You don't know her?"

"Does she not work on the mission compound?" He decided

to tiptoe close to a truth. "When I went to talk to Reverend Jim about the strike, I saw Jummai there. You want me to close my eyes when I go and see the Reverend? To not talk to anybody? Is that it?"

Nami gave him the back of her head, crossed her legs and looked out the window. "I won't have it. You understand? You with another woman and with me at the same time. You could leave me now and go and see her. What would I know of it?"

He suppressed the desire to confess. Not now. It was not the time. It would not happen again with Jummai. He had made it clear to her last night and to himself. Why should he worry Nami? "You are the one I want, Nami. Can you not see this?"

She turned and observed him with uncertainty.

"You must believe me. Are we not to marry?"

"Okay," she said, after a moment. "We will see."

⚜

"Your sister wants us to go to Jos next weekend."

Tebeya did not glance up at her mother. She continued reading an abstract that preceded a chapter on abdominal pains in *Harrison's Principles of Internal Medicine*.

"Tebeya," her mother said, tapping Tebeya's leg with a righteous jab of her cane.

"Mama, sorry o—"

"Are you not paying attention to your mother?"

"What did you say?" Tebeya kept her finger in the pages. She was conducting research on the grandmother's illness, searching in vain to see what other symptoms Nelson had missed. She despised her mother's interruptions when she was close to securing an answer. She remembered Nelson's erroneous incision, and how the white netted gauze had turned a frightening red as they brought the bleeding under control. She had been correct to concern herself with the grandmother's labored breathing during the operation. The grandmother suffered complications and died mere hours after the surgery. Because of Nelson and because Tebeya had not stopped him. And her mother, who never asked about the clinic or its patients, was sitting here going on and on about Bintu and Jos.

"Bintu wants to go to Jos."

"Okay, let her go, then. Has she finally decided to return to her husband?"

Her mother lowered herself into the cushions and scrutinized a tear on the cloth as she said, "You don't know why your sister has come. Have you talked to her?"

"It's Thomas," Tebeya said. "Everything that goes wrong in her life is because of Thomas. I warned her not to marry him. Did she listen? Atoh. That is her problem."

Tebeya had gleaned more details of her sister's marriage and surmised Thomas was part of the reason Bintu had come to Rabata and extended her stay for so many weeks. Thomas had offended a prominent governor by supporting his political opponent. He and Bintu stood to lose their status in the elite social circles comprised of commissioners and company presidents.

"Please, go with your sister to Jos."

"I cannot just travel to Jos. Is it anybody's birthday? Is there a celebration?"

Tebeya assumed her sister and mother were still colluding to marry her off to one of Thomas's boring, arrogant friends. She walked across the tiled floor to feign checking the calendar. "Just as I suspected," she said, stabbing the weekend date with her finger. "It's not anybody's birthday. It doesn't suit me to go to Jos this weekend."

"Haba, Tebeya. What else are you doing?"

"You don't know the things I have to worry about with these patients—"

"Is it not Dr. Landry's job? Is he not the director?"

"At this time," Tebeya said, clipped.

"Your brother has found a woman he wants to marry. She is from America. He is going to bring her back for us to give our blessing—"

"Good for Patrick. I will dance at his wedding."

"And you—you want me to die before you marry?"

"Mama," Tebeya said, reclaiming the seat next to her mother and searching her mind for how to distract her, "there are more important matters in this life. Have you not heard about this strike? What will you and Baba do?"

"Why are these people striking, eh? These missionaries have given much to this town. In my village, when our people were killing their twins, who made it stop—"

"I know, Mama, but that is not what I'm saying—"

"The people in this town can give their children an education now. Why? Because of the missionaries."

"We were educating ourselves without them," Tebeya said.

"Some of these people, they cannot pay the clinic fees. Haven't you said this to me? If they went to government hospital, would there not be payment required of them?"

Whenever he could, Nelson treated patients who were unable to pay the nominal fee. This had happened countless times, and Nelson would waive the fees or accept their forms of payment— yams or cassava or a catch of fish. A couple of the laborers they treated for chronic conditions had come to the clinic asking about the cost of their medications. Nelson said he would give it to them under credit. They could repay when the strike ended. "Separation of church and health," he said easily when Tebeya asked.

"But that is not what this is about, this strike." Tebeya sighed. "I've said to Baba that he should offer the laborers work in Glories and Blessings."

"How does this thing concern me?"

"They have wives and children—" She stopped speaking. It

was clear her mother was uninvested in mission politics or the welfare of the laborers, never mind that the men's wives were faithful
patrons of Glories and Blessings Ladies' Provisions Store and this
could affect business.

"What of you? Where are your own children?"

"Shouldn't you be happy that I'm not married, and that I've
remained in Rabata? Who will take care of you and Baba if anything happened, if you were to fall ill? Patrick in America? Selfish
Bintu and Thomas? I don't want to meet any of Thomas's friends."

"My dear," her mother said, "it is because you don't know this
friend—"

"It's a matter of probability."

"Listen to you." Her mother sucked her teeth. "Probability.
What is probability?"

"The probability of me having any interest in one of Thomas's
friends is close to zero, near impossibility, but please, Mama, if you
want to tell me about this one, tell me."

She succeeded in launching her mother into an extensive bi-
ography about Thomas's barrister friend, a man who had received
his LLD at King's College in London and currently served under
Nigeria's Minister of Justice. Tebeya arranged her countenance
into one she hoped reflected mild interest while her mind wandered to the girl whose grandmother had died at Nelson Landry's
hands. When Tebeya went to the ward to deliver the news of the
grandmother's death to the friend who had accompanied her, the
granddaughter sat on a cot, her short legs swinging back and
forth. Her oversized skirt had twisted around her waist so the
back zipper faced front, and above her white socks, dust covered
her calves and knees. Her skin was as dark as butter fruit, and
the girl's mouth, a shade lighter than the rest of her face, had
moved around her thumb mechanically, as if extracting fears.
Tebeya guessed her to be eight or nine years old, past the age
to be sucking her thumb. She carried the leanness of illness like

her grandmother; she might favor her in later years—short, thin, with pointed features.

"I'm sorry o," Tebeya had said after breaking the news to the friend and telling her when the family could come and wash the body and transport it for burial.

"The girl's father and mother are dead," the woman said, emotionless. Death, to her, was a state akin to eating or bathing. "Her grandmother was the one caring for this girl. I know her other relation. He will not want another mouth to feed."

"What is the girl's name?"

"Comfort. Imagine." The woman sighed and tapped the girl. "Oya, greet the doctor."

"Good afternoon, ma," Comfort said, without looking at Tebeya.

"This child," the woman continued, "now, she doesn't have anybody—"

"Surely, she has somebody," Tebeya said.

Tebeya looked down again at the granddaughter, and the conversations between the other nurses and patients stilled around her. In her peripheral vision she had seen patients coming into the ward to join a queue for Dr. Landry, and Katherine at the next cot preparing a vaccination, yet she focused on the helpless child in front of her.

The woman said, "She has one uncle—he cannot care for her."

"What of you, nko?"

The woman laughed. "Me, ke? Add to my four children?"

"Okay, take Comfort with you today," Tebeya said. "Bring her back to this clinic the following week. I will know what to do by then."

She had given the woman money for transport fare and food. The week would give her time to think about this desire that had come again and seemed to be rising within her.

❦

Katherine looked out the living room window in time to see Sayi escorting Elijah to the mission compound like a guard leading a criminal to his cell. Sayi held the hand of a dust-speckled Walu, and Yakwo trailed behind the three figures.

In a shy, grim voice, Sayi asked for Mai Hankali when Katherine opened the door.

"Gary's not here, sweetie."

Sayi said, "Please, ma, when will Mr. Gary return?"

"I'll tell him when he comes home," Katherine said, nettled that the girl found her an inferior substitute for her husband. "What's the matter?"

"Okay, ma," Sayi said with an expression showing she'd rather have Mai Hankali resolving this dispute. "Please, Elijah and Yakwo went and burned Mama Daga's lubu—"

"They *what*!" News had reached the clinic that Mama Daga's wooden lubu had caught fire and burned to the ground. Katherine had not expected the perpetrator to be her own son. A quick image flew into her mind: a wild-haired adult Elijah locked up behind bars, a convicted felon. "What in the world did you do, Elijah?"

Elijah pointed. "Yakwo dared me to do it."

Gangly and confident, Yakwo said, "Ma, Elijah was the one! Me, I didn't do anything. He was the one o!"

Elijah's lips quivered. "You did. You threw the match."

"Na lie!" Yakwo said.

"Okay, okay, boys." Arbitrating a case of arson was the last thing she needed today. "Sayi, where is Mama Daga?"

"She said she is coming. They had to stop the fire," Sayi said. "Elijah burned his hands. He's hiding them—"

Katherine reached for her son's elbow and pulled him forward. He had hidden his hands behind his back, and he cried out in pain. His palms had blistered, swollen and red.

"Get in here, now," Katherine said, moving aside and snapping her fingers. "Yakwo, Sayi, if you see Mama Daga, would you please tell her Gary and I will be right over, okay?"

Inside, Katherine inspected the superficial burns on her son's palms. "What were you thinking, Elijah? You could've been hurt. You could've killed someone!"

"I didn't mean to do it."

"Tell me what happened. I won't be upset if you tell me the truth. Did you do it?"

Elijah shrugged and looked up at the ceiling as if his memory were foggy. "Yakwo threw a match, then I threw one. Oh—wait, I threw the match first, I guess."

"Oh, Elijah."

She had him sit while she brought over a basin and washed the burn with soap and water. He winced when she rubbed antibacterial ointment and bandaged his hands.

"Now, why in the world would you do this?"

"They don't want to be my friend," he said, embarrassed to be admitting such a helpless truth. "I wanted to prove I could do it."

His shoulders sunk in defeat, and his legs were akimbo over the arm of the couch. His flaxen hair stuck straight up, a blessed distraction from the pimples pebbling his forehead. She saw how he hung around Yakwo and the other local boys, hoping he might be asked to play. On her way home from the clinic the other day, she had walked by a group of boys playing soccer, punting a rolled-up ball of cloth that looked as if it were held together with twine. They ran barefoot on the large field between the clinic and primary school, and Elijah was among them, dribbling the crude ball toward goals demarcated by rocks and branches. She thought he'd learned to fit in. On Friday, Gary had planned to lead the Boys' Brigade to the top of a hill near the church construction site to build crosses on the hilltop for the Good Friday evening service.

After the service, the boys would pitch tents to stay the night. Elijah had been looking forward to it, and Yakwo and Innocent were supposed to join.

Boys will be boys, it'll toughen him up, Gary would say. He'd be over to Mama Daga's tonight, face drawn and deeply apologetic, assuring Mama Daga and her husband that he understood the severity of the situation, making promises to discipline Elijah and the other offenders and to rebuild the storehouse. Within a few minutes, he'd have Mama Daga and her husband in stitches over an unrelated anecdote.

Elijah squared his face up, trying to make it look tough and impassive. His lower lip trembled, and when he sank his front teeth into his lip to control it, the tough guy act crumbled, and he was five again, frightened of the dark.

His voice cracked. "I *hate* Africa."

"Oh, Elijah—"

"I do, Mom. I hate it."

"I know it's hard, sweetheart. We're all making sacrifices to live here, okay? Next year, you'll be off to boarding school with Allison. It'll get better."

"You hate it here, too, Mom," he said, sniffling. "You hate it more than me."

"Elijah—" She was stung that her words had failed to soothe him, stung more so that he must have seen through her cheeriness and the smiles she worked hard to have ready for him before he trooped off to school. "We all have tough days, okay? Dad, too"— She did not know this to be true; Gary reacted with fervor and pleasure to everything— "but I don't hate it, okay? I'd rather these words not come out of your mouth again."

She sounded tired and unbelieving to her own ears, a middle-aged woman—gosh, was she really middle-aged already?—with dark bags puffing under her eyes. Her nurse's hat was lopsided on her head, and strands of hair tumbled out of a hurriedly arranged pin-up.

Elijah was studying her, flicking the gauze on his hand. His need for maternal comfort had passed, but she pulled him close and spoke into his hair.

"We'll leave Nigeria soon, honey. I promise."

CHAPTER EIGHTEEN

RUST HAD ETCHED TATTOOS on the front door of the diviner's house. The wall, located near a guava tree, looked set to crumble given a gust of wind. Two red-tailed lizards stole out of the corroded door hinges and disappeared into crevices in the walls. At the door's base, Jim glimpsed a stone carving, no doubt the woman's personal god, protecting the home.

"Reverend Jim," Zanya said. "We should not have come."

Zanya's expression telegraphed he'd rather be anywhere else. The diviner's gaunt dog barked and trotted toward them, panting in the late morning heat. Zanya shooed it away.

"I have not returned since the day I brought you here—"

"Well, that makes two of us," Jim said, attempting humor.

Jim had never come to offer gratitude to the diviner for saving his life. Yesterday morning, Manasseh had mentioned the diviner and said it was possible she had prayed to the ancestors for a strike to confuse the mission's work. It was surprising, he said, how the laborers in Rabata were coming against this station when it was not like this in other towns.

Manasseh had said, "I saw one laborer coming from her house on my way home one day. You know that I must walk a very long way to reach my house—"

"Yes, well, he could've been there for anything," Jim said.

Manasseh had poured him another cup of coffee. "Who is to say?"

"Do you think, though," Jim said, "that she'd know about the fire?"

"The fire?" Manasseh's expression put Jim in mind of Mrs. Smith, the organist at First Presbyterian. Her prying, old face, along with her pillbox hat and gloved fingers. "You know, me, Reverend, I did not think the story was true. I've been here wondering about Zanya since the day I met him. You know, our people say that hot water cannot be concealed in the mouth—"

"Yes, right," Jim said, to head off a digression. "She'd be able to tell me, you think?"

"The diviner knows things that even you do not know."

"Maybe I'll pay her a visit, then."

"Visit! You want to go and see her?"

"Yes. I think I'd like that very much."

"No, Reverend." Manasseh had shaken his head, the flask quivering in his hands. "You, a white man, you should not go and do this. Don't you know that people used to cross the road to the other side when they see her coming? They will cross so that they do not meet her. Our people will think you're going to spy on our ways.

"What will you say to her? If she is the one who has made this strike to happen or if she knows the truth about the fire, she will not tell you. And if she tells you, what will you do?"

"We'll just have to see," Jim said.

He did not believe the diviner had any power or clairvoyance. It'd be interesting, though, if she let it slip that the laborers had worked in tandem with her, employed her sorcery. It'd be a thing to preach about on Sunday morning, to turn the congregation against the men.

For months after the robbery in '67, he had transformed into a timid and fearful man, and he'd become watchful, suffering a little paranoia, which he thought must be a condition of any missionary, any outsider. Traveling alone to Pema and Shagye's village without meeting harm had boosted his confidence. He had not yet traveled to Yawari. Although he had a funny feeling about going out there on his own, he found himself possessed of adventure and curiosity at the prospect. He felt the same spirit of curiosity now, standing here in front of the diviner's door.

Zanya walked to the end of the veranda. "We should not be here, Reverend."

"Son," Jim said. "We should have no fear in speaking to her."

Jim raised his fist for the door, wondering if he was too confident an American, incautious about the woman's spiritual prowess. Maybe he ought to walk a bit with Zanya, hear more? Standing in limbo like this, hand raised, might create undue suspicion.

"It's now or never," he said, and knocked.

He heard the sound of slippers slapping against concrete before the door slowly opened to reveal the woman. When he saw her from a distance, he imagined her thin and hunched, with a face as darkened and shriveled as a raisin. She was none of these things. Dark brown sunspots flecked her forehead and cheeks, and she bore two tiny facial marks under each eye. Her wrapper, salmon pink and striped, was folded above an expansive midsection and sturdy arms, exposed in a sleeveless threadbare blouse. Her eyes alert, taking them in.

In mission training, Jim had learned that decades ago the Gbagyi had sought to avoid contact with missionaries, considering white men harbingers of evil from the spirit world and purveyors of natural disasters. He expected hostility from the woman. He flinched his surprise when she greeted them warmly.

"Please, come inside," she said in Gbagyi. "You are welcome."

They removed their shoes, and she instructed them to sit on a wooden bench while she went to another room. He observed nothing elaborate or eccentric about the house at first glance. Apart from the crumbling façade, the house was similar to other homes in Rabata: a mat, another wooden bench nestled against a back corner and a calendar posted to the wall. Upon further scrutiny, he noticed a table in the corner, and on it, a bowl containing cowries and feathers, and a long wooden stick leaned against it. Another calabash bowl held a collection of crushed dried leaves. He looked around the simple, confined room where he had been revived four years ago. This bare floor is where his head had lain, where he had gurgled and moaned when she forced the potion into his mouth.

The diviner reappeared. "For what purpose have you come?" she asked, carrying two cups of water and a plate of shelled peanuts. "I boiled the water."

"Thank you," Jim said, reaching for a cup. He held it in both hands, wondering if this was part of her ruse. Lure them in with hospitality, then poison him with a drink. This too had been in the mission training, to exercise caution when accepting meals from traditional healers. Jim allowed himself a tentative sip, enough to wet his lips, enough to not appear rude.

There was no evidence any other person lived in the house, yet he asked, "Do you have a son or daughter? Others who may want to join us?"

"My sons have their own houses with their wives and children."

He cleared his throat and said, "You may be wondering why we've come. You may recall my arrival to Rabata, the unfortunate circumstances that befell me."

"I remember."

"I've come to thank you for saving my life."

She said, "So you believe I saved your life? You have accepted this."

She spoke as if she knew about his restless nights, the internal turmoil he'd endured to come to terms with the version of the story dispensed to him. It was God, through her, who saved him; this was the version he had come to accept.

"You didn't have to help me," he said eventually. "You could've left me to die. You cared for a stranger. This is what my faith has in common with yours."

She remained standing, hands entwined. "I did not save you by myself. The other people who came before and taught us how to heal with these trees and plants, they are the ones who saved you. They are the ones you should be thanking."

"Were they alive," he said, "I would extend my gratitude to them as I have to you."

"They may not be alive in body, but they hear you in spirit."

Zanya, steeped in a palpable resistance, offered nothing to the conversation except to translate in halting sentences with his gaze fixed to the ground.

Jim set his water on the floor. "You saved my life—"

"I did not save your life, Reverend, and my life is not in your hands for you to save. Shekwoyi is the Supreme Being who gives us life."

"Yes, yes," Zanya said, having recovered his voice.

She said, "Reverend Jim, you have destroyed the personal gods of our people."

Was this what Manasseh had been alluding to? Was this the reason for the strike? He had offended her, and she had used her mysterious powers to bring down the church.

"Those who are believers are the ones who came and asked us to burn their gods," Zanya said, the plate of boiled peanuts balanced at an awkward angle on his lap. "We did not force them to do anything. This is what they wanted."

"Is this," Jim said, "the reason that you've—the reason for the strike?"

"Are you asking me why the house for your god has not been built?"

"I'm not saying you're responsible for the current situation…"

"My ears are hearing differently," she said.

"Please." Zanya looked sharply at Jim. "We are not putting any blame on you."

"Reverend," the diviner said, "when somebody harms you and you cannot avenge, we say it is Shekwoyi that avenges. If somebody cheats you, we say, 'I leave you with my god.' We come to Shekwoyi and ask of Him through our personal gods. I know this-your Jesus. It is how the white man reaches his god. He is the personal god of your people. Why can you not ask your god about the laborers? Why is it me you've come to disturb?"

The diviner looked at Jim and then she looked at Zanya, and something akin to a smirk played on her face. "The two of you. What is here?"

"Here? I'm not sure what you mean." Jim touched his clerical collar. It must have been the third or fourth time in minutes that he had lifted his fingers to the band of linen.

She stared at them both for a moment. She had not taken a seat, and it was uncomfortable looking up at her. "Do you know how our people learned the medicine for the bite of a snake?"

"Pardon?" Jim said. Where was this going?

"Zanya, do you know?" she said.

"Sorry, I don't know."

"You should know."

"Please tell us," Zanya said.

He was so obsequious and in such reverence of the diviner. Had he ever behaved this way with Jim? In the beginning, perhaps, when he'd had nothing to his name and needed Jim and the mission.

"A very long time ago," the diviner said, "when Rabata was still a village, two snakes fought near its entrance while the villagers watched. In their struggle, the two snakes bit one another, harming each other with wounds. One of the snakes was wise, ba? It crawled into the forest and ate the leaves of one particular plant. Do you know what happened? The snake that ate the leaves survived. The other snake was not as wise, you understand? Since it did not eat the leaves, it was not long before it died. This is how our people came to know that the leaves of this plant were a cure for the venom of a snake."

After a moment, she looked at them both and with a voice devoid of the disarming warmth that had filled it when they first arrived, she said, "I am not to blame for what has happened to the house of your god. You talk of this strike when something more than this will soon come."

Jim waited for her to speak again, yet she remained reticent. Her dog had ceased its restless barking outside, and silence expanded in the room.

"Reverend," Zanya said. "We should be going."

"No, not quite yet, son," Jim said. "I'd like to know what you mean by this."

The diviner did not respond.

"Reverend Jim," Zanya said, with more urgency. "It is time for us to go."

The atmosphere had changed, and Jim knew it. He and Zanya slipped on their shoes, and the diviner walked them to the door and swung it shut with finality. Outside, the sky was different, not the calming blue, but a whitish, blinding glare.

CHAPTER NINETEEN

THE TOWNSPEOPLE WHO WALKED to the mission primary school in a drizzle of rain for sunrise service on Easter Sunday saw the palm fronds littering the school steps before they saw the laborers blocking the doors of the classrooms. Palm branches had been ripped from the classroom windows and doors and scattered on the veranda in a brazen act they found blasphemous and titillating.

The early-goers who saw all of this would tell the latecomers that they should have woken up at dawn for the sunrise service to witness what had happened. If they had, they would have seen Reverend Jim and Zanya pleading on the veranda, in a desperate bargain with the laborers. They would have heard Reverend Jim say, "Fellas, I'd like you to step aside so we can have our Easter service," and seen how the laborers, ten of them, remained obstructing the doors. They would have heard Betabwi say, "You don't want to talk to us, Reverend, so we have come to you." And they would have heard Reverend Jim say, "Well, now's not the time," and Kago say, "When is the time, Reverend?"

They would have heard the laborers' chant start gradually and then carry power like this:

When is the time?!
When is the time?!
When is the time?!

They would have seen the white headmistress jump off her blue Honda CB175 and shoulder past the early-goers who were surrounding the school, some cradling their Bibles, wondering if there would be a service, wondering if they should return home. They would have heard the headmistress say, "This school is under my jurisdiction, gentlemen. I'd appreciate your cooperation in leaving the property," and they would have seen how the men ignored her and remained standing and chanting: *When is the time?!* They would have seen her trying to walk past Kago to step into her headmistress's office and two other men come beside him to stop her.

The early-goers would tell the ones who had decided to remain sleeping that if they had come, they would have seen Gary Parson and Katherine Parson arrive with their child, the one who was always frightened in the market if you greeted him. They would have seen Gary Parson join Zanya and Reverend Jim and Delores on the veranda to plead with the laborers, and Katherine Parson standing off to the side with Elijah in front of her, her hands on his shoulders, as if it did not matter one way or the other if the service happened.

They would tell the latecomers how Reverend Jim stopped telling the men to return to their homes. How he signaled to the missionaries and Zanya, and how they gathered near the mission car. They would tell the latecomers how you could hear the panic in their voices if you leaned your head to listen because they could see more people crossing the roads and the field, coming for sunrise service.

If the latecomers had come on time, they would have heard Reverend Jim saying, "We need to involve the local police. Zanya, you'll need to go down to police headquarters and request their presence," and seen Gary Parson putting up his hands and saying, "It's an awful idea, Jim."

They would have heard Delores agreeing with Gary Parson. "What would it look like for the laborers to be hauled off to jail on Easter?"

They would have heard Katherine Parson saying, "Why don't we just tell everyone to go on home?" and they would not have been surprised that this is what she said.

Moments later, they would have seen Reverend Jim come forward on the school veranda and face the crowd and say, "Christ has risen!" and Zanya translate, "Yesu la to!" in a voice that did not sound as passionate as the Reverend's. They would have seen Betabwi, the leader of the men, cross his arms and order the laborers not to move.

They would tell the latecomers how Reverend Jim decided to preach his Easter sermon while the laborers barricaded the doors, dry and warm under the eaves, and how the congregants stood in the drizzle in their Sunday clothes and shoes as the rain pelted their shirts and wrappers. If the latecomers had come on time, they would have heard Reverend Jim preach about the people of Jerusalem spreading their cloaks and palm branches to meet Jesus, who was riding on a donkey. They would have heard Reverend Jim say that the people of Jerusalem shouted, "*Hosanna! Blessed is he who comes in the name of the Lord!*"

But they would not have heard his words clearly because it would have been drowned by the laborers standing behind him, palm fronds resting at their feet, chanting above his sermon: *When is the time?!*

CHAPTER TWENTY

Two ARCED TREES GREW behind the huts in Betabwi's compound. He sat in the open yard in front of the huts, and nearby a young woman sprinkled dried corn as one chicken fluttered about her, nipping. Children squatted against the brittle walls. Zanya counted seven children—three girls and four boys. Some of the children looked slightly unkempt, hair uncombed, and most were old enough to be in primary school or starting secondary, not here at home. They watched Zanya with unguarded curiosity.

"See who don come," Betabwi said without rising from his chair. He sank his teeth into the yellow flesh of a cashew fruit, knees wide apart to allow the juice to drip to the ground and not stain his singlet or trousers. He snapped his fingers, and one of his sons dashed over with a wooden stool for Zanya. A leg on the stool was broken in half.

"Betabwi," Zanya said, distributing his weight on the stool to stabilize himself. "You're the one leading this thing, this strike. The thing yesterday at the church."

Betabwi chuckled. "Which kind me? You think say nah pikin de laborers be?"

His eyes had the satisfied look of a hunter returning to his village after outsmarting his prey. After preaching his sermon through the men's shouts on Easter Sunday, Reverend Jim had come to Zanya and said, "End this." Now, within two minutes of speaking to any townsperson, you would hear their opinion on the strike and who was in the wrong, the laborers or the mission and Reverend Jim.

"Your own men," Zanya said, "will not have money or food if this doesn't end."

"Everybody get their own mind o. Am I forcing them?"

"Okay, what if Reverend increases it small?" When Reverend Jim had told him to end it, Zanya had said, "End it with what? What can you give?" And he had agreed to a couple pence extra. Zanya had thought it a partial victory for the men, for himself.

"That is not enough," Betabwi said. "We want the same as the others."

"How can you not take it back to the others? Go and see what they'll say."

"It's not enough," Betabwi said, swallowing the last piece of fruit.

Zanya kept his voice steady. "They need work. Come and work, Betabwi. What is this going to solve? We have nearly finished. Reverend has said that the mission will be building a guesthouse. You want to spoil things so that he hires other laborers?"

Betabwi did not seem primed for compromise. He stretched out his legs and flattened his palms on his trousers. His corpulent, powerful body filled out the chair, and his singlet had rolled up on his ample abdomen to reveal a hairy, sunken navel.

"Moses get debts," Betabwi said. "Kago needs money for his pikin. And no be Reverend tell me say make I divorce two of my wives? Make I marry one woman? I hear wetin him talk, so I went and divorced two of my wives. You understand?"

"I remember." The mission's tenets were stricter than the Anglicans, who did not force their members to abstain from alcohol or to stop practicing polygamy.

The sun shone high in the sky, and Zanya wished to move into the shade of the trees. His shirt clung to the beads of moisture on his back. He had to force himself to listen to Betabwi, though he had his own worries. He had gone to his sister's village on Easter Sunday, and Pema and Shagye warned him that Reverend Jim had visited them and asked questions about the night of the fire. They said they had not shared anything, and Zanya had believed them because they, too, did not know the truth. But if Reverend Jim continued digging, he would find it, and Zanya would lose what he was working hard to gain.

"Now, my wives I divorced dey suffer." Betabwi pointed with his lips toward the hut to the far right. "One has come back to live with me."

"Sorry o. I didn't know."

"This is why I am here asking for more money."

"I'm seeing, Betabwi."

"These missionaries, they say, 'Stop doing this thing,' but they no know wetin go happen to the person when they stop. They don't know how it go be for our people. Was Solomon not the one with many wives? See how God still ask him to build temple? Did God ask him to go and leave his wives?"

"You're right," Zanya sighed his understanding. "If I was the one, I would have led things differently in the church—Betabwi, listen to me, I'm going to speak to the oga on top in Jos. Come back and work until I speak to him."

A slow-rising laughter flowed from Betabwi as he drummed drowsy fingers on the arm of the chair. "Which oga?"

"At one mission conference. Headquarters."

"Oga on top?"

"It will make the Reverend listen to us."

Betabwi stroked his chin. "See you, Zanya, trusting Reverend like this because you think he'll give you something." He laughed. "If Reverend has not given us anything, what makes you think oga at the top will give you something?"

Zanya resented the frank, knowing look from Betabwi. "Okay,

then, Betabwi, go to Reverend Jim yourself again. Make am hear you."

❧

"I have been caring for her," the woman said to Tebeya, "but I cannot care for her any longer. The money you gave me, madam—"

"Yes, I understand," Tebeya said, guiding the woman and Comfort into the corridor, away from the busy ward and the orderlies and nurses who might eavesdrop.

The woman pulled Comfort against her. "The money has finished."

"I expected it to last until now. Where are her belongings?"

"What she is wearing—that is all."

"Okay, that is fine. You'll come with me to her village now," Tebeya said.

The clock in the office read three o'clock. Katherine and Nelson could handle the patient load. She rarely missed a day of work or left early. She feared it might arouse Nelson's curiosity.

"I have to be going," she said when she found Nelson at the dispensary.

"You, Dr. Awyebwi? Taking a break?" Nelson said, and he made a show of opening his mouth and lifting his brows in mock astonishment. If she were not so worried about his behavior, she would have chuckled at his antics, because this is what she liked about him. He lacked the supercilious attitude of Katherine Parson, and he laughed and made terrible, self-deprecating jokes.

"There are things I must attend to," she said.

"Is everything all right?"

He appeared better today. He still arrived late on occasion this week, and when he did, he blushed and reeked a little of drink. But today, he was better, so she would go.

"Business," she said, and, thinking it not entirely true, added,

"Family business."

"Sure, okay. Godspeed," he said. "I'll hold down the fort."

Mama Bintu's houseboy hopped out of the clinic van, slammed the door, and asked Nelson Landry if he wanted the van washed. Nelson said it was fine, thanks. The houseboy had delivered a message to him at the clinic shortly after Tebeya went to handle her family business. Mama Bintu was requesting his immediate presence and discretion. It had sounded like an emergency, but now the kid was asking Nelson if he wanted the van washed, and none of the servants attending to the grounds appeared panicked. This did not seem like a house of illness.

Up here on this hill, one could look out over the town of Rabata. He found the Awyebwis' home ostentatious—the great green columns upholding the palatial structure, the glinting light blue roof. Iron gates barricaded the entrance to their estate. The house girl had propped open the door to the living room. She waited for Nelson to come up the porch stairs and offered him a seat, as if they had all the time in the world.

"Sir, will I bring you something to drink?"

"Water's fine, thanks."

She returned with a tray of soft drinks and water. "I can bring chin-chin."

He wondered if Mama Bintu might be upstairs, in some paralysis. "Is Mama Bintu waiting for me? Do I need to go up to her bedroom?"

The girl blinked. "You want to enter madam's room?"

"She's ill, right? Does she need me to check her vitals?"

"I am not understanding, sir," the girl said. Her perplexed expression shrunk her features. "Madam is well. She will come and see you in the parlor."

"Oh, all right."

"Please, you can sit, Likita."

"Sure," he said, and slapped his hands together. "Let her know I'm on a tight schedule, would you?"

He assumed Mama Bintu wanted to discuss the operation on the grandmother. Perhaps, Tebeya had mentioned it, and now it could affect the Awyebwis' financial contribution to the clinic. Tebeya had returned to her cool, practical self and had not referred to the surgical mishap. He had apologized after his outburst in the surgical room, and she, piqued, no ease in her voice, her sharp eyes looking straight into his, said she was fine and had no need for his apology, and of course, this had annoyed him to no end. What did she mean she had no need for it? It wasn't a matter of *need*, for goodness' sake.

Tebeya did not let a matter alone until she had analyzed it from a thousand angles. It made her an incredible physician and a formidable foe. If he did not deal with the situation, he saw ahead of him a dark, austere theater where operations were conducted in a distressing silence of head nods and sidelong glances. Oh, the operating room. He'd hated the insinuation in front of the rest of the clinic staff about his sobriety, or lack thereof. There was no drinking problem. He had attended an AA meeting in Rockford the last time he was home on furlough, signing divorce papers. Just to see. He had stridden into the room, looked around at the tired, ravaged faces in the circle and thought, "I'm not like them at all," then gotten into his Buick and left.

Now he paced in the living room, unable to relax. He equated sitting with contemplation, a deceleration of his body and mind. He preferred movement—weaving between patients, standing for examinations, rushing a patient into the operating theater, or bending over a patient with his stethoscope. He also disliked the heavy decor in the house, the too-plush, uncomfortable furniture, and the dark wood and velvet arms of the couches. The purple swirl-patterned rug in the dining room, the glossy straight-back chairs circling a large table, the wood and glass shelves, the polished framed pictures of the family. Furniture imported from America, not built by carpenters in Rabata. In the living room, lace curtains displayed a honeycomb design. Behind him, on the credenza, art-work depicted two women pounding yam under moonlight and men huddled on the ground drinking from a calabash dish.

He creased the frayed cuffs of his coat's sleeve, certain an hour had passed, though it must not have been more than five minutes. He was not yet habituated to the slow pace at which life transpired in Rabata.

Finally, the unmistakable thudding of Mama Bintu's cane echoed in the corridor. She stood at the base of the stairs with the same electrifying straightness as the Queen's Guards, her large, white turban mimicking their bearskin hats. "Do you want more water or something other than water? Duza should have brought you a tray of minerals. Which mineral will you take?"

"Water's just fine, thanks a lot," Nelson said.

Mama Bintu turned toward the kitchen. "Duza! Gbe ya!" She sucked her teeth. "This girl. She will test my patience."

He felt compelled to add that Duza had offered him soft drinks and chin-chin, but he doubted the additional information mattered. He steered the subject to the purpose of the summon. "I came as soon as I could. Are you ill?"

"I pray not," Mama Bintu said, reaching to pat her neck, where an innocuous black mole was nestled near a fold of skin. "My husband and I, we go to the hospital in Keffi if we are not well. You will never need to worry about my health, or about us needing your clinic."

He suppressed his impatience. He set down his glass and picked it up again to avoid a watermark on the polished wood. "I assumed this was an emergency."

Mama Bintu laughed. "I did not mean to frighten you, but the matter at hand is of extreme importance. My daughter—does she know you've come?"

"I didn't mention it. She left for the day. I thought she'd be here, actually. Anyway, I need to be getting back soon—"

"Have you seen my garden, Nelson? Why don't we walk together so that you can see it?"

Outside, the gardener rose from rooting weeds, removed his hat and bowed his head to Nelson. Nelson waved in annoyance at him to put it back on. He hated charades, which is what this whole thing was with Mama Bintu. Calling the white mission doctor at a time befitting her schedule. Mama Bintu saw the clinic as expendable, and therefore Nelson as less than a physician, the work he did insignificant.

"Do you know why I asked you to walk with me?" Mama Bintu rubbed a flower petal and poked a heap of soil. "Come and see how we've planted birds of paradise. Look at these yellow trumpets." The flowers were a buttery yellow, growing in clusters among the razor-sharp leaves. "They will grow like weeds if they are not properly tamed."

Nelson recalled what he used to tell Virginia's nephew when he threw a tantrum. Count to ten, buddy. That's right, count to ten. He followed his own counsel, but when he reached seven, he dispensed with it, finding it wholly inadequate for his present situation.

"Mrs. Awyebwi." He spoke forcefully in case his tone might hasten her languorous motions. "I need to get back to the clinic. Why'd you call me here?"

Mama Bintu stroked a leaf with the tip of her cane. "Dr. Landry, I don't want my daughter working for your clinic any longer."

"Oh, is that it?" He was instantly relieved that this was not about the operation. Surprise at her statement subsumed his relief. "Wait a minute, why? Your daughter's an excellent physician.

Quick to learn, focused."

"Since she was young, she's been focused," Mama Bintu said, looking up at him. "Do you know what honors Tebeya received in university? Better than her sister and brother, sef. Yet she's come back to work at this clinic. She's made no mention of marriage."

Marriage! So, this was the issue at hand. It had nothing to do with malpractice or the mission clinic, but Tebeya's rejection of suitors.

Mama Bintu was staring straight up at him, eyes unblinking, waiting for a response. What did she think he had to say when his own marriage was in shambles? The divorce had been finalized months ago, and his ex-wife was already stepping out with Kip Campbell, a lanky man in his late twenties like Virginia, a former love interest from her college days. What was the hymn the clinic staff had sung during their morning worship time? The hymn that nearly cracked his heart into two and prompted a welling of tears he managed to withhold. *Prone to wander, Lord I feel it. Prone to leave the God I love.* God knew he loved Virginia. God knew he thought he would grow old alone and had been surprised when his romance with Virginia crawled along and then picked up on two feet and ran full steam ahead.

Mama Bintu knew none of this.

"Look," Nelson said, clearing his throat, "I've got some seriously ill patients, all right? Now, we may not have the prestige of the government hospital in Keffi, but we do see an extraordinary number of patients for the small staff we have. Staff that has now been deprived of a physician because of this"—he waved a desultory hand—"meeting." He had hoped also to get a good game of tennis in with Monday before this evening, and this had eaten up some of his time. He remembered Tebeya wanted Monday fired. It had completely slipped Nelson's mind to talk to him about cleaning the clinic with more care.

"Tebeya won't listen to anybody," Mama Bintu said. "Don't

you think I've brought our relatives to talk sense to her? If this clinic were taken from her, she would see clearly."

His laughter was unintentionally aggressive. "You can't expect me to fire my best—the one other physician in our clinic. It's a harebrained idea, that's what it is."

"You misjudge my daughter," Mama Bintu said. "This clinic is what Tebeya wants above all else. There are matters more important."

"Tell you what," Nelson said, "you find me an exceptional physician—someone better skilled than your daughter—and I'll think about it."

They had come full circle, standing at the front of the house again. Compared to the vehicles parked in the driveway, the clinic van looked as if it had overturned in a muddy pool. He should've taken the houseboy up on his offer to wash it.

Mama Bintu said, "Do what I've said, Dr. Landry. I'm telling you."

"And I'm telling you it's a no-go." Nelson opened the driver's door. "It's been a pleasure, Mrs. Awyebwi."

❧

The road stretched ahead of them, and every few miles brought a new house into view. Dense weeds grew on the roadside. On the locust bean trees, seedpods dangled from their branches like desiccated worms. A deeply trenched dirt road led up to Comfort's village. Better to be traversed with motorbikes, especially when it rained as it had these past few days. The soil turned into sludge that could have suffocated birds.

Benedict made it safely through the muddied road. Upon arrival, the woman led Tebeya to a hut where a dejected, rangy man not much older than Tebeya walked out, unclothed save for a wrapper around his waist.

"Madam," the woman said. "This is the girl's uncle. Her mother's senior brother."

Sweat shimmered on his forehead. Black curls sprouted on his chest and grew down to the concavity of his stomach. He had hard eyes and gaps between his teeth, which were hidden under a prominent upper lip. Seeing the man created more doubt. What was Tebeya doing here in this village, trying to rescue this child? What an ill-considered decision.

"Good afternoon," Tebeya said.

"The woman has told us," the man said in Gbagyi.

He was the sole family member Comfort had, but he did not have the means to support her. Let the girl live with Tebeya, he said, where she would attend primary school and have enough to eat. He had nothing to give Tebeya except his blessing and gratitude. Comfort stood between them, her face devoid of emotion as her fate was decided.

"May God bless you," Comfort's uncle said.

"Thank you, sir."

He eyeballed her father's Mercedes and Benedict standing against the chrome bonnet. "Madam, you see we don't have anything..."

She ushered him into the hut and reached into her purse.

"God bless you," he said again as Tebeya ducked out.

As they returned to Rabata, a new confidence overcame her with this strange little girl tucked near the window, sitting trustingly in an unfamiliar car. Could the girl imagine how her destiny had changed? The girl had her hands tucked under her buttocks and a rag covering her hair. She needed new garments, well-fitting blouses and skirts. Tebeya would give the seamstress, Rhoda, fabric to sew clothes for Comfort. She needed sturdy shoes. New books, too. Tebeya would enroll her in the primary school and ask Delores Boyd to assess the girl's aptitude and ensure she progressed at the same pace as—or surpassed—her schoolmates.

She put up a hand to block the sun, which burned the side of her face closest to the window. She treasured how it had all come together, but she could not ignore the uncertainty lapping at her mind, the magnitude of what she was taking on. What if this little girl grew into an irresponsible woman? What if despite the care and provision offered, Comfort grew to despise her or see her as the doctor who had failed to save her grandmother's life? What if the girl faced tragedies that were a direct consequence of Tebeya's intervention? If Tebeya failed—and she had considered this, failure in knowing the specific needs of this child, failure in knowing how to raise a child properly—she could say the girl had come from another woman's womb and lived with her grandmother in another village before coming under her guardianship. The opposite could happen. If the girl excelled or grew to be elegant, hardworking, and genial, Tebeya could say her nourishment and guidance refined the girl and forged these qualities. Either way, she would own her failure or success—whichever came from this decision.

"Madam, she is like my youngest," Benedict said.

"Your son, you mean?" Tebeya said.

"Very quiet. It is as if their tongues do not exist."

She had not thought about the girl's reticence or observed if she had trouble with her speech like Benedict's little boy. She could not remember Comfort speaking or opening her mouth. The thumb sucking had distracted Tebeya from knowing if she was shy or mute. She could not recall now if she had ever bent down and said, "How are you doing, Comfort? Remove the thumb from your mouth and talk." She felt an urge to batter Comfort with questions.

Benedict asked, "You are helping her family?"

"Yes, she has no family, no relatives," Tebeya said. "I will see what I can do."

"Eh heh, okay," Benedict said. "What of your mother? What will madam say when she sees this child in her house?"

"Benedict, are you trying to worry me?"

With shaky hands, she cranked down the window to funnel a breeze into the airless car. She had not considered every angle as she usually did. She had to prepare for questions her mother, father, or Bintu would have about her decision. Her brother Patrick might call to voice concerns. How would she introduce the girl if she had no intentions of treating her like a house servant? People did this kind of thing all the time—caring for someone's child when the family did not have the means. Yet, her mother would treat this as an unusual circumstance and lament that her childless daughter was foolishly caring for another woman's child instead of bearing her own.

Benedict gassed the car as he turned off the main road, where women worked on the roadside, swaddled in wrappers or shaded under wooden sheds, selling their vegetables or fried goods despite the raindrops that threatened their fires and splattered the oil.

Tebeya would frame the situation to her family as such: a patient's daughter was in a precarious situation and needed a home for a little time. Before long, without them sensing, Comfort would become a regular presence in the house.

This night, the church building looked more unfinished to Zanya than it had in the day, though the walls were slowly growing with each layer of bricks. The scaffolding was against one side of the church. More layers of bricks were needed before roofing. Weeks ago, the laborers had preassembled the timber for the roofing trusses and stacked them against the partially completed wall, and he had ordered the ridged zinc sheets from the merchant days before the strike. The walls were incomplete, up and at the height of an average man. Dunes of sand and ballast still dotted the site. Abandoned wheelbarrows lay overturned near one side of the church, where the church doors would have been. Four more weeks, and they would have finished.

He still slept in his pickup during the week and faced the silence of the construction site every morning. No men stomping mud or pushing wheelbarrows. None pouring into the brick molders. He had halted the delivery of more cement bags and delayed the delivery of lumber. With no men to help unload and work, there was no reason to have these materials delivered to just sit.

He had continued working alone after meeting with Betabwi. He hauled bags of cement from his pickup into wheelbarrows. He mixed mortar and molded bricks and climbed up the abandoned rafters to spread the mortar and lay bricks. The muscles in his shoulders and back ached. It had been futile to think he alone could do what twelve men had done.

Startled by the roar of an engine, Zanya shot up and looked through the misted windshield into a rainy mirage—laborers walking toward him, headlights illuminating their dark figures. He searched the group for Kago's face. Kago was not among them. In the midst of them, Betabwi shouldered ahead, his bulky figure heaving with determination.

Zanya stepped out of his pickup. It was over. The strike had ended. They were coming to negotiate. Betabwi had heard what he said when he visited his home the other afternoon. He ignored the inner voice saying it was too late at night for the men to come for reconciliatory talks, that there was something menacing about how the group moved.

He lifted his hand in greeting. None returned his salute. More laborers jumped out of both vehicles and began loading bags of cement into the boots. The men knocked over wheelbarrows of sand and ballast, ransacking the site.

Zanya ran toward them, stumbling in the darkness, rain drenching his clothes. "Betabwi—what are you doing, na?!"

"You said make Reverend hear us. He go hear us now."

CHAPTER TWENTY-ONE

JUMMAI FLATTENED HER BACK on a woven mat in the sleeping area of the room she shared with her five siblings. She clasped her hands on her stomach and watched as a tiny lizard crawled down the wall and slipped under the door. Somewhere in the distance, she heard voices on the main road, striking her all at once so that it was a disorienting feeling hearing their cheerful greetings, the rumble of cars, the neighbor's radio, and knowing what she now knew.

She saw the sky from the open door, a wisp of clouds unfurling in the wind, their shapes thinning and thinning until they disappeared eventually into the blue. She thought clouds could be messages from Shekwoyi. Messages He gave to those paying enough attention to look at the sky and try to understand what He was telling them. It was the same when she was in the mission garden, digging through dirt with her hands, touching the stones and twigs. What was this stone saying to her? What were this stone and this twig together telling her? Why had she not paid attention to these messages so that she would not be here, feeling as if there were things nobody had ever told her?

Nobody had ever told her heartache could make her ill or make it difficult for her to fall asleep and wake her up with head and body throbbing. She did not know heartache could make her run to the toilet in the Parsons' house when she opened the canned bacon this morning or force her to ask Elijah's help with butchering the chicken because the smell of its offal and the gush of fluids left a nauseating, metallic taste in her mouth. Yesterday, Yakwo and Elijah, who had resettled into an uneasy friendship she did not believe would last, had trampled the house, drinking minerals and consuming the jollof rice and chicken she had cooked. She had cleaned the house after them, then rushed outside, hunched over in the bush, and vomited.

This morning in the mission garden, while uprooting weeds, her lower back had throbbed when she knelt. Of all the chores at the Parsons, she most enjoyed tending to the vegetables that grew in abundance near the water cisterns Zanya and the laborers had dug. She liked seeing the cabbage flowering, the large outer petals expanding and falling away, the inner layers protecting the small bulb. So when this pleasure, too, failed to relieve her aches, she had thought it was a deep, incurable heartache, manifesting as physical symptoms.

How had she not known she was pregnant? Like her mother who was pregnant now, too. This heartache that was not heartache would make her look like her mother; her feet would waddle and her stomach would grow and grow. She imagined hoisting Walu on her hip with one arm and carrying a newborn in the other and the thought alone made her weary, made her wish she could disappear from this room and this house and never come back.

It must have happened on the night of the fire, when Zanya had come to her, shaken. She felt the trembling in his bones and voice so that she knew it was true. People's bodies did not shake like this unless they had seen something. She had held her shaking mother after Tin City struck her many nights ago. Her sister Jecinda shook on the morning she saw a ghost while washing clothes on the riverbank. Zanya shook that night, like her mother and Jecinda had shaken. She remembered a faint smell of kerosene on his skin, as if it had been bottled with him from his time in the fire.

Yesterday evening, she had seen Zanya and Nami talking outside of Flo's. He had not seemed as loose and comfortable with Nami as he was with her. He looked worried. It might have been because of what happened at the site with the men destroying things and carrying materials away. Or it might have been that things with Nami were not going well. When was this wedding of theirs going to happen anyway? She had not seen him again to ask. Now, she would have to worry him some more and spoil this-his love. She would have to tell him she was pregnant, and it could not be anyone else's child.

The door to the room opened, and she pushed herself up on her elbows to see who had come inside. Tin City's shadow fell across the floor. Her mother was at the market, and he had limped from his place in the other room. He had gone back to the tin mines and returned three days ago with an injury to his right leg, so he wobbled into the room on a crutch he had received from the clinic. Miss Delores had visited him, bringing a canister of vegetable oil, a bag of rice, and a couple of plump, skinned rabbits. Jummai remembered the rabbits, how raw and gray they had looked. Her mouth filled with spit, and a burble of fluid flooded her throat.

"You get money, Jummai," Tin City said. "I've been looking for this-your money."

"Okay," she said, swallowing saliva.

They considered each other for several seconds. She was too tired and uninterested in his threats to say anything else. She waited for him to leave, but he stood halfway inside the room, angered that she did not have the presence of mind to argue with him.

"I will find it," he said.

He pounded the wall as if to dislodge the bricks and have them tumble down and crush her. What a foolish, foolish man. He had told her he was looking for her money, so she would take it with her when she went next to the Parsons' and hide it somewhere in their house.

❧

"I didn't know this was what they were going to do," Kago said, shaking his head when Zanya entered his home. "Betabwi did not tell me anything."

"Kago," Zanya said, "you can tell the laborers to stop—"

"My friend, we are not the ones who are wrong."

"It's too much now. What of rain? When the rains come, all the work we've done—"

"I said we should not build so close to rainy season. Did I not?"

They fell into silence when Kago's wife walked into the parlor, serving tuwon shinkafa and egusi. "See me here, feeding the enemy," Simi said to Zanya with a playful smile. "Isn't that what you people say? Feed my enemy? Are you not the one coming against my husband?"

You could not speak an unkind word about Kago in Simi's presence. Simi once told Zanya that she had wondered if Kago could truly be content with one child, their daughter Miriam, since Kago had a number of siblings and his siblings had a number of children. She said she had witnessed his contentment with their daughter, observed his patience as he taught her how to count her toes, repeating gently when he needed to and showing enthusiasm when she caught on to the simplest of concepts. He walked his daughter to the river and taught her how to catch frogs that crawled up the riverbank. Simi said Kago was not like the saka-saka men who divorced their wives for not bearing them male heirs. "It was because of Kago's faith," she had said; it was his faith that had made him think like this.

"Kago," Zanya said, "do you know that the Reverend is going to investigate with the police? He has already gone to the station to report what they did—"

"Let him go. Me and Reverend Jim, we are reading the same

Bible," Kago said, "and yet we have landed on different sides. How is that?" Kago spoke more freely when he was home; his tongue loosened in the presence of his wife.

"Zanya, answer me," Simi said, setting two tumblers of water on the table. "Whose side would Christ be on if Christ was here in Rabata? Isn't that what my husband is saying?"

"The men are being paid what they agreed to be paid," he said, parroting Reverend Jim. He balled the fufu Simi had made in his fingers, and the soup coated his fingertips in a warm and delightful heat when he dipped them in.

"You're not thinking bigger than this." Kago held his drink of water with both hands wrapped around it, and the bottom of the tumbler rested on his right thigh. "We are supposed to be brothers and sisters in this faith, but these people do not see us as brothers and sisters."

"What of Gary Parson?"

"Okay, you've named one," Kago said. "That Gary is my friend. Even now, he is on our side, and I cannot speak against him. But let me bargain like Abraham with God: if you find five righteous missionaries"—he spread his fingers wide on one hand—"then I will go and ask Betabwi and the rest of them to come and give you back what they went and took."

Simi laughed. "See how you've angered my husband, Zanya."

"Tell your husband he's losing opportunities for us."

"Have you listened to Radio Moscow?" Kago said. "Do you know what they're doing in America? In their own country, they're killing people who look like us. In their own country, they won't eat with people who look like us, and they are here. The thing doesn't make sense."

Zanya rested his elbow on his knee to keep the hand he ate with aloft. He had heard those reports, and he had tried to believe that the people who were in America were unlike the ones who had crossed the Atlantic to come to their country.

"I believe you, Kago."

"Yes, but you want Reverend Jim to promote you. Do you know what it is for us, these laborers, to see you standing in opposition?"

"Me and Nami, our wedding that is coming," Zanya said, as if this would explain everything. His reluctance. His fears. "Kago, do you know how things would come and change for me if I were to have this new position?"

"You're on the wrong side, Zanya," Kago said, and turned his head in silence.

CHAPTER TWENTY-TWO

THE SKY HELD A PROMISE of heavier rain as Katherine hurried across the compound carrying zucchinis from the garden. The trees relished the current drizzle, their leaves turgid and gleaming. The goats had huddled together for protection—a lumpy brown mass at the base of the lemon tree.

Gary had invited Delores to supper. "Get to know her when she comes," he had said again. "Give her a chance, darling. She might be the friend you're looking for here." She had wanted a Saturday night without demands or expectations, not to entertain Delores Boyd or have her sitting across from her and Gary.

Rain dripped down the roof, splattering duck droppings into greenish white swirls across the compound. Allison sat on the veranda, home for a weekend visit from boarding school. Compared to the rest of the family, Allison was a sheet of rock in Africa, impervious to the heat and insects, barely lifting her eyes from her book when Katherine walked up. Her daughter's neck was as rigid and smooth as a Roman column. A white polyester tag stuck out of her shirt, obscured by her ponytail. If Katherine fixed the label, like any sane mother would, her daughter would have swiveled her head and said, "Mom, why does a little thing like that matter when there are children who can't afford clothes?"

Allison saw the world through her father's eyes. She conceived of life like Gary: people were in need of hope, and they were the ones tasked to share the Gospel with them. It showed in the book Allison read now: *Through Gates of Splendor.*

Katherine wondered how Carole Brigham was navigating adolescence with her boys, wherever she might have been placed after Penang. Katherine had written multiple letters to the station in the Philippines, where Carole and Ralph transferred, and to their home address in Worcester, but never received a reply. They lived on Victoria Avenue, which sounded quaint and proper, with cobblestone streets and Tudor-style houses. She suspected they were no longer on the mission field, and it saddened her to think she was alone in all of this.

"Listen to this, Mom," Allison said, as Katherine joined on the chair next to her, setting the zucchinis aside. "'Am I ignitable? Saturate me with the oil of the Spirit that I may be a flame.'"

"Oh. Well, that's quite a statement, honey," Katherine said. "There's a whole set of my old Tippy books waiting for you at Grandma's, you know."

"I don't want anything from Grandma's," Allison said. Her lean legs, which served her well on her school's volleyball team, were crossed on the table. "I didn't like going over there last time we were in Missouri."

"She's your grandmother, Allison."

Allison shrugged and stuck a thumb in the book. "She spoke to us funny, that's all. Like we were dimwitted or something."

"Oh, you're not at all, darling," Katherine said, and she smoothed her daughter's hair and successfully tucked the wayward tag inside. "She didn't mean it, you know."

She thought the kids would have forgotten the awful visit last furlough. Her mother's lips had closed like a sphincter when Elijah and Allison spoke about Rabata. "Otherworldly," her mother had said to her, "that's what your kids are now, dear, and I can't recognize them as my grandchildren." As if Katherine did not know this herself, did not see the disappearance of a generation's worth of traditions and mannerisms, or how her children would never speak with the subtle drawl of a Missourian.

Her mother's missives evoked a similar tenor. She had written Katherine about her father, who was rushed to the hospital in time to prevent a ministroke. Katherine had read the letter with tears forming in the corners of her eyes for her ailing father whose hand she could not hold and whose heartbeat she could not listen to. Her former nursing colleague and friend, Sally Crawford, had taken care of her father at St. John's Hospital. Sally was just wonderful, her mother wrote, like a daughter to us.

Katherine's tears dried up as she read subsequent paragraphs stating her father's hypertension must have been on account of his never knowing the whereabouts of his children—Danny off doing God knows what with his girlfriend and Katherine running about in Tarzan's jungle instead of living like a normal person. Like Sally, who attended Bellhurst Baptist with her husband Frank and had purchased a new house near Fellows Lake.

She recalled her mother's most recent letter. She had slipped it back into its envelope, afraid its contents might spill if she left it out for long. This specific letter had not filled her with dread. It had filled her with an intangible optimism because she planned on sharing it with Gary, and her husband would be hurt that he had not known this secret about Jim, and he might be willing to consider leaving Rabata.

"Your Reverend Jim," her mother had written in irritatingly tiny cursive on the blue parchment, "was ousted from his last congregation before he joined your mission."

༃

Delores arrived; an abundance of auburn curls cascaded down her shoulders, as if she were twirling in a ballroom. "Hi! I'm sorry I'm a little early," she said, breathless.

"You're right on time." Katherine waved her inside. "Come in, won't you?"

"Did you walk or ride your bicycle?" Gary said, propping the front door open with his foot while Delores shook rain from a light jacket, the same purple as her ensemble.

"It's against the gate," Delores said. "My bicycle."

Gary volunteered to bring it under their veranda.

Delores wore a loose purple blouse and wrapper in the local fabric. She often dressed like the nationals—a bright-colored head tie around her curls or blouses with the traditional print or patterns—as she cycled through town or straddled a motorbike. Though the colors suited Delores's complexion, Katherine thought she looked absurd in the native getup. Gary dressed up like this too sometimes, and it drove her nuts.

"What a lovely blouse, Delores," Katherine said, leaving the door ajar for Gary.

"Rhoda sewed it. I was worried about the color. It's terrific, isn't it?"

"Yes, that's it. Terrific."

She led Delores into the parlor where Allison now sat, still reading her book, which she promptly placed down when Delores announced she had brought gifts for everyone. The first was for Jummai, so Allison ran to call her from the kitchen. Jummai entered, drying her hands on the bottom of her wrapper. She looked fatigued and a little feverish from all the cooking she'd done. Tonight, Katherine had shown Jummai how to make her mother's beef stew. Perhaps she had given her too much to do.

Delores handed Jummai a glossy purple book.

"I cannot read well, Mai Mulo," Jummai said, dubiously turning the devotional over in her hands. She flipped her braid over her shoulder. "I can read but not like my sister, Jecinda."

"Oh, that's all right, Jummai," Delores said. "Nami told me you'd be interested in advancing your reading skills."

"Nami?" Jummai said.

"I'm sorry. Did I get that wrong?" Delores said.

"No, ma."

"All right, so listen, why don't you come to my house on Saturday mornings? I'd love to teach you myself."

"With all the small-small girls?"

"Well," Delores said. "I can teach you privately, too, if you'd like."

"Okay." Jummai held the hardback in her hands and ran a thumb along the smooth spine.

Delores handed Katherine geraniums, red and pink ones, sliced diagonally at the stem and bunched into a handmade mug of indiscernible color with a bumpy, uneven rim.

"These are lovely." Katherine inhaled.

"I brought the seeds with me," Delores said. "Planted them outside my house."

"They grew?"

Delores laughed. "Of course they did! What do you mean?"

"Mom sounds like that about everything," Allison said, giggling. "She thinks nothing grows in Africa."

"We do have our own garden here, you know," Katherine said, knowing she sounded defensive. "I was surprised the geraniums bloomed in this season."

"Oh, yes." Delores touched the petals and raised a pink geranium higher than the reds. "There's no water in the mug. If someone could please fill it—"

Allison jumped from the couch. "I'll do it," she said, carrying the mug with care, like a newly trained horticulturist.

Candle flames flickered on the supper table. Jummai placed the beef stew and loaf of bread in the center of the table, arranging them between Katherine's candles and the mug of geraniums. She had brought the brass candleholders from Missouri, and not once did she regret tucking them into her suitcase. Better an extra bottle of malaria pills, Gary had said, or a Swiss Army knife. No, the brass candleholders were what she needed these days, these memories of home.

Elijah and Allison camped out in the living room with their supper, and Gary joined her and Delores at the dining table. Delores proved a proper guest, Katherine thought. She praised the beef stew and asked twice for the recipe, and Katherine was obliged to tell her it came from her grandmother's recipe book, and that Jummai had made it with Katherine's instructions.

Delores wanted to know about the mission clinic and patients. Katherine told a recent story of a woman who had come in suffering preeclampsia convulsions when it was too late for them to transport her to Keffi Hospital. Katherine found herself delving into excessive detail about how she administered medication to expedite the pregnancy, and as she spoke, she heard herself exaggerating the hours of work and her fatigue that day. She described how she had stood on her feet keeping watch over the pregnant woman and had slept in the clinic overnight to assist another nurse in tending to the complicated birth.

"What a terribly busy night," Delores said.

"Well, it wasn't easy," Katherine said, and noticed Delores's bowl was low on stew. "Have some more, would you?"

"Katherine works really hard," Gary said. "They all do."

"And how's the mother?" Delores ladled more stew and carefully circled around the potato chunks. Katherine wondered if she had done this with her first serving, not eaten the potatoes.

"Mother and son are well."

Delores nodded. "It's marvelous what you do day in and out."

"Isn't that why God sent us here?" Katherine's voice rang falsely pious. She manufactured a cough and corrected herself with a casual, "All of us—we're here to serve, right?"

"Sure, absolutely," Delores said. "I'm teaching these children to read and learn arithmetic, but you—you're saving lives."

"The kids need what you have to offer them, Delores," Gary said. "It's a good thing, I think, that you chose to live centrally."

Delores's house was behind the school, separated only by the large field where the kids played soccer. Katherine had walked past her small house many times, and once, a barefoot Delores had been standing near a rabbit hutch talking with two primary school girls and pointing to a pudgy white rabbit that sat on its haunches. Delores had waved and said, "Katherine! Come take a look at these kits. We've got six of them this time!" and Katherine had rattled off an excuse about needing to get to the clinic and quickened her pace.

"Have you given thought to moving over here?" Gary asked. "With the rest of us?"

Delores propped her elbows on the table, and the spoon dangled between her thumb and index. "Well, I don't think that would suit me, Gary."

For whatever reason, this response—which Katherine interpreted as a pointed barb about what kind of missionaries *they* were and what kind of missionary Delores was—set Gary chuckling. Katherine's eyes traveled to her husband's damp hair, fully taking him in for the first time. He had showered and taken time to comb his hair back and run some Brylcreem through it. He had owned the same tube of Brylcreem since they left for Malaysia, and he used it sparingly. Gary had also thrown on a red-checkered button-down and flat front trousers instead of showing up as he usually did to supper, with the sweat and grime of the day in his clothes.

Delores's eyes were beyond blue, a strikingly lucid azure, like a pair of crystal earrings. Katherine glanced at her husband to see if he had made the same observation, and her hands trembled as she struggled to cut the loaf of bread.

"Careful with the knife, honey," Gary said.

"I know how to cut a piece of bread." Her tone was unnecessarily sharp, and Gary and Delores blinked at her. She lowered her voice. "Care for a slice, Delores? It's still warm."

After dinner, with the kids off in their bedrooms, they moved into the living room, and Jummai soon had mugs of tea and a plate of cookies on the coffee table. Delores said she would wait for the rain to cease and then she would cycle back home. Katherine brought out a basket of yarn from her bedroom; she chose a skein of blue for the sweater she planned to knit for the infant who had been born a few nights ago.

"Have you heard, Katherine?" Delores said, selecting a sugar cookie. "The education edict from East Central State?"

Katherine recalled vague prayer requests about schools remaining with their rightful owners; she had never asked Delores to elaborate.

"Right," Gary said. "It might be just a matter of time before these changes reach us here, in Benue-Plateau, or the rest of the country."

"Yes, yes." Delores nodded. "Katherine, I mentioned it to you. Remember?"

"Well, you know," Katherine said. "I haven't really followed the news—"

"Oh, you *must* follow these things, Katherine." Delores reclined on the couch, her feet tucked under her skirt. Tiny feet in dainty purple slippers matching the material of her wrapper and blouse. She told Katherine that a local artisan crafted the slippers.

Gary helped himself to the plate. "These cookies are delicious, sweetheart. Really." He turned back to Delores. "It's easy to see why nationals don't want us teaching their children, their future leaders. They think we'll have them brainwashed."

She noticed her husband had also shaved his five o'clock shadow, the fine brown stubble speckling his face throughout the week. Was it the candles or did his skin seem more luminous? His eyes more alert and engaged than usual? His face glistened with a youthful, excited look, and he was relaxed in his chair, fingers striking the table.

Katherine's pins made quick work of the yarn. She listened for the rain outside. It had subsided, but Delores did not seem compelled to leave.

"I understand. I mean, really, think about what folks are fighting and marching for back home—equality, civil rights. We missionaries can't do the same to nationals here. It's why I don't agree with what Jim's doing to Zanya. He won't listen to a word anyone says."

"I thought it was just awful, wasn't it? The protest on Easter," Katherine said. "Then the destruction of the construction site right after. Just awful—"

"Jim didn't need to open a police investigation," Delores said. "These men don't need to be jailed; they need to be paid."

"Paid not jailed," Gary said. "It's got a ring to it."

"Right." Delores laughed. "All we need are picket signs—"

"I don't think," Katherine cut in, "we should reward their behavior, that's all."

"All I'm saying is that Zanya deserves a chance regardless of what the men are doing." Delores gripped another cookie with her teeth and secured her curls with a single ribbon.

"So, you'd be fine with nationals running the church," Katherine said, "but you're against the government running schools? Sounds to me like you and Jim are on the same page about who should be in power in this country."

"I'm concerned," Delores said, "about the capabilities of a government that's been critically weakened by a civil war. Jim wants to withhold power from a competent individual who's proved his readiness. We are *not* the same."

"I wouldn't worry too much," Gary said. "It'll all work out as it should."

Delores studied him with admiration. "Is he always like this, Katherine?" she said. "Seeing the best in everything?"

"That's his one flaw." Katherine averted her glance from the

BEFORE THE MANGO RIPENS   173

radiance and smoothness of her husband's face and the waves of hair he had tamed.

"How easy it would be to misjudge you, Gary," Delores said. She swiveled to Katherine and said, "Wasn't it just wonderful how Gary handled the situation with Mama Daga's lubu?"

"Oh, yes," Katherine said. "Just wonderful."

All had been forgiven with Gary as the mission ambassador to Mama and Baba Daga. The Boys' Brigade hilltop campout had gone on without a hitch. The two Saturdays since the burning of the lubu, Gary and Elijah were up at dawn, trooping off to Mama Daga's to build a new storage hut with Yakwo and Innocent. Both boys had started coming over to the mission compound more, asking to play with Elijah, and Elijah seemed less mopey and reserved.

The lights flashed twice and went out completely. They often went months with consistent electricity, but once in a while the electric company cut power for a spell.

"Gary," Katherine said. "Find a candle, a flashlight."

"It's okay, honey," he said. "Give it a second. It'll come back on."

Delores was speaking again, but Katherine was unable to follow. Darkness garbled her words. Katherine's mind seemed to fill with a dark, gelatinous fluid.

Gary and Delores laughed again, and their laughter fluttered toward her, embodying something both poisonous and fearsome. Had Delores moved closer to Gary when the lights cut off? She could not see Delores where Delores had been before. She could not see anything, and she could hear nothing.

"Turn on a light, Gary," Katherine cried.

"It's all right. I'll turn on the generator—"

"Now, honey. A candle or something, please."

"Okay, I'm up and going."

She listened for Gary's footsteps against the concrete floors. A brief moment, then the jangle of the drawer where they kept the matches, and a walk back to the dining room to relight one of the candles Jummai had placed on the table. Soon, the room was illuminated. Delores was where she had been before the electricity went out, her shadow a shrewd and elongated form against the wall. Gary blew out the match and positioned the candle in the center of the table, his face bright and innocent in the glow.

"Better, honey?" Gary said.

"Yes," she said, unable to meet his eyes.

Later, as they changed into their pajamas, Gary would ask about her behavior during supper, and when she slipped under the covers, he would sweep the tendrils from the back of her neck and say, "What got into you tonight, sweetheart?" If she told the truth, he would offer excuses for Delores as he tended to do for others, which was what made him extraordinarily gracious and empathetic as a missionary and what caused her immense frustration because his empathy made her seem equally ungenerous. She would not be able to explain the changes in his countenance. The exuberance as he spoke to Delores. How he absentmindedly stroked his chin and leaned forward in his chair toward her. And even now, as he and Delores spoke about their shared desire to remain in Nigeria long enough to see the progression of their work in the town, her husband was looking at Delores in a way that lodged like a stone in Katherine's throat. "Birds of a feather you two," she would want to say to Gary. But she would not say it.

When he asked what had been the matter with her, she would say that nothing had been the matter, sleepiness, perhaps, and the sad revelation that Delores was most certainly not a friend.

CHAPTER TWENTY-THREE

"Dr. Awyebwi!"

Tebeya slipped the prescription under a clipboard at the sound of Nelson's voice echoing down the corridor. She had come to the dispensary and requested carbon copies of the prescriptions he had written today. She had found a mistake within seconds of searching. It was clearly his handwriting—the overconfident swoops of letters, the slanted dashes that replaced full stops above i's and j's. He had written warfarin, a blood thinner, for a tuberculosis patient instead of isoniazid. The prescribed dosage a dangerously excessive amount. She had corrected it before the patient was sent home with the wrong prescription.

"Yes, Dr. Landry?" she said, turning to face him.

"What in the world are you trying to prove, heh?"

He crossed his arms against his chest. Behind him, a woman and her two sons who were waiting for their medications watched them with curiosity.

"Let us go and speak privately," she said.

"You're cleaning up my mess. Is that it?" He glanced around the low-ceilinged dispensary. "That's the message you're trying to send, isn't it?"

"I'm not understanding," she said cautiously.

It sounded as if he knew about the prescription pad hidden under the clipboard, or the records she had taken, which were locked in the desk drawer in the office. Had he learned what she had been tracking for the past month since the incident in the operating room? They were coming to the end of April, and she believed she nearly had enough evidence to use against him.

"The little girl," Nelson said. "She's living with your family now."

"Oh," she said. "You mean Comfort."

"Yeah, sure, Comfort."

"What does this have to do with you, Dr. Landry? Comfort no longer has anybody to care for her—so, she's under my care now."

"A regular Wonder Woman, aren't you? You're trying to make a point." He laughed and planted a hand on the counter. "You're blaming me for what happened, aren't you?"

"This is what our people do, Dr. Landry. What does this have to do with you?"

"Listen, we did the best we could in there," he whispered, and it seemed he was trying to convince himself. "I tried to save that woman's life. It wasn't my fault, you know."

"Dr. Landry." She came closer to him, her voice as low as his, for she could see that the woman with the two boys was delighting in the encounter, already picturing how she would tell her friends about the white doctor and Dr. Tebeya. *Eh! You should have seen them o! Fighting in front of everybody like ordinary people!*

She said, "You made mistakes during that operation—"

"I beg your pardon?"

"You rushed the procedures—why?"

"Why? Why did I try to ensure my patient received the best care?"

"Something was not right that day." She lowered her voice again. "Were you drinking before the operation?"

"Dr. Awyebwi," he said in a tone he'd never taken with her before. "I'm the director of this clinic, and it would be in your best interest not to insinuate that I was not in my right mind."

"I cannot question you? Is that what you're saying?"

"You work for me, not the other way around. Have I made myself clear?"

"Yes," Tebeya said, and she smiled and changed her voice for the sake of the nosy woman behind him. "You have made yourself very clear, Dr. Landry."

꙰

Zanya had come down from his flat and was standing outside his pickup when he saw Jummai strolling toward him. So used was he to seeing her under the cover of darkness that to see her walking in the daylight confused him, and he thought she was an apparition in the rain. She greeted one of his neighbors, a former officer in the Kenyan army who often pulled him into lengthy conversations, and the neighbor seemed unable to stop trailing Jummai with his eyes. She walked closer—that unhurried, wistful walk with which he was familiar.

He opened the driver's side door to signal the inconvenience of her timing.

She spoke: "Where are you going when you see me coming?"

He tucked himself into the driver's seat and jingled the keys. "You've heard what's happening, ba, with the men?"

"Yes o," she said.

"These rains, too, even small, it's not good for the building."

"Every time rain falls, I think of you."

It sounded like she was reciting lyrics to an American song he had once heard in a bar in Kaduna. He ignored it and said, "You understand, then, why I have to go now and take care of the materials." She did not move aside for him to close the driver's door. "Jummai, how many times have I told you to stop coming?" He made his voice sharp and unwavering. "Listen to me. We cannot keep doing this. It must stop."

"Zanya, you must hear me—"

"You are not the woman I want. Do you understand?"

She clamped her mouth shut. Her clenched jaw made her face compact and tense.

"Zanya," she said. "I am pregnant."

The words hit him with such force that it was as if the roof of the pickup had imploded, crushing him inside. He shook his head, for he thought he had not heard her correctly.

"What? What did you just say, Jummai?"

She did not repeat herself. She stood with both hands clasped in front of her with the rain wetting her face and arms.

"Enter, quick." He dove out of the driver's seat and helped her into it while he hurried over to the passenger side.

He looked around again once he was back in the pickup. His neighbors never spoke about a person's whereabouts or paid attention to what anyone else did—too occupied with their own misdeeds to bother with someone else's. Now, it seemed as if half of his neighbors were at their window or loitering outside their doors, observing him with Jummai.

"Jummai, na truth? Abi, you're lying."

"No be lie."

How could it have happened so quickly? A week ago, or was it two? It must be another man's child, and she had come here to trap him into believing it was his, as if he were an idiot.

"No, no. I don't believe you," he said.

"The night of the fire," she said, as if reading his thoughts.

Two months ago.

"No, you're doing this because you're angry with me."

"Angry, ke?" She laughed, covering her mouth.

"Because I sent you away. Because of Nami—" Just the sound of her name and the thought of having to tell her this news filled him with anguish. The muscles in his arms seemed to be fraying like a rope.

"So that's the one, ba?" She looked at him.

"You knew already."

"I am pregnant, Zanya," she said, "and you are the one who has made it so."

If she had taken his clothes and skin from him, she would have seen everything inside his body trembling at this news. Suddenly, the shock left as quickly as it had come. Was he to believe *he* was responsible? How many men could there have been other than him? All those times, she had meant to trap him in this situation. She was smarter than he had known. He had fallen for her show of obtuseness.

"Jummai, Jummai," he said, "there've been others besides me."

She said nothing.

"Am I to believe you?" He laughed. There seemed nothing else he could do, and he heard in his laughter a streak of cruelty, gratuitous and unfair, one that Jummai, who had comforted him in his pain, did not deserve. "How? It's not so."

She said, "Only you, Zanya."

Her voice echoed with sincerity, yet he did not want to believe her. He resented her now, rued the times she had come to his pickup in darkness, knowing he was too weak to resist her. Whatever power she had wrested from him in those moments, she wielded it now. Even seeing her, an irrepressible ache throbbed in his groin. He pushed his body toward the passenger window and put his head in his palms.

"You want to ruin me. Is that it?"

She remained composed and looked at him as if he were a misbehaving child.

"Jummai, listen to me. You cannot tell anybody—please, you will not tell Nami."

He saw the future he had dreamed about with him and Nami. It became real in front of him and then it vanished. It vanished completely, like an anchor disappearing under water.

Jummai remained calm. "I have not said anything to anyone. You will know what to do, Zanya. This is why I came."

CHAPTER TWENTY-FOUR

THE RIVER IN THE MIDDLE of Yawari had swelled up to the bank, and it flowed parallel to the road, yielding a gentle, meditative sound that would have lulled Jim to sleep had he not been at the wheel and had Manasseh not been in the passenger seat. From what he could glean so far, Zanya's village did not appear to be one of nightmarish incidents. Jim felt as if he could have walked on the smooth, sanded path that wound through the village and talked to the villagers and sat in their homes to eat with them.

Is this what had happened to Zanya? He had returned and been drawn to the splendor and quiet of his birthplace, and then his relatives had bound him up and set him on fire.

It was early evening now. Jim imagined Yawari at night, and he began to see how the tree boughs, verdant and tangled, arching silhouettes on the walls of the houses and huts, could become chilling, stark limbs in the moonlight. At night, without electricity, pitch blackness could envelop the wooded pockets of the village and conceal violent deeds. A tremor went through Jim and made him grateful he had not ventured here alone.

Manasseh must have seen him shudder. "We can go back to Rabata," he said, looking out with skepticism at the forest separating the huts and houses.

"Well," Jim said. "We've made it this far."

"My ancestral village, it is not far from here. We can go there."

"We'll find Zanya's family, ask our questions, and leave. My estimate is twenty minutes."

Jim allowed himself the thought that he might be taking things too far in his pursuit of truth. Why not just give the kid an opportunity? Train him, like Gary Parson suggested, instead of testing him with the laborers? His tactics with the strike had confounded Delores and the lot of them with his refusal to meet with the workers.

"I'd love to mediate a session between our mission and the laborers," Delores had said.

"I think," Jim said, "I'm well-equipped to handle it on my own."

She had given him a patient, put-on smile. "Aren't you at all concerned about the church building, Jim? The damage the rains could do? Aren't you concerned about what *that* will cost the mission?"

In his heart, Jim thought, *let it be ruined if it meant purging lies*. If it meant not giving into demands for higher wages, which would put the mission on faulty ground, leading to unceasing demands from the locals. Give them an inch, and they'd take a mile. There'd be expectations of the mission as a never-ending reserve. Jim was concerned about the spiritual growth of the church, not the physical structure.

Manasseh had closed the passenger-side door and was outside of the car. The villagers, especially the young children, had gathered to stare at the two of them. Well, at Jim in particular. He was accustomed to these outsider moments in West Africa—the perpetual feeling of exclusion and the instant kinship he could never create, regardless of his language study. He had perfected a passive, resigned expression to show his acceptance of such discomfiting situations. He asked the group in Gbagyi about Zanya's family. Seeing the confusion on their faces at his pronunciation, he disposed with his attempts and let Manasseh do the talking.

"Baba Pema?" a man stepped forward and asked.

"Oh yes," Jim said. "Could you take us there?"

"Come. I will show you."

The man led them to the house and signaled for them to wait outside. Broken cement blocks were mounted like a cairn outside the house, which was set apart from the others in the village. Though they had lost their trail of villagers, Jim had the distinct feeling it wasn't just the two of them out here. They were being watched by hidden eyes.

The man reemerged a few minutes later. "Baba Pema is coming to see you."

A man Jim presumed was Zanya's father, Baba Pema, stood under the lintel as if he had been disturbed while sleeping and had come out to discover the reason. Baba Pema was not as tall as Zanya. In fact, he was shorter than Jim. Zanya's height must have come from his mother's side. Baba Pema gestured Jim to two chairs on the side of the house, close to a forested area. The chairs faced the house and were so close to the shrubs and plants that branches dug into Jim's neck when he sat. Jim thought he saw Baba Pema exchange secretive glances with the man who had shown them the house before he walked off.

There was no offer of food or drink, so Jim started, "Baba Pema, I know your son, Zanya."

Baba Pema did not respond, and at first Jim thought he might not understand English.

"Oho 6i," Manasseh translated.

"I have ears to hear," Baba Pema said in English. "I have heard him."

"Zanya works with me for the Christian—" Jim caught himself. Surely, that had been the wrong word to mention in a place like Yawari. Zanya's father showed no change in countenance. "—the mission in Rabata."

"You are the one who turned Zanya from us," Baba Pema said. "Away from his people and his gods."

Jim laughed nervously. "Depends how you look at it, I suppose."

He wanted to add that people in Rabata knew his and Manasseh's whereabouts. Except nobody in Rabata knew. Gary thought he had gone on visitation nearby, a ten-minute drive and not an hour. Jim had sworn Manasseh to secrecy, but he'd had the presence of mind to alert mission radio about their trip to Yawari.

Manasseh had chosen to stand between Jim and Baba Pema instead of sitting. Jim wanted to tug him down. He tried to catch Manasseh's eye to have him take the seat on his left.

"Zanya has built many places in Rabata for the mission," Jim said. "He told me he learned these skills from you."

"Yes," Baba Pema said.

"I'd love to hear a little about this, if you wouldn't mind," Jim said.

Admiration might draw Baba Pema out of his laconic responses. It seemed the right currency regardless of culture.

"See this house?" Baba Pema said. "It is one the two of us built. See how strong it is."

"It's a wonderful home you have," Jim said.

This was the case with all the houses the two of them had built, Baba Pema said. There were houses in the village where the construction was an inferior quality than the buildings he and Zanya worked on. He had taught Zanya to build before he had ever entered primary school. He had only daughters, and it had saddened him until Zanya came along. Baba Pema had taught him at a young age how to put the clay mixture into the wooden molds. He had let him stomp in small pits with the rest of the grown men. Baba Pema pressed his nostrils together with his fingers and looked out at the house again.

Zanya had gone off to his studies in Kunama and returned, Baba Pema continued, turning his nose at the labor that had fed him. Zanya told Baba Pema about new tools and materials for building. He told Baba Pema about the gmelina trees in the forest around them, and how the trunk of these trees could be used for roofing. Baba Pema wanted to do things as he had done them before. What was wrong with the materials they had used in the past? Baba Pema seemed to speak about Zanya with a flush of contradictory emotions: pride, and what seemed to Jim like bitterness.

"And were you not pleased with Zanya after his studies?" Jim said.

Baba Pema looked at Jim.

Jim said, "It seems your relationship with him is not as strong as—"

"The boy left our village. His family. What else is there?"

"I'm sure his new religious beliefs have also caused some tension. Is that why the people of Yawari attempted to burn him?"

"Which burning?"

"It's the news that's been circulating—"

Twigs snapped, and branches and leaves rustled. Jim looked out into the thicket and turned his head to look down the path they had walked to Baba Pema's. Manasseh had heard the sound also. He looked from side to side, a frown developing on his face.

"Yes," Baba Pema said, "I've heard these stories."

"So it did or didn't happen? You lit the guinea corn chaff around your son's feet?"

Baba Pema chuckled to himself and looked at Jim. "Why did you come to our village? You don't trust Zanya?"

This time Jim heard footsteps loud and clear, and he turned his head in the direction of the noise. He thought he saw a group of men in the dwindling sunlight, walking through the forest behind the house, heading in their direction. They could be farmers taking a shortcut back to their homes. Or they could be women—it was hard to see with his eyesight from this distance—returning from the riverbank, buckets of water on their shoulders, giving the illusion of tall, strapping men. But there was something savage in how the figures approached.

"I'd hesitate to say that I don't trust Zanya," Jim said, finding that he was stuttering. "He's done a lot for the mission."

"Okay, then. Why did you come to Yawari?"

"Frankly, we're here to verify the testimony we heard about the fire."

"You want to know what we did to him?" Baba Pema said.

Jim's heart raced, and he searched for what he needed to say. "Zanya said his uncles came together, and I just thought it sounded quite terrible. Your brothers or your wife's brothers, I presume, would have been the ones who did this."

Baba Pema's leer was ugly and twisted. "You want to know what we did to that boy?"

Branches cracked and tree limbs fell as men emerged from the forest behind the house. One by one, they greeted Baba Pema and formed a crude semicircle in front of Jim and Manasseh.

"Reverend, this is not good," Manasseh said, stepping closer to Jim's chair.

"What's happening?" Jim said, rising slowly.

Zanya's father rose, and with a quick, authoritative flick of his head like a military general, he directed one of the men to stand behind Jim.

"Reverend!" Manasseh cried. One man grabbed Manasseh's shoulders in a crushing hold, pulled him back.

"You want to know what we did to Zanya?" Baba Pema repeated.

"No…" Jim said weakly.

"Please, we don't want to know," Manasseh said. "We don't want to know."

The man closest to Jim twisted a piece of cloth in his hands. Was that a blindfold? A gag?

Jim's breathing had become asthmatic—short, wheezing inhales and exhales. He stepped back and collided into a large, brawny frame.

Baba Pema smiled and said, "We will do to you what we did to Zanya."

"No, no, no—" Jim cried as he was pushed off his feet and lifted overhead.

CHAPTER TWENTY-FIVE

He was rigid and cold as a corpse as two men carried him down the village path. Dampness soaked his armpits and spread through the shirt and suit he had worn. The blindfold smelled of kerosene; it burned his eyes and his nose was inflamed and he could not release a finger to scratch, to pull the blindfold away. Red spots flowered and drifted to the center of his shut eyelids as he squirmed to escape the hold under his arms and the pair of hands grasping his ankles. They belonged to the man who had shown them the way to Baba Pema's house. Jim had seen him before they put the blindfold on him; he'd seen the man lunging for his feet.

This was how it would end for him. They were not going to make it out of Yawari alive. Jim had known death was a possibility. He had read about the Boxer Rebellion in China. Hundreds of missionaries slaughtered. *Slaughtered.* The article had used this word to capture the depravity of the horrific event. The diviner's words flashed in Jim's mind: *The other snake was not as wise, you understand? Since it did not eat the leaves, it was not long before it died.* He'd been the unwise snake, and he'd not taken the diviner's words seriously, and now he would be killed. He had flirted with death when he first came to Nigeria, and he'd walked away unharmed. The robbery had been an inauspicious turn of events. This, this he had walked himself into.

He felt the man's calluses cutting against his ankles. His

thoughts turned to how his sons would react to the news of his death. Walter stoic and proud, taking the news as if he had expected it to happen. Pete…would it lead him to repentance? Would it lead either of his sons to regrets about their strained relationship?

"Please!" Jim heard Manasseh implore. "We are begging you. Leave us alone."

He ought to speak and plead for his life, but the fear of what was ahead had tied his tongue. It was all he could do to keep breathing. The smell of the kerosene and the fear of the horror that awaited them choked him.

The men must have been carrying them into the center of the village. They were not talking amongst themselves. It was as if they had done this before and were coordinated in walking, on which route to take, how to do so with stealth. They had done this to other foreigners, to their own people, like Zanya who rejected their gods. Sheaves would be tossed to the ground. The villagers would gather. A match would be struck and the flames would writhe around Jim and Manasseh. For there had been a crowd when Zanya was almost burned.

He heard the ferocious rush of water. Smelled the change in the air. The mustiness of the river. Algae and roots and soil. The men must have carried them to the riverbank, and it was the same river he and Manasseh had passed driving into the village. They would be thrown into the torrent. He had never been much of a swimmer. He'd be caught into the current and would not survive.

"Throw them!" Zanya's father said.

"No!" Jim shouted. His words shot out like a cannon, and the men tightened their grip on him. "Please, please. Just a minute, Baba Pema—"

"You wanted to know—"

"I, we made mistakes. We should never have come—"

"Yes," Baba Pema said, "you should never have come."

Jim felt the swing of his body. The heave ho. He was like nothing in their hands. He was a sack of leaves as they swung him back and forth. He waited for the feeling of flying into the air. For the sharp descent. The explosion of water in his nostrils and mouth—

His feet hit ground instead. He was vertical again. What was happening? Had they heard his pleas and stopped, or were they planning something far more sinister and torturous?

His hands and feet were free. Hardly daring to believe it, he reached up a trembling hand to remove his blindfold.

Baba Pema stood in front of him. "You said you want to know what we did to Zanya." He laughed. "This is what we did to him."

Jim's hands trembled. His knees shook. He could not seem to orient himself. He had nearly lost his life, and now the men who had abducted him were laughing. Their eyes were merry with tears when these same eyes had been sinister and frightening at Baba Pema's house. He had envisioned a throng of villagers gathered around them. Yet nobody else was around except for Baba Pema and the men.

"What's that?" He was struggling to catch his breath though there had been no physical exertion on his part. "I don't know what you mean."

"I knew what you were wanting from the moment you arrived," Baba Pema said, rubbing his hands together as if closing a deal.

Nothing made sense to Jim. He staggered forward on shaky legs, feeling disoriented as blood rushed to his head and he felt suddenly faint. One of the men steadied him.

"Now, you can leave Yawari," Baba Pema said.

"I'm sorry, I'm having trouble understanding what you mean," Jim said.

They were not as close to the river as he had thought. He had believed them to be at the riverbank, close enough that the men might have fallen in while throwing him in. Manasseh had been released and had collapsed to his knees in gratitude, and Jim wanted to tell him to pick himself up and not look so defeated. And a part of him wanted to join him on the ground because he had thought he'd be at the bottom of a river just seconds ago. His ears were ringing now, and he felt as if the blood had drained completely from his head.

This had all been a grand joke to them. There had been no real threat of death.

"We let the boy go," Baba Pema said. "Just as we have let you go."

Manasseh had recovered and risen to his feet. "There was no fire in Yawari? Zanya did not escape from fire. Is that what you're saying?"

One of the men said, "We did the same to him as we have done to you."

"We did not burn that boy," Baba Pema said, as if it should have been obvious.

"What?" Jim said. He was surprised that the truth about Zanya, out in the open like this, had such a shocking effect after the time he'd spent doubting and pursuing it.

"You are the ones who said you wanted to know what we did. Now you have seen. Now you know. You will leave us now. You will leave our village and people alone."

"Yes, we will," Jim said, for Baba Pema seemed to be waiting for a response.

"We will go," Manasseh said.

The men pointed them back in the direction of the car.

"We'll speak of this to nobody," Jim said to Manasseh, warm with humiliation, as they walked away from the riverbank. "Understood?"

"Yes, sir," Manasseh said, and they trekked back through the brush in silence.

CHAPTER TWENTY-SIX

Tebeya soaked a cloth in a basin of shallow water and polished the soles of Comfort's shoes. She inspected Comfort's new dress—no spillage on the polka-dotted sash or stains on the sleeves. Nothing her mother would find fault with and take as yet another sign that they should never have allowed this elfin child into their home.

Tebeya parted Comfort's hair, and the wet curls sprang with each stroke of the comb. Comfort winced when the comb snagged a tiny knot. Tebeya recalled cringing in the same manner when her sister styled her hair. She had shunned the obsessive care some women put into their hairstyles while Bintu possessed a natural interest and skill at plaiting and twisting hair. In their youth, Bintu practiced faithfully on Tebeya, refusing to allow Tebeya to practice on her. Tebeya had never minded. She preferred textbooks and scholarship to finding her fingers greased with pomade. She had paid marginal attention to her own hair until Bintu's eyes would flicker over it and she would say, "You need to oil your hair," in a voice implying the dryness of Tebeya's scalp was a mild emergency to which she should attend.

Comfort swung her legs. "I want to go to school today."

"You will go next week after we return," Tebeya said. "We're going to important places today, so you'll have to come with me."

The essential item on her agenda was visiting Edward Hayes at headquarters to discuss the current directorship of the mission clinic. She might not have decided to move ahead with it if Nelson had not confronted her in front of patients this past Monday. Did she need to wait and see what he would do next? On Wednesday, a Canadian medical team had come to volunteer their services for a full week. It was the perfect time for her to leave.

Comfort sat erect as Tebeya brushed the last section of hair. The girl was not prone to quick movements or restlessness like other children. She was a reserved, precocious child, constantly studying her environment. This natural silence had made it harder for Tebeya's mother to welcome Comfort into the house.

"See how Bintu's daughter talks and talks," her mother said on Comfort's second day. "This one should talk like any other child. See other children running their mouths."

"Mama, her grandmother died. Let her not talk until she feels comfortable—"

"What is comfortable? See her eyes, Tebeya. How she'll just be looking at you."

What were eyes for but to look? Her mother made little sense sometimes.

Her parents and Bintu were at the dining table when she went downstairs with Comfort. Her mother did not resemble an approachable grandmother, one a child would want to climb upon and explore their bangles and earrings. Her eyes were lined with the same black thickness and ferocity as Bintu's. Her gold jewelry clanged on her wrists like bells around an animal's neck, and the expensive perfume she wore wrinkled Comfort's nose.

Daily Times hid her father's face, and in front of the creased pages, a bowl of cornflakes soaked in milk and a mug of tea grew cold. Duza had served the tea fresh and steaming from the flask. Her father read his newspaper, spreading a page out on the table before lifting it to his face, his need for worldly affairs taking precedence over sustenance.

"Good morning, Baba," Tebeya said. "Good morning, Mama. Comfort, oya, greet people. What have I taught you?"

"Good morning, sir," Comfort said warily. "Good morning, ma."

Tebeya's father answered from behind the paper, without bothering to flip the paper down so that they could see his face.

"See the new dress she's wearing," Tebeya said, spinning Comfort around.

"Am I not seeing it? Comfort, sit down and eat," her mother said, shunting the box of cornflakes over. "You know what to do. We don't have to teach you, ba?"

Comfort panicked whenever Tebeya's mother uttered a word to her. She glanced at Tebeya to know what she should do with the offer of cornflakes, as if it might be a trick.

"Sit and eat," Tebeya said. "Pour it."

How difficult would it have been for her mother to compliment Comfort's new dress? It was small things like this that made her glad that she had found her own place, a new property within walking distance of the clinic and primary school.

Bintu asked, "Why do you have to go to Lafia this morning? You could not come with me to Jos, and yet you are able to travel to Lafia."

"Hospital matters." She thought it best not to tell them where she was going.

"In Lafia?" Bintu said.

"Yes."

"But why in Lafia?" her mother said. "Is it for a new position? Is that it?"

"I'll be speaking with the administrators about a new health service." She hoped it sounded as vague and uninteresting as she intended.

Her father lowered the newspaper. "Do you have everything for the journey?"

"Yes, Baba. Thank you."

"They're just going to Lafia," her mother said.

Benedict had been given a few days off, so a new driver, Paul, was propped against the bonnet when Tebeya walked out with

Comfort. She preferred Benedict, but she was glad he was not taking her to headquarters this morning. He would have taken an interest in the affairs, and he might have led her to decide against the risk.

"Good morning, madam," Paul said, lowering his gaze as if he had been caught fondling himself. A chewing stick protruded from his mouth. He pulled the stick out and dropped it into his shirt pocket. "How you dey?"

"We have luggage," Tebeya said. "Comfort, greet Paul. Then come inside the car."

Paul went inside for their bags, and Tebeya examined the documents in her hands. She had started tracking incidents, writing them down as they happened, noting each incorrect diagnosis and prescription as well as Nelson's physical appearance. Her head nurse, Katherine, occupied with her own problems, failed to notice, only commenting initially that Nelson seemed tired or, in her nondescript expression, "out of it." She had whispered once, "He's going through a lot, Tebeya. Just give him time." Were they not all going through "a lot"? When Tebeya told Katherine about the warfarin error, Katherine had shut the office door and said, "Listen, I'm not supposed to be telling you this, but Nelson and Virginia got divorced six months ago, right around Thanksgiving. Go easy on him, would you? He'll be back to himself in no time."

Tebeya had been unable to sleep that night, thinking about Nelson's divorce and the action she intended to take today. Did the end of Nelson's marriage give him the right to misdiagnose and misprescribe? To show up intoxicated? She was a very good and hardworking physician, and now, her workload had doubled because of Nelson. She made sure she was in the operating theater with Nelson and attributed her presence to the desire to observe new assistants or procedures. She never mentioned his drinking, but he must have known she suspected. So this—what she was about to do—should not come as a shock.

She thought of Nelson, in the clinic right now, examining and diagnosing their patients. She had asked Vincent, a nurse she trusted to keep matters private, to observe Nelson in her absence, monitor his behavior and whereabouts. She had lied to herself when she first suspected his alcoholism and convinced herself it was better to have someone of his caliber in the clinic, an American doctor with more experience than her. By caliber, she later understood she had meant white, and she had carried a shadow of fear about what the clinic would become if others did not see him there.

The first time she met Nelson Landry, she had thought him commanding in his white shirt and creased white shorts, hale among the pained expressions of the patients. Other times, she had watched how helpless he was to control the changes in his skin, the white hue receding into a pinkish flush up his neck to his ears and cheeks when he was hot or frustrated, and at those times he looked pathetic and lost, an imposter.

Transition was afoot in Nigeria. With the government takeover of schools, it would only be a matter of time before they assumed control of mission-run hospitals and clinics, putting locals in charge. Was this, what she was doing, not just a matter of course?

⁂

Tebeya could not relax inside Edward Hayes's office despite the meeting proceeding better than she had hoped. She had expected more questions or opposition. After all, she was bringing accusations of unethical behavior against one of their own—someone they trusted to uphold the tenets of their organization. Someone who had broken their own rules. She had assumed there would not be much to the meeting besides handing the documents over and confirming what she had observed. Instead Edward engaged her in discussion, asking about her vision for the clinic and her overseas training in Ireland.

"Impeccable, Dr. Awyebwi," he said, flipping through the records she had provided him of the incidents. "Weeks, boy—all this? It's quite an allegation you're bringing against Dr. Landry. It's extremely serious, a dismissible offense."

She had evidence and facts, yet it was *her* allegation. It was personalized. It would be attributed to her. Her hands were empty, the material submitted. What more could she do?

"I would not be here if the evidence did not support my observations."

He sat on the edge of his desk and hiked up immaculate trousers. "Is there a reason you felt you could not speak to Jim Clemens or Gary Parson?"

"Not particularly," she said. "Should there be, sir?"

"Well, they do run the mission station."

"There are less complications this way," Tebeya said. "This should not be a situation—" she searched for the appropriate American idiom, "that is swept under the rug."

"I understand, and I won't argue with you there." He opened a leather planner. "I'll come to Rabata to do an investigation of sorts—I'd go today if I could, but we've got a lot going on. I know time is of the essence in a case like this. The best I can do is Tuesday. I'd like to talk to the staff individually and conduct some observations before presenting evidence to headquarters."

"That is fine with me."

"Listen, I can't promise you anonymity when this all comes out. Not in this situation. I'd have loved to do that for you. I'm sure you can understand why."

"One way or another," she said, "they'll have to know."

He looked at her with admiration. "And you're okay with this?"

"What choice do I have? What matters is that we reach a resolution to ensure the safety of our patients and staff."

Edward asked her to refrain from discussing his arrival with the missionaries. She assured him she would not be in Rabata when he came, since she was staying in Jos until Tuesday.

"Oh, really?" He untucked the part of his collar that had

slipped under his jacket lapel.

"Well, if that's the case—that you're staying—we could have lunch, finish this meeting over a meal. I'm due for a lunch break, and there's a restaurant here I'm fond of."

"Is that not what we're doing now? Meeting?"

"Well, sure it is." A husk came into his voice. "I mean, it'd be great, don't you think? To discuss the situation in more detail before I head to Rabata?"

He appraised her with a bold, interested expression. She had assumed he was married with a family on a mission station somewhere, with a wife she pictured as docile and agreeable, minding the children without complaint, which she realized was how she envisaged the wife of Gerard Nolan, and most wives, though her mother could not be categorized as such, nor Bintu.

She noticed Edward's naked ring finger and entertained the idea of joining him at a restaurant catering to expatriates. He was observant and thoughtful, unlike some of the missionaries she encountered.

Regardless, Tebeya preferred to keep intentions and working relationships clear. "Everything you need is there, Mr. Hayes," she said. "In those folders."

His eyes lost a bit of enthusiasm. "Oh. All right. I suppose I'll take a closer look."

"I come to Jos often," she said. "We will find another time."

"I'll look forward to it then."

"Yes, so, good afternoon, Mr. Hayes."

She strolled down the corridor she had come from earlier, passing signs for the various departments: treasury, seminary, education, and the general secretary's office.

Paul kneaded a cigarette butt into the ground with the heel of his shoe, and he beckoned to Comfort when Tebeya walked out.

Inside the car, her hands went to the swooped bangs of her wig in a self-conscious, congratulatory sort of pat. She knew the gossip that would spread if she accepted Edward Hayes's offer. That Tebeya had wrangled the clinic from Nelson Landry because of a dalliance with the regional coordinator. She laughed at such projections into the future when the man had simply asked her to accompany him to a restaurant. But she knew how easily simple matters could turn into complicated ones. Isn't this what happened with Gerard?

She had met Gerard Nolan at a dance hall in her third year at the University of Dublin, Trinity College School of Physics, in '57. She had never seen Gerard before in any of her medical courses. He said he had noticed her, and she said it was easy to be noticed, as she was one of four women and one of two foreign women in their classes. They had sipped on Club Orange and debated about the Church of England, the British presence in Nigeria and how this differed from its presence in Ireland, the Hungarian refugee crisis and the hunger strike in Limerick, the Nigerian footballer who had led the University College Dublin team to the Metropolitan Cup semifinals the previous year.

The attraction had been immediate, and even now, when she remembered him, a faint nostalgic feeling pulsed in her chest. Their relationship began to unravel when she bested him in their final medical examination results. It put her above him, and it was, to him, an unnatural order. It would have been fine if the scores had been reversed. If she had failed instead of passing with such high honors, Gerard would have thought it appropriate, and he would have comforted and reassured her and offered to help her study.

"I'm very sorry," Tebeya had said to Gerard that afternoon when they stood near the posted examination results. She had found her words inadequate, and disliked the roiling in her stomach, which she later knew portended the end of their relationship. "You can petition for them to review the exams."

"No, I won't do it," he said. "I failed. Fair and square."

"It is only three points, Gerard. If you go—"

"It's done," he said. "That's why there's a passing line."

He turned to her and, as a distant colleague to another colleague, not as Gerard to Tebeya, he had said, "Congratulations. Well done, mate."

Mate? Imagine.

Recalling her humble apology, she wanted to silence her younger self. She was with one or two men after Gerard—one Nigerian man in Ireland that she worked with briefly at Sir Patrick Dun's Hospital, and another when she practiced in Kaduna. In her interactions with these men, she found she had become as shut up as an oyster. She saw the possibility of a cruel twist in a kind gesture or charming word. She looked through them and saw them as their worst selves, what they were capable of becoming, and not the men they alleged to be. It was a subtle shift in her thinking to become the woman she had become.

She later learned—courtesy of a letter from her former flatmate—Gerard had indeed passed his retake later that September. He married an Irish woman shortly after, opening a practice in Dun Laoghaire. She reflected upon those years with Gerard or the others after him and judged them a waste of time. There were matters more gratifying and less injurious in life than the emotional turbulence of relationships.

She looked over at Comfort, who had made a game of counting each business and restaurant they were driving past. It was new, the tussle she felt between resistance and acceptance even as she declined Edward's invitation. She was tempted to ask Paul to turn the car around. She would tell Edward Hayes that her afternoon had opened up. She would agree that it was better to discuss more details face to face.

"How you dey, madam?" Paul inquired, looking at her in the rearview mirror. "See this junction coming? You want to stop and buy food?"

He did not yet know how to drive in silence and not bother people with questions.

Yet, she caught his glance in the mirror and said, "Turn the car around."

CHAPTER TWENTY-SEVEN

ZANYA LEANED AGAINST THE PEUGEOT, and the cold, a combination of metal and the cool plateau of Jos, shot like ice through his trousers to his skin. He leapt up. He had spent most of Friday outside, enduring the cold along with other drivers, going to buy some food with them. He opened the car door and rummaged for a sweater.

It was Saturday, the second day of the regional conference at the mission headquarters. He had arrived very early in the morning to the mission compound yesterday, and Reverend Jim said Zanya would be driving them to Jos. He had assumed this, and it had not bothered him. Before the first session, he discovered Reverend Jim had not intended he join the conference as a participant.

"Do you think you deserve to join the sessions?" Reverend Jim said in the cryptic tone he had taken with Zanya for the past few days. "Would it be honorable of you to join?"

Zanya had not known how to respond. At first, it had not bothered Zanya since he was still recovering from Jummai's news. He'd been content to spend the day contemplating his problems, asking himself if Jummai was lying to him and what she would gain by it. Some of his mates from Kunama had got a couple of girls pregnant. One had married the girl he impregnated. Should he marry Jummai when all was set with Nami and her family?

Zanya had thought about how he would tell Nami. If he

would tell her. It was not until the end of yesterday that his mind had cleared, not because he had come to any conclusions but because he could not think of impending fatherhood when he was here at this conference. The workers and the strike, these were the reasons he had come. He had dodged questions from locals asking him when the laborers would return to finish the church. They had the same worried look about the structure and the damage heavy rains could do to a roofless building. A few asked if it was true he would be given the associate pastor position. To everything, he said he did not know. Just the other day, he had encountered two laborers who had yet to find any work in the middle of this strike. Baba Bintu had hired a couple of them to drive lorries. He wondered how the others were getting on without a daily income.

"There's no work," the first said. "My family needs money. We cannot keep doing this." The other man's face was drawn. He looked as if he had not touched a morsel of food in some time. "Betabwi promised us that it wouldn't be long. We can come and help you."

Zanya had offered the men the change in his pocket and said he would let them know once the situation was resolved.

He looked once more at the headquarters building, wondering should he just go and enter. Yesterday, he had asked when he could attend conference sessions, and Reverend Jim had said, "Not today. I need you to be patient, son."

"When, sir?"

"Tomorrow," he'd said. "There's a specific session I want you there for."

Tomorrow was today, and he was still outside with the other drivers. And like the other drivers, he had slept in the car last night while Reverend Jim spent the night at the mission guesthouse. He had the sense of a wrong being done to him, that Reverend Jim wanted his body for labor but not the fullness of his mind. How had he failed to see this over the years? Since his request to progress in the ranks of the church, Reverend Jim had become adversarial, questioning and distrusting him. This issue with his laborers and Reverend Jim—he felt a plot was being orchestrated against him. How the Reverend had shut himself in an agonizing silence in the face of the strike, refusing to speak to the laborers even though the town supported them, waiting for things to fall apart so he might afterward say, "Did I not say you were unqualified?"

Zanya looked once more at the building entrance. He walked up the steps and bypassed the empty reception desk toward the end of the corridor, where he heard voices. He slipped inside the back door of the conference room and sidled against the wall until he spied an empty chair. Several long tables facing the speaker held about seventy men, suits interspersed with agbadas. Nigerians and foreign missionaries sitting side by side. Agendas, notepads, Bibles, and folders sat in front of all the participants. Nigerians from other stations exuded authority, showing they had every right to be part of the mission. They had not come in the same capacity as Zanya.

Bill Kent, the country director at the podium, reminded Zanya of his headmaster at Kunama—the determined expression, the ferocious eyebrows and graying mustache, the slimness suggesting athleticism. Zanya scanned the room for Reverend Jim and found him three rows ahead, his slicked gray hair visible above the collar of his navy suit.

Bill Kent quieted the room and spoke in a probing and sincere voice. "Many of you know John Gatu caused controversy by calling for a missionary moratorium." He quoted religious leaders Zanya had never heard about, and said Gatu, a Kenyan theologian, had asked American churches to reevaluate sending missionaries to Africa.

One of the Nigerian attendees introduced himself as a professor of missiology and said plainly, "How can we not agree with Gatu?"

"Quite easily," someone retorted, and others around him laughed politely. "It's not feasible. It's that simple. Gatu's running his mouth—"

"Let Africans reclaim their own spiritual identity," another voice spoke with ardor, "as they're reclaiming their independence, without Americans and Europeans holding our hands—"

"I'm sorry, I just can't agree with this," one of the few women in the room said. "Indigenous churches need Western assistance and funds to survive."

"Need?" the Nigerian professor spoke again. "We've complicated ecclesiastical matters. Give me a roof and three people, and I will have a church."

Zanya was acutely aware of intruding in this pastoral space, not like the others who sat around, confident and indifferent, used to coming and going in these rooms. He pulled out his notebook. So this was what Reverend Jim had not wanted him to see. The mission had strategies that involved the promotion of Nigerians, and it was happening at their other mission stations throughout the country. He felt the desire to speak and command the room too; it welled up in him. He thought some of these pastors spoke in theories about dependency and identity, while he had experienced firsthand the suppression of locals at the Rabata station. Reverend Jim, he noticed, remained silent throughout the discussion.

They were almost forty minutes into the conversation when Bill Kent looked toward the back of the room, pointed directly at Zanya and said, "You, young man. Lend us your voice."

"Me?" Zanya said.

"Yes, that's right. You, with the notebook."

Zanya glimpsed the confused looks of the attendees, and he saw Reverend Jim turning in his seat to see who Bill Kent had called upon. A flutter of whispers swept through the conference room that this random man, a driver no less, had managed to enter the room and was confident enough to contribute to the dialogue.

There was a flicker of shock on Reverend Jim's face. He drilled Zanya with a glare, one that said Zanya ought not speak at all.

Nevertheless, Zanya rose from his seat and pushed through the nervousness he felt. After all, hadn't he wanted to speak moments ago?

"Missionaries bring their books, their works written by their own people, and continue to teach us what they know as if it is the only truth. What about what we Africans know?" Self-consciousness ribbed his mind as he looked out again at the other leaders, trying his best to look past the Reverend to Bill Kent. He had enough courage to finish speaking. "It is the beginning, a moratorium; it is not the answer."

"Well said," Bill Kent said. "Anyone else? Let's keep this going."

Zanya continued to listen with a tangle of emotions as the fat, stout African pastor of Paiko station rose to give his opinion. A few minutes later, Bill Kent announced a short break. Zanya remained in his seat. He was not going anywhere. He would stay for the remainder of the conference sessions.

"What are you doing here?" Reverend Jim had come up to him. "What in the world was that about? Is there an emergency?"

"You said I could come to the sessions," he said simply.

"Well, you shouldn't be in here."

Bill Kent interrupted their conversation with a pat on Jim Clemens's back. "Jim, is this the young gentleman I've heard so much about?" He did not wait to be introduced but stretched out his hand to Zanya and introduced himself. "Call me Bill."

"Good afternoon, sir."

"Remarkable," Bill said, "the story about persecution in your village. It's pretty impressive. Jim said you've been a tremendous help to the mission station at Rabata."

So Reverend Jim had spoken to Bill Kent about him? He was ready to forgive the Reverend for bringing him as a driver and keeping him from the conference until Bill added, "He's mentioned your expertise in construction and how we might be able to use your skills for the guesthouse or the new station we'll be building in Takum."

Zanya's heart descended in hearing this, and the anger rushed back full and pulsating.

"Nigerians to replace the missionaries," he said. "It's what your mission headquarters desires?"

"Pardon me?" Bill Kent said.

"It's happened in Paiko and Kamba stations. Why hasn't it happened in Rabata?"

"Not to replace missionaries, to work in tandem," Reverend Jim interjected. "Bill, you and I have spoken at length about the progress in Rabata. No two stations are alike—"

Zanya said, "How can one know the proper time for Nigerians to lead? Who is responsible for deciding when this proper time will be? Is it Nigerians themselves or the mission?"

"Well, young man," Bill Kent said, looking at Zanya with renewed interest. "Both, I'd say. We want our churches to flourish, both are needed."

"How can things flourish," Zanya said, "if there is no church building in Rabata? When the laborers in our town have decided to strike?"

"What's this, Jim?" Bill Kent turned toward Reverend Jim. "Is this accurate?"

Zanya read Reverend Jim's disposition, the straightening of his tie and the blush creeping up the sides of his cheeks. He would be reprimanded later, in the car, on the drive back to the guesthouse, and if not, then on the drive back to Rabata tomorrow.

"He doesn't mean that exactly, Bill," Reverend Jim said. "I did mention to you some time ago that the building would take longer than we expected. There've been some complaints from the laborers. Nothing we haven't discussed. Nothing I'm not already taking care of—"

"Well, let me be the judge, Jim." Bill Kent folded his arms across his chest. "Tell me, Zanya, what are these workers of yours asking for?"

"More wages," Zanya said. "I'm afraid they won't return if we don't listen to their demands, and with the rains coming—it won't be good for what we've already built."

Bill Kent cocked his head. "What might these additional funds be used for? What political organizations are your men involved with?"

"I'm sorry, sir?" Zanya said.

"Any communist or anti-government sentiments?"

"Sir, no—my laborers?"

Most of the laborers were illiterate. They had either never attended primary school or never finished. None had attended secondary school. The image of Betabwi chairing a revolutionary meeting instead of going home to his first wife (and the second former wife still living with him) was laughable.

"Now, you wouldn't," Bill said, "want to unknowingly support any anti-government or communist activities. You understand?"

"No, there's nothing," Zanya said. He could not help but think that had he finished school, he would have known how to talk about such political matters.

After a long pause, Bill tapped the face of his watch. "Listen, I've got another conference session to oversee or we'd keep going." He studied Zanya with a curious regret. "I like you, son, and I hope you'd respect the authority the mission has in place at the Rabata station. The thing is, if Jim's not seeing this strike as a threat to the mission—"

"Oh, it's bound to fizzle," Reverend Jim said.

"I trust it, all right?" Bill said.

He went back up to the podium, and Reverend Jim beckoned Zanya out through the large, wooden back doors and into the bright fluorescent lights of the corridor.

"You weren't supposed to be in here," he said through gritted teeth.

Zanya felt a surprising calm, or perhaps a low boiling anger. Thoughts that Reverend Jim supported him or intended good were fading on a horizon of unbelief.

"I did what I had to do." The conference room doors had closed behind them, but the grainy voice of a new speaker at the microphone competed with his. "Simple wages, and you refused to give it to these men."

"Listen to me, son—"

"You've cheated them. It's not fair what the mission is doing."

"Cheated?" Jim Clemens's eyes crinkled. "You've got no idea, Zanya—"

"And you've not listened—you've done *nothing*—"

"Stop right there—"

"And me, I was here believing you."

"Quiet, Zanya!"

They both stared at one another. Zanya was mildly aware of the white receptionist in his periphery, hovering at the arrival desk, peering over at them.

"You want me to stop telling the truth?" Zanya said. "What of you?"

A blush of displeasure spread across Reverend Jim's nose and cheeks. His mouth worked, jaws moving like he needed to rearrange his teeth with his tongue after his sudden exclamation.

He spoke again. "It pains me to say this to you, son, but you're not ready. For leadership, for the pulpit, for any of this work."

Zanya laughed coolly. "Isn't that what you've been wanting to say all this time?"

"This story about the fire, Zanya, it never happened, did it?"

Heat flushed Zanya's body. So the Reverend had learned the truth.

"Tell me, son," Jim Clemens said, and his voice held an anger

Zanya had not heard before. "Tell me your testimony about the fire happened as you said."

Zanya swallowed a dry ache in his throat.

"Your silence speaks for itself. Listen, you've broken my trust, Zanya, and I'm in a sad state about it. When we get back to Rabata, know that you no longer have a position with this mission. We are no longer in need of your services—"

"What—"

"—construction, translation, or otherwise."

Jim Clemens jiggled open the conference door and disappeared inside before Zanya could respond. Words were not fast in coming to him, and so if the Reverend had stayed, Zanya was not sure he would have even found the sentences.

Within seconds, he was back outside, down the steps, ignoring the other drivers calling out to him, ignoring the rubbery feeling in his legs, finding his way to the car, which he thought he had parked close to the headquarters sign but now seemed so far away. Inside the car, he sat immobile for a long time. Anger, bitter and perceptible, burned within him, worked its way through him, like a carpet viper unspooling in the pit of his stomach.

CHAPTER TWENTY-EIGHT

RAIN CAME. It loosened fallow soil, pounding the earth with a force unlike anything Rabata had ever seen. In the faraway valleys, the palm trees swayed under the torrent. Leaves swelled, raindrops soaking into branches and roots. The serrated leaves of banana plants, once desiccated, greened and widened, flapping in the breeze.

The storms brought the delicacies of rainy season. Women hung fluorescent tubes over buckets of water and swatted swarms of termites that whirred around the lights. Farmers searched for termite mounds. They dug through the soil, plucking the insects' wings and towing small bucketfuls home for their wives and children. In the evenings, the crackling of roasted termites frying in skillets merged with the sound of ceaseless rain.

On the roadside, women worked while swaddled in wrappers or shaded under wooden sheds, selling their goods despite the rain threatening their fires and splattering their oil. Their children ran to school in the unending baptismal stream. After school, these same children tramped in the rain with friends, licking droplets from their lips, playing, and singing:

Rain, rain, go away
Rain, rain, go away
Come again another day
Little Walu wants to play

At night, when the townspeople slept, the children's refrain became a resounding and urgent prayer. Farmers previously pleased with the rains worried that too much of it might damage the crops. These men, who had never stepped into the primary school for service, found themselves awake on Sunday mornings, walking to the school to pray to the white man's god. On another side of town, the waters rose, flowing into homes. The same singing children ran to see the flooding, to see the water foamy and gushing, swirling around the mud houses. To see the men and women, wading in the water that rose to their calves, rushing to save their belongings, carrying pots on their shoulders and sleeping mats rolled under their arms.

And the church, the church that the men had built so close to rainy season, stood a ruined fortress in the storm. On some evenings, the townspeople said, one could see Zanya walking with the lank and height of a Fulani herder around the roofless building. It was impossible to see his face given the steady slant of rain, but there was a quality about his movements, an air of surrender in the delicate way he palmed the bricks.

PART THREE

CHAPTER TWENTY-NINE

THE DOOR TO JIM'S HOME OFFICE ricocheted against the wall, dislodging tiny wood splinters into the air. Nelson loomed underneath the doorway, a behemoth consuming most of the space. With his hair unkempt, he looked as if he had hitched a ride on the back of an open lorry. He was soaked from the rain that had fallen all morning. From the grime on his shoes, it seemed he had stepped into some puddles on his way to the mission compound.

"You *fired* me!" Nelson chucked a crushed wet ball of paper on Jim's desk.

Jim did not need to flatten it to know it was a letter of termination. Edward Hayes had come on an unscheduled visit to Rabata the Tuesday after the conference and stayed in town for a couple of days. This morning, two weeks after that surprise visit, Edward had returned again and this time disclosed to Jim that the reason for his initial visit was to investigate allegations of medical misconduct against Nelson Landry. He was here to let Jim know that headquarters had reached a conclusion to terminate Nelson.

"You fired me, Jim?" Nelson pushed the hair back on his head, but it fell into his eyes. He laughed and said again, "You fired *me*."

"Take it easy, Nelson. Less of the histrionics. Have a seat, would you?"

"I will not sit—"

"Lower your voice then, please."

"You screwed me over"—he laughed again—"'effective immediately'?"

"I did nothing of the sort," Jim said. "Headquarters is releasing you from your contractual obligations."

"Releasing me? I know damn well what this is." Nelson's face was red, the sleeves of his white coat wrinkled, and faint wet circles discolored the area under his armpits. "You brought me here, Jim. I left Rockford to serve with you, and now you've let those idiots—"

"Nelson." Jim kept his voice calm. "If you're unable to comport yourself—"

"For goodness' sake, why wouldn't you tell me this?" Nelson lurched across the desk. "I built this clinic. I staffed it. I funded it!" He pounded the desk. "This is *my* clinic."

"Nelson. I won't ask again."

"How long? Huh?" Nelson said, striving to keep his composure, his hands gripping the back of the chair now. "When'd you know, Jim? Tell it to me straight."

"What matters now," Jim said, "is what we need to do moving forward."

"Ha!" Nelson pushed away from the chair, and it almost toppled over. "Don't give me that, Jim. How long have you known?"

"It doesn't matter. You've got a problem, Nelson, and it pains me to tell you this."

"Yeah, all right."

"She's got incidents and dates—"

"Yeah, well, who's to say she didn't make it up?"

"I doubt she did, Nelson. It's particularly troubling, all of this. What you did to your patients and to the mission station."

The thought came to him quick. *We're losing.* Exactly what he was losing—losing ground, losing the town's trust after the men's protest last month—he might not have been able to say. Any doubts Nelson had would have evaporated if he had seen the precision of Tebeya's reports. Exact dates and times of procedures.

Detailed descriptions of Nelson's appearance and medical blunders. Patient names redacted. Nelson had not established the right boundaries, and Tebeya had usurped him, audacious enough to travel to Jos with incriminating documents. Not unlike Zanya, who had been truculent and self-righteous, swaggering into the conference against Jim's wishes, daring to participate in the session and voice an opinion about the moratorium. Bill Kent had taken Jim aside after Zanya's intrusion and expressed an interest in having Zanya participate in future mission conferences, seeing him move up the ranks in Rabata. Had Jim not traveled to Yawari and learned the truth about the fire, he may have responded differently to Bill's request. He had not yet informed Bill that Zanya no longer worked for the mission, and if Bill protested this decision, Jim would have to say that Bill, up in headquarters hours away, was too far removed from the daily work in the Rabata station and did not always know what was happening on the field.

Jim no longer needed Zanya or the other laborers. He had plans to hire new laborers to complete the church at the same wages. They would finish laying the bricks, putting up a roof to prevent further water damage to the interior of the structure.

"She must have falsified documents," Nelson was saying.

"Dr. Awyebwi?"

"There's no other explanation."

It was hard for Jim to see that he was looking at the same man who guided Edna through cancer treatments and patted her hands as the chemotherapy dripped into her thin veins. Nelson looked set to punch the wall behind Jim's head.

"I need you to be honest with yourself," Jim said. "Being here, in Nigeria, isn't helping you with your, you know—you and Virginia—well, I know it's been tough."

"No, no, no." Nelson pointed an accusatory finger. "Don't you bring Virginia into this. You are not allowed to bring my wife into this."

Jim did not dare correct him: *ex-wife*. Nelson stepped back from the desk, his energy diminishing. Exhaustion seemed to affect Nelson's muscles all at once, and he collapsed on the ground, his back against the wall, knees up. The divorce must have affected Nelson, but Jim had let Nelson's gaiety, his engagement with the locals, convince him that he was handling it with grace and acceptance. How easy it was to forget that those who came to serve with him were no stronger, no more self-sufficient, no less human, no less in need of spiritual succor, than those they had come to serve.

"I was good to her, Jim," Nelson said, looking up. "Virginia. I gave her all I had. Whatever she wanted, I gave it to her. She'll remarry, you know."

"It's not any reflection on you, if that's what you're asking," Jim said. *Flighty* was the adjective Edna reserved for Virginia on the few occasions they had them over to dinner in Rockford. Marriage was a game she had lucked into, not a covenant to steward. It was astonishing Nelson had not been able to see through this.

"Kip Campbell," Nelson said. "Kip and Virginia Campbell."

"Nelson—"

"I have a right to plead my case, Jim. I could keep this going. Make an appeal. You can't kick me out of the country."

"Leave it alone, Nelson. Let it go." Jim turned aside from the nakedness on his friend's big, open face—the anger and humiliation.

"Like hell I will," Nelson said, the edge in his voice returning.

CHAPTER THIRTY

NAMI LAUGHED FULLY this time and set down the oil-stained newspaper that had been filled with suya Zanya bought for them to eat in
his flat. His expression of confusion at her mirthless laughter made
her laugh more. He decided to speak as if her laughter were noiseless.

"She is pregnant," he said, again. "Jummai is pregnant."

"Pregnant, Zanya. She is pregnant."

"She came and told me before the conference—"

"She came and *told* you!"

Her eyes brimmed with tears brought on by her laughter, and
she was repeating what he said like a person losing her mind. The
oddity of her reaction—this high, effervescent laughter that was not
laughter—unsettled him. Before this news of Jummai, he had told
her about losing his positions as translator and laborer, and how
the conference had revealed things for him about the Reverend and
the mission, and she had received it well, listening to him speak
above the pattering of rain with legs crossed in an elegant, teach-
erly manner and leaning toward him, listening, the floral scent of
her perfume calming him. He had said things that must have been
there with Reverend Jim from the beginning. Things he refused to
see. Had he not been like this in Kunama Secondary School? Seeing a side to his mate Bashiru that left him dubious? Yet, he had
continued to consort with Bashiru so that he became absorbed into
the Kunama Four, as he, Bashiru, and two others were called. They

had risen in ranks to become head boys and house prefects, and they had charmed teachers with their high marks and studiousness. Once, the headmaster had even called upon Bashiru and Zanya to squash quarrels between two political student groups. It was worth those four years to gamble on Bashiru like this, and he remembered the four of them—young, skinny, cocky, striding through the school grounds, shooting off their mouths. He had gambled with Jim Clemens since the day he saved the man's life, and still, the man had not done nearly what Bashiru had done for him. Zanya had the wearisome, unshakeable feeling of having been tricked.

He had even told Nami how he had driven around Jos that Friday afternoon when Reverend Jim did not allow him to attend the sessions, and he had come upon Dr. Tebeya sitting in one restaurant with Edward Hayes, the mission regional coordinator. He had watched them for several minutes, seen how serious they appeared, and wondered if Dr. Tebeya had come to headquarters because of Nelson Landry. He had remembered but not shared with Nami about the doctor's drinking and what Jummai had told him. He considered the things he had wanted to say to Reverend Jim on the drive back to Rabata: What of your own missionaries? You protect them in their transgressions and me you will dismiss? When he shared some of this with Nami, she had listened with empathetic nods, holding his hand as he talked. She had not lost control or become angry about the situation with the mission and what it meant for the wedding.

Nami had stopped laughing moments ago, and he saw she was absorbing the news.

"Nami, talk to me. You must say something."

"You've known about this thing with Jummai for so long, Zanya? All this time. Where? Where did Jummai come and tell you? It's just now that I'm hearing it?"

He breathed a sigh of relief that she had stopped the repetition.

"You understand that this is not what I meant to happen," he said.

"The things you told me, Zanya, they were lies."

"I wanted to tell you before, but—"

Her eyes flashed with anger. "You've lost your position with the mission, and now Jummai is *pregnant*?"

He did not like the incredulity in her voice, nor the hands on her hips, the mocking lift of her right brow, the audible exhale of breath from her nose. He did not like it, but he deserved it and worse for what he had done to her.

"I asked you, Zanya. You remember? I said, 'How do you know Jummai?' Did I not?"

"The thing was a mistake."

"A *mistake!*"

Mistake was the wrong word. As if it were innocuous and fixable, like putting a brick an inch or two out of place. This was disastrous. This was learning that the foundation of a building had been irreparably damaged.

"Shameless man. You want to go and become one pastor, yet you are still chasing women. Hypocrite! My father was right not to trust you—"

"Nami, listen to me, I did not intend it to happen."

"What have you done to us, Zanya? My family, everybody thought we would—you've shamed us. You've shamed *me*. What about our wedding? Did you not think?"

She stood from the chair and went far from him, near a shelf that held his curated possessions: a comb, two singlets, a pair of trousers, two button-down shirts, the dysfunctional dictaphone, his notebook of ideas, and two other borrowed books.

Like him, she must have been thinking of what they had worked to have, the plans they had made together. Though he wanted to comfort her in his arms, he knew she would rebuff his attempts. Anger hovered, invisible, keeping them from moving toward each other. He knew her anger concealed pain, and beneath pain, disgust, and beneath disgust, humiliation.

He was about to lose Nami. The one thing making sense for him through these troubles. She was different than any woman—the type of woman who could stand with him and hold her own, and she made him want to give up things, like his freedom, to marry her. He considered how she might have consoled him if he had only told her news of his firing—with encouraging words, with approving glances, with laughter. If Jummai was sun, Nami was rain in the most bountiful of ways: cooling him, making him to grow, forcing him like a root to break through ground.

He had not yet even given her the worst news. He could not marry her even if she were to forgive him, which he did not think she would; his conscience would not allow him to marry her if another woman were to have his child. He would have to marry Jummai. He had done the wrong thing, and now, he would have to do the right thing by accepting the mistake he had made. It was why he had waited so many days after the conference to tell Nami. How could he be the type of father his surrogate father had been to him, absent and rejecting, behaving as if Zanya had been a thorn in his body? He refused to allow his child to be a distant, imperceptible disturbance to him. He did not want to carry regret if he abandoned Jummai. Was it possible that he had pursued Nami and desired marriage with her, when all this time it was Jummai? His mind had been like this for the past several days, muddled and unable to settle.

"Nami, please, see me begging—I did not think—"

"Do you intend to marry her?" It was as if she had jumped into his mind.

He felt a slick coating of mucus in his throat. It was strange that they were here, saying these things to one another, saying things about marrying Jummai.

He sighed. "It will be the right thing to do."

"The right thing? For *who*?" She looked at him and said, "You deceived me, Zanya," and went out the door without a backward glance.

※

"Madam, come and see." The girl angled a tray of freshly cut pineapple chunks and chopped coconut. "It's good o."

"No, no," Jummai said, maintaining her stride toward the main road.

A man approached her from his stall. He lifted a basket off his head, displaying records. He flipped a black vinyl over and spoke rapidly, "Come check am. We get your style. Marley, Kuti, Jimi Hendrix, Lijadu Sisters, The Wings—sis, you look like Marley."

A woman selling soaps and lotions pointed to a slim white bottle of cream. "Sis, it'll make you to look fine. Come and see!"

Jecinda had mentioned a recently vacated shop available to lease close to the provisions store. Jummai walked around the building then returned to the front, thinking of where she might put her signage and chairs outside. A man she assumed was the owner sat in front of the door as if he were guarding Baba Bintu's mansion and not this small-small building. She stood staring for so long that the man stamped his foot twice to get her attention.

"You never see house before?" he said, spitting his chewing gum on the ground. "The way you dey stand here go make people fear."

"Abeg sir, I fit see inside the house?"

He groaned as if it took considerable effort to rise from his chair and walk four steps to the entrance. Much smaller inside than it appeared outside, the place emitted a sickly, peculiar smell, like oranges or bananas rotting in the sun. It was a narrower configuration than she would have liked, but contained sufficient room for three or four tables. It had a door that opened to a yard, where she could cook and grill. She could sleep and live here too. Away from her mother's house and the commotion that started early in the day with Walu's cries and never seemed to end even through the night.

Seeing no signage, Jummai asked, "How much?"

The man named the figure. "The price na for one year. You hear me abi?"

"I will have it."

"The contract na one year. No come here with small money talk say you no hear."

"Yes o. Shebi I dey hear you na."

Within a year, maybe two, she could afford the cost of the lease. It would take all that she would ask from Zanya and what she had saved working with the Parsons and what she would earn working for them in the months to come. She would come back and bargain with this man. The quoted price was never the actual price. If things went according to plan, she would be out of her family's house and living the kind of life she had once thought beyond her.

❧

On her family's compound, a bottomless Walu, uninhibited by his exposed genitals, waddled around, dragging a bucket in wide circles. Next to Jummai, Jecinda threaded Sayi's hair, her fingers winding the black string around the fine strands that had never grown as dense as Jecinda's or Jummai's. Sayi clutched a comb and a nearly empty jar of pomade and handed Jecinda whichever she requested.

Jecinda wound the black thread around the last section of hair. When she finished, she handed Sayi the extra thread and said, "Take it back inside."

"Jecinda," Jummai said once Sayi had gone. "I need medicine from that-your clinic."

She had decided she would not have this child, no matter that it was Zanya's. This man and his dreams, so big and exclusive, she marveled at how he carried them in his head. His dreams had never included marriage to her or a child with her. And if she had this child, would the Parsons and the Reverend not force her to stop coming to the mission compound? They would tell her she could no longer work for them because she had not followed the beliefs of the church. But neither had she followed the ways of her people. If her mother and Tin City learned about this pregnancy, they would chide Jummai for disgracing the family. Her mother had brought shame, too—all these husbands going in and out of their house—but her mother would overlook her own disgrace. Jummai knew of other women who had gotten themselves into trouble and went to the diviner to have the problem taken care of, but she thought the white people would have medicine in their clinic that might make her problem go away.

"Bring you medicine?" Jecinda rubbed her legs with the remnants of pomade on her hands. She lifted Walu into her arms and uncurled his fingers from the rim of the bucket and set it on the ground. He looked at Jummai, and assuming that she might be a possible sympathizer, he let out a wild shriek at the loss of his bucket.

Jecinda laughed above his practiced screams. "You're not deceiving me," she said, bouncing him on her hip. "Now you're the one crying when you should have been sleeping like I told you. Where are your trousers, Walu? You see what you've caused now abi?"

"Jecinda, did you hear me?"

"You said I should bring medicine," Jecinda said. "Are you sick?"

Jummai sucked her teeth. "Why would I come and be asking for medicine?"

What kind of question was this? Were secondary school students not supposed to be more intelligent than other people?

"I can't o, Jummai. They lock it. Where will I find the key?" Jecinda sat against the wall and plopped Walu on her lap.

"Useless girl. Why are you working in that place?"

"Just come to the clinic and ask Dr. Landry and Dr. Tebeya? They will give it to you if you come and tell them what is happening."

"Are you deaf? I don't want people knowing," Jummai said,

feeling both the desire to pluck and chomp on a guava and the need to vomit in the bushes. Her body had changed with this child, and whenever she moved, she felt as wide and big as her mother was now, though she knew she looked the same. Nothing had changed on the outside, but everything had changed on the inside. The child was making itself known, reminding her that although others did not know of it, she could not ignore its existence. It was strong within her like the weight of a solid, mature melon.

"I can't go and be taking things from the clinic. You know what Mama used to tell us."

Their grandmother cautioned them that if a person stole food and gave the stolen food to somebody to eat, then death was certain for those who ate the stolen food.

"That is not what I'm asking you."

"It's the same, Jummai—"

"When have I ever come and asked you to do anything, eh?"

"What kind medicine? What is it for?"

Jummai cursed her younger sister in her mind. All this schooling had made Jecinda more bothersome. You could not tell her to do something simple without her wanting to know why and giving you her own suggestions when you had not asked.

"Medicine," she said, lowering her voice, "I come get belle."

Jecinda's mouth dropped open. "Jummai."

"Don't run and go and tell anybody. If you tell anybody, the way I will beat you."

Her sister closed her mouth, stung. She glanced around the compound. "I don't know if they will have that kind medicine. I don't know what to go and be looking for—"

"Bring it."

"If they catch me, nko?"

"Bring medicine," Jummai said, feeling a tenuous relief at the thought of salvation.

CHAPTER THIRTY-ONE

A COUPLE OF ORDERLIES pushing carts of surgical instruments stared at Katherine as she stood outside the clinic office. She had been standing there for ten minutes, and she was starting to draw attention. She'd made up her mind and changed it, thinking it'd be disastrous to confront Tebeya about the situation with mission headquarters and Nelson. She reached for the doorknob a second time and released it again. What would come from it, since she could barely speak to Tebeya without vines of resentment rising to choke her?

One of the orderlies returned empty-handed, cart stowed. "Nurse Katherine, what is the matter? Should I go and bring you anything?"

"No, thank you, Esther."

"You've been standing like this—"

Katherine waved her off. "Yes, I know. I just need a moment."

"Okay, ma," Esther said.

She'd go inside and get this over with, get the answers she deserved. How long had Tebeya tracked Nelson? Why had Tebeya hightailed it to mission headquarters without bringing it to Katherine's attention first? What tipped Tebeya off when Katherine, who prided herself on her observational skills, had noticed nothing amiss? She'd noticed once or twice that Nelson had seemed preoccupied when she asked about a patient's prognosis, as if his mind were far from the clinic, far from Rabata. It had not alarmed her, not with the situation he had been facing back home. Tebeya's portrayal of Nelson did not align with what Katherine knew of him; Tebeya had put Nelson on par with a drunkard slumped outside a bar.

Tebeya was a flutter of activity these days after assuming the acting role of director, uniformed in her white coat and stethoscope, barking orders to the nurses and orderlies, speaking of overhauling systems Nelson had in place. And she had fired Monday! Monday who had done his best to keep such a busy clinic clean and wouldn't hurt a soul.

Katherine pushed open the office door, and it was as if she had stepped into a different room; the desk and chairs, the shelves and cabinets, had all been rearranged. Tebeya sat behind the desk, immersed in paperwork and unaffected by Katherine's shock.

"Should I be worried?" Katherine said. "Do you have a dossier on me too?" It was pretentious and sarcastic. She had planned to start with something light and inconsequential. The unexpected furniture arrangement had given her a momentary lapse in judgment. She tried again. "We need to talk about what happened with you and Nelson. What you did to him." She shook her head and whispered, "After everything I told you."

"You want to talk at this moment?" Tebeya said, gesturing to the files on her desk and the crowd of patients visible from the window. She wore a weary expression, and Katherine had a sense of impinging upon the final hours of her day.

"I think you owe me an explanation."

Tebeya said in a flat, tired voice, "Okay, Katherine. Let us talk."

"I just don't understand. Why'd you do it?"

"That's not the right question," Tebeya said.

"Now you're monitoring my questions?"

"The reason why I went to headquarters should be very

clear. Before I say anything else, you must know I respected Dr. Landry—"

"Oh please. You wouldn't have done any of this if you respected him."

"Dr. Landry was dismissed over an ethical issue. Do you not recall that I came to you when I noticed his problem? What did you say to me then?"

"Oh, you can't possibly expect me to remember." Of course she remembered being accosted in the storage room over a month ago.

"I thought you might not," Tebeya said. The façade of kindness disappeared. A cool, unsympathetic tone took its place. She sat behind the desk with squared shoulders and her arms drawn together, hands clasped, the effect of it a stiff, intentional wall. "The decision to terminate Dr. Landry was made by Mr. Hayes. Will you be going to speak to him as well?"

"I do not," Katherine said, "work with Edward Hayes. I work with you."

"I see. It's just me that you've come to accuse."

"You had no right to—Nelson's *done*, ruined."

"Well, whether Dr. Landry left today or in a few years' time, he would be leaving Rabata. Just as you will one day return to America."

"What are you trying to say? You know Gary and I have given as much as we can to this town. We left everything in Missouri to come here—"

"Yes, and you will leave."

"All right," Katherine said, "so what's your point?"

Tebeya rose from her seat. She was magisterial under the white fluorescent lights, her figure intimidating and striking. Her eyes clear and discerning. "You accuse me of making this clinic mine. Do you know it's because I have no other choice? You've known Rabata is not where you want to be since the day you came, Katherine. We're a perceptive people—you don't have to say anything for us to know you never wanted to come to our country—"

"I don't know what you're implying," Katherine said, shame rising to her cheeks.

Tebeya's eyes focused in like darts in search of a bull's-eye. "Five years or fifteen years, you missionaries will leave Nigeria. You don't plan to be with us forever. You will not live the rest of your life here in Rabata, and if it were up to you, you might never have come. You see, Rabata is my home, where I was born, and where I will be buried. So, what I'm trying to understand is what problem you have with my leadership of this clinic, when you too will soon be gone?"

The dizzy courage Katherine had mustered minutes ago standing outside the office was transmuted into a stony and conscious embarrassment. Tebeya waited, out of courtesy it seemed, for her to speak, but Katherine pressed her lips together, having nothing else to say.

❧

"Forgive me for disrupting your dinner," Jim said to Gary. He'd knocked on the Parsons' door and asked Gary to come out to the veranda for a quick chat.

"You're welcome to join us, Rev," Gary said, and he waved toward the door. "There's plenty of food left, if you'd like some."

"This will only take a minute," Jim said.

He sniffed something different about Gary Parson, something confident and open. Could be that he was spruced up. No clumps of dirt falling from the ridge of his work boots. Jim wasn't sure, but he'd think of it later. Right now, he'd take it as a sign of his making the right decision.

He said, "I had to let Zanya go. I wish you'd seen him, Gary. I wish you'd seen how he spoke to Bill at the conference, went over my authority."

"What? What are you saying, Rev?"

"I had to let him go. I had no choice."

"Are you kidding, Jim?" Gary said, searching Jim's face. "How do you mean?"

"Listen, I need you to take this position of associate pastor. It's you, Gary. I'm giving it to you, and I won't take no for an answer. There's no one else more qualified. How about it?"

It had not been hard to arrive at this conclusion. Sure, Gary lacked Zanya's desire for the pulpit; nevertheless, the locals respected him.

"You'd be doing the Lord's work," Jim said, "and you'd be the best fit as we transition—well, when we transition to the new church building."

"I've got no words, Jim." Gary Parson massaged his forehead, resting his hands on the top rung of one of the chairs on the veranda, as if needing its support to digest the news. "I can't take that position. It's not right."

"Nationals aren't ready. The church would fall apart. You and I both know this."

"I wouldn't say that, Rev."

"The fire never happened, Gary," Jim said. He shook involuntarily thinking about the terrifying encounter with Zanya's father in Yawari, when he was certain Baba Pema and his mob had intended to drown him. "I figured out the truth."

But Gary did not seem to believe him. "What have you got against the kid? Listen, Jim, if this has anything to do with what happened to you in Rockford, if you're saying all this—"

"Rockford?"

Gary sighed. "I know. Well, we know, Katherine and I. We know what happened in Rockford, at First Presbyterian."

It was a statement so general yet ringing with such precision that for a second Jim thought he had misheard, but his body reacted to the question. His lungs deflated like a tire punctured, and he was fatigued in the face of Gary's declaration. Gary scratched the back of his neck and kept the other hand in his pocket, and they both retreated into silence. Jim gazed out upon the mud enclosure protecting the mission compound, and the kinked limbs of shrubs and grapefruit trees left shadows on the exterior of the cowshed. Seasoned missionaries had advised them to plant lemon and grapefruit instead of mango. It'd keep the locals from trespassing into the compound with baskets to help themselves, they had said.

"I resigned." Jim cleared his throat. "This is what headquarters was told."

Gary brushed his hair back with his hands. He seemed to forget he had thickened it with some kind of goop, and he rubbed his hands together. "Fiscal mismanagement. That's what the letter said."

"Letter?" A sharp pain emerged near Jim's ribcage—a thin, wiry pain, like a steel wire.

"From Katherine's mother. It's true, isn't it?"

Weariness descended upon Jim. He availed himself of the chair opposite Gary. It was a marvel how the past had reappeared, how it had reached ghostly fingers across the Atlantic and resurfaced in this humble town.

A couple of years before Edna's passing, Pete had come back to Rockford, twenty-seven and looking cleaned up and healthier than he had in the years since dropping out of his liberal arts college in Wisconsin. Within weeks, he was working part time as a janitor at Porter's Rexall Drug Store on West State Street. He had started waking up on Sundays, sitting next to Edna in the front row of First Presbyterian—his hair combed back and face alert, listening. Sure, Jim had felt a sort of pride, an expectation of God's restoration and renewal, seeing his son sitting in that pew. Six months later, Jim received the church's monthly statement from National Bank & Trust. For whatever reason, he had opened it instead of leaving it for Beverly, the church accountant. Two withdrawals totaling $8,376 deposited to a Pete Clemens. Pete had stolen the church's checkbook and forged Jim's signature.

He recalled how light flooded his church office in Rockford that afternoon, so that for an instant, the oil paintings and wallpaper blurred in a kaleidoscopic pattern. He had driven the short mile to the manse in a blind sort of haze, a white-knuckled grip on the wheel, passing down the neighborhood streets, which were wide and clean, the autumn wind fluttering the last leaves on his neighbors' lawns. He had gone into the guest bedroom. Pete's belongings had been cleared out, and Jim found the church checkbook in the bottom drawer of the armoire.

A couple of board members had accused Jim of plotting with Pete to drain the church coffers. The incident became a trigger for other grievances to be aired, and it wasn't long before the final decision was handed down.

Jim sighed into the evening air. "Take a seat, Gary," he said. "This will take a while."

CHAPTER THIRTY-TWO

ZANYA HAD NOT EXPECTED to see Betabwi and Kago when he walked into Shigudu's, though he had come looking for laborers. When he neared their table, the two men looked up at him and stopped their conversation. He tasted the bitterness of their sudden reticence. Before the strike, they would have welcomed him. He would have joined easily; whatever they chatted about, they would have been sure to include him and sought his opinion.

He heard that a few laborers had found other work upon learning that the mission was unwilling to negotiate. Reverend Jim had hired new laborers, and the walls of the church were going up. Whenever there was a day without rain, the new laborers were on the site working. Men who would not complain about their pay.

"You come spy abi?" Betabwi said.

"No, you're the ones I wanted to see," Zanya said.

"Ah, Fire Boy," Betabwi laughed. "Wetin oga at the top tell you?"

He could see from their expressions that he need not answer; they had already known the futility of speaking to Bill Kent at headquarters.

Kago said, "They did not listen to you, Zanya."

"Wetin we tell you?" Betabwi said. "Na how e dey be. Did we not tell you, but you had to go and find out yourself?"

Both Kago and Betabwi laughed.

"You been dey dance for them?" Betabwi said, folding his arms across his chest.

"It's not good what they did," Kago spoke, "but you refused to side with us—"

Zanya tapped a forefinger against the table. He had never seen himself as dancing for the Reverend. He had asked for the men to be compensated. He felt the same fluttery embarrassment he had experienced after Bill Kent refused to hear his plea.

"Na you dey support them before," Betabwi said. "Now you don see wetin we dey see since."

"I don see am now," Zanya admitted. "I don see."

"Na because they don drive you comot for work, that's why you don start to see."

"You know?"

Betabwi palmed the table. "Who no know?"

It had been three weeks without work. He had picked up odd jobs to do here and there, mostly small repairs. It was foolish to think people did not know already, and when he was not at the Reverend's side again during service, they would wonder and whisper.

"Wetin we tell you, Zanya?" Kago said. "These white people, them go use you, and then carry you throw way when they finish."

They had done everything to rise against the Reverend, and he had impeded their progress and sided with the missionaries because he thought they would remain faithful to him. Somehow, he must have thought he was better than his men, secure in the knowledge of his two positions, thinking that Reverend Jim needed him as a translator and someone who could manage the construction. He had made the mistake of seeing himself as indispensable.

"The two of you were right."

Betabwi said, "We already know."

"So, you go work with me?" He had thought about this on the drive back to Rabata, joining with the laborers. "We cannot let the Reverend continue to control this mission station. We have to stand for ourselves."

Betabwi reclined in his chair and looked at Kago. "During our own time, you no work with us, why we go follow you now?"

"The church should be ours. This building should be ours."

"Our own or your own, Zanya?" Kago said.

Betabwi said, "That one is true, Kago. For us or for you, Zanya?"

"Ours," Zanya said, looking from face to face.

He waited in anguish for their response, sitting in the silence of their distrust. He let his gaze slide from their hard faces down to his hands.

"What do you think, Betabwi?" Kago said, and it seemed he might be willing to listen.

"No," Betabwi said. "Make we no believe am."

๛

Jecinda was kneeling on the ground, rifling through a box of medication, when Katherine opened the medicine supply closet.

"Jecinda? What are you doing here?"

She looked up, guilty. "Ma?"

"I thought you were out back, doing the washing," Katherine said. "How'd you get in? Who gave you a key?"

Jecinda shoved the box back on the lower shelf and shot up, wiping dust from her knees. She was tall and curvy like her sister Jummai, except her stance and large eyes exuded a youthful innocence and not the wearied, blank looks Jummai gave.

Slipping a stray braid behind her ear, Jecinda said, "I came to look for medicine. My head was paining me." She seemed anxious to leave and looked past Katherine to the open door.

"Just a minute." Katherine pulled out the container Jecinda had pushed on the lower shelf. "This is not the medicine to take for a headache," she said, turning the bottle over. "Just read the label. Says here that it's for diarrhea, constipation. Stomach problems. See?"

Jecinda did not catch her eye. "Yes, Mrs. Katherine. I can read them."

Katherine rummaged through another box on a higher shelf, next to where they stored prenatal vitamins and powdered milk for breastfeeding mothers. She produced a bottle of aspirin. She twisted the top and plunked two pills into Jecinda's hand. "Take two with water."

"Thank you, Mrs. Katherine," Jecinda said, hurrying past her.

Katherine turned and called, "Jecinda—"

"Yes?"

Katherine was sure the girl had flinched at the sound of her name. "The key."

"Oh, yes. Sorry." Jecinda fished it out of her pocket.

"How bad is your headache? Do you need to go home for the rest of the day?"

"No, I am fine, thank you, ma," Jecinda said, and rushed out.

Katherine inspected the closet. Jecinda's hands had moved toward the pocket of her uniform before she leapt up from the floor. Was she pilfering medication? What would Jecinda do with it? Sell it on the black market and turn a handsome profit? Quiet, good-natured Jecinda? This sort of thing had never happened under Nelson's direction and charge. Nonclinical staff did not have access to this storage room. She would report this to Tebeya as evidence of her poor leadership. Make her feel as little as she had made Katherine feel the other day.

Katherine counted the medications in the box she'd seen Jecinda searching through and felt no relief when all were accounted for.

❧

"Dr. Tebeya," Vincent said, stepping in front of the next patient in the queue.

"What is it?"

She had been about to attend to a child suffering from dehydration with unexplained lesions on his upper arm. The queue of patients curved out of the ward and into the corridor. For some reason, the illnesses appeared vastly more complicated and urgent today than they had yesterday. It could be her exhaustion from sleeping on a cot in the office last night after dropping Comfort at her parents' home or the fact that they were short-staffed at the moment, each provider running on little energy.

"I saw Dr. Landry," Vincent said, leaning over the table that separated her from the patients and blocking the little boy from her view.

"See me working, and you want to come and disturb me."

Of course Vincent had seen Nelson Landry. A person could be miles away from Nelson and see his towering figure, especially since he was still wandering around Rabata, ostensibly saying his goodbyes. From what she had heard, he had a month or so before his flight back to America. She did not know why he had not left immediately. Perhaps, he had logistical issues to resolve about where he would live or where he would work when he returned to Illinois. She suspected that he planned to contest her allegations.

"Likita, I saw him today—"

"Why are you telling me? Are you not seeing this queue?" She beckoned a gloved hand to the patient, and he came close to her, twisting his body to show her the affected arm. She'd ask his father when the wounds had appeared and where the child had been playing.

"He came to the clinic," Vincent said, his face worried and frustrated, as if she was not taking him seriously enough, "walking around this afternoon."

"Is that all?"

"We must do something. Must we not?"

She adopted a more pleasant, understanding tone. After all, it was kind of him to be so concerned. "Dr. Landry is not supposed to come inside this clinic, you understand? So next time you see him, please, Vincent, tell him he should go, or come and tell me. I will take care of it."

"You should be careful, Dr. Tebeya," Vincent said. "I don't think he's happy with what you did to him."

※

Dr. Tebeya sacked the big, white doctor. This remained the talk around town, and it would be like this until Goliath departed for America. For a time, Mama Bintu had worried that a surreptitious romance was developing between Nelson Landry and her daughter with how closely they worked together in the clinic, all these shifts throughout the day and night. She had dreaded this possibility and worked herself into an unnecessary, all-consuming panic, considering how she would explain to her relatives about her daughter's fondness for the husky white man. She had asked Tebeya about his marital status and was reassured to learn he had a wife in America. She became dubious about the authenticity of his marriage when the woman never materialized in Rabata.

However, no romance existed. Tebeya had fired him, and the locals said it was the Lord's doing. See how the missionaries did not give Zanya the position due him? The hard rains they were enduring damaged the church. The locals said that God was rewarding them for their righteousness and humility, for accepting the missionaries, regardless of their maltreatment of Zanya. Foolish people with their parochial views, behaving as if they did not want the missionaries' presence and the progress they had brought to their town. The laborers had gone on strike when small wages were better than no wages. This would never have happened in her ancestral village of Yeruwa. People had respected the missionaries there. They had had their small problems, but it was nothing compared to how these ungrateful laborers behaved, complaining about the people who had given them money to have food and to send their children to school. And now, Jim Clemens had retaliated. The mission had fired Zanya.

She knew nothing about Zanya's family background. Despite these years of him living in Rabata, she had scant details about his upbringing. He seemed a thoughtful young man who preferred books to physical labor and construction. But he had been given a particular lot in life and was intelligent enough to let skill suppress desire, and it had fostered camaraderie with the laborers building the church, who were coarse and shabbily dressed men.

What a useless man, that Nelson Landry. Was he not at fault? She had not forgotten his arrogant dismissal of her request. She felt justified and hoped, with some conceit, that he might reflect on the afternoon she had warned him about her daughter's tenacity.

"Your daughter," she said, when she found her husband in the parlor. "You heard, ba?"

"Clinic director now," Baba Bintu said. "It will be good for her."

Mama Bintu removed her head tie to rearrange the wisps of hair sticking to the perspiration on her forehead. Fans rotated at high speed in the parlor.

Her husband straightened his newspaper. "She was right to sack the man. If any employee of mine were doing what this man did, it would be the same consequence—"

"She wants attention. That is all."

"We should support our daughter." Baba Bintu flipped back his newspaper and looked up. "We should send money to the clinic as we were doing before."

"No," Mama Bintu said. She had long learned that withholding money was how one could make people see your perspective and change their minds. "We decided against it."

"You, my dear, decided against it." Baba Bintu chuckled. "If I want peace in this house, what choice do I have? Tebeya will not leave that clinic regardless of whether we fund it or not. Why should we not support this daughter of ours?"

"Just wait. She'll come to her senses about the clinic and that child she went and found from the bush and brought to our house."

Imagine someone as attractive as her daughter choosing not to procreate. What a selfish act, withholding beauty instead of imparting it to a child. Mama Bintu told people Comfort was the daughter of a distant relative. They were not the kind of people to go and be bringing other people's children into their home without them intending to serve. Let other people do this kind of thing. One night, she had a frightening dream of the locals surrounding their gates, bursting through the chains, bringing deformed and helpless children into their home, crushing her expensive cushions and carpet, beseeching Tebeya to come and help them.

Mama Bintu had tolerated the girl when Tebeya first brought her to the house, asserting that no other relative had come forward willing to take care of her. "Mama, please let her stay until her relatives come for her," she had said. It showed Tebeya's desperation for a family, settling for a child belonging to someone else. She remembered the girl on her first night in the house, quiet and timorous, taking in the breadth and scope of the corridors and rooms and the house servants bustling through. And famished, too! The girl had shoveled jollof rice and fried croaker into her mouth as if hoarding it for a time of famine.

Both daughters were having trouble in their lives—Tebeya was inviting the trouble and Bintu misconstruing trouble where there was none. Bintu had called two days ago, babbling about leaving Thomas over the conflict with the governor and the damage to their reputation. Bintu liked to threaten. It gave her a sense of control.

"I have asked him to take care of this problem," Bintu shared.

"What is your problem? Why must you tell him what to do?"

"Am I not his wife?"

Mama Bintu laughed. "My daughter, you are creating problems. Do you not have food? Do you not have a house to live in? Ehen. It is a stubborn fly that gets trapped in the grave with a corpse. You should listen to your mother and leave this alone, Bintu."

The only thing bringing happiness to Mama Bintu was that her son Patrick had announced he was marrying and would have a wedding in Rabata. It did not please her that he had found an American woman. Nor did it please her that the American woman desired to marry next June, when the dry, sunnier climates of November or December were preferable. Despite all this, it pleased her that Patrick had the wisdom to bring this woman home for a true and proper wedding, one to be the talk of Rabata.

Mama Bintu relaxed next to her husband. Yes, this was what she would think about, not her daughters and the disappointments they had been to her.

CHAPTER THIRTY-THREE

TEBEYA RECHECKED THE MEDICAL SUPPLIES she had placed in boxes in the parlor of her new bungalow. The bungalow was an off-white color, and a side path led to a small walled yard with enough room for a couple of chairs. She had parked her borrowed car in front. Her father had loaned her one of his older models until she purchased her own.

This Saturday morning, she and Comfort were traveling to villages to the east. She feared working in the village without the appropriate equipment or medication to address the range of illnesses they encountered. Last Saturday, they had hooked a needle to an anemic child and hung the intravenous bag on the branches of a lemon tree. Another time, she had taken a few staff members with her to help slow an outbreak of cerebral meningitis in a nearby village, and they had needed to request the villagers' assistance to manage the number of cases.

She brought Comfort with her on these trips because she wanted to instill in her a love for medicine, and she did not want Comfort to associate the mission clinic with her grandmother's death. Comfort played with the children who waited for a sick parent's diagnosis, and she performed simple procedures. Tebeya had trained her to wear gloves and clean an abrasion with antiseptic or rub ointment on a skinned knee. Comfort's face turned serious when she had to soothe a child after Tebeya administered an injection.

"See you standing there," Tebeya called to Comfort. "Oya, come and finish helping."

"What of this one?" Comfort said, hefting a pack of large bandages from the cushion. "Should I put it in the box?"

"Yes, and don't forget that other pack, there," Tebeya pointed, "on the floor." She returned to counting the vaccines under her breath.

"Aunty Tebeya, is there enough? For everybody, even the small children like me?"

Tebeya lost track of her count. "Why are you bothering me with these questions?"

"You said to Uncle Benedict that the clinic doesn't have enough."

"We have enough—what do you mean? It's enough." Tebeya closed the flaps on a box. She had to remember to be careful with her words around Comfort. Children were like this. They listened and repeated what you had said to others, even when you thought they were not paying attention. "See how much we're taking with us? Now, go and wear your shoes."

She loaded the remaining boxes into the car with Comfort's help, and they started the drive. Less than a month since Nelson's termination, and a couple of donors had suspended their contributions, and another reduced their pledge, as if testing Tebeya's capabilities before reinvesting funds. She assumed the donors were Nelson's friends or former colleagues. She imagined him on a telephone or writing letters to America, telling these people she was unqualified to manage the clinic, telling his former wife, Virginia, about a belligerent Nigerian woman who had destroyed his life's work in West Africa. Edward Hayes had radioed and informed her that Nelson had indeed traveled to headquarters and contested his termination. Edward said not to worry, the evidence against Nelson was insurmountable.

This past week, their patient census was at the lowest it had ever been in the clinic's history, and it had to do with their tarnished reputation. It was more important now than it had been before to restore the locals' trust in the clinic. Patients had started resorting to traditional medicine after rumors abounded about the possibility of harm and death at the hands of the drunken white doctor. "Isn't it true what our ancestors believed?" one patient had said to Tebeya. "A white man is worse than a witch."

The clinic appeared to be falling into disrepair with the minor issues cropping up. Rainy gusts of wind blew through a cracked window in a unit of the clinic, and water lay like a thin film on a broken operating table. The lighting was insufficient. An essential machine to monitor a patient's heart rate sat nonfunctional and unused in the storage room. The walls needed repainting. Old, badly discolored cots were rolled into a corner. Outside, the generator shuddered and clanked. It had failed to work on a couple of occasions. Tebeya had called Gary Parson to repair it; he had come and tried and after several attempts told her it needed to be replaced. These issues must have been there even with Nelson, but the weight of this new responsibility had opened her eyes, made her more aware of duties she may have shunted to Nelson in the past. She must show the clinic could survive—this would be the best retribution.

She had worried a little after Vincent told her he saw Nelson loitering around the clinic, and she thought briefly about requesting one of the guards from her parents' mansion. She had asked Vincent to tell her if Nelson returned, but Nelson had not been anywhere near the clinic again.

"Comfort," Tebeya said, beginning their question-and-answer game as she signaled to turn on the main road, "what does the pancreas do?"

Comfort smiled, confident. "It helps with food and digestion."

"What else does it do?"

"It gives insulin to the body," she said.

"Okay. What is insulin?"

"Insulin," Comfort repeated, counting the syllables on her fingers. "It helps your body to chop the sugar—"

"No, not chop. What word did I teach you? What is the correct word?"

"I don't know."

"You cannot say you don't know when you have not tried."

Comfort scrunched her face, thinking. "Absorb sugar?"

"Correct," Tebeya said approvingly. "Now, tell me, what does your liver do?"

Comfort stretched her legs out in the front seat and fiddled with the window crank. "Aunty, did you take me from my village?"

"What are you saying? Do you not know what the liver does?"

"My schoolmate. She said you stole me from my village."

Tebeya clasped the steering wheel, and the skin around her knuckles tightened. Bintu had come to see her new home a couple of weekends ago. She had praised Comfort's manners and sense of responsibility.

"You took a bush girl and turned her into something," Bintu said, as a compliment.

Tebeya bristled at the notion of having *taken* Comfort as equally as she did with Bintu labeling Comfort a bush girl.

"Comfort, I did not *take* you," Tebeya said.

This must be what people were thinking. She was going around taking the clinic from Nelson, and she had also taken Comfort from her village.

"If someone goes and takes something, do you know it implies that someone stole what did not belong to them? Is that what you think? I went and stole you?"

"No, ma."

"I decided to *bring* you into this family—"

"Why did you bring me?"

"Because your relatives could not care for you. How many

times do I have to—have we not discussed this before?"

In a matter of weeks, Comfort was of sturdy build, her clavicle no longer bulging under a thin covering of skin. She had a bedroom to herself in their new flat. She attended the mission primary school, besting the students in her classes. She did not worry about meals or clothes. Yet, she wanted to know if she had been snatched from her family without reason.

"This girl is not your friend if she would say this to you. Do you understand?"

"Yes, ma," Comfort said, pushing her finger against the window. "Not even one of my relatives would take care of me?"

"*Could* care for you," Tebeya said, knowing she was giving the child an earful. "Your uncle told me this when I went to your village. You were there, na."

"Are we going to go to my village again?" Comfort said. She turned toward Tebeya with an attentive, excited look. "So I can see my uncle? Like we go to these other villages."

She had not returned to the village with Comfort since that bright weekday afternoon when she made the arrangements. She feared a relative who had not come forward before would decide Comfort should return to their family.

"Yes, we can go," Tebeya said. "We will go."

CHAPTER THIRTY-FOUR

"I don't want to marry you," Jummai said.

She could see Zanya thought this is what she should have wanted. She could see from his expression that he believed it the honorable thing to do. He had come to tell her he had ended his relationship with Nami so that he could marry Jummai, and she was here telling him that she did not want to marry him.

"You're not serious."

"Did I tell you to go and end things with Nami?"

He was angry now. "If you're pregnant with my child—"

"I am pregnant—" It was not *if.*

"Then why do you not want to marry? What is this foolishness, Jummai?"

He must not be sure what to feel—his pride must have been suffering, but she was certain he felt relieved. She watched as he moved toward the most intact wall, leaning with one shoulder against it. She wanted to jump inside his body and see how he might be seeing and receiving her. Behind the crossed arms, did his heart beat more rapidly? Was anger about to come?

The building they occupied was one that people passed without paying any attention to it. Dirt, rusted tools, and torn pages of paper littered the concrete floors. A section of the roof had caved, and someone had swept the broken boards and shingles into a corner. He had not wanted them to meet at his flat, and this morning he had come to the mission compound and asked her to meet him at this vacant building, at this time of night, so that they could discuss their situation.

Their situation.

He did not know that she had stopped thinking of it as *theirs.* The medicine Jecinda had taken from the clinic had not worked, and though she was a little afraid, she was planning to go and see the diviner. When Zanya had come to the mission compound this morning while the Americans were at Sunday service and said *their situation*, it had made her wonder why she should suffer this alone. For the rest of the afternoon, she had thought about how she would ask him for money to go to the diviner or she would lie and say she wanted to raise the child by herself. Then he had come here to this abandoned building, where there was no board or plac-ard to signify that it had once been a thriving shop or someone's house, to tell her that the best thing they could do in this situation was to marry.

"Zanya, if we marry, what would we do? Just sit there and be looking at each other? Is that it?" Her father drank after he married her mother, and he had *wanted* to marry her mother. Imagine what would happen if she married Zanya. If she married a man that did not want to marry her, even if he was here saying that he would do it because it was the right thing for him to do. What kind of life would that be? Days ago, it might have been what she wanted to hear from him, but now that she had her plans, she could not imagine them changing.

"This is foolish, Jummai. How many women in your situation would do what you're doing when a man is saying he will marry them?"

"I don't have to tell anybody about the child," she said.

"What?"

"Nobody has to know it was you—"

"And when the child comes, nko?" Zanya said. "And is there

looking like me?"

"The same. I can say it was someone else. I can take care of the child by myself."

"So that the child won't know his own father?"

She looked at him. Was he playing with her? Sounding as if he wanted to have this child. She remembered how he had looked at her that day when she went to tell him, when he said, "You are not the woman I want, do you understand?" His voice had been very sharp, so that for a moment it had sounded like someone other than Zanya was talking to her. Yet, he was here, sounding as if he wanted her to have the child, and she did not know why. She would play along and pretend she would have this child and take care of it, if it meant he would be willing to give her the money she needed.

"If the child comes," she said, "I can say someone else is the father. Or you can come and see him, but you won't have to care for him. You can go and marry someone else."

"Jummai, this is not—"

"It is what you want, Zanya."

He was thinking about this. She could see the way his mind was working. How he was thinking that if she did not say anything, if she took care of the child herself, he could go and be free of her. He could go and beg Nami to come back to him.

"What of you? What do you want, Jummai? This will cost me, so what is it?"

She wanted to lease the place she had seen and have a restaurant in Rabata. She would even cook American dishes for some of the white people, like mashed potatoes and roast beef. Food she had learned to make from working at the Parsons'. If she did this, then foreigners at the mission guesthouse that was going to be built the following year would come to her restaurant. Mr. Gary had said missionaries from various regions in Nigeria would come and stay at this guesthouse. It would have badminton courts and a swimming pool. She had also overheard Mrs. Katherine and Mr. Gary talking about British and Dutch administrators and new Peace Corps volunteers from America living in Rabata. She did not know what it meant, but it sounded like people who would like American food.

"There is a place I found, to open a restaurant," she said. "I will need money."

He rubbed the scar above his left brow. It was like a jagged line dividing a kola nut. She had traced his scar once, and the clean lines of his face, how smooth and unmarred it was.

"Money? How much money, Jummai? If we marry, you will have my money."

"That is not true, Zanya."

"You didn't hear that the mission fired me? Now, you're asking me for money—"

"I know you are not working for the mission. People know."

He lifted his right foot, as if he had stepped into dog shit and wanted to see what had been dragged at the bottom of his shoe. He set it back down again. There was nothing he would have been able to see in the darkness.

"So," he said, "you know, and you're still here asking me for money?"

He appeared determined to withhold any anger toward her, though his resentment was revealed in the rigidity of his body. She had become a vindictive and calculating woman to him. She was not such things. She had simply come and accepted the situation. She loved Zanya, and he did not love her. To see it any other way would be to complicate matters that needed no complication. She could determine to accept a circumstance, and once she did, complicated matters became simpler. If more people lived by this kind of thinking, then more people would find peace in their lives. Zanya had wanted her, but he had not loved her. He had not loved her the way that a man was supposed to love a woman, and she was not going to hold his inability to love her against him.

"You want it for something else," he said, looking at her as if he knew.

She looked away. "No. I've told you."

"Okay then. What are you going to call this-your restaurant?"

She allowed a small smile. "Jummai's Rice and Roast."

She imagined one day a wooden sign would display the name of her restaurant. It would have a bar area and ten round tables outside and inside with green plastic chairs of differing shapes and sizes. There would be a grill like Shigudu's, and there would be girls roasting the meat and cooking soup according to her instructions.

Zanya sidestepped a pile of broken concrete to move closer to her.

"Are you serious?" he said.

She looked at him a long time. "You can be free of me, Zanya."

"What if I don't give you this money?"

"I see Reverend Jim on the mission compound. There are things I can tell him."

He stared at her, then laughed. "When they've gotten rid of me? What does it matter?"

"What will people start saying about you when they learn what you did to me?" She saw his alarm. She knew he cared about his name and reputation in Rabata. Whether or not he had been fired from the mission, the locals still thought of him as the miracle man. People were blaming the Reverend for his firing. If they knew about this pregnancy, they would say Reverend Jim was in the right.

"Jummai—"

"What are you going to do, Zanya?"

"Let me think," he said. "Before you do anything, let me think."

She nodded, aware of what she would do. She would not wait for him to think. She would do what she needed to do. Gone was the Zanya others saw—this thoughtful, brave, unintimidated man who enchanted people with his preaching. He was not any of those things here. He was the man others did not see, vulnerable and slightly hesitant in his reflections, regretting his decisions.

Jummai felt the pregnancy was Zanya's way of punishing her for being a different woman than one he could have loved. Before he was the miracle man, she had known him and loved him when he was an ordinary man. She could not lie and say his escape from fire had not made her hope. His escape had made her think he would carry her with him and help her escape from her mother's house. Some days, she felt like Zanya must have felt on that fateful night—burning and burning, waiting for a miracle to happen.

CHAPTER THIRTY-FIVE

GIRLS LOUNGED ON THE VERANDA of Miss Delores's house, braiding their hair or working on sums and thumbing through the pages of books when Jummai arrived. Four occupied a table in the parlor, counting on their fingers and asking each other questions about the figures on the papers in front of them. A few years ago, Jummai would have known the girls, their families, and where they lived. With how Rabata was growing, she recognized people less and less.

"Would you like some biscuits?" Miss Delores asked.

"I've eaten," Jummai said, sinking down on the cushion in the parlor.

"There's always room for cookies," Miss Delores said cheerily, as if Jummai was the same age as the small girls.

She returned from her bedroom with a blue tin that held British biscuits, which they sold at Glories and Blessings. She offered them to Jummai before giving a couple to the girls at the table.

Miss Delores asked Jummai to read out loud from a book she described as her "all-time childhood favorite." Miss Delores explained that the children's story was about Stuart, a mouse born to human parents. Jummai thought it strange that the white people had not killed the rat-child. Imagine. The rat-child was allowed to go off having adventures. Despite the strangeness of the story, she could not concentrate with all that occupied her mind.

"Jummai, are you all right?"

"I'm fine, ma."

"I don't think you are." Miss Delores turned to the students doing their schoolwork at the table. "Girls, why don't you go outside? Give Jummai and I a moment alone?"

Jummai looked at Miss Delores, and for a reason she later understood to be loneliness, decided to share. She thought it was because she had gone and told Zanya about her plans for a restaurant, and his desire to marry her and be a father to the child had been unexpected, or because Jecinda's medicine from the clinic had sent her to the toilet but had not removed the child, or because she was tired of wondering and fearing, and she thought this white woman might offer another remedy, so she went ahead and told her about the pregnancy.

"Oh, Jummai," Miss Delores said. "I—I just don't know what to say."

"Mai Mulo, I don't want this child."

She was going to cry. She was going to cry in front of this woman.

"Of course, you don't want a kid right now. Not in these circumstances, when you weren't expecting it." Miss Delores rummaged through the drawer next to her side of the cushion. "Here, take this. Wipe those tears."

Jummai grasped the purple cloth, bordered with flowers and fruit, and held it in her hands, forcing the tears to remain in her lids and not fall.

"I'll help you take care of your child, all right?"

"No," Jummai said, patting her cheeks dry. Imagine, these tears coming like water in front of this woman. "My mother has enough children. I don't want to come and add another one to that small house. Where will the child sleep? What will the child eat? Me and Jecinda, we are the ones doing everything. It is too much."

"What about the father? Where is he?"

Jummai caressed the pages of the book, holding the tear-splotched handkerchief. "What of him, ma?"

"Oh, Jummai," Miss Delores sighed. Her skirt, bright as an orange, was like a big, flimsy sheet you threw on a mattress. "Do you mind my asking who the father is?"

"I mind," Jummai said. "I mind you asking."

"Whoever it is, he's got quite a big responsibility, you know. Even if he doesn't marry you, he should be invested in the child's welfare. Tell me, and I'll have a word with him."

How ridiculous Americans sounded sometimes, as if one person could make another do what she wanted by demanding to talk. She could say something to Miss Delores right now. She could tell her the truth about Zanya, mention his name, this man who had been persecuted for his beliefs but who had also impregnated her. He preached at the pulpit and came to her at night. But she knew Zanya would give her the money she had asked him for, and by the time he learned there was no longer a child, it would be too late.

It was raining again, and the rain made a comforting sound against the windows.

"I cannot tell you," she said. "I cannot tell you his name."

Miss Delores spoke. "Jummai, listen to me, okay? It's all right to have this baby. It shouldn't matter what the father wants you to do."

"Mai Mulo, you don't know how things are in Rabata. It is not like in America."

"You don't strike me as the kind of woman who cares what people say."

"Sometimes," Jummai said, "I get tired."

"Have the baby and live here. I've got an extra room, you know."

Miss Delores looked around her house excited at the possibility. Jummai looked too, at the ugly, flower-patterned curtains with the long, dangling gold strings, how it hung over the doorframe to where Miss Delores slept. The house had a small parlor with two cushions. A short corridor to the left of the front entrance led to a latrine and farther back, an indoor kitchen with a kerosene stove. Near a guitar on her parlor wall, Miss Delores had taped photos of her family, and the adhesive had blistered and flaked. A couple of chairs faced the back wall instead of the open space; books and record covers were spread along the floor. She also had a shelf of books adjacent to the curtains; the books had titles like *The Gleaner, Gift from the Sea, The Pilgrim's Progress, The Woman's Bible,* and *The Christ of the Indian Road.* Miss Delores said this was only a quarter of the book collection she had when she lived in Pennsylvania. She had given them away and sold them before she came to Nigeria.

"It's modest, the room, but it would be good enough for you and the child. I'd buy a mattress for you tomorrow if you say you'll stay. The two of us, well, three of us eventually, could live here together until you figured things out—"

"No, ma," Jummai said.

"No?"

"No."

Miss Delores held her reading glasses against her mouth, and the curved tip of the temple split her upper lip. She did not wear lipstick like Mrs. Katherine, so her lips were thin, and if she pressed them inward when thinking, they disappeared, reappearing when she wanted to speak. "Jummai, don't do anything out of fear, all right?"

"I'm going to see the diviner," Jummai said. She had not said it aloud, and it seemed the type of thing she needed to say in case it sounded different to her ears than it had in her head. Most people knew where the diviner lived, even the ones who converted to Christianity, including those who said they had rejected traditional beliefs. Jummai's mother went to the mission church, and still, she had placed their family's god in an old, rusted pot behind their compound and had visited the diviner about Tin City's whereabouts one time. Other girls who had gotten themselves into trouble by lovers or relatives had gone to the diviner.

"What? What do you mean you're going?"

"She will know what to do—"

"Oh, Jummai," Miss Delores said, reaching for Jummai's hand, as if to ease her own fears. "You could hurt yourself going over there. Listen, God says he has set before you life and death, okay? He says choose life so that you and your children may live. Shall I read it for you? It's there, Jummai, in Deuteronomy."

"I am going, Mai Mulo."

After a long silence, Miss Delores said, "Toh, shi kenan." *That is it.*

Jummai, in surprise, repeated, "Shi kenan."

"All right. Well, let's go ahead and finish reading. Where were we?"

"I said I'm going to the diviner—"

"I know, Jummai. I've heard you."

"You won't make me pray?"

Miss Delores sighed again and removed her reading glasses. "Jummai," she said, rubbing the sides of her nose, where her glasses left red marks. "You know I don't agree. I'm happy to pray if that's what you want, but I don't think it is what you want, dear. I think you've made up your mind, and I can't take that choice away from you, even if I don't support it." Miss Delores lifted the handkerchief and pointed to the top of the page. "Now that you've decided what you'll do," she said, "abeg, let's finish this sentence."

Jummai read on, relieved.

❧

Later that night, Jummai walked to the diviner's house. She was used to walking at this time of night, whether moon shone or moon was little. She had with her a small amount of the money she had earned from the Parsons. It was enough, she thought, for the diviner to rid her of this pain in her body.

She stopped walking to remove a pebble that had tumbled into her sandals. Stopping allowed the elephant-sized fear she had pushed down to jump into her mind. A paraffin lamp lit the diviner's home as Jummai walked toward the door. Unlike Miss Delores, the diviner would ask no questions about the greater circumstances surrounding her situation; the woman would simply cleanse her of this pregnancy that had come disguised as heartache.

Zanya peeled off his shirt inside his room, arranged it on top of the singular shelf nailed to the wall, and unlocked his window. He looked out at the specks of light on the roads below—the strolling and chatting people who in this part of town nursed desires thick as sugarcane, and nevertheless accepted their lack, allowed the unfulfillment to live with them, like a never-properly functioning limb. A trio of boys listened to a portable radio at full volume, sitting outside a nearby food stand, shouting in jest to one another. One woman washed clothes near the side of the building, turning the tap on to fill the bucket, and another rinsed a bowl, cursing when the dish slipped from her hands. Advertisements posted on the outside walls of his complex had fallen off and been trampled on the ground.

At times like this, he felt like a visitor passing through Rabata, and it seemed that the locals would have gone on with their lives whether he had come from Yawari or not. He was here simply watching how they lived, breathed, and existed in a world where cattle trampled islands of grass, women bartered for cassava and sugarcane, farmers hewed guinea cornstalks, and motorbikes wove between lorries on roads that dissolved unexpectedly into the rust-colored trails so characteristic of Rabata.

He sat in his chair, eating dry garri with a teaspoon of sugar and groundnuts. Two weeks ago, his life had been different. Two weeks ago, Nami had waited in this chair for him to dispense good news about the conference instead of the news he delivered.

She had stopped speaking to him. He no longer had use of the pickup, and so he had walked to the primary school several times and waited. Nami would walk out, see him, and walk into the headmistress's office or in the opposite direction.

He hated her obstinacy, how she could decide so easily what she wanted or did not want without going back on her decision. He deserved many things for how he had lied to her. He deserved erasure from her memory. He deserved her contempt. He had never yearned for a person, and it crystallized within him, this mystifying feeling to which he was unaccustomed. He had learned to yearn for meals, to yearn for his lectures in school, to yearn for work and opportunity. But he had learned over time not to yearn for people, for the disappointment and fickleness of them, for their disloyalty, or their inability to offer understanding when you most desired it. Yet, he yearned for Nami.

What an idiot he had been to tell her before he had settled matters with Jummai. Before he had known that she did not want to marry him. They would have kept things quiet and not told anybody, and he would have been able to see his son (he imagined it was a boy) in Rabata, take care of him, give him what his surrogate father had not given him, and still have his life with Nami. That is what he should have agreed to with Jummai. His panic had made him move too quickly. He had not wanted to deny it, to add another lie, another burden of guilt to the ones he carried.

He put the empty bowl back on the shelf. Since his talk with Betabwi and Kago, he had also thought he should go to Jim Clemens and beg for his position back. He could say he was willing to do any work the mission found for him. He would not speak to Jim Clemens about what the locals needed from the church. Things the Reverend refused to see. No, he could not stay in Rabata if Reverend Jim maintained power over the mission station. The pain was still there in the center of his chest, the shame of being spoken to as an inferior. These missionaries were the same, displaying compassion when they hid cunning and apathetic sides. Blowing fan and smoke. They came to tell the locals what was wrong with their conduct, what was wrong with their town, what was wrong with their medicine and spirituality, but if you sought to suggest that they too might have failings, things they ought to confess, they reminded you of your place.

He had failed the test from Jim Clemens to bring the men back and failed the men in raising their wages. Imagine if somewhere in his village, his mother learned the church her son had sought to build would be incomplete. She would say in a steely voice: *Why did a devil's child believe he could touch a holy place?*

He should leave Rabata. He should listen to the same stirring impulse he felt on the day he woke and left Yawari and his father and his father's buildings. He could go to his sister's village and live with her and Shagye. He could aid Shagye in caring for Pema and his nephews. He had not seen her since Resurrection Sunday. He could go to Kaduna and see if Bashiru might have work for him to do in his company. His life would be nomadic like this, never staying long in one place. He threw his shirt back on and walked outside. The din of canteens and businesses rang in his ears, and the smells of firewood and exhaust choked the air as he crossed the street and walked the roads he had come to know so well.

CHAPTER THIRTY-SIX

JUMMAI HELD TIGHTLY to the side of the passenger seat as Gary Parson drove over another bump in the road. She pressed her legs together, feeling the insistent wetness she had come to expect since the night at the diviner's. She remembered the warm ground in the woman's house, and the sharp pain of the long needle, like the spoke on a bicycle wheel. She remembered the medicine the diviner gave her afterwards. She had walked home alone that night, breathing like an infant taking its first breaths, and the wetness had begun immediately, trickling down her thighs. She had been afraid and wanted to walk to Zanya's pickup at the church construction site and tell him what she had done. But he was not there any longer. There was nothing to guard.

The blood had kept coming and coming since that night, and all the cloth and rags she used had not stopped it from coming. This afternoon, Mrs. Katherine had allowed her to go home early because she had struggled to cook. She had dropped a bucket of water and broke three of the plates and tumblers. Mr. Gary was driving in the same direction to Mama Agatha's house and offered to take her home.

"It was great, really," Mr. Gary was saying. He used both hands to steady the steering wheel. She remembered how Zanya used to hold the steering wheel of his pickup as if they were coasting on a palm tree leaf. His right hand would grasp the bottom of the steering wheel. Not even one full hand, just four arrogant fingers guiding the pickup.

"Yes?" Jummai said.

She had forgotten what he was talking to her about just now. Somewhere he had wanted to take Mrs. Katherine and the children. She winced at the sharp pain in her stomach and looked toward the window, away from Mr. Gary so he would not see her face.

"You all right, Jummai?"

"I'm fine. Thank you, sir."

"You sure?" He slowed down the car. "We can pop into the clinic and see if Dr. Awyebwi could have a look at you."

"I will rest, then I will be fine—"

"Well, okay. If you're okay, then I'll quit pestering you."

"Thank you, Mai Hankali."

"Right, so I was telling you about Yankari, how we went there the first year we came to Nigeria. Me, Katherine, and the kids."

Yes, she would listen to this story so that she did not think about the pain. He told her how baboons had roamed the grounds of the park along with tourists. The more reserved squatted on stumps with their babies attached to their backs, while the audacious ones approached people or stole into their chalets if they left the doors open. "The springs were an aquamarine color," he said, "flowing from a crevice into a large open pool." She imagined the water though she could not understand what "aquamarine" would look like. She pictured falling into the water in Yankari. The blood coming down her legs now would seep into the water and change its color. Was there not a story Reverend Jim had told in the church one Sunday about how water had turned to blood in the Bible, and the fish died and the frogs jumped out of the river, and blood was everywhere, even in their cooking pots, and no one could drink any water?

"You ever been?" Mr. Gary said. "To Yankari?"

"No, sir."

"You should go one day," he said. "Your mother, your family. I think they'd enjoy it. We could arrange for it to happen. Just say the word."

Jummai imagined riding the four hours to Yankari with her mother and Tin City. The fighting that would ensue, which was often the case whenever Tin City returned from the mines, and they had to become accustomed to living in a confined space. He would be squeezed in next to her mother, short-tempered and hankering for a cigarette or tobacco. Jecinda would be angry that she did not have time to finish her schoolwork. Yakwo would be bickering with Innocent and Sayi. Walu, who currently believed every enclosed space a trap from which he should escape, would be squirming on her lap, scratching in desperation at Jummai's face and hair.

"Yes, thank you, Mr. Gary," Jummai said. "One day we will go."

"I told Katherine we ought to go again," he said. "But she's not having it." By now, he had driven past her neighbors' houses to her family's compound. "Anyway, Jummai, you take care, now. Don't hesitate to let us know if you need anything. All right?"

She inspected the seat once she stepped out of the car. There was nothing there. No blood. No stain. She thanked Mr. Gary again, and she walked as straight as she could because she knew he might be watching her to see if she was feeling sick. When he pressed the horn two times and drove off, her limbs and legs weakened in relief. She should go back to the diviner and tell her something was wrong. But she did not know if it was true. What if what she felt was wrong was actually how it was supposed to be happening? Maybe she needed to feel this pain, and it was how she knew that the diviner had done what she was supposed to do.

Tin City was standing in the room Jummai shared with her siblings. He no longer needed his crutch, and his feet were planted on the mat where she slept.

His smile was crooked, threatening. "Did I not tell you?"

"Tell me?"

"What I say I will do, I do."

It was how he said it—the deliberate, cunning way he turned and glared at her—that made Jummai look around the room with dread pulling at her body. She saw that behind him, the trunk the Parsons had given her was broken open, the few items she owned thrown like rubbish.

"Where is the money?" Her voice was hoarse.

"Ah, so you have more money than you've been telling us?"

"Where is it?" she said, a little louder.

She had forgotten to take it to the Parsons' house as she had intended. With everything else, she had not taken the bag and put it in the drawer they never used, the one in Allison's bedroom. The wetness had started again, and she felt it trickling down her thighs.

Tin City jangled the bag of pounds. "Ashawo! Is that how you earned this money?"

"Please—"

"Imagine when I learnt that all this time you were lying to us. Make you no come rob me for this house."

"I didn't lie—"

"This money na my own—" He spat tobacco through his two front teeth. "Don't you know that I own you? Don't you know I own your mother? So I own this money."

He was not too far from her. If she tried, if she found all of her strength, she could seize the bag of money out of his hands. It was all that she had worked for and saved. She lunged for it, and Tin City swung it high above his head and leapt back. Jummai stumbled over the mat that separated them, and it caught and twisted around her ankle, spiraling her out of balance so that she landed hard on the ground.

"Get up!" Tin City said.

Jummai groaned.

"Get up!"

She tried to push herself up from the ground, but her head and arms would not move. The room widened, seemed to grow bigger and bigger. She wanted to ask Tin City to help her stand because she could not move her limbs and her eyes were making things look like dreams. This was when she realized there was nobody in the compound. There was always somebody in the compound, and today, there was nobody.

Tin City's feet loomed above her head, becoming bigger and bigger like the room, coming closer and closer to her face. She gasped. Tried to cry for help. His feet floated away from her face as he stepped over her and walked out of the room.

CHAPTER THIRTY-SEVEN

NELSON LANDRY HAD SLIPPED into the mission clinic undetected so that when Tebeya entered one of the private examination rooms expecting a patient, she found him waiting against the wall, arms folded. Her heart was that of a fowl facing an ax and stump, seeing him in here like this. They had not seen each other since the day Edward Hayes terminated him.

Vincent had reported no signs of Nelson this morning. She had asked him when she found him eating his lunch in their staff room. He had become her unofficial guard, taking a few minutes to secure the perimeter, advising her that it would be wise if they fenced the area around the clinic. It was late afternoon now, and Vincent had long finished his shift. No one else would have been surveying the grounds, looking for Nelson.

She had to show Nelson she was unflustered at his unannounced visit; she would behave as if she were expecting him instead of the patient with obstetric fistula, the one whose urine she could have smelled even with the door closed. Nelson's face was impassive as he glanced around the room, his hand a proprietorial clamp on the examination bed next to him.

"Dr. Landry," she said, tucking a pen in her pocket, as if it were perfectly ordinary to walk in and find him fuming in the room. "How are you doing? Where did my patient go?"

It seemed he had not prepared any statements, and she could

see that the ease with which she greeted him—as if they were speaking under ordinary circumstances—unnerved him.

"I know that this may not be a social call," she continued. "Were you in need of a medical examination? If you are—"

"Drop the act, Dr. Awyebwi." His words were garbled. He had been drinking. Maybe more than usual; she'd never heard his words like this.

She had the sudden sense of being in danger. He was such a big man. Everything in the room—the shelves, tables, chairs—felt miniscule and low with him in it. Long before his termination, Tebeya had once suggested Nelson sit or kneel when speaking with their patients. The dual threat of his height and the redness of his skin intimidated them; instead of sharing their ailments, they clammed up at the important white man with the hair like yellow straw, who lumbered into the examination room and hulked over them. Sitting, she said, allowed patients to see his face level with theirs.

He came toward her in a swift, frightening motion, and she confirmed that he smelled of drink. She steeled herself to remain calm despite his closeness.

"You know you should not be at this mission clinic, Dr. Landry—"

"You should have come to me. Not gone off to headquarters."

"Everything I wrote in my report was accurate."

He sneered. "I never saw your report—"

"Well," she said, speaking slowly. "I told Edward he could show it to you." She took a step backward, and she looked at her feet as if to ensure the tiles had not floated away. She had never seen physical aggression in Nelson, and she did not think of him as a dangerous man. In fact, she had marveled at how gentle he appeared despite his largeness. Still, she knew that anger and drink could drive one to violence. She scanned the room for an instrument she could use, a mislaid injection perhaps. "I don't want you to think I'm ungrateful for what you taught me—"

"That's not going to matter now, is it?"

"I would not say so."

"How many hours did I operate on Moses? Huh? What about Agnes? Hours, hours. What about Shizawu's femur? How many hours?"

"Yes, I remember—it was a very complicated operation."

"Oh ho. You *remember*? I should be so grateful."

"You did good for this town," she said to assuage his anger. Maybe he had on the days he had not been inebriated. Surely, he had done some good in the beginning.

Eyes alert and fixed on her, Nelson said, "More than *good*."

"Yes, yes—"

"What do you know?" he said, inching closer. "Traitor—that's what you know. Your mother wanted me to fire you from the clinic. I protected you despite your mother's request—"

"She what?"

"Why do you think your family stopped donating to the clinic last month?"

"What are you talking about?"

He had slurred his words, but she had grasped most of what he said. Her question sprang from her astonishment. It could not be. He was lying to anger her, to seek revenge.

Nelson smiled. "I see. You didn't know."

"You're telling stories—"

"Check the records then," he said smugly.

"Well," she said, faltering, "you assumed I needed your protection from my own mother."

"My mistake was assuming my loyalty to you would be reciprocated."

"By allowing you to cut into patients drunk? Is that your idea of loyalty, Nelson?"

She had forgotten to be afraid, and she felt anger driving her forward. Anger at her mother. What had she ever done but try to please that woman? Anger with Nelson at his obtuseness and lack of contrition. Did he not understand his culpability? Did he not understand that he had jeopardized the health of their patients and the integrity of the clinic?

"Listen," she said. "I may have been mistaken about how I handled the situation, but I am not mistaken to think the people of Rabata deserved better treatment than what you gave them in a compromised state."

"This is what you wanted all along, isn't it? You wanted me out of here. You in charge."

"Nelson," she said, with a bit of spirit, "it is time for you to leave the clinic."

"You'll flounder without me, you know." His laughter had a menacing, hysterical ring in the empty patient room. "You won't cut it alone."

"We'll see, Dr. Landry."

"Oh, you'll see all right, you'll regret this—"

An explosion of honks cut through Nelson's words, drowning the drone of the clinic's generator and the chatter outside. They both looked at each other and then toward the door. She was quick, springing to the door before he could, fumbling blindly for the knob. With her hands clammy, the knob felt slicked with ointment. She thought she heard Nelson's thunderous footsteps rushing to slam the door shut, lock her in here with him. But when she glanced over her shoulder, he was sitting on the examination table, his face buried in his palms.

She hurried out to find patients in the waiting area, swiveled toward the window. At the blasts of the horn, they must have parted against the walls in anticipation of a body being carried through the corridor. Some hobbled over to witness the commotion outside.

A car had swerved in front of the clinic's entrance. The back doors swung open and a man and a boy scrambled out of the driver and passenger side. She recognized the boy as Jecinda's brother, Yakwo. She had seen him at the clinic from time to time.

"Please, Likita. Come and see!" Yakwo cried.

"What happened?" Tebeya demanded.

"My sister—"

"Is it Jecinda?" Tebeya asked. "What happened to her?"

"She has fallen!"

It took several seconds before Tebeya recognized the unconscious woman as Jecinda's senior sister, Jummai: the red streaks down the sides of her wrapper near her thighs, the dusty pallor of her face. Tebeya's fingers tapped Jummai's wrist for a pulse.

This was not good. This was not good. She would die.

This was an emergency for the larger hospital to handle. She might need an operation, and with Nelson unable to perform surgeries, they had to take her to Keffi in this car. The clinic's medical transport vehicle was in use elsewhere.

One of the male nurses had run up to the car with what Tebeya would need to stabilize Jummai on the journey. "Is Jecinda working today?" Tebeya asked. "Yes, okay, so tell her what has happened to her sister. Don't frighten her. You understand? And please, quietly see if you can escort Dr. Landry out of the clinic. You will find him in examination room two."

Then they were gone, speeding down the path that curved through grass and maize, hurtling to the hospital in Keffi.

CHAPTER THIRTY-EIGHT

JIM HAD ASKED KATHERINE to coordinate Nelson's goodbye dinner, and with Jummai hospitalized, she had displayed her culinary ineptitude. She overcooked the spaghetti and forgot to simmer the tomato sauce, leaving the flames so high the sauce burned, and a foul, grayish cloud drifted near the kitchen ceiling. Her guests ate the meal without complaining, furtively expelling charred chunks of tomato from their mouths onto the sides of their plates.

Gosh, she missed Jummai. She had not realized how much Jummai ran their house with efficiency, each meal a feast to look forward to—slices of buttered bread and boiled eggs halved to reveal moist golden yolks, or yam slathered with a rich egg batter and deep fried, served with a tasty stew of bell peppers and tomatoes. Katherine had no details about her condition; she only knew it had been critical. She should have paid better attention when Jummai came into work on Monday looking ill. She had not bothered to check her temperature or pulse. She had simply allowed her to go home to rest.

"We hate to lose you, Nelson," Jim said after supper, when they were seated in the living room. "You've worked tirelessly for the people of this town."

To Katherine, Jim looked older than sixty-eight sitting on their couch, his left hand resting on the wooden frame. The quartet of wrinkles across his brow was more defined, and his face paler in the dim light. His hair had not receded, and had molted, in the past few years she had known him, from a grayish brown to fully gray, and it made him look nobler, a lean-faced Cary Grant.

"It's my time to go, I guess," Nelson said. He looked embarrassed about the whole affair. He was no longer the enthusiastic doctor she had met at Kano airport when they first landed here. He had crackled with a seize-the-day energy she found off-putting at that time. She had been jetlagged, ready to sprint back toward the tarmac to the BOAC VC10 to fly her out of Nigeria and through the cities they had connected through—London, Cairo, Nairobi.

"We'll miss you," Gary said. "That's for sure."

Katherine nodded. "It won't be the same at the clinic. It's not the same now."

"It's been wonderful," Nelson said. "Really wonderful."

Delores, sitting in the sling chair, did not chime in. She gave a conservative, general sort of smile and traced a finger on the fabric coaster. Earlier, they had all exchanged words of praise at supper except for Delores, who had said bluntly, "Honestly, Nelson, please get the help you need back home," and brought the conversation to an awkward, flustering halt.

"We'll take a trip north to see you," Gary said, leaning forward from the lip of the couch. "When we get back to Springfield for furlough. Isn't that right, dear?"

"Yeah, that's right, Nelson," Katherine said.

"It's a pretty long drive, isn't it?" Delores said. "Missouri to Illinois?"

"About eight hours, I think," Gary said.

Nelson lifted his mug of coffee and said with pained cheeriness, "Well, you're welcome to Rockford, all of you," and he drank from it in a desperate, speedy sort of way.

Katherine excused herself and went to the kitchen to prepare tea and dessert. Hands on hips, she glanced around in search of a kettle or small pot to refill the hot water flask. She planned to serve fresh-baked rhubarb pie. The double crust had turned out quite nicely, a little too golden. Jummai would have cut up the pie and also popped her head into the parlor from time to time and figured out what needed to be replenished without instructions from Katherine.

"I say let one of the men do it for once, right?"

Katherine looked up. "Oh, Delores. Hi."

"You know," Delores waved, "put a kettle on themselves."

"Oh, it's all right," Katherine said, spotting the kettle behind the stack of dirty plates.

Delores said, "Could we go somewhere private and talk, Katherine?"

"Is something the matter?"

"Oh no, I only wanted a chat. Just you and me."

Delores stood confident as ever, with a lithe figure that had never suffered the effects of childbearing or rearing, and her crown of dark curls in a messy bohemian updo and those intense blue eyes. Except for a barely conspicuous twitch of her lower lip, Katherine would not have guessed anything was wrong.

"Well, all right," Katherine said, once the kettle was on.

She led Delores into her and Gary's bedroom, regretting her choice of location when she recalled its simplicity. Their bedroom in Missouri had been a haven. Big windows left open to allow the fresh smell of mowed grass to drift in. A floral chenille spread—one she had bought at Marshall Fields on a short vacation to Chicago with her mother. She had flung it with abandon, watched it billow like a parachute.

In this bedroom, the two pillows at the head of the bed were plain and sunken, as if no acts of love had occurred in months, which was not untrue.

"It's lovely in here," Delores said, and she studied a photograph of Gary, Katherine, and the children in a pearl-trimmed frame on the dresser. Elijah was squinting and grinning wide, and

Allison gazed up at Gary. It had been taken on the front lawn of their yellow-icing-colored house.

"Let's talk, shall we?" Katherine said. "I've got the kettle going."

Delores sat on the edge of the bed and smoothed the sheets. "I wanted to let you know—well, the thing is, I'm being transferred to Ethiopia in a few months."

Ethiopia! Katherine could have sworn her heart had leapfrogged in her chest. It was in these moments that God felt close and real.

"I'll be in Addis," Delores said. "Addis Ababa."

"Well," Katherine said. "Congratulations are in order, I suppose."

Delores continued, explaining that the mission planned to transfer her. It could be right away or in six to eight months. The government would replace her with a Nigerian woman who had served as a school administrator and bursar in another region of the country.

"Katherine, I know we don't agree on many things," Delores said, observing her with doleful eyes. "See the thing is, well, I just wanted to assure you nothing untoward ever happened between Gary and I. Before I left, I guess I wanted you to know this."

Katherine tilted her head. "Now, why would you feel a need to say a thing like that to me?" Delores had ambushed her and planned to humiliate her in her own bedroom. Delores and Gary must have whispered about Gary's miserable little wife, reading into situations, needing to be placated like an infant.

"I hope I'm not out of line with what I'm about to say. I feel we ought to be able to share things with each other."

"Go on," Katherine said, impressed with her own composure. One quick look at her fingers clenching the hem of her apron would have told anyone otherwise.

Delores smiled, her eyes dewy and bright. "Gary needs a wife who wants to be in Rabata as much as he does. He's a man of such intelligence and commitment. He's linguistically gifted, and his heart for the people, for this work, it's unmatched—"

"I know who my husband is."

"Right, of course. I guess what I'm trying to say is that Gary needs a wife who weeps with him and really feels as he does for the souls of the people in this country."

"Weeps?" An image of her husband and Delores embracing flew into her mind, sharp and clear as if it were happening right in front of her. Gary caressing Delores's back, her curls sweeping across his fingers. The two of them crying over the souls of the Nigerian people, crying in Delores's small, eclectic home.

"You love Gary," Katherine said. "You love my husband."

A wild, fearful look entered Delores's eyes, and she turned from Katherine. "Sure I do, as a Christian sister ought to love a Christian brother," she said. "Yes, you can say I love Gary, as I love Nelson and Jim, you and your children—"

"Oh, *bullshit*, Delores."

"What?" Delores said, taken aback.

"Did you and Gary—did you sleep together?" The strength of her voice at this moment surprised her, and so too her own equanimity.

"No, Katherine, all right? No, I would never—and frankly, I can't believe you'd ask me such a thing. We're friends, Gary and I. We understand each other, that's all."

The suggestion of a deeper intimacy lurked in Delores's words.

"Listen, Katherine, Gary's going to accept the position of associate pastor. Things will change for you here in Nigeria. That's all I was trying to tell you."

Katherine's throat closed. "Gary's going to do what?"

"Oh gosh."

"He accepted the position with Jim?"

Delores bit her lip. "I'm so sorry. I thought you knew. He's just thinking it through. I don't believe anything was finalized."

The door opened, and Gary poked his head inside. "How's everything going here? We were wondering where you both went off to."

Katherine rose from the bed. She didn't know what to say to Gary. She was looking at a complete stranger. Her husband had become a stranger. Fifteen years of marriage, and it was possible to look at your husband and feel as if you had never seen him before.

"We're just fine," she said.

"All right." He leaned against the doorjamb, uncertain, and looked past her. "Delores?"

"It's nothing," Delores said. "We're okay."

Katherine turned to Delores. "I hope," she said, "that your next assignment in Ethiopia brings you the fulfillment you need."

Gary moved aside for Delores to pass, and he waited for Katherine, reaching for her elbow when she neared. "What happened, honey, are you all right?"

"We have company, dear," she said, and freed her arm from his grasp.

CHAPTER THIRTY-NINE

ON THE KITCHEN COUNTER, a metal bowl teemed with peeled yams, and starchy water dripped down its side. White tomato seeds swam in a gelatinous liquid on the cutting board next to a halved red onion. A stone forced open the kitchen door leading to the backyard, where Tebeya found Duza loitering near the tomato vines, chatting with the houseboy.

"Duza!" Tebeya called, and Duza whipped around.

"Yes, ma. I'm coming."

"Where is Comfort?" she asked.

Duza came inside, her gangly body folding into the kitchen entrance. When Tebeya left for Jummai's emergency, she had asked a nurse to bring Comfort here, to her parents' home. She was grateful for the Dutch physicians who had recently arrived to offer a month of volunteer service; they had managed the clinic while she stayed in Keffi to make sure Jummai had appropriate supervision. One of the doctors intended to remain in Nigeria, in Jos or Kaduna, or possibly in Rabata if she could convince him.

"She is in the room," Duza said.

"No, she is not in her bedroom," Tebeya said. She had gone there when she first came inside. "Where is Mama? Where is Baba?"

"They traveled to Wukari."

"Did Comfort go with them?"

"No, ma."

"Duza, if you don't tell me this instant where she is—"

"She was here. I will go and find her, ma."

Tebeya's body ached from the uncomfortable hospital chairs. She must have slept a total of six hours over the past few days. The surgeons in Keffi had performed a surgical repair that saved Jummai's life and womb. What a senseless, tragic circumstance. If Tebeya had known that Jummai was pregnant, she might have arranged for Jummai to enter a program in the city for unwed mothers or to consider an alternative solution.

She looked around for something to nibble on and picked up a half-eaten meat pie. This situation with Jummai would have been the kind of thing for people to know—that diviners were fallible beings—so they could trust the mission clinic again. Yet, she had ensured Jummai's surgery was reported to the Parsons and the locals as an appendectomy, something inoffensive and forgettable, to protect Jummai's reputation and position with the mission.

Duza returned fifteen minutes later. "I cannot find her, ma."

"What do you mean you cannot find her?" She found a pot of stew in the fridge and took it out to be warmed on the stove. "Did you look very well?"

"I don't know where she is—"

"Were you not supposed to care for her?"

"She was here, ma," Duza stammered.

Duza's hesitation gave rise to fear in Tebeya, so slight that just to think of it was to give it actual weight. "When did you see her last?"

"She was playing outside when I was peeling yam." Tears had formed and spilled down Duza's cheeks. "I don't know where she is, ma."

"Stop crying this instant. Let us go and look."

Tebeya, along with the guard, the houseboy, Duza, and the gardener, searched the house and the grounds for Comfort. Tebeya's exhaustion vanished, and worry appeared. Not another thing, after such a week. What if Comfort had fallen down the hill that led to her family's mansion? It could be treacherous in rain. She might have crossed the main road and been hit by a car or motorbike. She envisioned Comfort slumped on the ground, a grotesque lump on her forehead, the unnatural angle of an arm or a leg, a twisted bloody ribbon in her hair.

She didn't trust herself to drive. She hurried to the gate. "Benedict!"

"Yes, madam?" He had been carefully wiping the side mirrors with his own shirt.

"Please, take me to the primary school. We must hurry." It was Saturday. There would be no primary school in session. But they had to search everywhere.

They were soon on the road to the school, with Benedict speeding like a madman before another thought dawned on her: *Nelson*. Nelson must have taken Comfort. Had he not charged into the mission clinic and threatened her the other day? He had cut a wretched figure, his body tumbling menacingly at her. His flight to America left on Monday, and he must have decided upon a final act of revenge. She recalled the day he accused her of parading Comfort in front of him, making a point about correcting his blunder. Had he not spoken of regret when he accosted her in the examination room? Her calmness subsided, slipping away, and a cold, cold feeling replaced it. "Go to the mission compound, Benedict," she said. "*Go!*"

PART FOUR

CHAPTER FORTY

KATHERINE GAZED AT THE PEOPLE milling about and walking outside the gates of the mission compound. Stray dogs roamed, yelp-
ing and nipping at each other's tails and legs. One crouched on its
hindquarters and defecated before straightening up and sniffing a
new trail. Ugliness resided in this town. All of it a chaotic, tum-
bling-down place, with its smoky and disorienting arrangements
of shops, eateries, and shacks. She was done with all of it.

Zanya stood across from her on the veranda, propped up
against the wooden beam, waiting for her to tell him why she had
come to his flat this morning—which she had found bare, either
because he could not afford any furnishings or because he was
gearing up to move or to leave Rabata—and asked him to come to
the compound this evening.

Earlier in the morning, while dusting the nightstand, a slip of
paper had fluttered out of Gary's journal: *I don't know how I'll cope
in Ethiopia without you. I'll miss you terribly. Yours, Delores.* Katherine had held the note and read it, feeling like a colony of bees was
trapped under her skin, pushing to escape. She had thought there
must be other letters and notes Delores had sent her husband,
and while Gary showered and ate his breakfast, preparing to drive
Nelson the full day's trip to Kano Airport, Katherine had stalked
through the house, rifling through his papers and books.

"She doesn't mean it how you think," Gary said when she confronted him. He had thrown up a hand to glance at his wristwatch. "I'm sorry, sweetheart, Jim and I really need to get going with Nelson. Could we talk about this later, do you think?"

"How does she mean it, Gary?"

He had closed the zipper on his overnight bag. "What's that?"

"I said, how does she mean it?"

"Let's not do this now, Katherine. Please, when I come back?"

He had planted a soft peck on her cheek and headed out to the car. With Elijah at school and Jummai in the hospital, she and Manasseh had been the only ones on the compound available for goodbyes to Nelson.

On the veranda, Zanya had remained standing instead of taking the bench she offered. His guard was up; she had shown up asking to speak about the mission when she had never exchanged more than greetings with him before.

Nervousness slunk into the pit of her stomach and burrowed. She inhaled, then said, "Did you know Jim was let go in his last pastoral position in America?"

"Let go?"

"Yes."

"You mean he was sacked?"

"Oh, well, sort of. Jim says he resigned, but it seems he was fired from his last church in Rockford, Illinois. You know, Jim lived in Rockford before coming here—"

"Yes, I know where he used to live in America."

"All right, of course," she said. "Well, according to my mother, he led the congregation astray and mishandled the finances. He resigned shortly after. It's a little fuzzy, but it's all there in her letter." She pinched her mother's letter from her pocket and held it toward him. "It's all in here if you don't believe me. Read it for yourself. See what it says."

Zanya did not reach for the letter. He looked at her instead, holding an unopened bottle of soda she had brought out for him.

"Okay, well," she said, flustered. "Jim was voted out of his congregation. He told us he resigned, and you can guess how that looks now, finding this out. My mother's friend—she's the one who told my mother this—attended Jim's church, First Presbyterian. She still attends actually. Apparently, they replaced Jim with a younger pastor, a Dave Turner—" She stopped, hearing her rambling words reverberating in the night air.

Zanya rubbed the condensation on the bottle. "Did Mai Hankali know?"

"My husband?"

"About Reverend Jim and his church? Did Mr. Gary know?"

She knew why he asked. Gary, trustworthy and sensible, concerned about the Nigerians and their rights and lives. It'd be devastating to the nationals if they thought Mai Hankali had been in cahoots with Jim all four years.

The truth was that Gary had agonized over her mother's letter and Jim's revelation. She knew he must have mulled it over with Delores even though he had talked a little with Katherine about the right decision to make. Protect Jim or alert mission headquarters to Jim's lies about resigning from First Presbyterian? "We ought to fast and pray about the proper course of action," he had said, worried Jim's history was evidence that he was mismanaging church funds again. He wondered if assuming the role of associate pastor would allow him to resolve any financial issues before turning the church over to nationals. "We can't make a mess of things and then hand it over," he had said. "It wouldn't be fair or right."

"Gary knows many things about Jim, about the mission," she said to Zanya.

Zanya pulled the bottle from his mouth. "Mai Hankali?"

"Yes."

"I don't believe what you're saying."

"Well, my husband is Jim's confidant, you see. Why else would he have accepted the associate pastor position with Jim?"

Zanya let out a nervous chuckle, as if attempting to reconcile the Gary he knew with the image of Gary she was painting. "That doesn't sound like—you're pulling my leg."

"I know it's difficult to think that Gary could do such a thing…"

Zanya shook his head and crossed his ankles. "Mai Hankali knew? The whole time."

She remained quiet, letting the misunderstanding bloom.

"What of headquarters? Did they know?"

"I'm not sure," she said. "I doubt it, actually." She put the letter forward again. "Take a look at this. See what my mother wrote."

He set the bottle down and crossed his arms. "So, why did you want me to know?" he said, brows furrowed. "Why all of a sudden?"

"Excuse me?"

"You must have had this letter months ago, maybe years ago. Why now?"

"Does it matter?"

He laughed, and in those waves of laughter, she heard impatience at his being here, having to speak to her. She feared he might end the conversation if she did not hurry.

"Listen," she said, confidence ebbing because the letter remained untouched, and she was questioning the wisdom of having involved him. "I thought you should've been given the position. I never wanted Gary to work under Jim. I wanted us home in Missouri—"

"Ehen," Zanya said. "You *want* something."

"Well, I guess I do."

"That's why you want me to know about Reverend Jim's troubles in his former church. It is always the same with you white people. Only when it privileges you do you take an interest in someone else's affairs."

"I see you're upset," she said, slowly, for she felt his assessment unfair. How had being in Nigeria privileged her? Sally, whose new house they had visited while on furlough last year, had flitted about, showing off her rattan chairs, asking Katherine if she cared for a midday cocktail. Sally would never in a million years understand what Katherine had given up to come to Nigeria, and neither did the locals. "I guess I understand what you're saying—"

"No, you cannot understand, and it is fine. You will never understand."

She crossed her arms in a self-protective hug. She had gone about this wrong, assuming Zanya would be appreciative, praising her for coming to him with this information.

He remained against the column. "Tell me what it is you want. It's better to be truthful with one another. You're not here because you want to help me or my people go against how Jim Clemens is running this mission station. If you were, you could have done so in other ways."

She flinched. "Well, what do you want me to say?"

"The truth," he said. "People I trust more than you have lied to me in this life."

She looked him straight in the eyes. "All right. I'd like my family to go back home to Missouri—and if it means Gary losing this new position with Jim, so be it."

"Ah. There is the truth finally."

"I don't know what this letter can do by itself, but in your hands, it could do something. If Jim could be convinced, or forced, I suppose, to retire, to let the church be headed by nationals, Gary will agree. He'll be convinced it's our time to go home. When they finish this church building, Zanya, which they will, who do you want leading it?

"Take the letter. At least see what's in there. Do with it what you will."

He was silent a moment. Finally, he reached for the letter.

Jummai woke to another woman's cries, and it took her a moment to recognize them as the cries of childbirth. Her eyes remained closed, and her mind worked to figure out how many days had passed in Keffi Hospital. There were no windows in the room she shared with three other patients. She did not know when day turned to night.

Her swelling had not subsided, and the bruises on her arms and lower body had not faded. She could not sit up fully. Her stomach, the place where they had cut her body open, was wrapped with white bandages. She thought she could remember the physical pain of the surgery—the sensation of muscular arms wringing her womb in a merciless twist, and the sense that they were scraping everything within her—ligaments, organs, intestines, and bones. She remembered afterwards, sinking through the sheets and cot and tiled floors and into the ground. Her vision had blurred, and the faces of nurses dissolved into a giant mass of bodies looming over her. Jecinda had told her how her skin felt cold to her touch, and how her body was there on the cot, but her spirit absent.

"Jummai, you nearly died," Jecinda had cried.

Jecinda told her Yakwo and Innocent had run into the compound and found her on the ground, fainted. They had sprinted to the main road and waved for a car to stop and help. All those times Jummai had thought of her brothers as foolish, unhelpful boys, and here, when it mattered, they had come and saved her life.

It was restful in the hospital despite the pain. Imagine having to nearly die before you could rest. She could not remember when she had last lain like this, doing nothing. She was to be released soon, and the Parsons had arranged to come and drive her to Rabata.

Dr. Tebeya had stayed with her when she was admitted, refusing to leave the first few days, asking the doctors questions, ensuring they followed proper procedures. Dr. Tebeya had a frightening manner that made you want to answer her questions, and quickly.

You feared you had to tell her more than she had asked. She was not as intimidating as her mother, Mama Bintu, though her presence demanded the same respect and deference. It was the broad shoulders and queenly stature, the eyes that seemed to want to look at you with ease but instead looked at you like a commander did his soldiers.

"Who impregnated you?" Dr. Tebeya had said to Jummai when she was here. "Was it any of the missionaries?"

"The missionaries?" Jummai would have laughed if she could. Imagine sleeping with those old men! Imagine having a child with a white man. Would he not come out looking like the rat-child in Miss Delores's story?

Jummai had not said anything else. She had looked away from Dr. Tebeya's inquiring eyes and studied the sign above the door to the ward: THANK GOD ALWAYS.

"They have been good to me," Jummai said. "All of them have been good to me."

"Okay," Dr. Tebeya said, as if she did not believe her. She leaned over the side of the bed. "Perforated uterus. It means there was a hole where the baby was growing. It was serious, Jummai. If things had not happened as they had, you would not be alive. The doctors repaired your womb. We don't know what this will mean, you understand? We don't know yet if you can become pregnant again and carry a baby to term. But I will help you. If this is what you want in the future, I will help you."

Jummai rubbed dry patches of skin around her fingernails. The words Dr. Tebeya said had not made sense to her, and they still did not make sense to her now. Her mind had become like a well as Dr. Tebeya was speaking, and Dr. Tebeya's words were like stones. Dr. Tebeya had flung the stones into the well, and the well was deep, so very deep that it was taking a long time for them to descend and break the surface of the water.

She grimaced now and sucked her bottom lip as a heavy, searing pain made its way through her body. It felt as if someone had taken an iron full of hot coals and pressed it against her bandaged stomach, pressing and moving, pressing and moving. That day, Dr. Tebeya had asked her again the question that made her body feel the same kind of soreness.

"Whose child was it, Jummai?"

Jummai had remained quiet.

"Jummai, you must answer me."

"I don't know, ma."

"How can you not know—" Dr. Tebeya stopped herself, as if realizing it was possible that a woman might not know the father of her child. "Is this person important? Is he in the church? Is that why you do not want to tell me?"

Jummai had touched the sheet on the cot, felt its worn roughness against her fingers.

"Okay," Dr. Tebeya said, rising, as if she knew.

Jummai pressed her hands against the cot, unable to turn onto her side. She thought she might be able to move her legs if she looked at them. Pain pinned her to the cot, and she needed to summon her strength simply to lift her head.

She wondered if Zanya had heard that she was in the hospital in Keffi. What if Zanya were to come? A warm, reassuring feeling went through her chest at the thought of seeing him standing at the door, his hands on the doorframes, greeting her with concern. He had traveled to Keffi for building supplies many times. It was possible he would travel to Keffi to come and comfort her. He would sit with her as she had with him so many nights. She would know then that he had loved her, and she had been mistaken about his love.

A long time ago, her grandmother told her a story about why the heavens are so far away from the earth. The story went that the sky used to almost touch the earth, but one day, while pounding grains, an elderly woman asked the sky to move up and give her room to raise her pestle. The sky moved a little. The woman asked again, and the sky moved again. She kept asking and the sky kept moving until finally, tired of the old woman's requests, it moved very far away to where it is today. Jummai sensed the weight of the sky—as the old woman must have sensed it—hovering so close she did not have enough room for all the things she was feeling.

The dull desire to sleep weighed upon her eyelids, and when she closed her eyes fully, the shrill cry of a newborn filled the hospital.

CHAPTER FORTY-ONE

ELBOWS ON KNEES, Zanya conversed with patients as Tebeya approached the clinic. Like most people in his company, they grinned their pleasure, delighted with his attention. She took umbrage with the patients laughing unabashedly with him, though she believed laughter a palliative for pain.

"Dr. Tebeya." Zanya stood upon seeing her. "Good morning."

"Good morning, Zanya." She unlocked the front entrance. "Look at how you're making our patients laugh this early morning."

"Just talk and laugh, and sometimes, people will forget their troubles."

Imagine if simple laughter could bring more money to the clinic.

"Is something the matter, Zanya? Why have you come?"

"I wanted to speak with you."

"Let us go to the office," Tebeya said. "We must speak quickly. You see this line."

Tebeya pushed the door open and held it with her foot while she wrangled the keys back into her medical bag. She lost a grip on the bag, and he saved it before it hit the cement.

He moved with determination as they walked the corridor, as if somewhere within him a vibrant force lent strength to his motions. She understood why townswomen were infatuated with him, and why married ones glanced at him when they thought no one was watching. Or why one woman was in a hospital now, having endangered her life for him, if Tebeya's presumption was correct. She sighed her irritation at Zanya's youthful appeal, though it was unfair to be exasperated with him for such petty, irrational reasons. He did not mean to parade himself. It was like being angry at an ostrich for displaying its extraordinary stride, or a tree for growing a bounty of lush, sweet fruit. It was only because she felt drained, overworked, and saddled with mounting expenses from the clinic she had saved from Nelson.

She was also driving Comfort to her village later this afternoon, and she worried about which relatives the girl would find, and if they would say Comfort needed to return to them.

On the day she thought Comfort had been stolen, Benedict had sped to the mission compound.

"Where is she?" Tebeya had said, barging into Nelson's house.

Nelson jumped up at the intrusion. "What?"

"Where did you take Comfort?"

"Whoa, now, wait a minute—take her? You mean, *kidnap* her? That'd be a criminal offense you're accusing me of." He swore he knew nothing about Comfort. "I'm leaving Rabata in a couple of days, Dr. Awyebwi. Why in the world would I take your kid?"

She had refused to believe him, but there had been no sign of Comfort in his house or on the mission compound. She and Benedict later located Comfort walking on the main road leading out of Rabata toward the hills. She had trekked a good distance alone. She confessed that she had been going to her village to find her uncle, because she thought Tebeya had forgotten her and was not returning from Keffi.

Now, Zanya leaned back in his seat in the office, waiting for her to lead the conversation. Tebeya brought her hands together and repeated, "Why have you come?"

"How is Comfort?" Zanya asked.

"She is adjusting. We thank God," she said. "Like you, I have

many things I must complete today. What is it you have come
for?"

"I see how you're handling things here, Dr. Tebeya. You will
soon be medical director of this clinic, having gone and demanded
Nelson Landry be sacked."

"You have to be careful with what the wind carries to you."
The spread of gossip was pollen to an insect in the wrong person's
mouth.

"There's no wind o. I saw you at headquarters in Jos."

She frowned. "What are you saying, Zanya?"

"I saw you in Jos," he said again. When she said nothing, he
continued in a self-assured manner, "I was there for a mission conference with the Reverend, one for pastors and ministers, and I saw
you there, eating with Edward Hayes."

Tebeya had foreseen no harm in asking the driver to return to
campus so she could meet with Edward to discuss details of the
case. It had been a pleasant meal. Quite pleasant. Now, Zanya was
revealing that he had spied her there. It was June now, and so much
had happened since that Friday afternoon in April that the lunch
was a hazy memory.

She wanted to stand for no reason other than giving her feet
something to do. She remained in her chair and said, "Is it a crime
for one to go to Jos?"

He grinned. "I, too, went to headquarters with the expectation that I would speak to Bill Kent, and he would care about the
laborers. Do you know what happened? He dismissed me, and
he listened to Jim Clemens's lies about the strike. Do you think
Edward Hayes will keep his promises to you? Are they not of the
same mission?"

"Mr. Hayes has already fired Nelson Landry."

"Has he permanently made you the director of this clinic?"

Her father had once said Zanya was sharp when he came to
ask about the purchase of land for the church, and she was here

seeing it. She had questions she did not yet have the answers to and had not posed to Edward Hayes. Would the mission continue to support hospitals run by locals if the government did not take over? She was not sure where the money would come from for a Nigerian-run clinic, as most of the clinic's support currently came from overseas. Staff salaries would have to come from the charges for patient fees and surgeries, and this was not a consistent and sufficient means of support.

"Suppose," she said, "you are correct about Edward Hayes, that he does not uphold his promise. What is it you have in mind?"

"We have the same vision, Dr. Tebeya." His voice had not lost the bravado and strength it used to carry in church services. "We see the situation in this town in a way other people don't see it. The primary school will soon belong to our government. Nigerians, because of what you did, will soon lead the clinic. Why must you wait for Edward Hayes to allow you this position? Why must we wait for the church to belong to our people?"

"Our situations are different. Nelson Landry was drinking and seeing patients—"

"Jim Clemens was dismissed from his position in America. Why did they consider him unfit to run a church there but good enough to do it here, in our country?"

"Dismissed? What do you mean?" He seemed unusually confident about a rumor sure to do damage if it were to come to light. "How do you know this information?"

"I didn't go searching for it," Zanya said. "You understand? One has not finished making ridges for the planting of okra, and suddenly the okra appears. That is how it came to me, this thing Jim Clemens was hiding. We should have known for ourselves what happened to him at his former church and decided ourselves if we wanted him leading us."

"You're speculating."

"No, I'm asking questions. Just as you did with Nelson Landry."

She resented that Zanya had solicited her, as if she were someone to enlist in a coup against Jim Clemens. She had not become
an interim clinic director through devious means, regardless of
what others thought. But there was something too about not fighting this alone, if Edward Hayes went against his word and this
formal directorship failed to materialize.

"You can understand," Zanya said, "that since the thing was
hidden from us, people will wonder: Did mission headquarters
know and refuse to tell us? If they are refusing to tell us this, what
else have they withheld?"

"Okay," she said. He was as passionate and eager as she had
been when she first assumed control of the clinic. "Let us say this is
the truth. You have to know it may be difficult to lead the church.
What will happen to the laborers? Who will fund the completion
of the building? Who will it belong to if Jim Clemens is gone and
the mission does not want you in charge?" She took a risk, one
that had more to do with her intuition than any logical conclusion
or evidence. "You cannot run away from situations—they will not
take care of themselves. You were able to escape what happened
with Jummai. You cannot do the same here."

He grew silent. "You know about me and Jummai."

So, she was right. He had been the father.

"Were you not the one who asked her to go to the diviner to
end the pregnancy?"

"When did Jummai…?"

"To abort the child, Zanya. Because of you."

His eyes widened in disbelief as she spoke. "Is that what happened?" he said. "I learned the news that she was in the hospital.
Stomach problems is what I heard."

"It was not stomach problems, and you are the only other person who will know the truth in this town," she said. "And where
were you? You intended to go and abandon Jummai after impreg-
nating her."

"Ask Jummai. I was prepared to marry her. She is the one who did not want to marry."

"Is that so?" This information Tebeya hadn't known.

"Dr. Tebeya, I understand the mistakes I have made. I have learned from them." He stood to leave. "Please, consider what I have asked. Stand with us when we come against the mission."

She sat behind the desk after he left. She had to begin seeing patients; yet, she was unable to leave her chair. Imagine him coming to her, thinking she had power, when she was working without sleep to keep this clinic afloat.

Perhaps Zanya's experience would not be like hers. He had rescued Reverend Jim from certain death and served him faithfully for many years. He was right about the church leadership, how they had prevented locals from rising into higher positions. It could not be denied how much he had given to the mission, and Jim Clemens had refused to reward it. Zanya could do without her help. Whatever he was planning, the shrewdness she witnessed this morning would sustain him. It would not be long before he took the reins.

CHAPTER FORTY-TWO

KAGO SAT SQUAT AND RECEPTIVE next to Zanya. The RIGHT ON!
cap was gone from his head, exposing a gleaming, dimpled scalp.
The conversation in Kago's home was unfolding much better than
Zanya had planned.

"This is exactly what we needed," Zanya said. "Are you reading
it well?"

"Financial mismanagement?" Kago said. "Reverend Jim?"

"That's what Katherine Parson told me."

Kago held the letter. "With her own mouth?"

"All of her mouth and teeth, everything."

He waited for Kago to read the letter in its entirety again. He
knew Kago was wrestling with this development as he had wrestled. The other night, Zanya had studied the handwriting on the
thin blue paper, concentrating on the paragraph disclosing details
of Reverend Jim's tenure at First Presbyterian and a vague story
about his son stealing money from the church. It was unclear what
Jim had known about his son's plans and if they had worked together. He had held onto the letter for a couple of days before going to Dr. Tebeya and now Kago. "Use am," Chubz urged when he
shared his initial ambivalence. "The water that is not sufficient for
a bath should be used to wash the face. That woman give you this
letter so you go dey look am?"

But this was not how Zanya had wanted to progress. If Jim

Clemens had not fired him, he would not have been in this situation, exposing the man's history.

He did not know if he could trust Katherine Parson. She maintained a cordial, reserved manner whenever he interacted with her. The night she gave him the letter, he had noticed a change in her demeanor. If she had had more secrets, she would have willingly given them to him. When he had still been considering if he should leave Rabata, she had come to find him.

If he had left Rabata, he also would not have known what happened to Jummai. Now he knew why Jummai had wanted money. Not for her restaurant or to care for the child on her own as she had promised him, but to go and abort the child.

"Na wa o," Kago said, holding the letter.

"What did I tell you?"

"You said Mai Hankali knew?"

"The whole time."

Kago curled his lips and whistled. "Gary Parson, my friend."

"Like you, I thought we could trust him."

"The things he did for me and my family—I don't know, Zanya."

"All this time, Kago. It is no longer about the strike, you understand? All of them knew. Us, in Rabata, we are the only ones that did not know." Zanya sat back. "I don't want to turn you against anybody. I want you to think about Rabata. I want you to ask yourself why our people are not advancing at this station."

Kago reread the sentences, and at the middle of the page, he whistled again and looked at Zanya. "Before the ripening of fruits, what were the birds eating? We were fine before these missionaries came, were we not? We can do without them and will be fine when they depart. If this letter here"—and he shook it again—"is true, we must use it. See how Reverend behaved against us with this strike."

"Yes, yes. This is what I have been saying—"

"You nko?"

"Me? What do you mean?"

Kago probed his lower lip with his tongue. "You did not side with us when you should have sided with us in this strike. How are we to know you will stand with us?"

"Abi o. Yes, I failed to stand with you."

Kago turned his head. He seemed to have been gearing up to hurl more questions and appeared a little disappointed by Zanya's capitulation.

"It was wrong of me not to stand in solidarity. I want these missionaries to know they have not shown our people fairness," Zanya said. "Look at the Redeemed Christian Church of God or ECWA, both with indigenous leaders. See the other stations the mission has in the east of our country. They, too, have Nigerians in leadership. But here, Reverend Jim has not treated us as equals."

"I am hearing you," Kago said.

"You understand, abi?"

"So, how are we supposed to reclaim things?"

Zanya leaned in. Kago's question did not bother him; his question was a sign that he was willing to come with him against the mission.

"We will start talking to people," Zanya said, "telling everyone what we know."

⁂

They had driven past Comfort's village many times on their medical outings with the mobile clinic. Tebeya hoped Comfort would not notice that with one simple turn they could have visited her village on the way. The wheels rolled easily on the road as Tebeya parked in front of a one-room school made of mud brick. This was the school Comfort would have attended if Tebeya had not intervened, and when she could attend no longer, she might have worked on the farm, digging tubers. Comfort might not know the capitals of the world's countries as she did now. She would not have a satchel of books and her own room. She'd be selling moi-moi and fetching water from the stream, like the small girls with buckets who were trekking along the trail now, staring at her and Comfort.

A few curious children followed them to the uncle's hut. Tebeya's shoes dipped into the soft earth. She reminded herself that it was a simple visit.

Comfort's uncle was alive, shuffling out of the hut again, wearing the same cloth Tebeya had seen him in the last time.

"Good afternoon, Uncle," Comfort said.

Panic was in his eyes. He yanked the chewing stick out of his mouth and spat. "What happened? Why are you bringing her back to us?"

Tebeya said, "We wanted to come and greet you."

"Is that all?" he asked, suspicious.

"Yes, your sister's daughter, Comfort, wanted to come and visit with her family."

"Come inside," he said.

"Comfort. Oya come," Tebeya said. Comfort had maintained a safe, respectful distance.

"No, no. You, madam." Comfort's uncle gave an aggressive shake of his head and put up a hand. "Not the girl."

Inside the hut, Comfort's uncle told Tebeya he was going to be remarried. A good woman, but she would not want Comfort coming and disturbing their lives, causing trouble. He had even forgotten his younger sister's daughter was alive and living in the big town with Tebeya. He spoke rapidly and loudly, and his chapped lips made hissing noises from the spittle frothing in the corners.

"We will not come and disturb you any longer," Tebeya said. "But you will have to talk to Comfort. We have come all this way. Please, tell her about her mother."

She shepherded Comfort inside. When the uncle started by saying Comfort's mother had been useless and bullish as a child, Tebeya regretted inviting Comfort inside this smoke-blackened hut to listen to her uncle's disparaging stories. Eventually, he veered from listing his sister's faults to praising her as quick-minded and kind. Tebeya listened and made herself inconspicuous as Comfort asked tentative questions, which the man failed to answer with his long-winded digressions.

Tebeya could not help but take solace in the appearance of the man and his humble hut. She had done the right thing for Comfort, and she thought this had been the purpose of the trip—assurance that she had adopted the girl as much for Comfort as for herself.

CHAPTER FORTY-THREE

JUMMAI'S MOTHER ROCKED a suckling baby while a little boy, with the wobbly, determined gait of a toddler, crashed into her legs and struggled to clamber onto her lap. Jummai's mother did not care that Zanya had come to speak to her daughter. He had thought he would have to explain his presence and feign being a part of the mission—coming to minister or evangelize—in order to speak to Jummai.

He had never visited Jummai's home before. She presented herself well so that no one would know from looking at her that this deteriorating house was the kind of home she came from. He looked around at Jummai's siblings and understood that this was what she had not wanted. Another mouth to feed among all her brothers and sisters.

"Go and call Jummai for me," he said to one of the boys.

Jummai ambled outside, taking tender, inefficient steps. She walked as if in need of a cane, and he went to take her arm and aid her in sitting in a chair against the wall.

His eyes explored the changes in her. She was a beauty still, though she seemed to have aged in a matter of weeks since he had last seen her in that abandoned building. She wore her hair in the same single braid down her neck. He was at once surprised and relieved to find he was not in thrall to her beauty.

"How have you been?" he asked.

"I've been fine." She gestured for him to sit, but there were no other chairs.

"I learnt you were sick."

"Okay."

"You didn't tell me that you were not well—"

"Did I die?" Jummai said. "Am here, am I not?"

He had the envelope in his pocket, and he handed it to her. It was a portion of the money he had saved all these years he worked for the mission, thinking he would use it for the wedding and the house he had planned to build for him and Nami.

"What is this, Zanya?"

"You will see."

She peeked into the envelope, looked at him, peeked again, and then laughed. He saw she was missing a tooth, a back molar he would not have seen if she had not laughed as she always had, with her head thrown back and her shoulders shaking. Seeing the missing molar saddened him. It was as if an unexpected pain undergirded her laughter. He remembered her past laughter in his pickup, how it echoed against the ceiling and windows. In this present laughter, sorrow emerged abruptly like a legion of crows taking flight from a tree.

"What did you go and do?" she said. "Why are you giving this to me?"

"Is it not what you asked for?" he said.

"Zanya—"

"I know what happened." He did not say it to cause her any guilt. He said it so that they would both be released in the acknowledgement of the truth.

She avoided his gaze and tucked the envelope into her wrapper. "Thank you."

Her face contorted, as if it were excruciating to sit near him with her aching, injured body. It seemed as if she wanted to weep with him about the loss of the child and what she had experienced.

He could have led her to a shaded area or given her food or offered more money than what he had given her. He could do those things, but he could not indulge her desire to cry about a child he had never known because what he felt was a welling of relief—a quiet, palpable relief for the possibilities and opportunities yet in front of him.

⁂

"See what you've done, Zanya," Betabwi said. He nodded toward a group of men who had congregated around three tables in Flo's restaurant, in furious debate about Jim Clemens's past, like ants swarming a crumb. Kago had convinced Betabwi to come on board with asking Reverend Jim to step down.

Zanya said, "What have I done but told the truth?"

"Listen to them talking about this church." Betabwi was pleased. "People who don't even go, who have never put one of their toes are angry—"

Zanya laughed. "This is what we wanted."

"This is your doing. Fire Boy!"

The majority of locals were with him and his laborers. Reverend Jim had taken advantage of the men, and Nelson Landry had harmed his patients. These white people considered themselves invincible; they did not think the locals would discover their misdeeds. How could these missionaries be trusted?

This time, Zanya would not be the singular voice. His voice alone had carried little clout. That had been his mistake and conceit, believing his lone voice sufficient. Zanya had promised to raise the issue to Jim Clemens in front of the congregation this Sunday.

He said to Betabwi, "We will come back here tomorrow—"

"And next tomorrow, until this Sunday happens, ba?"

"Now you're seeing."

※

Within an hour, Zanya was in front of the provisions store counter, standing next to Chubz, listening to the complaints of people who had gathered. Two were university students, less reserved than the other locals, pontificating about Reverend Jim's disgraceful exit from his American church. Zanya had noted their names and could see that they would be instrumental in the future: possible leaders to court.

One of the university students said, "Missionaries are here under the pretenses of Christianity, saying that they want to help us when they're only ruining our culture, our affairs—"

"These are African affairs to be dealt with by Africans," the other student chimed. "Since independence, other churches have brought Africans forward. Why is the church in Rabata moving backwards when others have indigenized?"

"If the church in America did not want Reverend," someone said, slapping down money on the counter for a case of tinned sardines, "what made them think we would want him here?"

"It's not right for him to have come," Chubz added. "He never told us the truth of what happened. When people hide things like this, it makes you to wonder."

"What about the doctor who worked for him?" one of the women said, her face sheathed with condescension. "Let us not forget what he did."

"Yes! What if people died because of that Nelson Landry they brought to us?"

"What about when Gary Parson's son went and burnt Mama Daga's lubu?"

There were groans of remembrance.

A voice from the back said, "Who knows what else he will go and burn?"

"They think they can come here and be doing anything to our

town," someone said. "How do we know one of them didn't send that child to go and burn the thing?"

"Zanya," the man said. "Tell Reverend Jim that we don't want him leading the church."

"Yes o!"

"Let us tell him!"

Someone shouted, "Missionary, go home!" and others laughed, but soon a chant was taken up throughout the provisions store.

"Missionary, go home!"

"Missionary, go home!"

"Missionary, go home!"

Zanya raised his hands to settle the crowd. "We should give Reverend a chance to explain what happened. We were not there to hear the complaints that his church raised against him."

People grumbled aloud again: Why were they giving Reverend chance to talk more of his lies? Let them just be done with it. Why did they need to hear his excuses?

"I'm not defending anybody," Zanya said. "Am I not simply asking that before we come to any conclusion, we should consider how to address this problem? Let us not allow them to see us as they want to see all Africans."

He held their attention as he walked near the counter. "You see, they want us to believe we are unenlightened. Were our people not governing ourselves for generations before they came?" There was laughter from the crowd, and he waited for it to settle. "Do they not want us to think we are uncivilized? That we are backwards people?

"What did this university boy say? African affairs, ba? Are we not equipped to deal with our affairs ourselves? We don't need their interference in our own matters."

He had not felt like this in months—this certainty, this same revival and energy. He no longer doubted. He was on the side of the town and the laborers, and the thing was sweet, like the slow, unctuous pour of oil into his bones.

"They must hear your voices and not only my own," he said. "Come to the mission compound this Sunday. Let Jim Clemens answer us."

⋇

Gary inquired again, "Are you sure you never said anything?"

"I swear, Gary, if you ask me one more time."

"I know. You said no."

"All right," Katherine said, guiding the butter knife over her piece of bread. She had become used to the texture of bread here, how spongy it was, like Texas toast, just a little softer, a little sweeter. She might miss the taste of it once she was back home.

Zanya had met with many people over the last couple weeks, on a crusade after receiving her letter. There were whispers about practices and traditions needing to be overturned in the mission church. Some of the locals were requesting a public assembly with Reverend Jim on the mission compound on Sunday. It was electrifying to see these events unfolding.

"You knew Jim left his church, dear," she said. "You might have let it slip to someone."

"No." Gary sighed. "I wouldn't have, and I didn't."

She shrugged. "Tebeya's brother lives in America. In Minnesota."

"So?" Gary turned his head sideways. "So what?"

"It's a small world, that's all I'm saying, okay?"

Gary had not touched his egg stew. He rubbed the handle of his mug, following the curve with his thumb. "They're saying I knew about this from the beginning. I just wish—I don't know how it got so out of hand."

"Well," Katherine said, licking the corners of her mouth for a stray dollop of butter, "Jim should have been honest from the beginning—with all of us."

"Sure, that's exactly what he should have done," Gary said. She could see he was starting to get worked up. "All I wanted to do was straighten things out, take a look at the finances—"

"We need to accept that God is handing the church over to the Africans, like they did in Congo. Isn't that what you said happened in Oicha?"

"Right, so what would it look like to leave right when the Africans want to take over church leadership? It'll send the wrong message, that we feel like we're too good to be under their spiritual guidance or authority, that we can't work with them—"

"Gary, stop it. We're coming to the end of our time here in Rabata."

Gary scoffed. "Katherine, you've always been at the end."

"Don't you dare say I've been at the end. After all I've done for our family, after all I've given up for you, don't you dare say that to me."

Gary pushed his coffee aside, and a little wave of it splashed over the sides and pooled around the mug. "All I'm saying is that we can serve somewhere else in Nigeria or another country. This doesn't have to be it for us—"

"Where else? In Ethiopia with Delores? That's what you want. To keep me on this godforsaken continent"—she gave a wry, apathetic laugh—"for your *mistress.*"

They had not mentioned Delores's name aloud since Nelson's departure. Yet her presence hung like filaments of a spider's web, sweeping across tree branches, invisible until times like this, when you walked smack into it.

Gary blinked, struggling to put his turmoil into words. Whatever feelings he had for Delores were plain as day on his face—the hooded eyes, the beleaguered expression.

"All I did was talk to her, Katherine, like I wanted to talk to you. About the mission, about being here and how good it felt to be here and do this work. I talked to her when you closed up and didn't want to be in this with me."

He was hurting her. He wanted to hurt her with his declarations.

"We never—I never slept with her, Katherine. I swear to you I never did."

She tinked her fork on the plate's rim to silence him. She had survived these months without any discussion of whatever might have transpired between him and Delores Boyd. Survived his miserly affection. If she reached for him, he stroked her hair perfunctorily, not as he had before. She had endured this for months. She would not allow him to speak now.

"Take me back to Missouri," she said.

CHAPTER FORTY-FOUR

JUMMAI COUNTED THE MONEY Zanya had given her. She had counted it many times after he left yesterday. She had planned to put it in the trunk that Tin City had broken, but she needed a new hiding place. Her mother said Tin City was never returning to the house, but Jummai could not trust her mother. He could come tomorrow or next tomorrow or the following month. The little trust she had given her mother before was no more.

The money was enough to start operating a food stand, and a restaurant could come in time. Or maybe it would never come. What did she know of life? Outside, the way the sun was shining on the trees made the leaves look a lighter color than usual. Was that not life? To think a thing was one way and for it to become another?

This morning, Dr. Tebeya had come to the house to inspect her bandages, and she had said, "Jummai, I don't think you understood what I said to you about your surgery and what it might mean for you." Dr. Tebeya had thrown her sentences of stone again, and this time, the stones had descended into the well of Jummai's mind.

Too many stones had been thrown into her well these days. She was a woman who accepted things. This is what she thought about herself. But the things she was being asked to accept had become too much. She did not know if she could have a child again. She would not marry Zanya, this man she had loved. She had lost the money she saved because of Tin City. All of it—gone. One day a thing was here, and the next day, a thing was gone. She understood now that she was the type of person things liked to leave. And she was supposed to keep accepting how things happened to her. She was supposed to wake up and keep going as if these things that were gone did not matter, as if these things had never mattered.

No, it would come to pass, the things she wanted. The restaurant. Leaving her mother's house. She could return to Miss Delores who had said, "Raise half," and show her the money from Zanya and see if Miss Delores would ask her church in America to help Jummai as she had asked them to help Jecinda. Her womb would heal, Dr. Tebeya said she would help, and there would be marriage and another child one day. In time, she would be well.

"Jummai." Yakwo was at the door, dragging a branch back and forth across the ground.

"What is it?"

She waited for a rambling complaint or for him to tell her Innocent was misbehaving.

He said, "You want me to bring you food?"

She looked up at him.

"Jecinda is making food."

"Yes. Go and bring it."

He had become protective since the trouble with Tin City. More than Sayi and Innocent, or Jecinda, he sensed when she needed to lie down or when she needed help to walk. He would fetch water for her. Sometimes, he would sit with her and not say anything. It was as if the accident had made him recognize that things happened in life that were serious, and so he had become serious to be able to handle these things.

Yakwo went off to where Jecinda was pounding yam. He threw the branch aside and fetched a bowl for Jecinda to dish the soup.

Jummai could have given birth to a child like her mother had recently given birth to a new sister for them. Jummai's child might have been a boy, and he would have grown up to be as kind and good as Yakwo was these days. She would have wailed during the birth, weeping not for the pain between her thighs but for Zanya. The child would not have come clean and silent; it would have come screaming and wanting like its father. It would have come with the defiant eyes of Zanya, boasting his strength and tenacity.

She folded part of her wrapper to her face because the tears she had not cried since she went to the diviner were coming now, rising in her chest and turning into a low, inaudible sob. It became a strange groaning that seemed not to come from her. She could say it was something about the afternoon, the dampness in the air, the sun low in the sky like fruit to be plucked, but it was the realization in her spirit of the things that were now gone.

CHAPTER FORTY-FIVE

ZANYA STEPPED OVER THE THRESHOLD into the Reverend's parlor, aware that he had interrupted the two men. There was a momentary lapse in their conversation, and it was clear from their expressions they had not expected him to arrive early to the requested meeting.

Gary Parson sprung up from the cushion to greet him.

"Zanya, it's good to see you." He seemed to mean it. Since Katherine Parson told him about Gary's duplicity, Zanya had trouble seeing him with the same eyes. This man had taken the associate pastor position after saying Zanya should be the one in leadership. Gary Parson had seemed content in Rabata, doing what he could do to support the mission, no matter the role. Had this been pretense? Gary Parson seemed like less of his former self, less ebullient, as if he had suffered loss. Or was Zanya sensing loss everywhere he went, when none existed?

"Won't you come in?" Reverend Jim rose to grip Zanya's hand in a firm shake, as if they had not parted with anger, as if he had not fired him.

Since receiving the invitation to come to Reverend Jim's house, Zanya had rehearsed this moment, and yet when it was here, and he was in the house, hearing their voices destabilized him. Reverend Jim was willing to have a meeting now. When his laborers had requested one months ago, Jim had ignored them.

"I'm sure you know why we've invited you here," Reverend Jim said.

"Yes, I know," he said.

Zanya's glance traveled to a familiar black-and-white photograph. Reverend Jim in a suit at a young age—the serene, thoughtful expression on the bespectacled face, the stern mouth, and the same elongated forehead. Next to the Reverend was a stoic, dark-haired woman—Edna, the wife who had died before he came to Rabata. Reverend Jim often said Edna would have loved serving the people of Nigeria along with him.

"I'd like us to come to some sort of agreement," Reverend Jim said. Both him and Gary Parson were seated on the cushion across from Zanya. "If word of this rumor gets to mission headquarters, well, it won't reflect well on me, you see."

Zanya said, "News of your financial mismanagement?"

"It's not as you've portrayed it—"

"What is it then, Reverend?"

"Listen, this has gotten a little out of control, Zanya," Reverend Jim said. "I'd be happy to reinstate you to your position. I'm sure it'd go a long way for you and your lovely bride."

Zanya had a sudden awareness of the cuffs of his shirt nuzzling his wrists. He had not expected them to offer him his position back.

"We'd start small, you see," Reverend Jim said. "A trial period, to get us going. Perhaps, we can have you translating again for me this Sunday."

"That's not what we decided, Jim. We didn't talk about starting small," Gary said. "We said everything back to the way it was."

"Well, I think gradualism is the answer here," Reverend Jim said. "We've also considered the possibility of enrolling you in a seminary program, Zanya. We'd take on the cost."

Zanya looked at Gary Parson. "Did you attend seminary?"

"Well, no," Gary admitted. "Not exactly."

"I see," Zanya said. "Yet, you are here leading."

"I wish I'd gone," Gary said. "Take the opportunity, Zanya."

"And the laborers? What happens to them?"

"What about them?" Reverend Jim asked.

"Will they be rehired? Will they be given what they asked for?"

Sunlight streaked Reverend Jim's hair, and crinkles cradled his eyes, signifying like the rings of a tree his years in Rabata. He looked the same as he had when he arrived from America in '67 and Zanya came upon his beaten body after the robbery. Yams, guavas, pineapples, oranges—all the nourishing foods of Rabata had had little effect on him.

"It'd put me in a bind, you see." Reverend Jim uncapped and recapped a fountain pen before laying it on the center table. "We have new laborers getting the job done."

Zanya knew. These new laborers had come from nearby towns hungry for work, pleased with receiving the same wages the other laborers had fought against. Zanya had walked by the construction site the other day to find that the walls of the church and the roof had been completed, and it looked a solid, impermeable structure undefiled by the heavy rains. He recognized a childish pride that had desired its destruction, desired things to fall apart for these new laborers without his expertise to guide them. He had resisted the curiosity to wander inside and search for defects in the church's interior—irreparable cracks and splinters in the wooden beams, gaps between the walls and window panes.

"What about other mission projects?" Zanya said. "You said there was a guesthouse that would be built in the next year."

"Well, we can't reward the sort of behavior the laborers displayed with more work," Reverend Jim said. "These same men could cause strife with future projects—"

"Jim, just a minute now." Gary Parson looked a bit exasperated. "Why don't we take some of this under consideration? Let's think about it."

"Listen, Zanya," Jim said, "we need to take this one step at a time. Trust me in this."

"After what happened in America, sir, how are we to trust you?"

A flush of color crept across Reverend Jim's jowls. He seemed to be taking Zanya in, comparing him against an earlier memory. He looked at him as he had on the Sunday Zanya had given his testimony. Then, the Reverend's dubious, contemplative face had not bothered him. He had listened to Zanya from his place near the classroom window, close to where the young boys had leaned their heads inside, and Zanya thought that the look had more to do with the heat and the noise and the elbowing of the congregants.

The Reverend looked at Zanya with the same eyes as Zanya's father used to look at him. The eyes that said: *This boy has become something. How did he become something?* When his father got this look in his eyes, he would take to beating Zanya, and those looks often coincided with the times he returned on break from Kunama Secondary School. His father had seen this change in him as an affront against his own work as a builder.

"Our people," Zanya said, "should have known from the beginning."

"The people of this town were fine with our leadership," Reverend Jim said. "You've made them angry, Zanya. You've made them turn against the faith."

"Reverend, they're not turning against the faith, you understand? You cannot make us turn against what we have chosen. We have turned against what you're doing in this town under the guise of Christianity."

"Listen, Zanya," Gary said. "There's a lot you don't understand at the moment, and I hate that things have gotten out of hand. If you'd give things a little time—well, we'd love to squash this and come to an agreement that pleases everybody."

Zanya pushed his sleeves up to his elbows, feeling unusually warm and confined in the spacious parlor. These people were afraid, which meant the letter held truth.

"Put Nigerians in leadership," Zanya said. "In your position, Reverend Jim."

"My pastoral position?" Reverend Jim leaned forward and said, "You mean, put you in leadership, is that what you're saying? Allow *you* to fill it?"

Zanya stayed silent.

"Now, Zanya, how would you feel if the town learned about some of the things that never happened in Yawari?"

"Jim," Gary Parson rushed in. "I don't think that's necessary."

"Well, I think it is, since we're revealing our pasts," Reverend Jim said. "Why don't we leave this up to you, Zanya? How'd you like to go about this?"

It was the same. Nothing had changed with Jim Clemens. He remembered the diviner's tale about the two snakes, and he wondered if the diviner had been cautioning him against Jim, that Zanya might die if he did not forage elsewhere.

"I will see the two of you tomorrow," Zanya said, and took his leave.

CHAPTER FORTY-SIX

THOSE WHO HAD AIRED GRIEVANCES with him and Kago under the strung lights of Shigudu's beer parlor or at the tables of Flo's or the counter of Glories and Blessings Ladies' Provisions Store or under the orange trees in their yards had come. The temperature rose as people shifted in agitation, bumping shoulders, waiting for Reverend Jim and Gary Parson to come out of the Reverend's house. Manasseh, the Reverend's house helper, stood outside on the veranda, glaring at the people entering the compound as if he wanted to chase them out and lock the gate.

People had found chairs or were sitting on benches. Most stood, leaning against any structure they could find: the cowshed, the chicken coop, the gates.

At the front of the crowd, Zanya waited with Kago. He leaned over and whispered, "How are you, Kago?"

Kago had donned a clean shirt and shaved his stubble. He refastened the top two buttons of his shirt as his face worked with emotion. "It is time," he said.

Another fifteen minutes passed before Jim Clemens and Gary Parson walked out on the veranda. Gary stood behind Jim, running a nervous finger along the crease of his Bible, and looked out at the crowd.

"My fellow congregants," Reverend Jim said in a voice that surprised Zanya with its firmness, its readiness to buck accusations. "It's come to my attention that you're questioning my ability to lead this church." He raised his voice. "We must denounce slander. We must strive for uprightness and mercy instead of sowing seeds of distrust."

Zanya took intentional steps to stand on the veranda. He had not meant to react so quickly. He had wanted to wait for the Reverend and Gary to speak. He sensed immediately the direction the Reverend planned to take to solicit sympathy.

"We, too," Zanya said, turning to face the crowd, "are people who denounce corrupt talk. Reverend, we are asking you to tell us what happened in your church in America. How are you positioned to lead after you were unwanted in your last church?"

"Yes!" It was the voice of Kago.

"Tell us what happened," came another voice.

Zanya said, "You were dismissed from your former church—"

"No, no, I was never dismissed," Reverend Jim said.

"Let your yes be yes and your no be no." Zanya's voice, loud and strong, carried through the compound. He would press into Jim Clemens like a boil until the truth erupted. "Did you leave your church because of financial mismanagement? What is the truth?"

"The truth?" Jim Clemens's face twisted in bitterness. "Yes, in a way, you could say I resigned from my last position. The reasons are complicated, having to do with my youngest son Pete. He was the one who took funds from the church."

"You see!"

"We knew!"

"Wait," someone said. "Is Reverend innocent then?"

Reverend Jim looked at Zanya. "I knew nothing of Pete's ploy."

"And did you try and prosecute him when you learnt what he did? Instead of prosecuting him, you allowed him freedom to escape. You did this for your son, and you came to us and did the opposite. What freedom have you given us? What protection?"

"Zanya is right o," someone shouted.

"Reverend, look how you came and treated us," a laborer said.

Zanya allowed the whispers and accusations to flourish. Out in the crowd, Zanya saw Katherine Parson, sitting on the Parsons' veranda across from the Reverend's house. Elijah was at her side. She appeared unworried about what the letter had unleashed. Delores Boyd stood on the other side of the Parsons' veranda. He thought she would have marched to the front by now and asserted her opinion, as she had on Resurrection Sunday. Today, she seemed to know this was not a battle for her to join.

Gary Parson came forward. "I know the past two weeks have been difficult for many of us, hearing that a trusted leader is not what you thought he was. You allowed us into your town and into your homes and we failed you. On behalf of the mission, I am deeply sorry. We will do what we can to regain your trust."

There were reluctant nods of agreement from the crowd.

"It is not enough," Kago said, and it seemed to pain him to speak against Gary Parson. He joined them on the veranda. "All these years, Jim Clemens has led this church, and now that we Africans are saying 'enough,' you want to silence us."

Reverend Jim said, "I've given much to this town, to your families, to the education of your children." Surrounded by the locals, he had been on edge when he first walked outside, but now he was reinvigorated, and his voice was raised and defiant. "Let's not take drastic actions over what is most certainly a misunderstanding. I want to lead this church as long as I am able—"

"You cannot," Zanya said. "Not anymore, Reverend."

"The time has come for a transfer of power," Kago said.

The four of them were the only ones standing on the veranda. Him and Kago on one side, and Gary Parson and Jim Clemens, next to each other.

"Reverend Jim," Zanya said, and his tone shifted subtly. He was here accusing the Reverend, and he had not taken responsibility for his own deception. "I know men like you. Men who do something, like you did in protecting your son, and you believe that this *one thing* might define you. I was like this, too. I was like this with the lie I told about my testimony of fire. It happened, but it did not happen in the way that I said."

He proceeded to tell them the full truth about that night in Yawari. There was silence, as if people had not heard the confession, before a chorus of voices came at once:

"Did Zanya say he never burned?"

"What is he saying?"

"All those months—"

"He *lied* to us?"

He had imagined the people rising up in arms, rushing toward him. But they were staring in surprise at him, waiting on him to say more, to explain, to help them understand.

This thing with the fire had felt so large, so looming he had felt he needed to hide it. How easily the truth had come out of him now, and it felt like this moment had happened a long time ago, and he was simply reliving it, confessing for the benefit of those before him. He felt the shift as he looked out at the faces, and he saw the baffled expressions, eyebrows raised in surprise, and within himself he felt the relinquishing of something he had not known he was holding. He turned to Kago, who looked bewildered. He would explain to him later and pray he would understand.

Looking back out at the crowd, he saw Nami. He had not expected to see her, sitting on a bench in her confident yet unassuming manner, not wearing the same expression of surprise sweeping the faces of the locals. Had she known that this had not been true, or did she no longer care? He looked at Reverend Jim standing on the veranda in the shame of his past, and he appeared defeated, the defiance gone in the wake of Zanya's admission.

"You lied to us like this and you want to lead us?" An older man spoke up. "How can we have this? How can we take one liar away and replace him with another?"

Someone shouted, "We cannot!"

"No! We cannot," others reprised.

"The persecution happened," said one of the university boys who had come to the front. "It did not happen exactly as Zanya said it, but he was attacked for his beliefs."

"Na lie still o."

"He nearly burned for his beliefs. That part is still true."

"How can we even know," one congregant said, "if his accusations against Reverend Jim are true—"

"Reverend said it was true!"

Another shouted, "How can we trust Zanya?"

Kago said, with a voice full of conviction, "I have seen the evidence with my own eyes. It is true what the Reverend did in his former church."

"Rabata, my town," Zanya said, "this town, you are more of a home to me than the village where I was raised. Whether you forgive me or not, my desire is that you are wise enough to see that the practices and traditions of this church should be our own." Zanya looked out at the congregants' perspiring, expectant faces. "I must prove myself to you again. I must regain your trust. So until I do, choose someone else to lead. Choose Kago to lead you. Whoever it is, choose one of our own to lead you."

His words stirred a change in the air, and he saw agreement in the glances of the crowd that had gathered and heard it in their murmurs. Kago nodded his head, as if he had been waiting all this time for someone to see him, to say that he, too, could lead.

The crowd parted. Zanya looked to see Tebeya walking to the veranda to join him and Kago. She stood with her hands clasped, waiting for some of the locals to quiet down before speaking. Zanya had forgotten about his request to her, and he had not known if she would come and support his petition.

No one knew what to make of Tebeya standing there like an elder. It was uncommon for a woman to speak at a moment like this. But this was Tebeya. She had gone off unmarried to be educated overseas, and people educated abroad brought back strange behaviors. She appeared unperturbed by the stifling humidity and unaware of the slight awe in the eyes of the other women, their curious envy at her courage, and the men's raised brows at perceived impudence.

Her voice carried through the compound, elegant and unafraid. "Church, it is not often that I stand before you," she said. "You know me as your doctor. You have entrusted me with your children, wives, mothers, and fathers. Please, listen to me when I say that whether Jim Clemens resigned or not from his previous church in America—it is not the correct question. What we should ask ourselves is if the time has passed for the mission to continue overseeing this church. Has the time come for us to lead ourselves?"

Zanya nodded his appreciation as Tebeya reclaimed her seat. He stepped toward the crowd. "These missionaries told us our drums were wicked, and we believed them. They told us our medicine was evil. We did not ask: Why is it that anything of ours is wrong, and all that is theirs is good? We did not say, which thing of what they say is of this faith and which thing of what they say is their own way, their own judgment?

"Power has been relinquished to our people in other places. It's happened in our school, and it's happened in our clinic. Let it happen in this church. Let us declare that we can lead ourselves. Let us declare ourselves powerful."

The people clapped, slowly at first, and then it gained momentum until it seemed no one else could stand up to speak. Jim Clemens was forgotten. No one listened for his voice any longer. It was greater than him, what was happening all around them.

CHAPTER FORTY-SEVEN

THE SUNSET LEFT FEATHERY LINES of pink and orange across the expanse of sky. The overlay of colors bestowed a golden hue on the mission compound, bronzing the sun-wilted leaves of the grapefruit trees and bougainvillea vines creeping along the walls and gates. The beauty of the compound failed to serve as a salve for Jim's remorse and embarrassment, both of which had not abated since the confrontation with the town.

Gary sat with Jim on the veranda, looking out at his own home. Jim could see the shadows of Katherine and Elijah behind the drawn curtains, preparing to eat dinner, waiting for Gary. He and Gary had sat in silence since Zanya and Kago and their retinue of disgruntled parishioners called for Jim's resignation afterwards in a private meeting. Zanya and Kago requested that a committee of Nigerians be established to appoint the next pastor. Jim knew once headquarters learned of his past and the town's growing resistance to him, there was little chance he would stay on board with the mission.

In the early days, Jim had stood in the primary school with Zanya as his translator, staring into the sun-weathered faces of a handful of curious locals. He had prayed deeply for them to know the hope of Christ. He had sought to master their language. He had prayed with their sick. Looking out at the congregation this morning, he knew he had lost them for good.

"We lost their trust," Gary said.

He wore the dark charcoal suit he had worn earlier. He looked diminutive, and his eyes were possessed of an uncertain, over-whelmed look as he fiddled with his tie, undoing the knot at the hollow of his neck and slipping it over his head.

A chicken squawked inside the coop, and then came the brief flutter of battling feathers. The compound had once brimmed with activity. Nelson Landry rushed to and from the clinic, his footsteps loud and unmistakable whenever he stomped through the gates. Before Allison left for boarding school, her friends had banged on their door, asking if she was allowed to come outside and play. Chickens and ducks pattered around in abundance, squalling and pecking at scraps while Jummai fried yams in the kitchen. There had been the steady thud of Manasseh chopping firewood, or his palm-frond broom scraping the cement.

"You should've told the mission—Bill Kent—the truth about First Presbyterian."

"I would never have been able to come here if I had."

Gary rose, and in a very tired voice said, "Maybe it would've been for the best."

"Now, Gary…"

"Goodnight, Jim."

Gary walked off in a cheerless gait toward his house, at one point stopping in the middle of the compound and looking up, allowing what Jim imagined was a prayerful exhale. There was nothing he could have said to Gary that would yield forgiveness right now. He had marveled all week about how these events had transpired so rapidly, how the past had repeated itself.

He'd book a ticket back to Illinois. Once there, he would tend to Edna's grave, uproot dandelions, and set fresh flowers. He might reunite with his son Walter and Shirley, dote on the grandchildren who had dubious knowledge of him. Pete, who had written once in Jim's four years in Africa—a short, unapologetic note—might board a plane from his commune in San Francisco to visit him in Rockford.

Returning home should have filled Jim with hope. So, why did the thought of reuniting with his own sons depress his spirit? He thought about how brittle and strained these relationships had been before he left America. How little pleasure his children brought him or how little pleasure he could see he brought to them.

Jim breathed in, knowing he'd miss the smell of Rabata. And perhaps, one day, he would be sitting in Rockford, the night air redolent with the scent of mangoes and firewood, and he'd think about his time in West Africa, and he'd wonder, as he wondered now, if he should have ever come.

Benedict had driven Tebeya's mother to Tebeya's new home. They were picking up Comfort to take her shopping for a new dress and new shoes in Keffi. At least her mother was trying. Something had shifted in her, and she had decided to start accepting Tebeya's invitations for her to spend time with Comfort.

"Where are you going?" her mother said, at the door to her bungalow.

"Where else, Mama?" Tebeya said.

She was due at the clinic in the next hour. She had decided to never speak to her mother about the scheme to have her fired from the mission clinic.

Her mother said nothing. She simply called Comfort to the door. This was how it would be between them from now on. Tebeya waited until Benedict had driven off and she could no longer see the red taillights before getting into her car to drive in the opposite direction to her family's mansion. Her father would be home from his travels this afternoon, and she thought he might be amenable to her proposal. She had considered securing a partner-ship with a hospital in America through her brother Patrick. She would petition her father to resume donations to the clinic and ask him to fund the church building for its completion.

She recalled Zanya's words. They were not people dependent on foreigners for assistance. Things were going to change in Rabata, and it was both daunting and exciting. Delores Boyd was leaving the primary school, and it would survive. The church had undergone a strike and Jim Clemens's deception, and yet it would survive.

So, the clinic, too, would survive.

Katherine examined a sleeveless periwinkle dress she had bought years ago after her and Gary's fourth wedding anniversary. Since they were returning to Missouri, her desire for new clothes in eye-catching colors—an emerald green or rose—had surfaced, and already, in her mind, she had planned a trip to Heer's. She'd go with her mother or Danny's girlfriend, and while there, they would stop at the mezzanine to nibble on a cold raspberry sherbet. They'd meander to the hairdressers for Katherine's new 'do, a flipped style like she had seen in a photo Sally sent. She worried it might be out of fashion.

These small uncertainties were reprising her anxieties—the fear of not knowing the fashion trends, what was popular or anti-quated. She had been doing this all week since the confrontation with the locals last Sunday: thinking about going back to America, what would be new and different. She'd sound different after near-ly a decade in Penang and Rabata, and there'd be new expressions and social etiquettes to learn. Still, she experienced a lovely jolt knowing a date would soon be set for their permanent departure to Springfield. By the end of July or early August, they would be home.

Elijah had come to her earlier in the week and said, "Mom, does this mean we're leaving Nigeria?"

"Yes," she said, smiling brightly. "It does, sweetheart."

"Oh."

"It's what you wanted, isn't it?"

"Yeah," he'd said. But her son, who had cried months ago and said, "I hate Africa," had descended into a sullen, touchy mood after learning they would leave.

Allison said she planned to come back to West Africa after college. She wanted to be a missionary and work with the Voices of the Gospel radio station in Jos.

"Sure, honey," Katherine said, because she knew her daughter would change her mind. Allison would return to Missouri and acclimate to the comforts of home. She'd have a network of friends or a steady boyfriend she would refuse to leave by the time she was college-aged.

Katherine removed another dress from the leather Samsonite, one sewn by Rhoda with fabric they purchased in Malaysia; it was the color of a pink peony, imprinted with teal blossoms. Leave or take to America? She wanted to arrive unburdened by memories of Southeast Asia and West Africa. She would leave it with the others. She would give them all to Jummai.

Jummai had come in today to do some light chores. She looked much healthier than she had in the hospital. Katherine had given her the news of their departure.

"You are going back to America?" Jummai said.

"That's right. It seems to be the plan at the moment," Katherine said.

Jummai had not asked when they would go, and she had not said how wonderful it had been working for their family these four years. She simply said, "Okay, ma," as if she had expected them to go, as if their leaving had no consequences for her. Her indifference left Katherine feeling rebuffed.

"She doesn't care," she said to Gary.

"I think she does, honey," Gary said. "A lot more than you think."

People had come to her and Gary after the confrontation on the mission compound and expressed their sadness about them returning to America. Her patients asked if she would be coming back in a few years' time. Every little *no* gave Katherine a great satisfaction.

Gary walked into the bedroom and surveyed the piles of clothes. "Packing already?"

She dropped the dress. "I was just looking through a few things."

"It's all right, Katherine," he said. "There's no need to pretend."

He placed his book on the nightstand and sank down on the bed, folding a couple of her dresses to avoid sitting on them. He looked every minute of forty-two, with a spattering of gray in his beard and a slight paunch that had formed on his slim frame.

"Suppose," she said, "suppose you don't like it back home, in Missouri—"

She had found herself asking him this question, rephrasing it multiple times. She lacked control over his happiness, yet she wanted reassurance that he would not grow resentful.

He gave a half-smile. "Is that really your concern, honey?"

"I just want to know you're happy with our decision to go back home."

"Well, it wasn't really a decision, now was it?" he said.

Tiredness and sadness hunched his posture, and he rubbed his temples. God had taken what was most precious to Gary, and her heart softened a little for his pain. She longed to wrap her arms around him and nuzzle into the warm, familiar crook of his shoulder, and tell him the truth, tell him that she'd had a hand in how this all came to pass. It might help them to share things with each other again. A clean slate before they returned home. But there were things she knew she'd never share with Gary, not in a million years.

She did not move toward her husband; she remained standing where she was.

"There's nothing left for us here, Gary," she said.

"I know, sweetheart," he said.

꙯

"I did not know things would happen like this," Zanya said. The song "My Lady Frustration" was an accompaniment to the conversation in Shigudu's.

"You should be saluted," Kago said.

"No, we should salute ourselves."

Over the past couple of days, Zanya had asked himself several times: What had they done? Did they understand the undertaking? Would headquarters move the mission station from Rabata? Congregants who had sided with the mission might leave the church once a new pastor was elected. He remembered the days he and his laborers shouted instructions back and forth on the construction site, and the women roasted corn and plantains or sold bags of chopped coconut. The bricks and sand on the site were piled so high it made a person wonder where all of it would go. This felt an abrupt, improper ending after all those months. The same as it had with Nami.

He had run into Nami the other day. He maintained his distance before they greeted each other superficially, affecting cordiality. She had walked toward him and said, "If you want to talk, Zanya, we can talk." There had been nothing in her tone of voice to offer him hope. But somewhere deep within him, hope stirred. It was possible things could return again as they had been before his transgressions.

"So," Kago said, "what will happen now?"

Distant noises—that of insouciant laughter and chatter—
seemed far removed from him minutes ago, and now they roared in
his head, along with the motorbikes and taxis rumbling down the
main road in Rabata. The tables in Shigudu's were full of people,
and Fela Kuti's voice blasted from a radio outside, rising above the
conversations, and in the back of the beer parlor, women pounded
yam as if nothing at all had changed.

"We will carry on," Zanya said.

ACKNOWLEDGMENTS

I MUST EXPRESS SPECIAL GRATITUDE to my late maternal grandfather, Nyayisa Koche Chidawa, for entrusting the traditions and his stories of the Gbagyi people with me. Thank you to Awyebwi Wanwyegni Jatau, Jecenuda Esther Jatau, and Aba Keziah Chidawa; though you are no longer with us, your faithfulness lives on. The early version of this novel could not have been transformed into this final work without the kindness of my aunts and uncles, who shared memories, proverbs, and resources: Phoebe Ayenajeh, Naomi Jatau, Jacob Jatau, Gloria Acheme, Roxie Bako, Ibrahim Katampe, and Angela Katampe.

I'm grateful to my agent, Ellen Levine, for her discerning eye and for working patiently with me on the original manuscript in order to bring forth the true work. I thank the entire team at Dzanc, notably editors Michelle Dotter and Chelsea Gibbons, for their dedication, expertise, and shepherding of this novel.

I'm thankful for the time and space I received at artist residencies and workshops: Vermont Studio Center, Ucross Foundation, Ragdale Foundation, and Callaloo Creative Writing Workshop. I am indebted to my brilliant instructors at the Iowa Writers' Workshop: Sugi Ganeshananthan, Ayana Mathis, Amber Dermont, and Paul Harding. I needed your collective wisdom and insight to finish this work. Thank you to Lan Samantha Chang for her support and advice throughout my time at the Workshop. I'm grateful to

Connie Brothers, Deb West, and Jan Zenisek for their administrative guidance. Thank you to Maurice Wallace and Patricia Elam, two mentors who served as catalysts in my creative journey. Special thanks are due Curtis Sittenfeld and Ravi Howard for their encouragement.

To those who read drafts or excerpts of this manuscript and offered feedback, thank you: Dawnie Walton, Eliana Ramage, Regina Porter, Monica West, Melissa Mogollon, Jade Jones, Grayson Morley, Yvonne Cha, Jianan Qian, Mia Bailey, Tameka Cage Conley, Anna Polonyi, Angela Tharpe, Kiley Reid, Nathan Machart, Mark Prins, Robert Lamirande, Bentley Reese, James Frankie Thomas, Matthew Kozlark, Ifeoma Peters, Osita Peters, Vanessa Small, Doris Acheme, Onjefu Ochai, Baleja Saidi, Barclay Bram Shoemaker, Jennica Dotson, and Sara Birmingham. Thank you also to those who contributed to research for this novel: Rachel Gabler, Nola Galluch, Naomi Gustafson, Waheedah Masinga, Brian Naess, Cesuwo Paceyi, Keith and Carol Plate.

I'm beyond grateful to innumerable friends and former colleagues who offered support, prayers, and a listening ear during the writing process. To my extended family, thank you for your support in small and large ways throughout the years. To my mother and father, thank you for your unwavering faith, open-mindedness, and grace, beyond the writing of this book. Thank you for sharing your childhood stories and allowing me to ping you via email and WhatsApp with random questions at random times of day. To my brothers, thank you for your selflessness and willingness to always lend assistance without complaint. To Philip, thank you for your commitment and devotion, amidst the concrete tasks of reading and editing multiple drafts. Thank you for nurturing the seedling of an idea and standing with me until it became a thing to hold in my hands. Above all, I'm grateful to God, without whom there would be no vision or creation of this work.

A CONVERSATION WITH AFABWAJE KURIAN AND PAUL HARDING

Paul Harding is the author of the Pulitzer Prize–winning *Tinkers* and *This Other Eden*. He is a Distinguished Professor of Creative Writing at Emerson College.

Paul Harding: From the very opening, I love the complexity of the characters and of the setting in which they are placed, that of (at least) two different worlds or cultures. How did the idea for this novel come to you?

I visited Nigeria in 2015 and conducted interviews with my relatives. My paternal uncle told me a story about a relative of mine in the 1920s, who—out of compassion—carried a missionary on his back when they walked long distances together and the missionary got tired. My uncle was nonplussed as he recounted this story, stating it in a matter-of-fact voice. It was what it was. But for me, it sparked many things—curiosity at what was behind the story, disbelief, a sense of injustice at the thought that the missionary may have used my relative in this way. I mean, was this a mutual exchange? Was my relative's charity reciprocated? Did the missionary carry my relative on his back? So I wrote into this image, turning it on its head in the process. In my version, Zanya carries Reverend Jim to save his life, and in that action, there's a physical entwining of their two worlds, and eventually a spiritual and relational entwining follows. Zanya becomes Jim's savior, and it bothers Reverend Jim for years.

Tell us about the first line, "By sunrise, the town knew…"

I'm hoping to immediately signal to the reader that this novel isn't about a single individual. It's about a community, and a communal knowing. I hope to also introduce an element of mystery. Which town is this? What does the town collectively know? The town becomes a character.

What is the significance of the title, *Before the Mango Ripens*?

There is a Gbagyi proverb that inspired the title: "Before the ripening of fruit, what were the birds eating?" A common interpretation of this proverb is "We can do without," and this is the proverb Kago says to Zanya in reference to the locals being able to do without the interference or presence of the Americans. For me, the title also signifies the characters' desires and dreams. Many of the characters are "before the mango ripens," so to speak. The period of ripening represents a liminal space. It represents the maturing of dreams, not the actual fruition of them. When I think of Jummai, she is before the mango ripens. She's diligently saving, wishing for a different situation than her home circumstances allow. I think the same for Tebeya and Zanya and Katherine as well. Zanya is no longer content in the role of laborer. He believes there is something greater in store for him, and it hasn't ripened yet. I think the title also represents the political state of the nation in that time period. Nigeria was newly independent, about a decade old, having shaken off the yoke of British subjugation and moving toward defining itself as a nation—a ripening. I think the questions a new nation would ask itself are: Who were we in the past? Who do we want to be in the future? What are we ripening toward?

This novel fully humanizes its characters. You give readers an incredible range of lives here. Zanya, by the end, is legitimately changed. Jummai is wonderfully conflicted and torn by sorrow. Tebeya, too, is softened by her relationship with Comfort. You show us Reverend Jim's hardly pious will-to-power, Katherine Parsons's jealousy and incurable bigotry, and Deloris Boyd's apparent enlightenment. They are complicated, not simply one "good" cut-out image or another.

There's a short quote from Janet Burroway's *Writing Fiction: A Guide to Narrative Craft* that I used when I taught fiction to my undergraduate students. It says, "All of us are gentle, violent; logical, schmaltzy; tough, squeamish; lusty, prudish; sloppy, meticulous; energetic, apathetic; manic, depressive." We are all contradictions. We are not good cut-out images. Chubz, who works behind the counter of Glories and Blessings Ladies Provisions Store, used to be more present in the novel. At the end of an earlier draft, I had a scene where he was speaking to his wife. She, a faithful churchgoer and supporter of the missionaries, was upset that Zanya was easily forgiven by the locals for his deception and saddened that Rabata turned against Reverend Jim. In the scene, Chubz smokes his joint and quotes the Bible, saying, "All have sinned and fallen short of the glory of God." Essentially, he's saying, look, Zanya did what he did, and Reverend Jim did what he did. They both told half-truths. They both misled each other and the town. They're both hypocrites. So who's really the villain? Who's really the hero? Aren't we all complicated, layered, broken, and searching? Which one of us is purely good or purely evil? For me, Chubz's response sums up the human condition.

Because of the (still, essentially) colonial superimposition of American and European Christian missionary culture onto Nigerian culture, it'd be easy to make all the white characters into

flat cartoon villains, or all the locals into epic heroes/heroines. Tell us how you managed to retain all of the unsavory aspects of the missionaries' often unenlightened, paternalistic attitudes, while simultaneously giving them real human lives.

I like to complicate my characters, try to give them understand-able motivations and fears. I want them to be compelling on the page, whether they're the antagonist or protagonist. Villains have mothers, too, right? Even a simple statement like that humanizes a villain. I approach writing with a lot of empathy for my characters. I remember a workshopper saying something akin to, "I really love Katherine. I know she's racist, and I don't think I'm supposed to like her, but I do." I loved hearing this wrestling. Showing Kather-ine as hurt, jealous, suspicious, ignorant, and ultimately as human allows readers to see her more fully, which I personally enjoy as a writer. I find that conflict within myself. I see gray in people, where others may see black and white. I think I'm wired to try to find the good. I'm always seeking explanations—some might say excuses—for what leads us to behave as we do.

The novel depicts a clash between Western and indigenous faith practices, and among competing interpretations of Christian-ity. The locals, in particular, demonstrate a wide spectrum of theological and cosmological viewpoints. How did you wish to portray these various embodiments of and reactions to Chris-tianity? And to what extent is your novel about reclaiming a distinctively African Christianity?

Christianity has largely been depicted as being forced upon Af-ricans and rarely willingly or intelligently received. There's no question that Christianity was weaponized, a tool of the colonizer to oppress and exploit. But I think to reject the fact that many Africans thoughtfully considered and accepted the faith is to infantilize them or portray them as lacking agency, which also robs them of their intelligence. Just like there was a spectrum of reactions to British soldiers and administrators—staunch opposition, physical and spiritual warfare, or surrender—there was also a spectrum of reactions to missionaries. Those who rejected Christianity outright; those who accepted it superficially, for education or economic progress (or for their safety when force was involved); those who accepted specific teachings and practiced syncretism with their traditional faiths; and those who accepted it genuinely. I think the locals, both minor and major characters, highlight the varied reactions. Africans were not simply passive observers. The roots of Christianity also run deep on the African continent, so it wasn't always and only accessed through Western missionaries. Christianity was in Africa in the first century. The ruler of the Benin Empire sent religious scholars to Portugal to study Christianity in the fifteenth century. Many Christians in the Philippines, Congo, Kenya, and other nations fought against Western teachings and interpretations of the Bible and created indigenous-led churches, striving to make this faith their own.

How did writing about this specific decade differ from your other works of fiction, which have not been explicitly historical in nature?

I conducted far more research for this novel. I relied on interviews with relatives, and on many secondary sources, like *The Gbagyi Journal*, Joseph A. Shekwo's *Gbagyi Folktales and Myths*, and *An Introduction to the History of SIM/ECWA in Nigeria 1893-1993* by Yusufu Turaki. I read letters that Vera Thiessen, a medical missionary for the Africa Inland Mission to the Congo, wrote to her mother and sister from the 1940s to the 1970s. I read self-published memoirs from missionaries who had lived in Nigeria for twenty to thirty years, and Lamin Sanneh's *Whose Religion Is Christianity?*

The Gospel Beyond the West. It was also important for me to try to capture the ethos of the seventies. So to get myself into that mindset, besides watching video clips from that time, I wrote certain scenes while listening to music from the seventies. When I listen to music from the nineties, I'm instantly transported back to childhood, and specific scenes and memories appear, and I'm filled with nostalgia and emotion. I hoped music from the seventies would serve as an emotional gateway for me. When I wrote the scene with the laborers in Shigudu's beer parlor, I listened to other artists I named in the novel, like The Wings or the Lijadu Sisters. During a particular writing session, I had Fela Kuti's "Teacher Don't Teach Me Nonsense" on repeat for two or three hours.

At its best, the novel leaves the reader with the deepest aesthetic sense of lived experience, expressed through a rich multiplicity of consciousnesses. How did the ending come to you, the final confrontation between the locals and missionaries?

I knew I wanted the novel's final scene to mirror its opening scene in a way that shows a transformation of the town. Zanya is no longer as centered in the final scene as he was in the opening scene. It's about the town and not about an individual. Initially, I also had the final confrontation between the missionaries and the town taking place in the primary school where the missionaries held their church services. I changed it to the mission compound in the final draft. I wanted the locals to stake a claim to their land by encroaching upon the mission compound property. The takeover is not drawn out or explicitly mentioned as other takeovers, but retaking the mission compound—which has been gated and locked and never really sees the presence of many locals throughout the novel—is the town's quieter and final act of reclamation.

READING GROUP DISCUSSION
QUESTIONS

CHARACTER ANALYSIS: How do Jummai, Tebeya, and Zanya each embody different aspects of Rabata's society? Discuss their personal journeys and the challenges they face.

THEMES OF SECRECY AND REVELATION: Many of the characters in Rabata have maintained secrets or told half-truths. How do these secrets and half-truths shape the characters' actions and the overall plot? What are the consequences when these secrets are revealed? What are the consequences when the secrets remain undisclosed?

IMPACT OF THE MISSIONARIES: How do the American missionaries influence the social and interpersonal dynamics in Rabata? Discuss the effects of their presence on the town and its people, and the impact of the town on the missionaries.

CULTURAL AND HISTORICAL CONTEXT: How does the setting of 1970s Nigeria, a period of post-colonial transition, influence the story? What historical or cultural elements did you find most compelling? Which of these elements were you unaware of before this novel?

FAITH AND RELIGIOUS BELIEFS: Faith is a central theme in the novel. In which ways do the locals accept or reject the Christianity of the missionaries? How do the locals and the missionaries, as individuals, differ in their practices and articulations of Christianity? How do the characters, in general, grapple with their beliefs and humanity, and how do these struggles reflect broader societal issues?

PREJUDICE AND BIASES: In what ways are the characters struggling with their own limited knowledge, worldviews, or perspectives? How do prejudices and stereotypes affect how the characters interact with one another? What role do race and power play in the characters' relationships and personal journeys?

FEMALE EMPOWERMENT: How do the women in the novel (Jummai, Tebeya, Katherine, Delores) challenge and/or conform to traditional gender expectations?

IDENTITY AND BELONGING: Discuss how the characters search for belonging and identity within their community and beyond. How do their personal quests intersect with broader societal changes?

CONFLICT AND RESOLUTION: The novel builds up to the crucial question of whether to let the American missionaries stay, or make them go. How do the characters' decisions reflect their personal growth and the evolving identity of Rabata?

MORAL COMPLEXITY: Many characters in the novel operate in ethical gray zones. Discuss how Afabwaje Kurian portrays the challenges of moral ambiguity and its impact on the reader's perception of the characters.

CONTEMPORARY SOCIAL ISSUES: Though this novel is set in 1970s Nigeria, in what ways do the issues faced in Rabata feel relevant to the present moment, and your locale? Are there similar issues of race, culture, faith, identity, and belonging in your community, even if superficially distinct from the town of Rabata?

LITERARY COMPARISONS: Afabwaje Kurian's work has been compared to that of Imbolo Mbue and Chimamanda Ngozi Adichie. If you have read works by these authors, how does *Before the Mango Ripens* compare and contrast in terms of plot, themes, style, tone, and impact?

Tell us about your book club! Email info@dzancbooks.org
to share your experience with this reading guide.